KU-506-325

MERCEDES LACKEY

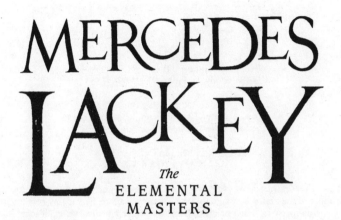

The
ELEMENTAL
MASTERS

THE BARTERED BRIDES

TITAN BOOKS

Bartered Brides
Paperback edition ISBN: 9781785653544
Ebook edition ISBN: 9781785653551

Published by Titan Books
A division of Titan Publishing Group Ltd
144 Southwark Street, London SE1 0UP

First Titan edition: October 2018
1 3 5 7 9 10 8 6 4 2

This is a work of fiction. Names, characters, places, and incidents either are the product of the author's imagination or are used fictitiously, and any resemblance to actual persons, living or dead, business establishments, events, or locales is entirely coincidental. The publisher does not have any control over and does not assume any responsibility for author or third-party websites or their content.

Mercedes Lackey asserts the moral right to be identified as the author of this work.
Copyright © 2018 by Mercedes R. Lackey. All rights reserved.

Cover art by Jody A. Lee.

No part of this publication may be reproduced, stored in a retrieval system, or transmitted, in any form or by any means without the prior written permission of the publisher, nor be otherwise circulated in any form of binding or cover other than that in which it is published and without a similar condition being imposed on the subsequent purchaser.

A CIP catalogue record for this title is available from the British Library.

Printed and bound in Great Britain by CPI Group Ltd.

Did you enjoy this book? We love to hear from our readers.
Please email us at: readerfeedback@titanemail.com

To receive advance information, news, competitions, and exclusive offers online, please sign up for the Titan newsletter on our website:
TITANBOOKS.COM

THE BARTERED BRIDES

The
ELEMENTAL
MASTERS

527 830 04 8

To the memory of Harlan Ellison. Irreplaceable.

1

The calendar read June 3rd. The weather agreed. There was a fine, light summer wind sweeping down the London street where Nan Killian, her friend Sarah Lyon-White, their raven, their parrot, and their ward Suki lived. It frisked in through the open windows of their flat, bringing with it the scent of the daffodils blooming in the flowerboxes outside their window, a scent that just managed to counter the less pleasant odors of London as summer began. At this time of the day there was minimal traffic outside, but you could have heard a pin drop in the sitting room. Not even the birds were feeling chatty.

Sarah, Nan, and Suki sat on the sofa on one side of the cold hearth; their friends and fellow occultists John and Mary Watson sat on the matching sofa on the other. Between the sofas, the table was laden with tea-things, completely untouched so far. Mary was dressed in full mourning, and John had a mourning band around his upper arm.

John was, in Nan's estimation, a very fine looking gentleman. He kept himself in shape, and the hard line of his jaw gave the lie to the kindness of his eyes. His wife Mary was not a beauty, the way Nan's friend Sarah was, but she was something between "pretty" and "handsome," and her own expression was generally as kind as her husband's.

Nearly a month ago a mysterious telegram addressed to both of them had arrived from Germany. Unsigned, it had said merely this: *Do not believe what you read.*

Then, before either of them had been able to find John or Mary Watson, both of whom were out of London, or consult with Lord Alderscroft—the *what* of the mysterious message became clear, as within hours headlines across London screamed *SHERLOCK HOLMES DEAD!*

Alderscroft, when they finally contacted him, knew nothing. Mycroft Holmes was unreachable. And John and Mary, when at last they appeared in London again, were no help. They went into outward mourning. John Watson simply said in print that Holmes had had a "misadventure" in Germany, and had fallen to his death at the Reichenbach Falls—in private, he thinned his lips and gave the girls a look that suggested they needed to go along with that story.

Mary Watson sent around a brief note a week ago suggesting they should gather for a wake for Holmes, but oddly specified the girls' flat, not 221B nor one of their own flats—neither the seldom-used one above John's surgery nor their real home at 221C. So here they were, regarding one another across a laden tea table covered with cups and edibles that no one had touched, silently staring at one another. Even the birds, sitting behind the girls on their perches, were uncharacteristically silent. No one had said a word aside from the initial greetings. To say that the atmosphere was "strained" was something of an understatement.

Of course, Nan could probably have used her mental powers to read John's mind, or Mary's—but Sarah and Nan had discussed that, and without their permission, that was something Nan simply would not do, and nothing either of the Watsons had said or done had indicated to *her* that she had said permission.

And as for Sarah, her mediumistic talents were not of much use here.

So for the course of the last month, they had alternated between being certain that it had been Holmes who had sent that telegram, and that he was alive and well, and certain that it had been a mistake or a cruel hoax, and their dear friend Sherlock Holmes was dead.

"Tea?" Sarah ventured, breaking the silence. But before either of the Watsons could answer, they were interrupted by the sound of the bell downstairs.

All of them started, and strained their ears. Mrs. Horace, the girls' landlady, answered the door on the second pull of the bell. There was the sound of quiet murmuring, then footsteps, two sets, coming up the stairs to the girls' flat.

Mrs. Horace tapped on the door, and opened it. "A Mrs. Stately to see you," she said, in tones that suggested she felt very doubtful about their visitor. "She says she is here on invitation from the Watsons."

"Show her in, thank you, Mrs. Horace," Nan replied before Sarah could say anything. The door opened fully, and a hunched old lady—at least, Sarah *thought* she was old—clad head to toe in black, with a black veil, entered the room. Mrs. Horace closed the door.

And as soon as the door was firmly closed, the old lady suddenly stood up straight, gaining almost a foot in height, pulled back her veil, and revealed the face of Sherlock Holmes.

Sarah stared; she would have sworn that a moment ago the face beneath that veil had been pinched and wizened, and nothing at all like Holmes—save, perhaps, in the beaky nose. But now, there was no doubt—although Holmes looked thinner than usual, and a bit more pale. Still, it was Sherlock Holmes.

Mary and John just looked as if an enormous burden had been taken from their shoulders. Suki squealed, and threw herself at Holmes; he smiled very slightly and patted her on the back as she hugged his skirts. The birds both flew to Holmes as well, landing one on each shoulder, Grey bending down to gently mouth the top of Holmes' nose, and Neville pressing himself up against the side of Holmes' head. Nan felt like flinging herself at Sherlock as well, but what he tolerated in children and animals made him uncomfortable when coming from adults, so she confined herself to sighing as she felt a surge of unimaginable relief.

Then, suddenly, John burst out laughing. "By Jove, I get it. Stately Holmes, indeed!"

Sherlock smiled slightly and took a seat on the one remaining chair, as Suki returned to the girls and the birds to their perches. "The last four weeks have been unpleasant enough for all of us that I thought I might amuse you with a small pun." He lost the smile. "Unfortunately, the unpleasantness is just beginning."

"Wait!" Nan said, before he could continue. "Before you do that, for heaven's sake, tell us what happened! Why did you and John vanish? What happened in Germany? Why did you pretend to be killed? You *did* send us that telegram, didn't you?"

Holmes raised an eyebrow and glanced down at the laden tea table significantly. Sarah hastened to pour out for everyone, while Nan passed around ham sandwiches and cakes, the birds returned to their perches for their shares, and only when Holmes had eaten and drunk did he put his cup aside and begin,

"I have been on very short commons these last few days," he said by way of apology for eating more than half the sandwiches all by himself. "Well, to begin at the beginning, you will recall my campaign against that villain, Professor Moriarty, and his fiendish gang?"

They all nodded.

"Last month, the campaign had nearly reached its ultimate goal; I was about to spring my trap, when I became aware that Moriarty was going to escape it—and in revenge would not only seek to destroy me, but everyone I had allied myself with. Mary was safely out of harm's way for the moment, so John and I slipped off to the Continent with Moriarty in pursuit. To make the story as brief as possible, I hoped that we could occupy him at the least, and possibly bring him to justice, and while he was concentrating on us, the police would be able to swoop in and round up his gang."

"We stayed as close to water as we could at all times," John put in at that point. "It would have been much easier if we'd had Mary along—"

"I absolutely forbade that," Holmes interrupted with a frown. "Not that I do not believe Mary perfectly capable, but it was enough of a risk bringing John in. Moriarty would have immediately made Mary his target as the weakest of the three of us; he would have used her ruthlessly against us, and in the end, brought all three of us down."

The Watsons exchanged a look. Mary shrugged, a tendril of her dark blond hair escaping from her chignon. She pushed it back behind her ear with an impatient gesture.

But Nan had a good idea of why Holmes had not wanted to

risk her presence—and a good idea of why having Mary along would have been more useful than having her husband. Holmes still did not have much of an idea of what an Elemental Master could do with his or her powers. It was entirely within the realm of possibility that had Moriarty seized Mary Watson, she could have sucked the very breath out of his lungs—or rather, her Elementals could have. Under the normal course of things, no Master would ever ask her Elementals to kill, but nothing about the threat that Professor Moriarty posed could be construed as "normal."

"So we stayed close to water so we could employ the protection of my Elementals, knowing they would warn us of danger. And it was in Germany that they finally did. The Professor finally caught up with us. We chose the falls as the place with potentially the most power for me to use, and the likeliest place for Moriarty to attempt an ambush," John continued. "And as we had hoped, Moriarty took the bait as we hiked on a brief sojourn to view the falls close at hand. He sent a false message that there was a dying Englishwoman back at our inn who requested my services. We didn't fall for it, of course."

Now that they were no longer guarding their minds and memories, glimpses of what they had done in those moments flashed across Nan's mind. There was the steep, mist-soaked path leading to the falls. The roar of the falls themselves, like a roar of thunder that never ended, almost obscured the boy's speech. There was the boy; blond, bareheaded, in short leather pants, long white woolen stockings, a green wool jacket, much patched, and sturdy clogs. He wouldn't look at Watson, his eyes shifted as he gabbled out his message, and he fingered something obsessively in his right-hand pocket. The money by which Moriarty had bought him?

Holmes nodded. "John pretended to believe it, and sent the messenger back to tell them he was coming. In actuality, he only went a few hundred yards, then doubled back, warned of exactly where Moriarty was by his Elementals. Moriarty expected me to fight honorably." Holmes uttered a dry laugh. "I think, Doctor, he was rather too much a consumer of your fine stories. Watson and I got him between us; he was concentrating on me, and between the noise of the falls and his own eagerness, Watson crept up on him completely undetected. Watson, I believe you shot first?"

Again, the memory washed over her; first from Holmes' point of view. The Professor faced him, fearlessly, a cold arrogance over his features. The falls thundered at Holmes' back, and if he had not been so keyed up, he would have shivered in the cold spray. But he *was* keyed up; like a racehorse, waiting for the signal to spring into action. Behind Moriarty, Watson crept up the path, step by cautious, sideways step, a little crouched over, revolver in hand. In that moment she knew, with utter certainty, that Holmes had not exaggerated when he had told Watson that as long as Moriarty perished, he would be willing to die as well.

John nodded, an expression of grim satisfaction on his face. "You don't do a mad dog the courtesy of letting him have the first bite. I got him in the back. I wasn't taking a chance on missing, so I aimed for his torso. I reckoned on the shock of the first shot allowing me to get off more, even if the shot itself deflected on a rib."

Now Watson's view; and within Watson was an anxiety that was tearing him apart. He was afraid, desperately afraid, that Holmes *would* be honorable, be chivalrous, would offer to fight the fiend man-to-man. Watson did not intend to give Holmes the chance to make that offer—indeed, his one fear as he had doubled back was that Holmes would initiate a fair fight before he had a chance to get in place. So when he saw Holmes' gun hand twitch, ever so slightly, he did not hesitate, bur fired a burst of three shots into Moriarty's back. By the time the second had struck, Holmes had fired his own gun, reflexively.

Holmes continued. "And I shot once you had, as well. He was . . . surprised. He staggered over the side of the path and into the falls."

It was uglier than that. Moriarty staggered, gasped, bled, snarled—tried to reach for his own gun, but his right hand would not obey him, and he could not reach the pocket where it was with his left. He stumbled toward Holmes, arm outstretched, as Holmes skipped out of his grasp with great agility, despite the slippery path.

And then a half dozen long, white arms made of mist snaked out of the falls and seized him.

They were not strong, those arms, but they were enough. They pulled him off-balance, and his stumbling feet carried him to the edge of the path and over. Both John and Sherlock approached the edge of the path cautiously, lest he be somehow lurking on a ledge just beneath it, ready to seize one of them to end the victory in defeat—but there was nothing there, nothing but mist and thundering water. Moriarty was no more.

"And I made sure my Elementals pulled what was left of him down underwater and held it there for a day and a half. Between that, and after four shots and the plunge, we were sure he was finished. Holmes disappeared, and I reported his death along with that of Moriarty."

The memories let go of her, and Nan took a deep breath and a sip of her lukewarm tea. She wondered if either of them guessed what she had just witnessed.

"I stopped in a small village just long enough to telegraph you young ladies, because I did not want you to do something . . . untoward." Holmes added. "But I didn't dare do more. As it transpired, I had been too sanguine in my surety that my trap would catch *all* of Moriarty's gang. Much to my chagrin and alarm, I underestimated the number of his followers by fifty percent. I have been tracing and dealing with individuals for the last four weeks, and I am only halfway through what is proving to be a gargantuan task, a true Labor of Hercules."

Nan frowned. "And you think that anyone who is connected with you is still in danger," she stated.

Watson and Holmes both nodded. Holmes started to open his mouth, then gestured to Watson instead. John sighed. "I've had several close calls over the last month. They might have been sheer bad luck and coincidence, but they might not have been."

"In my estimation, that much bad luck is improbable," Holmes observed with a frown. "Moriarty did not engage stupid henchmen; they learned from him, and they will not have forgotten what they learned. Moriarty's men probably are not motivated to avenge *him,* but they certainly have personal reasons for seeking to revenge themselves on me—and perhaps on John. We have been instrumental in sending most of their comrades to prison, and they probably are aware that their own hours as free men are numbered. And until I have them all in custody it is better to take no chances."

"Do you think we're under any hazard?" Nan asked. "Sarah and me, I mean."

"I do not *think* Moriarty was aware of my work with you, but it is better to take no chances," Sherlock repeated. "This is why I will remain 'dead' and you will not see me until every last man of his is behind bars."

"We need a point of contact with you, Holmes!" Watson protested. But Sherlock shook his head.

"Every point of contact is a risk. *This* was a risk, and contacting my brother was a risk, and these are things I do not intend to repeat twice. Don't worry, old man," he added, with a faint smile. "Mycroft is taking steps to make sure I don't starve to death, or catch pneumonia from sleeping under a Thames bridge." He looked at the tiny pendant watch in a jet case he wore about his neck. "And now it is time for me to go. Don't see me out."

He pulled the veil over his face, and suddenly his visage seemed to shrink in on itself; and as he stood up, Nan saw he was hunched over again, and back to being the old lady who had arrived at the door. "Good evening, my dears," quavered a high, thready voice from behind the veil, as he opened the door. "Thank you for inviting me."

And then he was gone.

"Stubborn goat," John Watson grumbled, as Mary patted his hand. "Well, at least he's gone to Mycroft. Hopefully he has a place to lay his head and a ready source of food now. Judging by the way he ate, he hasn't had a proper meal in a month."

"Well, he got those widows' weeds from *somewhere*," Mary pointed out. "And they weren't rags, either. I think he can manage. Don't fret too much."

Nan leaned back in her seat, and her raven Neville hopped from his perch to the back of the sofa and from there into her lap. "Well, despite the fact that he was *finally* able to accept the factual existence of your Elementals, John, I'm still concerned that magic is a blind spot with him." She scratched the back of Neville's head as Grey climbed into Sarah's lap to be cuddled. "I don't think Professor Moriarty was as stubborn. And this worries me. Holmes doesn't himself know who the magicians and occultists of Britain and the Continent are. And now that he has run off on his own, he's not going to have someone he can ask. He scarpered before we could tell him anything that might protect him."

It was Mary's turn to frown. "Now that you mention it . . . you're right. Moriarty was powerful and ruthless, and I find it unlikely that he ever rejected *any* form of manipulation and control. Even if he himself did not believe, he would be aware that some of his henchmen were believers, and he would have taken pains to acquire at least one magician among his followers."

"I'll go further than that, my love," Watson agreed, frowning under his handsome moustache. "This could be a critical area of omission for Holmes. He doesn't have our abilities, and literally won't see an attack by magic coming. So we must be doubly, triply alert, and take care of such enemies for him. Remember, we are all fast friends, and united, nothing is beyond us."

Mary smiled wanly. "I wish I was as sanguine as you, my dear," she replied, but then she relaxed a trifle. "Still, you are right. And I must say I am relieved to be unburdened of that secret." She finally took an interest in the tea tray. "Did Holmes leave us *anything* to eat?"

"Do you think Mycroft would have told Lord Alderscroft about Holmes?" Sarah asked as Nan returned from setting the depleted tea tray out on the landing.

"I think it very likely, but unless Alderscroft contacts *us,* and says something about it, we should continue the charade," Nan replied, and looked down at Suki.

The little girl with a head of beautiful black curls and a complexion of *café au lait* looked back up at her. Nan didn't have to say anything. Suki bobbed her head so hard her ringlets danced. "Won't tell nobody about nothin'," she volunteered. "I dun think we should tell Memsa'b neither," she continued, with a little frown. "Mus' Holmes didn' say nothin' bout Memsa'b."

Nan considered that, and nodded reluctantly. "I think you're right. Besides, she isn't as close to Sherlock as the rest of us are. It will do no harm to keep her out of the secret for now." She had no fear that Suki would blurt out anything by accident. The child's life previous to her being adopted by the girls had taught her how to hold her tongue better than most adults.

"Well, now that the interruption to our day is over—," Nan began.

Suki sighed, and went to fetch the box that contained her testing cards.

The cards consisted of three decks shuffled together—one deck of ordinary playing cards, one deck of Tarot cards, and one deck of the cards used to drill children in their letters and numbers. To be fair, this exercise was as much to keep Nan sharp as it was to strengthen Suki's telepathic abilities. They took it in turn to be "sender" and "receiver," and did not stop until they had been through all the cards three times. Meanwhile, after tidying the flat, Sarah resumed her self-appointed task of going over all their summer and spring clothing, making sure that no repairs had been overlooked when they had put the clothing away last autumn, and checking that moths had not had a chance to damage things while in storage.

Sarah sighed audibly as Nan put away the cards. "We did our best, but I think we are going to have to invest in new stockings," she said mournfully. "They're more darn than stocking, and I hate wearing lumpy stockings."

"You'll get blisters if you try," Nan pointed out practically, and checked her watch. "We've just time to go round to the shops, then the park, before dinner."

Suki looked up with hope in her eyes at that.

The child looked nothing like Nan or Sarah, of course; she had curly hair as black as a raven's wing and a dusky complexion, with a sweet, round face. Sarah was a true English rose, blond and blue-eyed and pink-cheeked, while Nan was taller than her friend, with plain brown hair and an equally plain face. But any impertinent observations on the fact that Suki did not look sufficiently "English" were swiftly quelled with one of Nan's dagger-looks, and Sarah's frosty, "Suki has been our ward for several years."

Sarah tossed all the stockings in the rag basket. "Get your bonnet, Suki," she said, and the child ran off joyfully to do so.

Not more than an hour later, new stockings duly bought, the two of them were in one of London's many parks. This one was smallish, with a round pond in the center. There were four benches spaced equally around the pond, and a circle of heavy bushes shielded the pond from the streets around it. As it was teatime, they had the park to themselves.

They sat together on one of the benches, with Neville on Nan's shoulder and Grey the African parrot on the back of the bench beside them, and watched Suki romping with the pigeons and starlings, who were more than used to her, and knew that she was a good source of crumbs. She wore her currently favorite dress, a blue and white sailor suit, with a straw sailor's hat. Nan, as usual, wore a plain brown Rational Dress gown; Sarah a light blue gown of similar design. "You were hoping Puck would show up, weren't you?" Sarah said in an undertone.

Nan shrugged. "It was a thought. I was hoping Puck could put a watcher on you-know-who."

"Except that you-know-who is quite likely to go places a watcher won't want to go," Sarah pointed out practically. "You know Earth Elementals do not much care for the city. Let John and Mary tend to that side of things. We can find out from Memsa'b if there are any occultists she would suggest might have been Moriarty's henchmen. A telepath would have been extremely useful to him, after all."

"That is a very good point, and we can do so without letting the secret slip," Nan agreed. She watched as Suki stood balanced perfectly on the curb around the pond, walking the stone as easily as if she was on the flat pavement. "We should get Suki a toy boat."

"So we should. It will be worth it to watch the horror in every nanny's eyes as she outsails their male charges. How long, do you think, before she starts begging to march in suffragette parades?" Sarah chuckled.

"Any day now—" Nan replied, when suddenly, the pleasant day turned horrific.

Three things happened simultaneously. Nan got a sudden surge of nausea and panic and a glimpse of horrific visions of Suki being treated as no child should be, Suki whirled and screamed, pointing, and Neville launched himself off Nan's shoulder, bellowing a challenge. A moment later, there was more screaming, but it wasn't Neville or Suki.

"*Gerim orf!*" screamed a male voice behind Nan as she lurched off the bench and whirled. "*Gerim orf!*" She stared, unable to move for a moment. There was a man, roughly dressed in shabby clothing, thrashing his way out of the bushes behind her. Neville had fastened his talons into the man's scalp and was plowing furrows into his skin with his beak, then, as Nan watched, stupefied, whipped his head down and clamped down on the right ear, scissoring it completely off. The man screamed incoherently and tried to pummel the bird, but Neville was already in the air again, hammering the man's skull with his beak as he hovered above his head.

Suki ran, not toward Nan and Sarah, but toward the man, her face a mask of fury. Before Nan could stop her, she reached him and plunged her little knife into his leg behind his knee. He shrieked, and before anyone could react, he ran off, stumbling and limping, covered in blood.

Now Suki turned and ran for Sarah and Nan, throwing herself against Nan's legs, wrapping her arms around Nan's waist and sobbing into Nan's skirt. Neville landed on the ground beside them, looking equally concerned for Suki and very proud of himself, ear still held in his beak.

"Get rid of that, Neville," Nan said absentmindedly, as she embraced Suki's shaking shoulders. "You don't know where it's been."

Neville looked disappointed that he was not going to be allowed to eat it, but obediently flapped off and returned without the ear. *I don't think I want to know where he left it.*

By this time a bobby had appeared, attracted by the screaming. Nan continued to comfort Suki, letting Sarah handle the situation.

*He was gonna—he was gonna—*Suki cried in Nan's mind.

He was going to try, lovey, but we're here, Neville got him, and so did you. And if he hadn't run away, Sarah and I would have turned him inside out. She gathered from the murmurs on Sarah's part that she was convincing the bobby that the man had actually attacked Suki, rather than merely thinking about it, and that he'd been frightened off when all three of them screamed. Certainly

Suki's hysterics were convincing enough, and by some miracle she hadn't gotten any blood spattered on her where it would show. Nan held her little ward tightly while Suki showed her, in *much* more detail than Nan found comfortable, exactly what she had sensed in her attacker's mind. It reminded her far too much of what she herself had seen in the minds of the men her mother had sold her to when she was a child, before Memsa'b took her in. Nan continued to reassure her until the bobby had gotten enough detail from Sarah to hurry off and make his report.

"He's never going to catch the bastard, you know," Nan murmured under her breath, as they both sat down on the bench again, with Suki between them, and Grey and Neville both now trying to offer their own sorts of comfort. "You described him *before* Neville savaged him."

"*Eyes.*" Neville croaked angrily, making it very clear what his next target would have been if the man hadn't run off.

"And how was I going to explain that our pet raven turned his skull into a dissection exhibit?" Sarah replied, reasonably, petting Suki's hair and wiping her eyes. "We're just lucky the park was empty and no one else saw what happened."

Suki hiccupped a couple of times, and took the handkerchief out of Sarah's hand to blow her nose. She took a long, deep breath, and the horrific images faded from her head. "Oi 'ope 'e bleeds t'death," she said, hoarsely.

"Well, he's likely to die of an infection," Nan replied grimly. "Neville's beak is anything but clean."

"*Oi!*" Neville objected.

Nan looked over Suki's head to Sarah. "Are you thinking what I'm thinking?"

"That this was what you-know-who warned us about?" Sarah replied, just as grimly.

"Either the man was completely mad, or it seems a strange thing to do." Nan set her jaw. "There's no other reason to attack a child in broad daylight in a public park. And it wasn't an impulse attack. It was Suki he wanted." She looked down at their ward, who sniffed and nodded confirmation.

But then Suki spoke up. "I don' thin' 'e was gonna grab me 'ere. I thin' 'e was gonna foller us 'ome t'see where we lived. On'y,

I screamed an Neville went fer 'im." She managed a watery smile and petted Neville, who purred. "Yer a 'ero, Neville."

"Yes he is. And . . . damn it all. Whatever the cause, I don't think we dare take the chance that this wasn't aimed directly at us. I think you need to go back to Memsa'b, and I think you need to be a boy for a while, my love," Nan said firmly, and Suki's face looked a little less forlorn. Although she loved her pretty things, and preened in the lovely dresses Lord Alderscroft spoiled her with, she also loved the freedom being dressed as a boy gave her.

"All right," Suki agreed, blowing her nose again.

When they got back to their flat, they sent messages, first to Lord Alderscroft, who replied immediately that his carriage would be there within the hour to take Suki straight to the school, then to Memsa'b with the particulars. Neville was better than a telegraph office; he returned with Memsa'b's short reply, *Send her here at once!* just as the carriage also arrived. And in the carriage were two very burly footmen. Lord Alderscroft obviously was taking the situation quite seriously.

One of the footmen stowed Suki's small trunk on the roof of the carriage, while the other handed her in as if she was a princess, much to her delight. The girls stood on the stoop and waved to her until the carriage was out of sight, then went back into their flat. Already it seemed emptier.

"Sendin' Suki back to school?" their landlady, Mrs. Horace, asked from the door of her own flat. And without waiting for an answer, she nodded wisely. "Almanac says it's going to be a dreadful summer. Heat always makes sickness spread like wildfire. You're wise girls to get her back to somewhere healthy before it starts."

"That's what we thought, Mrs. Horace," Sarah replied. "I'm glad you agree."

"I wish *we* could leave," Nan said, as they closed the door of their flat behind them. "I wish Alderscroft would find us a job that needs doing somewhere on the other side of the country."

"Wales would be nice," Sarah sighed wistfully. "Or Scotland. We've never been to Scotland. The Scottish Highlands sound so romantic in Scott's novels."

Nan cleared away the supper things and put the tray out on

the landing for Mrs. Horace. When she came back, Sarah was cuddling Grey in her chair at the hearth. Neville was in no mood for cuddles; Nan sensed he was still angry about the near-attack on Suki.

"Well," Nan said aloud, settling into her own chair, where Neville was already perched. "Here's the question. We've had a chance to calm down and our thoughts to cool. Was this random, or was it one of Moriarty's henchmen?"

"You're better equipped to determine that than I am," Sarah pointed out. "Was there anything in his thoughts that suggested he was sent after us, specifically?"

Nan frowned as she examined the repugnant memories. "He wasn't thinking about anything but Suki," she admitted. "I didn't see anything about him being ordered to find us . . . but I didn't *not* see anything, either, if that makes any sense."

"So it could be he was just looking for a victim—and it's possible he wouldn't have actually tried to abduct Suki at all?" Sarah persisted. "Yes, I know he wanted to, but she was with two adult women in a very public park. And we live in a respectable neighborhood where everyone knows her. One hint of a scream from her and half the neighbors would come boiling out with fireplace pokers and brooms in hand." She rubbed her head as if it ached. "What I am trying to say is, yes, he was an absolutely horrible man and I have no doubt he has done horrible things to other children, but all we can tell for certain is that he was only *thinking* about doing them to Suki."

Nan swore under her breath. "Which means, we know nothing, other than we certainly administered just retribution to someone who absolutely has earned it by his actions in the past."

Sarah nodded. "We may have been jumping at shadows. But I think we did right in sending Suki away. Until we know that Sherlock has eliminated all of Moriarty's men that are inclined to look for revenge, we should be alert enough to jump at shadows."

Nan glanced over her shoulder at the nearest window, where the last light of sunset touched the roof of the building across the street. "Well, I *still* hope he comes to a horrid end," she growled. "Maybe even more, now."

Sarah nodded.

"And if we run across him again, I'm going to *let* Neville have his eyes!"

"And I won't stop you," Sarah replied. "In fact. . . ." She bared her teeth in something that was not a smile. "I'll help."

2

Mary O'Brien looked about herself with wide eyes. She had never been to a place like this in her short life. In fact, for most of her twelve years she had never been anywhere except to play in the streets, or work in whatever cramped little room the whole family shared, so this place was like one of those fairy palaces in a song.

She knew it was a pub, but she had never dared to go *in* a pub. Not because she would have been chased out because she was too young to be there—but because she would have been chased out because she was too *poor* to be there. Pa was a crossing-sweeper and she and Ma mended clothes for pawnbrokers, and her three little brothers collected dog shit for tanners and there was just never enough money to go around even for basics like food and rent. In summer especially there were weeks when they all slept rough in the street, their meager belongings stowed underneath them against thieves.

There were lots of places where you just didn't go when your dress was more patch than dress and you wrapped your feet in rags in the winter because you didn't have shoes. She probably would already be in service if she'd had one good, clean dress to be interviewed in, but nobody hired even a tweenie who didn't have a good dress and a pair of shoes. As it was she'd been helping her mother with her mending and sewing work since she was old enough to be trusted with it. Never mind they were all supposed to be at school. School was only for days there was no work. At least she could write her name, and puzzle out words, and add good enough that she didn't get cheated, so that was something.

But now . . . they were inside the door of a real pub. And she was openmouthed with amazement. To begin with, there were the loveliest food smells . . . the floor under her little bare feet was clean and polished, not greasy or full of splinters. There was *glass* in all the windows! The people here were all very much better dressed than Ma and Pa and herself; and as the three of them lingered in the doorway, she felt a rising fear that someone was going to come to send them out with hard words and blows.

But instead, a man dressed like the other people here came forward to greet them. "Ned, Meggie, yer in good time!" he exclaimed, as Mary's sharp eyes saw money pass covertly from his hands to her Pa's. But she didn't get a chance to wonder about that.

"Now, I got us a table over 'ere." He ushered them to a quiet, dark corner, out of the way, a table pushed up against the wall, near the door where people were coming out with dishes of food and going in with dirty dishes. There were two bench seats, one on either side of it. There was a big plate of food waiting there, and smaller plates to dish it into, and three glasses of beer. Mary's mouth watered as she smelled fried 'taties and sausage, and she started to climb up onto the bench seat to sit beside her mother.

But the man took her by the shoulders and prevented her. "Not now, Mary, me luv," he said. She looked at her Ma, who nodded as she shoveled 'taties and sausage into her plate. The man turned her around and gave her a little shove, and she saw he was shoving her at a big, red-faced woman enveloped in a huge white apron. Mary stared. It was the cleanest garment she had ever seen in her life. It was certainly whiter than any snow she had ever seen, at least where she lived, where all snow was gray by the time it fell, gray and dirty from the soot and smuts in the air. "Now you just go along of Rose there, an' do what she tells ye. We'll be along when ye're ready."

"Do wut 'e says, gurl," her father told her, mouth full. "Yer gettin' leg-shackled t'day. Jerry 'ere is goin' ter Canada, an' 'e wants a wife ter take wi' 'im."

Suddenly it all fell into place, and she got a funny, sort of scared, sort of good feeling in her belly. Mary's older sister Sally had married a man that Ma and Pa had found for her that was going to Australia, just three years ago. They'd said it was better than going into service—if you weren't being transported, the land was there for taking, you'd have your own farm before you could blink, and if you didn't like farming, there were a hundred things a man could make his fortune doing. She didn't care about a fortune, but going to Canada—that meant always having a full belly, and never being cold in winter, and living in a place where the wind didn't whistle through cracks in the walls you could stick a finger in.

So Mary didn't object, she just followed the lady named Rose through the big room, crowded with tables, then up a steep little stair, and from there, into a room like something out of a dream. There were rugs on the floor, and pretty pictures on the walls, three chairs that were all soft and padded, and something bigger than a chair that was just as soft and padded, and a table that had four good legs and wooden chairs around it that matched. And a fireplace, though there wasn't a fire in it. In the middle of one of the rugs stood a big thing made of tin, full of hot water. Steam rose off it, that was how she knew it was hot. She stared, wondering what it was for.

"Take yer thin's off, missy, an' get in there fer yer bath," said Rose.

Mary obeyed, meekly. She'd had "baths" before, but only rough ones, where Ma would take off her clothes and scrub her under the pump in the yard. Getting into a big tin pan full of hot water was strange, but after a moment, Mary decided she liked it. A lot.

She also liked the soft, sweet-smelling soap that Rose scrubbed her with, and used to wash her hair. She was sorry when the bath was over, and Rose wrapped her in a big piece of cloth and two men came to take the tin pan away.

But then Rose combed out her wet hair and braided it up on the top of her head, like a grown woman, and gave her new clothing to put on, and she nearly burst with pleasure. Stockings! She'd darned plenty, but she'd never had any of her own. Soft drawers with a row of lace on the bottoms! She'd only had drawers but the once, and that was when her skirt was so short it was a scandal, even in the East End. A sleeveless chemise with more lace! Then a real *corset* to go over the top, like a woman grown, and then *two* petticoats, not just one like Ma wore, and they were soft, creamy white, and light, not heavy flannel. And then a white blouse with lace at the neck and sleeves and all down the front, and a white skirt with three rows of lace, and a wide, white ribbon sash. And *shoes!* Beautiful white leather shoes! She'd never had shoes before, and even though they were too big and Rose had to stuff the toes with paper, she couldn't stop admiring them. And then Rose put a square of lace on the top of her head and pinned it there, pinched her cheeks and told her to bite her lips.

"Yew clean up right pretty," she said, genially, and handed Mary a bunch of violets with a white ribbon around them. "Now hold onter thet, stay where ye are. I'll jest be going t'fetch yer Ma and Pa an' the lad."

Mary stood as still as she could in the middle of the rug, but standing still didn't prevent her from looking down at the rows of ruffled lace on the bottom of her white skirt, or marveling at the pink color of her own hands, now completely free of grime. A little giddy giggle escaped her. Sally hadn't gotten it *half* so good when she'd got leg-shackled! Just three skirts and waists from the pawnshop, and a few underthings, and she'd been married off in a little street chapel by a street preacher. Not even church, and they were church people. Church gave out better things to the poor than chapel did.

But it wasn't just Ma and Pa and the man she was going to marry that came up the stairs, it was Ma and Pa and two men. One was the one she recognized, Jerry, who was going to be her husband. The other was an old man, dressed in rusty black with a bit of white at his collar, and carrying a book. That must be the preacher.

He looked at her dubiously. "How old are you, child?" he asked. She started to open her mouth to say she was twelve, but Ma stepped on her foot and Pa said loudly, "She's fifteen. Jest small fer 'er age. She'll fatten up right quick i' Canada, an' sprout up like a weed."

Fortunately Ma had stepped on the paper the toe of her shoe had been stuffed with, but Mary took the hint. *Don't speak until you're told to.* So she stood quietly, clutching her flowers. When the preacher asked her if she would take Gerald Baker as her husband, she said yes. When he asked her to repeat the words he told her, she repeated them. It was all over very quickly. Everyone shook hands. Her new husband gave the preacher some money, and she was told to make a mark on a piece of paper, which she did, printing her name carefully and with great effort, and her tongue sticking out of the corner of her mouth. The preacher gave the paper to her new husband, and just like that, she was a married woman.

"You folks go an' hev yerself a time," said Mary's husband. "We'll be go board ship now, she's off fust thing i' the mornin' an' we don' wanta miss 'er."

"But what 'bout—" Ma began. "Jerry" laughed.

"I got clothes fer the wee gal, same as I bought the weddin' dress, an' it's all aboard with me bags, in a good stout case," he said, and patted her shoulder. "Don' yew worry. I'm doin' Mary right."

"Well, all right then," said Pa. "See, I tol' yew this'd be Mary's big chance!" And before Ma could say anything else, he took her elbow and hustled her away down the stairs.

The man looked down at Mary, who was still clutching her violets with both hands. "Yew c'n call me Jerry," he said. "Or 'usband. Time t'go."

"Yis, 'usband," she said meekly, and took the hand he held out to her, even though she was dreadfully disappointed that she wasn't to get any of those 'taties and sausage. But she was more used to going hungry than not, and maybe there'd be food where they were going.

He led her down the stairs, and then they began a long, long walk, far out of the neighborhoods Mary knew. It had been about teatime when she and Ma and Pa had arrived at the pub, they walked for miles and miles, until the sun had started to really drop, and she and Jerry were still walking. In fact, it was so long she began to wonder; the docks weren't that far, surely?

But why would he lie about going to the ship?

It was nearly sunset when they finally arrived—but it wasn't to a dock or a ship. She was so tired that her head drooped, and all she paid attention to was putting one foot in front of the other. Then he suddenly turned to the left, pulling her hand so she would go with him, and she looked up, and saw they were approaching a big house, set off the street a little way, with its own bit of yard around it. It was a nicer house than she had ever seen before, all white. It was set back from the street, and had a set of three white stone steps leading up to the big front door. As he led her up the stairs, she thought about saying something about them supposed to be on a ship right now—then thought better of it. He'd lied, but maybe he'd had his reasons for lying. Like maybe he thought Pa and Ma would drink off all the money they'd been given, and then come looking for more. Which . . . was pretty likely.

And the dress was real. The shoes were real. The money he'd spent to marry her was real. The house he was unlocking right this minute was real. How was this worse than going to Canada?

So she looked up at him just as he got the door open, and asked, voice tremulous with weariness, "Is this yer 'ouse, 'usband?"

He looked down at her, unsmiling. "'Deed 'tis, wife," he replied. "I mebbe fibbed to yer Pa 'bout Canada so's 'e'd let us get hitched quick an' make no fuss. Now we're gonna go inside an' 'ave our weddin' supper."

Before she could answer—and tell him the truth, that she only knew how to cook a very few things, like a sausage, or a baked 'tatie—he led her by the hand inside, locked the door behind her, and then led her through a dark passage with closed doors on either side of it. He took her all the way to the back of the house. There he opened a door on what proved to be the kitchen with a lovely lit oil lamp in the middle of the table and a red-checked oilcloth on it and not just the bare table. She'd only seen a kitchen but once, when there'd been money for a room in a house with a shared kitchen. This one was nicer, and much cleaner.

"Sit yersel' down," he said, gesturing at the little table pushed against the wall, with a chair on each side of it. She was so glad to get off her weary feet she didn't even ask what he wanted cooked.

But it seemed he didn't need a cook. He went to a cupboard and took out food; ham, cheese, onions, pickles, bread, butter. She recognized "ham" only because she'd had it a bare couple of times—at Christmas parties for poor children given by whatever parish church they were nearest at the time. And then the slices of it had been so thin you could practically see through them, just one slice per child. As she stared hungrily at the food, out came plates, glasses, and knives and forks, and he laid out the table himself. He cut ham and cheese for her, indicated that she was to help herself from the bread, onions and pickles, and turned back to the cupboard. She stared. Such *thick* slices! Why . . . he must be rich! No wonder he'd lied to Pa. If Pa knew her new husband was possessed of such a house and such bounty, Pa'd come touch him on a regular basis for certain. Or maybe even try to move the family in! Suddenly she felt rebellious. Why should *she* share this lovely place and this wonderful food with them? Half the time when there was food in the house, Pa and Ma ate it, or gave some to the boys and let her go hungry. It would be horrid having them here!

When her husband turned around again, after she had taken a little onion and pickles and piled it all on a slice of buttered bread, he had a bottle in his hands. He poured it out into the glasses; it was a beautiful color, a deep red. Gingerly, she tried it, when he gestured to her to drink.

She almost spat it out, but didn't. So sour, though! At least it wasn't as bitter as beer. Still . . . whatever it was—wine?—it must be expensive and she shouldn't waste it by not drinking it. She watched him closely before starting to eat herself. He had piled his bread with ham and cheese and pickle and onion, but instead of picking it up with his hands and cramming it into his mouth like Pa would have done, he cut it into neat bits and ate it with his fork. She did the same so he wouldn't think badly of her.

They ate and drank together in silence, and when she had finished the glass of liquid, he poured her another. By this time she had gotten somewhat used to the taste, and drank it with a bit more enthusiasm. But when the meal was over and he had put the food in the cupboard and the dishes in the sink and she went to stand, she found herself a bit wobbly and light-headed.

He didn't seem to notice. Instead he took her by the hand again, and led her up a set of stairs at the end of the kitchen, down another passage, and into a bedroom.

She knew it was a bedroom, because there was a *real bed* in it. Not just the sort of broken-down thing that the whole family had crowded into to sleep when they had a bed and not the floor— and in winter, piled every scrap of clothing they had on top of themselves to try and keep warm. This was a tall, proud, brass creation, with pillows and blankets and a coverlet, with a rug at the side, and a china thing under it instead of a leaky bucket if you need to "go" in the night. And there was a stand with a pitcher and bowl for washing up, and a big wardrobe, and a chest at the foot of it. And it was all so splendid all she could do was stand on the rug and stare with both hands to her mouth.

"Bedtime," Jerry said, and she nodded, because this was something she knew about—after all, Ma and Pa just went *to* it all the time, regardless of whether the kiddies were awake or asleep, so she knew she was going to have to get undressed and into that splendid bed, and he'd put his tackle in her cunny. Then there'd be some heaving and grunting and then she could go to sleep in this beautiful, soft, wonderful bed!

So she began by untying the lovely ribbon sash, and laid it over the chest, then took off her skirt and did the same, unbuttoned the waist and folded it neat and then came the petticoats. She was a little worried about getting the corset off by herself, but it hooked up the front and hadn't been pulled at all tight, so that was all right.

And then, just as she unfastened the last hook, she heard the door close, and looked up, and realized she was alone.

Well . . . that was odd.

But maybe he didn't want to undress in front of her? Peculiar, but today had already been full of peculiar things, so she just shrugged, and slipped out of the drawers and stockings and that pretty little chemise, and climbed into bed naked, and waited.

And waited.

And as the last of the blue dusk light faded, and out past the curtains it turned into black night, she fell asleep, still waiting.

She woke with a start, still in an empty bed.

It was *long* past when her Ma usually woke her, in the first light of predawn. And the reason she had awakened was because there was someone else in the room.

Not her new husband. This was a wizened little thing in a dark dress with a white apron and cap, who had placed the jug from the washstand on the floor and was filling the jug from a pail of steaming water. The little old lady put the jug back on the washstand and turned, and saw her staring from the bed.

"Breck-fuss i' kitchen," the old woman said, abruptly, and turned and left, taking the pail with her.

There was a breakfast? In the kitchen? That *she* hadn't cooked? She knuckled both her eyes, expecting all this to be a dream, because surely she, ordinary little Mary O'Brien, hadn't married a man who had a house, a servant to tend it, and money to eat ham whenever he chose!

But the bedroom was still there. The jug of water steamed enticingly. She got out of bed and had a wash, then peeked in the wardrobe. Sadly, there were no dresses in there; she'd hoped for some, because her sister had gotten three whole new outfits to wear out of *her* husband, and Jerry was obviously better off.

Well since her husband had managed everything else, perhaps he'd manage some dresses too. Perhaps he'd just been waiting to be married so he could get things to fit her.

Meanwhile she had the clothes she'd been married in, after all, and she was used to wearing the same things all the time, so she put those back on—leaving off the corset this time. She discovered, looking at it, that it couldn't be pulled any tighter than it was, so there really wasn't any use in wearing it.

She remembered the way down to the kitchen, so down she went, her new shoes making a satisfying clicking sound with each step she took. When she emerged into the sunny kitchen, the wizened old lady was scrubbing pans and paid no attention to her. But there was a big plate of cooling food on the table, and a cup of tea, so she took her seat and contemplated the bounty.

Eggs, she'd had—she and her brothers and sister had often stolen pigeon eggs in season out of the nests in the roofs of any house they could clamber on without being chased away. So she recognized those. And sausage, bacon, and toast. But not the slices of red things with crisped edges or the odd brown things. And she knew beans, but these beans were swimming in a sort of orange-brown sauce and not boiled up plain. But it was all food, and food was not to be wasted, so she waded into it, prepared to like everything.

The red things were strange, but in the end she decided she

liked them. The brown things had a strange texture and an earthy taste she wasn't sure she liked, but she ate them anyway. But she had never had that much food in one sitting before, and when her plate was empty, she pushed away from the table feeling as if she wanted to sleep again.

The old woman snatched the plate and cup away and turned back to the sink. Since there didn't seem to be anything she could do here, she went back upstairs to see what the other rooms were.

The first one she found was obviously where Jerry had spent the night. The bed had been made, but there was a man's dressing gown flung over a chair, there was shaving stuff on the washstand, and when she peeked in the wardrobe, it was full of men's clothing.

The second room held a bed with no bedclothes on it, but *three* wardrobes and two chests. When she looked in the first, it was full of skirts and waists and dresses, all white. One of the chests was full of underthings. She perked up at that. She knew how to alter clothing. Some of these might already fit her, and if they didn't, once she could find a sewing kit she could have more than one set of clothes! She didn't mind wearing white. In fact, she liked it. It made her feel . . . elegant. Like someone who didn't have to work or worry about getting dirty. She helped herself to two sets of drawers that looked like they'd fit, two sets of stockings, and two chemises. That way she could have one set on, one set clean, and one set drying all the time. She could wash the dirty ones up in the basin in the morning. She went back to her room and carefully put the stockings and underthings in the drawer of the wardrobe. Then she went back to her explorations.

The fourth room was storage too, but of things like bed linens and curtains and rugs.

There was a door that must lead to a staircase going to the third floor, but it was locked, so she went back downstairs to discover what was in the rest of the house.

When she went out of the kitchen into the passage, she realized there was a second staircase leading up from the passage. That must have been the one that was blocked off and locked on the second floor. She went up it, only to discover another locked door on the landing, so she went back down again, disappointed.

There were three doors off the passage itself. The nearest to the kitchen had a door that was slightly ajar. She peeked inside. The wizened maid was on her hands and knees, cleaning the rug in what looked like a parlor, so Mary just peeked in the door, and quickly went on to the next. That one was . . . disappointing. There was nothing in the room but a chair and a lot of books. She went on to the room nearest the street.

That was better. This was how she imagined rich people lived, with a room like this, carpets on the floor, overstuffed furniture, and crowded full of interesting things to look at. Glass-fronted cabinets, display domes on tables, shelves, all crammed with things.

And . . . these things all belonged to her husband! He was richer than anyone she had ever seen in her life. No wonder he had lied to Pa about going to Canada. If Pa ever saw all of this, Jerry would never be rid of him, always coming around looking for money.

The things in this room were a funny lot enough, all right. Under the glass domes were monstrous little preserved creatures, looking very alive, posed in the act of eating other monstrous little creatures. Were these insects? Sea-life? Something else? She couldn't tell. On the shelves were ranged crystals and odd little sculptures, some of which made her feel very queer indeed, and what looked like tiny models of buildings, and medallions with strange writing, and many more things of that sort. The crystals in particular attracted her; she kept picking them up and taking them over to the window to hold them up to the light and see them sparkle, or discover their colors. For some reason, she didn't like to touch the medallions. And the sculptures—well they all seemed remarkably ugly, and she couldn't imagine why anyone would want them around.

Still, they were fascinating to look at.

Finally she picked one up and peered closely at it. It looked a little like a human with a goat-head. And as she held it, it warmed to her touch—

—it moved in her hand!

With a squeal she dropped it, then got to her hands and knees in a panic, afraid she'd dropped and broken it. But it had fallen on the carpet and it was fine.

Scolding herself for being silly, she picked it up and put it quickly back on the shelf, and rubbed her hand against the arm of one of the chairs to take away the strange feeling she'd gotten when she touched it.

She was disappointed to discover that the glass-fronted cabinets were all locked, though they were full of things she wanted to pick up and peer at and play with. Jars and jars of seashells, polished stones, and different colored sands. Astonishing-looking insects mounted on framed boards. More jars full of clear liquid in which odd things floated. Tiny, beautiful little painted and glazed jars, and jars made of stone of every color, and vials of colored glass. And jewelry! All of it old and strange; necklets and necklaces, bracelets, rings, even what looked like two crowns! She wanted badly to take those out and try them on. She began to search the room for a key to the cabinet holding the jewelry, but in vain, and as she went back to the cabinet to stare at it all with longing, she heard a step at the door to the room and turned.

The maid stood there, glaring. "Lunch on table," she rasped, and turned and left.

Mary had thought she couldn't possibly be hungry after that breakfast, but she was, so she trotted along to the kitchen. The maid was nowhere in sight, but the same food as last night— ham, pickle, onions, cheese, bread and butter, augmented with a glass jar of glistening red jelly—had been laid out with a single place setting.

Mary helped herself with suppressed glee. Biting into buttered bread spread thickly with sweet red jelly evoked a sensation of such visceral pleasure she shuddered. She had *never* tasted anything like that. In all her life she'd gotten a "sweetie" three times, all on memorable occasions; once a bit of barley-sugar at a church parish Christmas dinner for the parish children, once a peppermint a more fortunate child had dropped in the street that she had spotted before it got trodden on, and once a piece of licorice from a Salvation Army lady when she'd had a cough that wouldn't stop. She'd made each last as long as she could, but the sensation of pleasure on sucking on the sweeties had been nothing compared to this. And people ate like this *every day!*

She was going to eat like this every day!

Since there was no one here to stop her, she had a *second* piece of bread and butter and jelly.

She washed up afterward at the sink, since her hands were sticky from the jelly. The old lady had finished in the parlor and moved on to the room with the books, so into the parlor she went.

There were none of the interesting things to look at here that there had been in the sitting room. In fact, this seemed to be a room intended for a man. The furniture was all covered in leather, there was a desk, two chairs at the fire and one behind the desk, a jar filled with what she discovered to be tobacco on the desk, and a rack of pipes beside it. The room smelled like tobacco and smoke, actually. And there were more books.

She took one down and leafed through it, but the printing was all odd, and there were no pictures. She put it back, then decided to look through the desk.

The middle drawer was locked. The ones on the right and left side, however, were not. In the top right she found a key that looked as if it would fit those glass cabinets, and in the top left, she found a door key. She picked that up with a tingling sensation of excitement. Would this fit the locked door on the second floor, or the one on the landing?

She took it, leaving the smaller key for now. The cabinets could wait. She wanted to see the rest of the house. There might be more dresses. There might be toys. She'd looked with longing in at the windows of toy shops, knowing she could never have so much as a ball, much less a doll—and if Jerry wasn't going to need her to cook or clean, then why *shouldn't* she play?

She thought about trying the door on the landing . . . but the old woman was on this floor and might try to stop her. So instead, after making sure the old woman was still cleaning the parlor (she was), Mary went back upstairs and carefully approached the locked door on the second floor.

She put the key into the lock and turned it.

It worked!

With some vague idea of putting the old woman off the scent, she went back into the bedroom and packed a pillow under the blankets, as if she was taking a nap. Then she went back to the now-unlocked door.

When she opened the door, she found herself on the landing of a staircase, as she'd thought. There were small, dirty windows in the outside wall at each landing, allowing some dim light to filter in. She closed the door behind herself, and went up the stairs, slowly, and as quietly as she could.

She half expected another door at the top of the stairs, but there wasn't one. She found herself in another hall, like the one on the second floor. But this hall only had two rooms on it. Two doors.

She went to the nearest, put her ear to the crack, and listened.

Silence.

Good. That meant Jerry wasn't in there. He must have gone off to whatever work he did. She put her hand on the handle, and turned it, opening it just the smallest amount. She peeked in through the tiny gap.

It was dark. She couldn't see anything.

She pushed the door open a little more and stepped inside—

And an iron-hard hand closed about her wrist and yanked her completely in. The door slammed, the hand pulled her tightly into someone's chest, while another hand clapped a sickly-sweet smelling rag over her mouth and nose. She took in a deep breath to scream, and then a different sort of blackness descended.

She woke. There was light in the room, coming from a single lamp overhead. She was strapped down to a cold metal table, with heavy, wide straps holding her at the ankles, knees, waist, above her breasts, at her wrists, elbows, and a final strap across her forehead. Her mouth had been stuffed full of rags, with another rag tied around her head to hold the rags in place. The metal table wasn't flat; her heels were significantly higher than her head. If the straps hadn't been holding her skirt down, her skirt and petticoats would be up over her head. Terror engulfed her, and she started shaking.

"Curiosity kills the cat," said Jerry, somewhere in the darkness beyond the pool of light cast by the lamp. "Mind you, I was counting on that curiosity."

He'd lost his commonplace accent, she suddenly realized.

He sounded educated now. Posh, even. She struggled with her bonds, but they were stout leather straps, and far stronger than anything she could break. She could hardly breathe, she was so frightened.

He moved into the light. He was wearing . . . something strange. A long black dressing gown? No, this looked more like something a priest in a high-class church would wear, only without the white bit at the collar. Except it had things embroidered on it in dark red thread.

"Are you still curious, my little wife?" he said, looking down at her impassively, although there was a sneer in his voice. "Don't you want to know why you're here? Of course, you didn't have a choice in what's been happening to you, after all. I wonder if your mother and father were still sober enough to notice the significant differences from the norm in our wedding ceremony? Probably not. I gave orders for them to have as much gin as they could drink. They should have been seeing double by the time they came upstairs."

At this point she couldn't even think clearly. Her throat was too paralyzed to produce so much as a squeak.

"Our ceremony bound you to me, little wife, forever. You are obliged to obey me in life—" he reached over his head, and turned up the lamp. "—and in death."

The light glinted off a row of bucket-sized glass jars on a shelf a few feet to her left, and *now* she let out a muffled, strangled shriek.

Because each of those jars was full of clear liquid, and floating in that liquid, in each jar, was a girl's head, their hair floating loose like seaweed. Their eyes were wide open and. . . . staring at her.

Their lips moved.

She thrashed, or thrashed as much as she could, and tried to scream again. But the restraints held her firmly, and the man who had married her looked down at her with no trace of feelings whatsoever.

Then he pulled on the pins holding her hair on the top of her head, making no attempt to be gentle. When it was loose, he wrapped it around his left hand, and reached down with his right.

"Remember," he said. "You are mine, forever. You obey me forever. You can never leave me."

He raised his right hand. He was holding a butcher's cleaver. She froze, unable to think, to move, to make a sound.

"You are mine, forever," he repeated. Then he smiled thinly. "Don't worry. This won't hurt for long."

3

It was always too quiet in the flat when Suki was away. Even with the windows open and the street noise filtering in, it was too quiet.

It didn't help that Sarah was alone in the flat today, while Nan was out with Neville, seeing if they could find Suki's attacker. Over the past year, Nan had gotten a bit of tutoring from Sherlock on disguises, and now she was able to present herself as quite a believable young man. In that guise, with her own knowledge of the bad back streets and her abilities at self-defense, she could go anywhere. And with Neville following her from above, hopping from roof to roof, she and Sarah were quite confident that she would be safe, especially in daylight.

In fact, may heaven help anyone who interferes with her. If he's lucky, she'll just leave him unconscious in the street. And if she actually finds the perverted wretch that wanted to hurt Suki . . . he'll wish the police had gotten him instead.

Sarah doubted they'd actually find anything, especially not if the blackguard had crawled off to some hiding place where his wounds would fester and infect, but they both felt but it was worth going out on the chance that something would turn up.

Meanwhile Sarah had something of her own to do. Work that didn't need Nan, only Grey as an assistant; work that only she could do.

It was not just places that could be haunted. Objects, too, could have a spirit attached to them. This was particularly true of those souls who had no attachment to a particular place, but had a particularly treasured object.

There were a lot of reasons why a spirit would linger, halfway between the material world and the next. Sometimes, especially in the case of children, they were not aware they had died. Sometimes they left urgent business unfinished.

Sometimes they feared what awaited them due to their own misdeeds, whether perceived or very real.

But as a medium, Sarah felt it was her duty to send them onward. In some cases . . . whether they wanted to go or not. So when she and Nan were not actually working a case for Lord Alderscroft or with John and Mary Watson, she hunted out stray souls and did just that.

She made a habit of scouring pawnshops for haunted objects and buying them, releasing the spirits to move on to the next world. But a few weeks ago, she had come across an anomaly: a very expensive piece of jewelry in a very humble shop.

It was a haunted locket, quite a good one, in fact, and something of a surprise to come across in a pawnshop, especially at such a low price. She assumed it must have been stolen from the owner in her coffin before burial—or, perhaps, after, since medical students needed bodies to practice on, and corpse thieves were not unknown in London. She had sensed the spirit attached to it and bought it without asking any questions, intending to do as she usually did and send the spirit on. At the time, she had wondered if the reason the price was so low was because the pawnshop owner had encountered the spirit himself and was desperate to be rid of the piece, but in all the time it had been in the drawer of her bedside table, nothing had happened to *her*.

Still there definitely was a soul attached that needed release. She was sure of that. And this would be a good time to do it, with Nan out of the house and Suki off at the school.

Normally she would have waited until nightfall. Sunlight had a powerful effect on spirits. If you tried to invoke one with daylight coming in the windows, you might see it appear for a moment or two, but you would quickly watch it wash away in the light, as if it was a figure made of sugar dropped into a rushing stream.

Spirits just couldn't hold their form against sunlight. However, if you excluded sunlight from a room, it was perfectly possible to invoke a ghost by day without any such problems.

Sarah had made heavy pasteboard inserts for the window in her room, and already had thick drapes that would take care of anything leaking around the edges. She lit a small candle—she would need something to see by, but the less light there was, the better, so using the gaslight was not an option. She fitted the inserts into the window, pulled the drapes tightly closed and pinned them in the middle with a wooden clothes-peg, then shut the door and blocked the light coming in from the bottom with a rolled-up mat, while Grey watched with interest from her perch.

When she was sure she had blocked out as much light as was humanly possible, she got the box containing the locket out of the drawer of her bedside table, opened it, and cradled the locket in her hand, preparing to invoke the ghost.

Except—she didn't have to.

Even as the gold of the locket warmed to her hand, the spirit appeared before her.

"My goodness," the young woman said. *"I thought you would* never *call me!"* and she smiled.

Like all ghosts that were able to muster the psychic energy to speak, her voice came as an echoing whisper, barely audible. The ghost herself was a young woman, simply but tastefully dressed in a neat lace waist and long skirt, with her hair done in a chignon on the top of her head. As ghosts always did, she looked like a chalk drawing painted in the air, tinted only faintly here and there with color.

It was obvious immediately what she had died of—at least to Sarah, who had a great deal of experience in these things. She was thin, with a hollowness to her cheeks that spoke of consumption—although, had her clothing been poorer and the locket gold-washed base metal instead of solid gold, Sarah might have also suspected lead poisoning, as the young women employed to paint china often ingested fatal amounts of lead by licking their brushes to give them good points.

Sarah stared at her, very much surprised. "You knew I had your locket? I mean, you knew that I would be able to see you?"

"I . . . I am not quite sure how. I just felt it," the ghost replied. "Oh. I'm Caroline Wells. Call me Caro. You must be some sort of mediumistic person?"

This was, without a doubt, one of the sanest and calmest spirits that Sarah had ever encountered in her entire life. And she could not account for how such a levelheaded soul had not passed on. "Yes, I am," she answered simply. "I'm Sarah. Among other things, I look for objects in pawnshops that are . . . attached to spirits."

Before she could continue, Caro interrupted her. "Well, I don't want to be sent on just yet. Please. This is why I clung to my locket. It's not for any selfish wish, and heaven knows I never did anything to speak of, much less anything terrible. The thing is . . . I don't want to be sent on if I can help you. I spent most of my life in beds in sanitariums and nursing establishments and other such places. I want to do something useful before I move on. Do you understand?"

Sarah frowned a little; this was . . . a new development. And it made her a little uneasy, given what she knew about ghosts. Could this one be trying to pull some sort of deception on her? "I think it's only fair to warn you that the longer you remain in this form, the more of yourself you are going to start losing. Old ghosts . . . are more than a little insane."

"Oh, I don't mean to stay forever," Caro said, with cheerful practicality. "Just a year or so. Until I've done something really useful and helpful. So I don't meet Saint Peter with a sad little list of non-accomplishments."

For the first time Grey spoke up. "Yessssssss," the parrot said, drawing out the "s" into a long hiss. "Good idea."

Sarah was startled. Again.

Sarah turned to look at the bird, who bobbed her entire body enthusiastically. She turned back to the ghost. Grey has never been wrong before. She knew when someone was dangerous, even when I had fallen under her spell. But I should, in all good conscience, make sure of this spirit.

"It won't bother you if I don't call on you for days at a time?" she asked, carefully.

"It's not as if I'm a djinni that has to live in a lamp," Caro laughed. "I'll be fine. There are a lot of things I can do 'over here.'"

"And if I take the locket with me, you can go with it," Sarah mused. "To the theater—"

The ghost literally brightened, and her expression changed to one of such pathetic eagerness that Sarah's heart went out to her. *"Oh, would you? I've never been to the theater! Or the ballet, or the opera or—"*

That cemented it. Sarah was reasonably sure this was no act. It was Sarah's turn to laugh, as she rummaged in the bedside table drawer for a ribbon and strung the locket on it temporarily until she could find a good strong chain, tying it around her neck. "I'll take it with me everywhere. If you're going to help me, you certainly deserve some reward."

"Thank you, Sarah," Caro replied. *"I had the feeling you were a good person when you touched the locket. I'm glad I was right."* She tilted her head to the side, abruptly, as if she had heard a sudden noise. *"I think there is someone coming to your flat."*

"That would probably be Nan, my friend. We live together. We also have a young ward, but she's at school."

"Then I'll disappear, and you can introduce us later." Caro wiggled her fingers. *"Tata, my new friend. Thank you ever so!"*

And with that, she vanished, as abruptly as she had come. Just as Sarah heard Nan's key in the door.

"Well, your afternoon was more fruitful than mine," Nan said ruefully, having changed out of her masculine disguise and into a comfortable tea gown. "I discovered exactly nothing. Well, other than that there apparently are a few fellows on the prowl for pretty young men who are bold enough to walk about looking for them in daylight."

Sarah shook her head; Nan chuckled inwardly to think how shocked John Watson would have been to overhear this conversation. "Well, that seems to indicate that there are pretty young men willing to give them what they want that also walk about in daylight, doesn't it?"

"So it does. And I don't know *why* that never occurred to me, but the first time one of them came sidling up and whispered in my ear it was a bit of a shock. Fortunately they were willing to take

'No thenkee, guv' for an answer. But tell me more about this ghost of yours."

"I suppose we probably ought to see if there is any recent record of someone by her name passing away of consumption," Sarah said thoughtfully.

"I suppose we could ask her *directly* when she died, and where, and where she was supposed to be buried," Nan countered. "That would make verifying what she says much simpler. If she really is what she says she is, she won't be reluctant to tell us."

She waited warily for Sarah's reaction to her challenge. After all, Sarah had shown herself to be susceptible to falling under the control of another before this.

But Sarah only nodded eagerly. "I was about to get to that myself, but that was when you arrived, and she told me to call her again once night fell."

Hmm. Seems promising. "Grey, what do you think?" she asked, turning her attention to the parrot on the back of Sarah's chair.

Grey bobbed her whole body, her feathers slightly fluffed with cheerful exuberance. *"Good! Good!"* she said enthusiastically.

Nan did laugh out loud at her reaction. "Do you mean it's a good idea, or that you think this ghost is good?" she asked.

"Both!" said Grey.

Nan didn't really need the answer; she was satisfied that Grey had been convinced by this ghost. "Well, shall we do this after sundown, then?" she asked. And then something occurred to her. "Wait a moment. Doesn't it seem to you as if she is offering to be your spirit guide?"

Sarah blinked owlishly at her. "I always thought that 'spirit guides' were the hallmark of charlatans . . . but now that you mention it, that is exactly what it sounds like."

Nan shrugged. "The idea has to come from somewhere. Perhaps it came from a situation identical to this one."

Any response Sarah might have made was interrupted by the appearance of their landlady and her maid of all work with their dinner tray. Nan was starving after all the walking she'd done, and Mrs. Horace had outdone herself with a lovely soup and cold sandwiches.

Once the last crumb was gone and the tray outside their door

44

with the empty dishes on it, Nan locked the door to prevent interruptions and turned back to Sarah. Outside the windows, the sky held the clear blue of twilight.

"So—" Nan began.

And then there was a third, transparent figure in the room, standing on the hearthrug. The young woman turned toward Nan.

"You'd be Sarah's friend?" she said, though it came out as a whisper.

Nan raised an eyebrow at her. "Nan. Nan Killian." She glanced over at Neville.

The raven was so perfectly relaxed in the presence of the ghost that he wasn't even paying attention to her. Instead, he was giving his wing and tail feathers a vigorous grooming.

"I hope you don't mind answering some questions," Nan continued.

"I expected them." She folded her hands at her waist, looking as relaxed as Neville. *"Ask away—or, wait, I think I can anticipate them, if you'd like to sit down and take notes?"*

Sarah got a pen and paper from the writing desk, while Nan took a seat in one of the hearthside chairs. "You seem . . . very composed for someone who's dead," she said bluntly. Truth to be told, she was a little startled. The only other time she'd seen Sarah's ghosts had been when Sarah had summoned them to help all of them with the operatic diva, Magdalena von Dietersdorf. And then, they had not spoken to her.

"I had a very long time to get used to the idea I was going to die," Caro told her, just as bluntly. *"The fact that I lived as long as I did was more of a surprise than the dying part. Honestly, to be this free to move about, to be able to breathe without pain, is glorious. I prefer this state. I feel better now than I ever remember feeling in my life."* She glanced over at Sarah, saw that she was ready, and nodded at her. *"As I told Sarah, my name is Caroline Wells. I died last year, December 28th, and I was buried in the churchyard of St. Mary's Church, Wimbledon."*

Sarah wrote all that down. "Parents?" she asked politely, as if she was interviewing one of Sherlock's clients.

"Mother died giving birth to my brother, Stephen. Her name was Charlotte, and I am buried next to her. Father is Brandon Wells, and is

a solicitor in London. Please don't trouble him or my brother—" for the first time she lost her cheer. *"My illness and demise were very hard on both of them. I do not wish to renew their grief."*

"Oh, we won't," Sarah assured her. "How did your locket get into the pawnshop?"

"Stolen by the gravedigger after the service. I didn't mind, you see, because I was hoping I could get it into the hands of someone like you. So I haunted him until he sold it at a pittance to the pawnbroker, then haunted the pawnbroker so he hurried to do the same." A mischievous smile creased her lips once again. *"And then until you came I gave anyone else who touched it an extreme dislike for it if I felt they were the wrong person for me. I fancy the gravedigger will never rob another corpse again, and the pawnbroker has been cured of taking stolen grave goods."*

Nan couldn't help but laugh as she shook her head. "You are a terror, my dear," she said.

"I am making up for all the pranking I was never able to do when I was sick," Caro admitted shamelessly. *"But I promise, aside from throwing a fright into any boys in this neighborhood that terrorize their sisters, I shall be quite sedate. You'll scarcely know I am here."*

"Now, what fun would that be?" Sarah demanded, and Grey bobbed her head. "I trust your discretion, but I see no reason for you to have to conceal yourself if we're alone here of an evening."

Nan was a little torn . . . after all, they had not yet verified the ghost's story. But on the other hand, Neville was also nodding his approval, and if the birds approved, there really was no reason to object. And Caro seemed the sort of "person" who would be amusing to have around in the evenings.

"I follow the locket of course, so if you want me to find something else to do, just put it in a silk handkerchief in a drawer, and I'll amuse myself," Caro continued.

"Well, tonight I was going to read some of Mr. Kipling's Indian stories aloud while Sarah does the mending for both of us," Nan told her.

"That would be heavenly," Caro replied with a wistful sigh. *"The nurses never had time to read to me, and it was a great trial to hold up a heavy book."*

"Then you should definitely join us," Sarah pronounced.

And so she did. It was possibly one of the oddest evenings they had ever spent in this flat, with a silent, transparent wraith perched attentively in the corner of the settee that Suki usually occupied, with one of Suki's dolls showing through her middle, as she had absentmindedly "sat" where the doll was. She was highly appreciative, and suggested that she take her leave just before Nan was about to beg off.

"Now is the most active time for my sort," Caro explained, *"And I would like to look about your neighborhood and see if there are any other spirits, perhaps ones that might need your help."*

"By all means," Sarah agreed, and Caro stood up, made a saucy little sketch of a curtsey, and drifted out through the street-side wall, waving a cheerful goodnight as she did.

"Well!" Nan closed the book and looked at Sarah, who was smiling. "I don't think I've had such an entertaining evening since Robin shared our stolen bread and ham that one evening in the garden at the school."

"It makes me wonder if this is what John and Mary go through of an evening," Sarah mused. "There are ever so many more Elementals about than there are walking spirits."

"Probably not. I get the impression from Mary that Elementals are supremely uninterested in what we humans do, for the most part," Nan replied, as she put the book back in its place and turned down the gaslights. "Perhaps Beatrice?"

Sarah shook her head. "I get the impression that Beatrice's parlor is full of her young writer and artist friends in the evening. I actually envy her. If this flat wasn't so comfortable and convenient to everything in London I'd be mightily tempted to ask you to move."

"You'd get quickly tired of a lot of artists lounging about, eating our food, drinking our wine, and burning holes in our furniture with their cigarettes," Nan laughed. "I think I prefer ghosts!"

"I think I do too," Sarah confessed, setting the last stitch, and patting one of the two piles of mended clothing next to her. "These are yours. Don't stay up too late."

She took her own clothing with her back to her room. As was her habit ever since Suki had been attacked, Nan settled back into her chair in the darkened sitting room with Neville on her lap, cautiously opened her mind, and passively allowed the uppermost thoughts of those around her to trickle into her mind.

Mrs. Horace was preoccupied with her own bedtime preparations, thinking of how nice it was to have a bakery around the corner so that she didn't have to make her own bread anymore. Mary Ann, the little maid of all work, was already asleep—Mrs. Horace was a thoughtful woman and made sure the girl went to bed right after the last of the washing-up was done, so when she rose at five to get the stove started, she'd had plenty of sleep the night before. In her little room in the garret, Mary Ann was dreaming of sitting in the middle of the kitchen eating all the bread and jam she could hold.

The neighbors to either side were either asleep already, or engrossed in getting ready to do so. Across the street it was the same, as well as behind the house. There were a few late strollers in this fine evening air, and one lone policeman. There was no one lurking about in the shadows, hiding in the alley, or even flattened on a rooftop. All was well.

She shielded her mind again with relief. *Maybe I am being too cautious—but I would rather be overcautious and feel foolish than be cavalier about this and regret it later.*

"All right, my lad," she said to the dozing raven in her lap. "It's off to bed for us. No eyes for you to peck out tonight."

"Bugger," said Neville sleepily, and laughed.

The next morning as the girls were enjoying their breakfast with the birds, they clearly heard the staccato hoofbeats of a horse in a hurry and the two wheels of a hansom stop in front of their house. All four of them—girls and birds—brought their heads up like hounds hearing a fox horn, and a moment later, they heard the bell ring, Mrs. Horace answering it, and footsteps on their stair.

But of course, Nan had already detected the familiar flavor of John Watson's mind, and had sprung up to answer the door before he could knock on it. "The hunt?" she asked, using one of Sherlock's favorite phrases.

"Not precisely 'up,' but Lestrade has begged me to come have a look at a corpse that's got him all of a tither in the absence of Holmes." Watson shook his head. "Poor Lestrade. He's not nearly as much of a fool as I make him out to be in my stories, but he's much repenting some of the hard things he's said about Holmes at the moment, and I feel very sorry for him. He's out of his depth again, and he knows it, and now there's no Sherlock to fall back on."

"Just how awful is this corpse?" Sarah asked. "I'd like to know whether I'd be well advised not to finish my breakfast. The oatmeal will probably stay settled, but anything excessive and I have doubts about sausage and eggs."

"I'd advise you not to finish," John said soberly, and Sarah immediately folded her napkin and set it aside, rising from her chair.

Neville immediately jumped to the table and helped himself to their eggs. Nan thought about chiding him . . . but why waste perfectly good eggs?

"Eat some of the tomato too," she chided him. He looked up at her and made a disgusted noise, but she stared him down. "It's good for you," she reminded him. "The Warden told me so. Pretend it's an ear."

Reluctantly, he ate half a tomato slice. Roughly the size of the ear he'd sliced off.

"And eat neatly while we're gone!" Sarah ordered, tying on her hat. "It's not fair to Mrs. Horace or Mary Anne to make them clean up your mess."

"Yes, Mama," Grey said, and laughed at her.

Sarah rolled her eyes, as Nan suppressed a smile. She had the feeling this was going to be the last amusing thing that happened today.

The young woman's corpse had been in the water for quite some time. Both Nan and Sarah had tied neckerchiefs around their faces soaked in lavender oil. It helped, but not nearly as much as Nan would have liked. The stench was appalling—but it was one that both of them had endured as children. Sarah's doctor parents had lived in a part of Africa where death was commonplace, and Nan in the worst parts of London. Neither were strangers to death and decay.

The most notable thing about the body was the fact that it had no head.

Strangely, that actually made the sight of it a little easier to bear. Without a head, it just became a thing, an abstract. At least, Nan felt that way. *Odd, how much of personhood we assign to having a head.*

Inspector Lestrade stood behind them with a handkerchief of his own pressed up against his face. He generally looked distressed or worried when Nan and Sarah saw him, but today the upper part of his face was contorted in a way that suggested that he might go have a good cry when he was assured of privacy. Nan didn't blame him. The poor child on the morgue table couldn't have been more than fifteen, and for all his bluster and officiousness, Lestrade was human, after all.

Sarah had a far-away look to her eyes that suggested to Nan that she was hunting for a spirit to go with the body. Nan, however, had fish of her own to fry. She was examining the stained, water-soaked dress the corpse wore.

"Who'd murder a girl on her wedding day, I'd like to know—" Lestrade choked out from behind his handkerchief.

"It's not a wedding dress," Nan corrected him. "Or . . . well, there is no telling if she was wearing it *as* a wedding dress, but it wasn't originally one. It was a lawn-party tea gown. An expensive one, before it was sold on to a ragman too."

The handkerchief came away from Lestrade's face for a moment, before he clapped it back. "Sherlock me, then, miss."

"The lace is of very high quality, but worn. See where the edges of the flounces have started to fray?" she told him, pointing out the places on the first flounce showing the wear; in fact, there was probably a good quarter inch of the bottom of the lace that was worn away. She pinched a bit of the fabric carefully in her thumb and forefinger, and turned part of the skirt up to show the underside. "Now look here—this is a very fine hem along the bottom, the stitches are almost invisible. But look at this seam. It's much clumsier, and no one who could afford this lace and this quality of dress would ever have seams that were not frenched— never mind that term, ask your wife about it, she'll explain it. This is a gown that was worn by a wealthy lady, discarded, sold on, discarded again, sold on again, and remade by a much less skilled seamstress into a smaller size. And possibly turned as well, although that's not as likely with light gauze like this."

Watson had bent to examine the corpse's hands, and stood up with a grunt. "This was a working girl; someone in service or employed in scrubbing floors until very recently. I'll lay my life on it that there are the beginnings of housemaid's knee under that dress. She didn't have an easy life."

"All the more reason to marry young—" Lestrade began.

"True, although Inspector, most poor married women still work." Sarah had come back out of her trance. "She might have been a good religious girl at First Communion?"

"Too old for that," Lestrade replied, obviously feeling on certain ground with that statement.

"Can we cut the boots off, Lestrade?" John asked. "I want to get a look at her feet."

Lestrade motioned to the morgue assistant, who went about the gruesome task with care and delicacy to make sure he didn't take off parts of the foot with the boot. He did so by first cutting the laces, then cutting the seams of the boot, so that he could peel the boot off the swollen flesh. The girls stepped back several paces as John moved in.

"This girl's never worn shoes in her life," he declared. "In life her soles were harder than leather."

Sarah and Nan exchanged a look. Nan spoke up. "She'd never be able to afford anything like what she's wearing," Nan said flatly. "She was one of the poorest of the poor. She may have been in service, but it was somewhere that no one would care she was dressed in rags and shoeless. She was more likely to have been employed as a scrubwoman somewhere. So *how* and *why* she's dressed in this gown is as much a mystery as where her head went."

Silence reigned in the morgue. It was Lestrade that broke it. "Is there anything else you need from this poor wench?" he said. "Because if not, I'd as soon get out of here."

John shook his head. "She's been in the water too long. I'd like to know the stomach contents when the coroner completes the autopsy, but that's all. Not even Holmes would get more from her than we have at the moment."

"Another look at her clothing would be helpful," Nan added, as Lestrade headed for the door with a haste that suggested his stomach was likely to rebel if he remained much longer. "Off her, of course. It needn't be cleaned, but dry would be good."

"I don't suppose you'd be able to Sherlock me up anything about what part of London she's from with bits of dirt or the like?" he asked wistfully.

Nan shook her head as the morgue door closed behind them, thankfully closing the stench behind them. "She's been in the water too long, I think."

"I'm sorry, Lestrade, but none of us have the depth of knowledge that Holmes had of soils," Watson said apologetically. "I wish we did, for your sake."

The Police Inspector had stuffed his handkerchief in his pocket, and Nan was moved to sympathy by the distressed expression he wore. "I know he and I didn't always get along . . . but damme, he was a genius, and . . ." Lestrade's face crumpled a little and Sarah patted his arm.

Lestrade took a deep breath, and got control of himself. "I miss him. And not just for what he could do."

"We all do," Sarah said, simply. "We'll just have to carry on."

They took their leave of the Inspector, after extracting a promise that they could see the deceased's clothing once it was removed and dry. "And try to cut it off cleanly, at places where there are no seams," Nan cautioned. "I'd like to figure out, if I can, just how many times it was sold on and remade. If we can get an idea of that maybe we can trace it through used-clothes dealers." She didn't have any hope there would still be a dressmaker's label in it. The first owner would have had such things cut off before she handed it down to her personal maid, who was usually the recipient of such garments.

John put them into a hansom, sending them home on their own; he intended to check the records of where the girl had been pulled out of the Thames, hoping he might have an idea of where she had gone *in*. "And what's become of the head, I'd like to know," he was muttering as the cab pulled away.

"Wouldn't we all," Nan observed, biting her lip. "Whoever did this—*why* kill an unknown, impoverished girl in this way? None of this makes any sense."

"Well, remember the Battersea case. We never knew the *why* until we uncovered the *how*. Stop trying to think of the *why*," Sarah replied sensibly. "Sherlock never bothers about the motive in a case like this, this early. Remember that."

"That's true," Nan admitted. "We need to concentrate on evidence. But I wish we had some way of contacting him."

"Right now, I think no one wishes that more than John Watson," replied Sarah. "Poor John. I hope his Water Elementals can give him some help."

4

The tiny room smelled strongly of rotten fish and sewage, which was not surprising, Spencer supposed, considering that the wharf was right outside the broken window. But that was by no means the only stink in this room; it also stank of blood, dreadful body odor, and infection. If he hadn't possessed an iron stomach, he'd have been gagging by now. He gazed with distaste on the man sprawled under the inadequate covers of the iron bedstead, the only furniture in the tiny room besides a stool beside the bed with the stub of a candle stuck in the grease of dozens of candles before it. Spencer was pretty certain these rooms were generally let by the hour, not the night.

As for the fellow he'd been summoned to attend, well, he wasn't worth tending to. The man looked as if he'd gotten in a knife fight with someone who had concentrated on carving his head up like an apple.

"What happened here?" he asked the thug who had brought him, a flunky from the very lowest ranks of the Organization, whose name he had already forgotten.

The man removed his greasy cap from his equally greasy head and stood uneasily beside him, turning the cap in his hands as if it was some sort of prayer wheel. "Dunno, guv," he replied with hesitation. "'E wuz on me doorstep this mornin', 'arf outa 'is 'ead. I figgered yew'd want 'im somewheres no one 'ud arst any questions. I brung 'im 'ere, an came ter fetch yew, cuz I didn' know if 'e wuz on some sorta job fer yew or if 'e jest got 'isself inter trouble all on 'is own."

"He wasn't doing any jobs for me." Spencer's lip curled as he noted the swollen, red skin, the pus oozing from the wounds, the man's flushed face and shallow breathing. "I don't know what you thought I could do," he added testily. "He's too far gone even for a doctor to help."

Round and round went the brim of the cap as the man's dirty hands shuffled along the edge. "Oi thunk . . . wut if mebbe 'e blabbed." The cap went faster. "Arter wot's been 'appenin', an yew sayin' we couldn' be too careful, like. . . ."

Though it was well after sunup, the noise (and the stench) of the docks really didn't change much no matter what hour it was. Both poured in through the broken window as Spencer considered that statement, frowning. The shouts, the sounds of cargo being loaded and offloaded, a drunk singing in the streets, it all interfered with Spencer's ability to think. But think, he certainly must. The thug was right. It *was* possible that could happen. . . .

And it was imperative that he not give the impression to the flunkies that he considered them expendable. It was hard enough holding the Organization together right now without giving the underlings a *reason* to desert. For many of them, the promise of protection was as much, or more, important than the money they were earning.

"Let me think about this a moment," he replied, stalling for time. "Have you *any* idea what happened to him? Did he get into a knife fight? Did he—somehow fall into some machinery somewhere?" This sort of horrible mutilation *did* happen in factories, but what would a petty thief and a man more used to being hired for his fists be doing in a factory? Had he taken a side job to intimidate some factory workers?

The cap stopped moving for a moment. "Oi . . . dunno," the man admitted, "'E wuzn't real clear. 'E *said* it wuz a raven. . . ."

More than likely that was a hallucination. Spencer snorted. "Preposterous. Why would a raven attack a man who wasn't bothering it? Besides, the only ravens in London are at the Tower, and what would he be doing at the Tower?"

The man (what *was* his name? Geoff? No—George) shrugged,

his shaggy brows furrowed as he struggled with the question. "Dunno. That wuz wot 'e said. Wutever, it took't 'is ear clean off."

"I can see that." Indeed, the entire side of the thug's head was a crusted mass of blood and pus, so it wasn't possible to see if the ear had actually been cut off, or torn off—or even bitten off. But it did seem likely the ear was gone, one way or another. And why would a raven even do that? Ravens pecked, they didn't leave gashes in a man's scalp or bite off his ear.

No, he'd probably gotten into a stupid fight . . . in fact, now that Spencer thought about it, he was fairly certain this particular idiot was the one with a penchant for little girls. And that was a recipe for trouble.

Probably what had happened was that instead of being smart and just *paying* for one at a brothel that specialized in such things, he'd likely tried interfering with a child who had a brother or father who took exception to his "interest."

And this did not give him an answer as to what he should do with the man *now*. What he wanted to do was just leave him here to die, which he surely would soon. But that would give a bad impression to the flunkies.

Plus, there was always a chance the landlord would come up here and the idiot would say something in his delirium. Or worse, the landlord would take exception to the idiot dying on his property, and get him dumped in a charity ward, where he might babble.

That was the problem, of course. Right now, what was left of the Organization was probably safe. But the wrong word carried to the right ears would change all that, and England would be too hot for any of them.

If only there was a place where he could leave this fool to die without. . . .

Wait . . .

"'E's gonner die, ain't 'e?" George asked, but in a disinterested tone of voice that suggested the man was not invested in the outcome one way or the other, except as it might apply to him in the future. Well good. At least there also wasn't a messy friendship involved here.

"He's dying now. If he'd come to me in the first place I could have at least cleaned him up and cauterized those wounds," Spencer told him. "That would have given him a chance. Remember that for the future, George. No matter what stupid thing you've done to get hurt, have the decency to come to me so I can fix it and keep the Organization safe. Now the only thing we can do for him is see he dies quietly and painlessly. Can you get someone to help you move him again?"

George's brow furrowed again. "Aye, but . . ."

"Here." Spencer dug into his pocket and brought out a purse, handing the man a carefully calculated number of sovereigns. "Take him to Lee Chin's opium house. It's barely a block from here. Tell Chin I want the man to die free of pain and give him half of that. Keep the rest for yourself."

That should solve multiple problems. If the idiot made it as far as the opium den without dying, Chin would drug him up, rendering it impossible for him to babble to anyone. Probably Chin would just administer a fatal dose at once and pocket the rest of the cash. And the body would be no problem for Chin. The Chinaman disposed of bodies all the time; his was one of the opium dens where the proprietor didn't care if you drugged yourself to death as long as you paid for all the hashish you ate or opium you smoked. George would be satisfied that Spencer had done all he could, and he'd have enough cash to ensure he kept his own mouth shut.

And if the idiot *did* die on the way to Chin's, George could just pocket all of it and dispose of the body himself. And he would still be sure that Spencer was taking care of his underlings.

For that matter, George might decide on his own to get rid of the idiot so he could keep it all. And that would be just as good of an outcome. Better, really.

"Roight, guv." George pulled his cap back on his head. "Oi'll get me mate. Yew c'n go on 'ome."

"You did the right thing by coming to me, George," Spencer replied. "I like a smart fellow who can think on his feet. I'll keep you in mind when jobs in your line come up."

Much pleased, George pulled at the brim of his cap by way of a respectful salute, and Spencer got out as quickly as he could without seeming too hasty about it. He stopped long enough in the bar to get the landlord's attention, drop another couple of sovereigns on the bar, and say "I'm arranging for the wounded man upstairs to be moved to a hospital. Thank you for your trouble."

"Weren't no trouble, guv," the landlord said, pleased, but he was already on his way out.

Halfway back, it started to rain, which just put the cap on what had begun as a miserable day. And even in the relative comfort of a hansom, he was still subject to the rain blowing in the front, which put him in a foul mood as he ran up the steps of his house and opened the door.

But he'd had a visitor arrive while he was gone, and his temper changed immediately, for he found someone waiting for him in the hallway who put him in a much better mood.

One of his regular suppliers sat patiently on the bench in the hall, a thin girl in a dull gray dress so small for her that it strained at the seams sitting beside him. When he entered, the man stood up and held out his hand.

To see him on the street, you would never look twice at him. He was clean and neat, dressed in an old brown suit showing a respectable amount of wear, and a good bowler hat that fit him properly. His moustache was neither so large as to be ostentatious nor so small as to be laughable. His face and expression were pleasant, but not notable. This was as it should be. Workhouses would trust that a man like this was looking for a cheap servant girl. They'd never trust anyone dressed shabbily.

Spencer placed a sovereign in the outstretched hand. The man grunted appreciatively and shoved it in his pocket. "Lambeth Work'ouse," he said. "Put to service a year ago. Caught wi' 'er marster. Sent back wi' big belly. Lost it. 'Ere she be now. Name's Peg."

And with that brief history of the girl, he tugged on his hat and left. Spencer approved of this man's way of business. Get the goods, deliver them, give just enough information to be useful, collect the fee, and leave. Spencer put on a pleasant expression and sat down on the bench next to the dull-eyed girl.

Fortunately, he didn't need his girls to be virgins.

"Hello, Peg," he said. "I'm your new master."

"Yus, sor," she replied in the faintest of voices. She looked as if she expected to be beaten or raped, or both, at any moment.

Well, he needed to change that, as quickly as possible.

"I'd like you to come with me. I'll introduce you to my housekeeper, she'll give you a nice, hot bath, and new clothing to wear. Would you like that?" He scrutinized her carefully for any sign of response to kindness. He thought he saw something stirring, but he couldn't be sure.

Well, let Kelly do what she could with the girl. Then they'd feed her. Food often worked small miracles with the dull ones.

"Yus, sor," she repeated, and followed him obediently to the kitchen.

His housekeeper—the only other person in this entire city who knew what he was about and what he was—was making luncheon. "Mrs. Kelly," he said. "When you are quite ready, would you please do the usual for our new girl, Peg?"

The old woman turned around, looked the girl up and down, and grunted. Long familiarity with her allowed him to discern that she was pleased. Well, she should be; she was as invested in this project as he was. "Let 'er eat, fust," the old woman replied, "Poor gel looks like she ain't et roight since she was born." She finished her preparations, and slapped down three plates on the kitchen table, one for each of them. Each plate held a generous portion of steak-and-kidney pie. A moment later, a platter of bread and butter, a pot of jam, and a bowl of apple pudding joined those plates. He sat down in his usual chair. He preferred eating in the kitchen, and the girls that were brought here ostensibly as servants were too impoverished to realize that people of his stature were not *supposed* to eat in the kitchen.

"Excellent luncheon as always, Mrs. Kelly," Spencer told her. Long ago he had learned the value of a well-placed compliment. Properly used, they accomplished far more than ranting and raving. And the truth was, the old harridan really was an outstanding cook. She grunted in reply, though it was a pleased grunt, pushed the girl Peg into the middle seat, and sat down in the remaining one.

Peg stared at the food as if she didn't believe her eyes. When she made no move to start eating, Spencer put on his most coaxing tone of voice, and said, "Go on, Peg. Eat. The pie, and the pudding. It's all for you. And all the bread and butter and jam you like, as well."

As he had come to expect from workhouse girls, once she started, Peg didn't finish eating until everything on the table was gone. She even picked up her plate and licked it clean, which didn't surprise him in the least. These workhouse girls didn't have any more manners than a dog. And when she was done, old Kelly put the dirty dishes in the sink then seized the girl by the elbow and got her up out of the chair. The girl followed her, unresisting, to the bathroom.

Spencer went to his study, where he waited for Kelly to return. Meanwhile, he studied his notes. It never hurt to refresh his memories, after all.

Kelly returned about the time he was finished and, as was usual, sat herself down without an invitation. He looked up and smiled at her, and set aside his notes. He allowed behavior that would have been unthinkable in an ordinary housekeeper. This project would not have been possible without her full knowledge and assistance. She was as much a partner of no indifferent skill as she was his housekeeper.

"Put the girl to bed," she said shortly. "Exhausted. Ain't been that long since she lost 'er brat, an' they musta put her straight back to work. Reckon she'll sleep till breakfast."

"Is there anything in the wardrobes that will fit her?" he asked.

Kelly pulled at her lower lip as she thought. The old woman had once been a beauty, but her looks had gone long ago. Her big eyes were surrounded with frown lines, her neck looked like a chicken's, and her blond hair was like dry straw. Fortunately she knew better than to try her wiles on him, but he'd caught her trying to flirt with some of his underlings as if she was still twenty. Pathetic. But he never told her so.

"Reckon so," she said, finally. "Can always put a sash 'round 'er, and she ain't gonna need a corset."

"Good." He linked his fingers together and stretched them. "She seemed rather emotionless and not very bright. How long do you think I'll need to woo her?"

Kelly pulled at her lip again. "Gi' 'er two days with food an' rest, then start. Reckon it won't take long." She shook her head. "It'd be better if ye didn' 'ave t'woo 'em. Quicker."

"But I must have their complete assent in the ceremony," he pointed out, and she nodded.

"Yew know best," she agreed. "I jest want 'im back. Things is gonna fall apart soon without 'im."

He sighed, but she was right. He simply did not have the strength of character, the charisma, or the blinding intelligence that *he* did. "Well to that end, did she talk in the bath? What did she tell you?"

For the first time Kelly cracked a smile. "Did she talk! Fust 'int I was gonna be nice, an' she wouldn' shut her mouth!"

What Kelly had to say was very enlightening, and gave him a clear path for winning the girl over to him in the shortest possible time. She'd gone to the workhouse as an orphan at six, and the workhouse had been a terrible shock to her. She'd been sent out to work in service at age thirteen, one year before she would officially have been deemed a "woman" and sent to the adult women's section of the workhouse. At the time she'd been grateful she wasn't being sent to a factory. But no sooner had she arrived that the master of the house had forced her to accept his advances, and had continued to have his way with her until they were caught by the mistress.

When she'd been sent back to the workhouse, she'd discovered she was pregnant, and almost immediately lost the fetus. Spencer suspected the workhouse nurse had probably dosed her with something to get rid of it. They'd have wanted to put her back out to work as soon as they could, and no one would take a girl with a big belly.

Kelly had coaxed this part of the story out of her by dint of lying. She was very good at making up whatever tale would extract a girl's history the quickest. Her ability to lie was a talent that Spencer valued immensely.

"Well, that seems simple enough," he said, when Kelly finished the last of her story. "Is the girl at all religious?"

Kelly rolled her eyes. "It's all tears and contrition with 'er," the old woman told him. "She thinks 'twas *'er* fault 'er master ruined 'er."

"Excellent. I think a combination of *God sent me to redeem you,* with *God wants you to be mine,* will be the swiftest path." He smiled at the thin harridan sitting in his best chair. "You're invaluable."

"Pish," she replied. "Since I 'spect we'll be eatin' supper alone, will cold tongue an' pickles do?"

"Admirably," he replied, and she got up, smoothed down her dress, and left.

But he did not. Instead, he sat back in his chair to contemplate the work ahead of him for the next week. And it would most certainly be a great deal of work, work he was growing weary of.

He didn't like young girls at the best of times. His taste was for solitude. On the rare occasions when he felt the need to exercise other bodily urges, he liked beautiful, mature, attentive, silent women, women who got on with the important business of arousing him without any unnecessary chatter. There were several such at his favorite brothel. All attractive, all clean and sweet-smelling, always freshly bathed, always exquisitely dressed (even if they were not wearing much), and not one of them demanding anything more of him than his money.

These girls were so *needy.* The best of them had been like the last one he'd bought from her parents—silently accepting their fate, delighted it was better than anything they'd ever experienced before, and perfectly obedient. Perfect obedience was all he needed.

The problem was the girls like this one—broken things that had to be coaxed back to life, then convinced they should give him their trust and devotion. But he couldn't buy girls from willing parents too often, and he was running out of poor neighborhoods in London to prospect for them in. The broken discards were common—just as easily bought from a workhouse, and with no more questions asked—but they required so much more work.

He was sick and tired of it. He wanted his old life back. He longed for the day when this would be over, when he could rid his house of gowns and girls, when he could go back to his studies, sifting through the mysteries of life and death and life beyond death. Back to when he would be required to practice his art no more often than every fortnight or so, and be paid handsomely for doing so.

He knew *why* he was doing this. Kelly was right. The Organization, traumatized, and shaken by losing its leader and half its members at a single blow, was close to falling apart.

And without the Organization, *he* would not have the pleasant way of life he had become accustomed to. Not for long, anyway.

And he was tired of all of the killing.

No, that wasn't exactly true. It wasn't the killing he was tired of. It was the mess and cleaning up afterward that he was tired of. Granted, he used his Elementals for it, rather than actually doing the work with his own two hands, but it was still an effort to control them. The more blood they absorbed, the more difficult they became to handle.

Kelly could do that, but he preferred to handle it himself. She was an Earth Magician—not a Master, so *he* had to invoke Elementals for her and bind them to her, but once she had them under her control, she ruled them with a fist of iron. Never once had he seen her domination of them slip for even an instant. But those were Elementals he had never allowed to taste blood. He didn't think she'd be able to control the ones that had so easily.

Still, even without that assistance, she was a fine underling who very much appreciated her easy life with him. Although she was his "housekeeper," in fact very little of the housework was actually done by Mrs. Kelly; most of it was accomplished by her Earth Elementals. The only thing she did herself was cooking, in part because she enjoyed it, and in part because she was particular about her food, and it was just easier for her to make it herself in order to get it done the way she liked it.

If there was a girl in the house, Kelly would feign doing the work, but it was all pretense. Ordinary people couldn't see the Elementals, and usually the girls were so preoccupied with their new circumstances that they didn't notice Kelly wasn't actually doing anything if they saw her "working."

And of course, if there wasn't a girl in the house, Mrs. Kelly could simply sit back in a chair and enjoy a nice cup of tea, a biscuit, and an illustrated magazine while the Elementals did her bidding.

It was an excellent arrangement for both of them. *He* had reliable, trustworthy help, while not taking the risk that an apprentice with potential equal to his would decide to challenge him. That, after all, was how he had gotten as much power as *he* had; he had challenged, beaten, and killed his mentor, and taken his power and his Elementals. But a mere magician couldn't possibly challenge a Master, and wouldn't try. And she got Elementals to command, as many as she wanted or needed, plus a very comfortable living situation.

And all she had to do was tend to the occasional girls until he disposed of them.

The fact that she was almost fanatically loyal to the Organization and to *him* also helped keep her cooperation.

That brought his thoughts back around to the new girl. Initially, he hadn't been impressed, but the fact that she'd revealed so much to Mrs. Kelly suggested her spirits would revive much more quickly than he'd first thought.

It almost made up for being dragged out of the house with no breakfast but a cup of tea and a slice of buttered bread to deal with that wretched thug.

Kelly had been right. The girl slept right through supper, through the night, and only appeared in the morning when Kelly went to wake her and give her something to wear. She turned up at the breakfast table looking very young and vulnerable in one of the white tea gowns he'd bought from secondhand dealers. And pretty in a faded, soon-to-age-into-plainness way. Well now she would always be pretty.

In fact, he thought he would use that line with her. "You will always be pretty to me." She'd be even prettier, in fact, with her head in one of his jars.

She stood uncertainly in the door of the kitchen; he motioned to her to come sit down in the same chair she'd used the day before.

"Dun think I c'n work in this," Peg said, looking a little desperate, and plucking at the folds of the gown with one hand.

"Sit down and have some breakfast, Peg," he said patiently. "Mrs. Kelly told me all about you. You're not well, you're not healthy. It would be wrong, truly wrong of me, to make you work while you are sick. I forbid you to do any work until you are rested and feeling better."

The sweet simpering he put on when he made that last statement sickened him. Oh, the things he did in order to achieve his goals!

She was so startled she actually raised her eyes and looked straight at him with a stunned expression on her face. He smiled at her. "That's right, you are to rest and eat, and get better. Then we will speak of your duties." He remembered what Kelly had said about the girl being religious. "Jesus told us that we are to take care of the weak and sick, did he not?"

To his surprise, she suddenly burst into tears, snatching up the napkin from her place at the table to sob into it.

He reacted quickly, however, patting her carefully on the back as she sobbed incoherently about being a "sinner" and "undeserving," and how if he knew how bad she was, he'd cast her out.

And then she wailed out her misdeed. That she'd let a man have his way with her, and that it wasn't illness she was suffering from, but the effects of losing his baby.

Well, now what should he do? This was the first girl that he'd gotten that had ever reacted in this way. He glanced at Kelly, who mouthed the words "blame the man." Taking the hint, he also took a firm grasp on her wrists and pulled her hands away from her face. "Look at me, Peg," he commanded.

Instantly obedient, she did. Her eyes, swollen and red, reflected her apprehension and fear. He could guess what she was thinking, that she expected that he'd send her back to the workhouse.

"I know all about your troubles, my poor child," he said, in a soft, coaxing voice. "Mrs. Kelly told me what you told her. And I know you are not to blame. Your former master took advantage of the fact that you were under his authority and had to do whatever he told you to do. If you had told him no, if you had fought him, he would have beaten you and done what he did anyway. That was very, very wrong of him, and is a betrayal of his position as a master. He is the wicked one, the evil one, not you. He is the one who will have to answer to God for his crimes, not you. You are the victim. You are to be helped and pitied."

She looked at him with mingled hope and doubt, so he added, "If you need me to find a priest to tell you this so that you will believe it, I will go right out this minute and visit my priest at St. Michael's and convince him to come here to tell you himself."

Most workhouses, of course, were associated with the established church, not something like a Methodist chapel, so he was perfectly safe in assuming she'd respond to the word 'priest.'

Her mouth dropped open and she stared at him. "Yew'd do that?" she gasped. "Afore *breakfast?*"

"I would," he replied, then transferred his grip from her wrists to her hands, folding them inside his, and looking earnestly into her eyes, thinking as he did so that he was a better actor than most of the ones he'd seen on stage. "But I should think you would be willing to believe me without that."

She flushed and dropped her eyes. "I'll . . . try," she said.

He carefully hid his elation. She was responding already! Perhaps, despite the coercive nature of the relationship, her former master had awakened her sensuality. If that was the case, this would go much faster. She would not only have her feelings of gratitude to urge her toward marrying him, she would have the stirrings of her own body helping that urge along.

He let go of her hands. "Good," he said. "Now I want you to eat your breakfast and grow stronger. Can you read?"

She *should* have been able to. The workhouses were *supposed* to see to it that the children they sent out were literate. But of course, given that the girls were generally destined for a life as housemaids and the boys as factory workers, most didn't really bother.

"Not . . . good," she said, picking up her fork and starting, tentatively, on her eggs. She glanced sideways at him, as if she was still afraid she would find disapproval in his face.

Of course, he smiled. He would control himself so that she never saw a frown on his face. "That's all right. I was just trying to think of something you might do to amuse yourself while you rest. Do you knit?" That was usually a skill that the girls were taught in the workhouses.

She nodded shyly.

"Well then, I shall give you some knitting to do. I would very much like stockings," he told her.

Of course, he didn't need or want stockings, but this would keep her out of trouble.

She ducked her head a little. "Oi make good stockin's," she managed.

"I'll see t'it Marster," Kelly said, as she brought her own filled plate to the table. He nodded. "I got knittin' tackle I can share."

"In that case I will be in my study." He finished his breakfast, gave her another encouraging smile, and left the room.

He almost felt like going back to bed himself. Being nice to that girl was exhausting.

But she had what he needed. Youth. All the energy of the years she would never live. And of course, her soul, which would be bound to him.

His lip curled as he thought of the job of work he had before him with her, and he decided, early as it was, that he needed a drink.

He gave nod to the early hour and poured himself a brandy instead of a whiskey, and instead of sitting at his desk, took his comfortable wing chair and put his feet up on a footstool. Downing half the glass, he leaned his head back and closed his eyes.

He heard Kelly come in and shut the door behind her, and opened them again. "Cor," she said, pouring herself a gin and sitting in the chair across from him. "What a milksop! Surprised th' work'ouse gave 'er up so easy. She's *just* th' kind uv pathetic little beast they like."

"Possibly they felt that having fallen once, she was more likely to do so again, and again, and again, with the same result each time." He finished the rest of his drink.

"Big bellies and babbies. More mouths to feed on the parish." Kelly nodded. "Well, she's tucked up i' bed wi' needles an' wool, an' she *can* knit, at least."

He grimaced. "I do *not* want stockings."

Kelly grinned. "I'll 'ave 'em, then. It'll pay me for puttin' up wi' 'er tears an' vapors. I tol' 'er I'd bring 'er lunch an' supper on a tray."

"You don't have to do that, Mrs. Kelly," he said, not really *objecting*, because he wanted to keep his contact with her to carefully measured and calculated moments, and not have to deal with unexpected outbursts like the one over breakfast.

"'Tis a small price t'pay t' keep 'er from weepin' an' spoilin' my dinner," Kelly replied. She eyed him with calculation. "If I was you, I'd go read 'er a bit uv Bible whilst she knits."

He groaned, but he knew she was right. The comforting verses, of course. Well he supposed that it all had to even out. That last little girl he'd bought from her parents had been ridiculously easy to process. Slightly less than twenty-four hours, and her head had been in the jar. So, of course, this one was going to be twice the work.

"Have you any other suggestions, Mrs. Kelly?" he asked. "I bow to your expertise in such matters."

As a matter of fact, she did.

When she finished, he sighed, but he had to admit he agreed with all of the suggestions, insipid as they were. Reading at her bedside would reassure her immediately that he wasn't going to ravish her. Bringing her a modest little picture or two and flowers to brighten her room was a hint that he felt she was something more than a servant. Praising her knitting would raise her spirits and make her feel that she had accomplishments.

But oh, the boredom. . . .

"When do you suggest I start?" he asked, and Kelly smiled with satisfaction.

"Leave 'er be 'til arter luncheon," she advised. "Gal really *is* peaked. I thin' she might fall asleep over the knittin'. An' we want 'er 'ealthy."

"So we do, Mrs. Kelly," he agreed, and leaned toward her, over his knees. "Now, having been so very helpful, what is it you would like in return?"

"Oh," she replied, her eyes bright with greed. "I got a list. You c'n pick one."

5

Nan had the feeling when John Watson sent round a dinner invitation that it was not going to be the good news that he'd discovered the identity, or the origin, of the headless corpse and Lestrade had been successfully placed on the hunt. But, well, she figured that they might as well hear the bad news over a good dinner, and Mrs. Hudson was planning "something special," according to John's note. Whatever the news he wanted to give, at least they'd have a lovely dinner and please Mrs. Hudson at the same time, which was always worthwhile. Mrs. Hudson was more than just a "good cook" as Mrs. Horace was. She was an extraordinary cook, and it pained her that Sherlock regarded food as mere fuel and would absentmindedly shovel whatever she gave him into his face without noticing what it was. In fact, she had seen him eat his dinner cold, congealed, and conventionally inedible without even noticing the difference, more often than not. When Mrs. Hudson had a group that appreciated her cooking ability, she loved to show it off.

The invitation specifically included the birds, which relieved Nan. After the scare with the man in the park, she didn't want to leave them alone in the flat at night. Mrs. Hudson had fed them in the past, so she could be counted on to supply some lovely fresh veg for Grey and raw meat for Neville.

When they arrived, John's sober expression confirmed Nan's fears. But she was determined to put all that out of her head for as long as it took them to eat what promised to be an excellent meal, and so, it seemed, were John and Mary.

She couldn't help but notice that all three of the ladies had worn light-colored summer gowns in the Artistic Reform style, but not white, as if they were trying not to echo the headless girls. Mary Watson wore a blue Liberty of London print, Nan was in light green, and Sarah in pink. Not formal "dinner wear," but then, all three of them cared far more for comfort than fashion. No one said anything at all until the dishes were cleared away and they had all settled down in the sitting room. And then John brought out the brandy, which did not bode well to Nan's way of thinking.

"All right," she said, when John had poured all around, excepting the birds, of course. "What's the bad news?"

John sighed. "Another headless body," he said reluctantly. "Fundamentally identical to the last one. I didn't bother to call for you for that reason. My own attempts at discovering anything more were fruitless. The Elementals couldn't tell me anything other than the general area of the Thames where the body first turned up as far as *they* are concerned. As you know, they won't go into the worst of the river, so to them it appeared just outside the heavily contaminated area."

"I was afraid of that," Sarah told him, echoing Nan's thoughts. She toyed with her glass, a little frown line between her brows.

Grey uttered a heavy sigh, which at least made them all smile.

"But that is not why I asked you here," John continued, after a sip of his brandy. "I know we more or less agreed to help Lestrade but . . . there is a limit to what we can do. And I believe we have reached that limit." He let that sink in for a moment. "We are none of us, neither singly, nor together, the equal of Sherlock. His kind of deductive reasoning is not our forte, and I will be the very first to admit that. He was an excellent teacher, so we are better than Lestrade at it. We are good, very good. But not *that* good. And so far, utilizing *our* strengths has had very little result."

"I can't think of anything we missed," Nan said, shaking her head. "Which probably means we missed seventy five percent of what Holmes would have seen."

"But that's not all. To be honest with you, with the exception of his self-appointed mission to destroy Moriarty, Holmes always worked for clients. We don't have a client. No one has commissioned us officially to pursue this." John raised an eyebrow. "Furthermore, we are not working for Lestrade. And not to put too fine a point upon it, the one person we *do* work for is Lord Alderscroft. Not Lestrade. Not Scotland Yard. What we *should* be doing is standing at the ready for Alderscroft's call. Well, you two should. I should be seeing to my patients."

"I see your point," Sarah replied as Grey bobbed her head. A profound silence descended over all of them, a silence broken only by the street noises from outside, coming in through the open window.

Nan saw his point, too. In fact, this was something she herself had been wondering about. With all the good will in the world, what on earth use was *she* to Lestrade, now that they'd spent their budget of "expertise"? If he had someone whose mind he wanted her to read—not that he would believe in such a thing— that would be one thing. But he didn't have so much as a hint of a suspect yet. Sarah had done what she could—but without a ghost haunting the body, she was as useless as Nan. *Sherlock* would have known how to effectively use their talents in ways they just couldn't see. And that was the problem. They couldn't see how to do more than they already had.

And of the two Elemental Masters, only John *might* have been able to get any information, and he'd tried and failed.

"Well, let's at least do this logically and make a list of points for helping Lestrade and against," Mary said into the silence. "I'll get paper and a pencil."

John shook his head as if he thought the effort was futile, but didn't stop her. When she returned, she had a sheet of writing paper and a book to use as a desk. "Arguments for?" she asked, sitting down.

"Lestrade clearly needs help," John said, with a little laugh. "Always has, once a crime traveled out of the realms of his understanding."

"Sherlock would say that was not a very long journey," Nan pointed out.

And then there was silence again, as they all tried to think of another reason. "Well one reason could be because it's possible this may be a crime that involves the occult?" Sarah ventured. Grey bobbed her head.

"It also could just be a madman," John pointed out. "We've got absolutely no evidence that it involves the occult."

"I'll put that down anyway," Mary replied. "Two bodies, both headless. The heads missing. The bodies both found in the water— and we know running water washes away signs of magic."

"But dumping bodies in a sewer to wash into the Thames is a safe way to dispose of them," John reminded them.

"I can think of another reason. Where else is Lestrade going to get help, if not from us?" Sarah asked. Mary noted that, and they all sat in silence. Neville *quorked*, and roused up all his feathers.

After that, no one seemed able to think of anything else.

"All right then, arguments against." Mary had barely spoken the words when Nan spoke up.

"We're not the police, and we're not consulting detectives," she said firmly.

"We've already given Lestrade all the information we know how to extract," Sarah put in, though she sounded reluctant.

Mary sighed. "We properly work for Lord Alderscroft, and by extension, the Crown, not Scotland Yard."

"We seem to have far more reasons against helping Lestrade than for," John observed.

Mary put the list down on her lap. "I'll tell you one more, John, and it goes past this particular situation." She put her hand on his knee, and looked into his eyes with an expression of entreaty. "I am your wife, and I need to consider these things. I am extremely concerned that if we give Lestrade more help than we have, you will become the 'new Sherlock Holmes,' and your life will no longer be your own." She gazed earnestly at him. "Sherlock never had a problem saying 'no.' You however, have a much softer heart. How can you tend your patients, who rely on you, *and* do what Alderscroft asks of us, *and* go haring off every time Lestrade feels timid about a crime? You can do any two together, but not all three."

Nan nodded, as did Neville, as John looked as if he was going to make some sort of retort to that. Nan was the one who spoke, knowing that John knew she was blunt, but never unfair. "She's right, John Watson. You've such a soft heart you can never say no. Especially with women. You've seen Sherlock turn weeping women away without a qualm, but all a woman has to do is present you with the merest hint of a tear, and you are putty in her hands."

Watson looked chagrined. "Am I that—"

"*Yes*," all three of them answered at once.

He looked from one to the other of them indignantly . . . then the indignation faded, and he sighed. "I hate to admit this . . . but much of my reason for helping Lestrade was that the victims thus far have been young women. And that brings me to *my* objection." He looked around at them all again. "I am not so much concerned about the danger of the cases that Sherlock and I solved. I know all three of you, and I know you are brave, skilled, able to defend yourselves, and above all, prudent. What does concern me is the sheer *nastiness* of some of the cases. The ones I have not written about, because the public would shrink in horror. Some of them I have not even confided to *you*, my darling." He glanced over at Mary, who compressed her lips, but nodded. "I was a soldier, and I witnessed many terrible things in Afghanistan, but they pale beside some of the horrors I have dealt with at Holmes' side. I am not trying to *protect* you. That would be foolish of me. I am trying to *spare* you, and if you were all young men, I would be saying the same to them."

"I think we are all agreed, then," Sarah said at last. "We have no business doing Lestrade's work at this point. We've done all we can."

"Perhaps Sherlock himself will turn up and give us some information to give him," Mary said at last. "One would think it is macabre enough to pull him away even from something as pressing as hunting down the last of Moriarty's minions."

John reached for her hand. "I hope you are right, my dear," he said. "I hope you are right."

With the birds in their travel boxes, John put the girls into a cab and bade them good night. Nan felt . . . perhaps a little more depressed than just merely "sober" or "subdued." She knew in her head that they had made the right decision in deciding to let Lestrade know they couldn't help him anymore, but . . . it felt like giving up. And she hated giving up.

But what else were they to do? They certainly couldn't take on every case that Lestrade had difficulties with. And Lestrade *knew* Sherlock's methods, he had to. He had certainly listened to Sherlock explain them often enough. And *they* were at the limit of what they could do for him.

So why did it feel as if they had abandoned something?

Because we have. And we should take no shame in that, she told herself. *There is no shame in admitting when you are bested.*

Sarah seemed a little depressed over their decision, too. So as they ascended the stairs to their flat, Nan decided that they both needed something to lift their spirits.

"I think we need a treat," she said, as Sarah put her key in the lock, and Mrs. Horace peeked out to make sure it was them. "I think we should visit the theater tomorrow night."

Mrs. Horace nodded, as Nan glanced down at her. "I agree. You two 'aven't been out in ages."

"But the birds—" Sarah objected.

"Oh bring down their perches and I'll let 'em doze in the parlor, ducks, while I mend." said Mrs. Horace cheerfully. "They'll be no trouble at night."

Mrs. Horace did not ask them why they were suddenly concerned about leaving the birds alone when they never had been before, and Nan was just grateful that she had volunteered to watch them. "Shall we come tell you all about the performance when we come back, then?" she asked instead.

"That'd be lovely, as long as it's something cheerful, like Gilbert and Sullivan, or a pretty ballet," Mrs. Horace replied. "Just not one of those dreary operas where everyone dies."

Nan had to laugh at that. "Cheerful it is, then," she promised.

When they closed the door behind them, Nan felt a smile coming on. "You're going to wear the locket and bring along Caro, aren't you?"

"You don't—"

"Actually I am strongly in favor of this. Unless you have other information for me, she's been helpful about the spirits in this neighborhood, she did her best to find out about the headless girls, and I think she deserves a treat," Nan said decidedly, as she took off her hat.

The transparent form of their resident ghost manifested next to the cold fireplace. *"The resident spirits in this neighborhood are all cozy ones,"* Caro pointed out. *"Sarah has taken care of anyone troubled or troublesome. But thank you for thinking of me! Where are we going?"*

"I don't know yet. I think we should consult the paper. Of course, we can always have our fun vulgar and go to one of the big music halls," Nan said, picking up the evening paper from where Mrs. Horace had left it for them and settling down next to Sarah on the couch. Caro leaned over the back of the couch between them as they turned to the advertisements for various theaters.

Nan could not help thinking how strange, and yet how droll this was, to be perusing the advertisements for theatrical productions with a ghost. And yet, Caro really was a great deal of fun to be around. She had even found a way around the fact that she could not turn pages in a book to read to them in the evening—she had somehow got Neville to do it for her! He would carefully pick up and turn the page with a twist of his head, then quickly run his heavy beak down the crease to make sure it stayed.

"Well, all the music hall productions look equally enticing to me," Caro said finally. *"And you'd have a lot to tell Mrs. Horace about."*

"We could arrive and leave when we pleased, too, which is an advantage," Sarah mused. "There really isn't much else that we haven't already seen."

"It's not really theater season," Nan pointed out. "There are some smaller companies doing plays I don't much care about, but no ballet and no opera." She sighed. "I wish Lord A would send us to Blackpool."

Sarah cast a startled glance at her, and Caro a quizzical one. "Blackpool! Why on earth?"

"Because, according to my actor friends from Beatrice's little gatherings, there's a great deal going on in holiday season in Blackpool. Not only big music halls, but little halls on the pier, with concert-parties—"

"What are those?" Sarah demanded.

"Like music halls, only with much smaller groups. There's usually one handsome young male dancer and singer, the same for female, most of the group can play instruments, so they can do small concert numbers, there's generally a comedian and someone who sings 'serious' songs, and from there it can be all sorts of acts, a juggler, or an acrobat or two, or even a dog act. Sometimes they're called 'pierrot troupes,'" Nan told her triumphantly. "They're all up and down the seaside. My actor friends pretend that it's a great comedown to be in one, but secretly they'd much rather be in one of those than starving in the summer."

"If I'd had any idea Beatrice's evenings were that entertaining, I'd have come along," Sarah said. "I thought it would be all cigarette smoke and ego."

"Well, it is, but you do pick up things," Nan admitted. "Anyway . . . we could go see those, and at night there's the illuminations. I think Caro would love it."

"*Oh, I would,*" the ghost sighed.

"Well, in absence of that, I think a music hall is going to be our best venue," Sarah sighed. "Which means we need to find one that is respectable after dark."

Nan laughed. "Why? Don't you think we can take care of ourselves?"

She expected Sarah to respond with something like "No, I'm worried about the mess we would make," or something of the sort. But Sarah said, soberly, "If Moriarty's men are truly looking for *us,* a rowdy music hall with ladies of ill fame would be a good place to do away with us."

"Bother your logic," Nan sighed, but nodded. "All right then. The Alhambra. They have very good ballet dancers and nothing could be more respectable."

"Lovely. We'll go tomorrow night. And meanwhile, Caro, perhaps you can tell us the latest ghostly gossip." Sarah set the paper aside.

"*Nothing you want to hear about,*" Caro laughed, then sobered. "*I have asked about after your headless victims, but thus far, no one has brought me any information. It's a bit frustrating, and a great deal like the children's game of 'Whispers.' I have to ask someone who is at the limits of where I can go, who has to ask someone at the limits of where he can go, and so on. And then information will only trickle back, and one has to decide just how much it has been distorted, based on the number of hands the information has passed through."*

"Except that you've gotten nothing, so there is no information to distort," Nan stated.

"Alas, yes."

Nan glanced over at Sarah. "Then we have absolutely done everything we can, to the limits of our abilities. We have *earned* a respite from the work, and tomorrow night we shall have it!"

Caro applauded.

With the birds safely in Mrs. Horace's care, they caught a hansom cab just after dinner, and directed the driver to go to the Alhambra Music Hall, Caro's locket safely around Sarah's neck on a strong steel chain. Once there, they joined the pleasure-seekers that streamed inside, having secured tickets for a very advantageous spot in the first row of the first balcony.

They arrived just in time for what, according to the programme, was a "fairy dance" by the ballet. Nan rather thought that Puck would be rolling on the ground laughing to see what the silly "Sons of Adam and Daughters of Eve" thought were "fairies"— these long-legged girls with gauzy skirts and ridiculously tiny wings at the small of their backs. But the music was good and the dancing was very good. Caro did not put in an appearance, but Nan actually expected her to stay invisible.

Act followed act, and Nan found herself happily engaged. The Alhambra really was living up to its reputation as a first-class music hall, and of course, the advantage to coming to a music hall was that if a particular act was not to your taste, it didn't matter, because in a few minutes, there would be another act along. The orchestra was exceptional, something Nan noticed particularly, since she preferred instrumental music over vocal.

Sarah much preferred vocal music, which puzzled Nan a little. *If I'd been used and manipulated by a semi-Elemental Opera Diva, I think that would have put me right off singing.* So while some fellow bellowed that *"Maaaaaany brave heeaaaaaarts are asleeeeeep in the deeeeep,"* she amused herself by looking around at the Alhambra's opulent interior. Chiefly red and gilt, she was fairly sure the owners fondly supposed it to be the epitome of

Moroccan decor. Having *been* in Morocco, she begged to differ, but that was of no matter. It was attractive, and certainly not as overwhelming in its intent to impress as some other music halls with their baroque interiors.

In the interval, she and Sarah remained in their seats while those around them made a stampede for the refreshment salon. With the seats around them mostly empty, Nan suddenly felt a breath of cold on her neck, and heard Caro whisper, *"This is amazing! Thank you so very much!"*

Nan glanced over at Sarah, who smiled. "You're welcome. We're glad you are enjoying it."

"Every bit. But I haven't been idle. I've asked the spirits here to send our need for information onward. Leicester Square is quite some distance from your flat, and it seemed like a good opportunity to pass on our request."

Nan glanced over her shoulder, but Caro remained invisible—prudent, to Nan's way of thinking. But she was touched that in the midst of her first real outing ever, Caro had thought about being helpful. Very helpful, in fact. "Thank you," she murmured. "Now I think you have earned the right to just enjoy the rest of the program." She glanced at the program in her hands. "It seems the second half is devoted entirely to a short ballet, *La Fille Mal Gardee.*"

"The Girl Who Was Poorly Supervised? *Well that certainly sounds promising!"* Caro laughed. *"She sounds like a very naughty girl indeed!"*

"I believe that's the case," was all Nan got to say, when their seatmates began making their way back, having fortified themselves with cigarettes, orange squash, lemonade, or something much stronger.

The ballet was everything Nan had hoped for. She had not expected a ballet to form the entire second half of the program, but evidently there were more than enough enthusiasts to support such a program. She was glad, however, that they had not chosen to attend at the height of summer. It was warm enough by the end of the production that she and Sarah elected to make use of the fans provided for free by the management, and they weren't the only ones.

As the rush to leave began, they remained. For one thing, it would give Caro a little more time to interrogate the local ghosts. For another, there was no point in getting caught in the crush. They wouldn't be able to get a cab any faster.

They were nearly the last people out of the balcony . . . and Nan suddenly felt uneasy, though she had no idea why.

"Let's go down to the main floor, and take our time getting out," she suggested. "I've got a funny feeling. . . ."

Sarah didn't object. Instead of making for the exit, they took the stairs down to the refreshment salon and managed to convince the weary staff to serve them a last lemonade, which they sipped until Nan's feeling of unease passed. When they left the theater, there didn't seem to be anything untoward going on, and Sarah gave Nan a questioning look as they hailed a passing hansom. The driver had had a disappointed look on his face; he'd probably thought he'd missed a chance of getting a last fare. He cheered right up when Nan hailed him, pulled up his horse, and jumped down off the box to open the door for them—something hansom drivers didn't often do.

Nan gave him the address, and off they went. "I don't know," she said, in answer to Sarah's unspoken question. "I just had the feeling that we really needed to delay going out."

"You don't suppose . . . you-know-who's people were actually waiting for us?" Sarah began, when the cab began to slow, then stop.

The driver opened the little door above them. "Beggin' yer pardon, leddies, but there seem t'be a narsty accident ahead. Any objections if Oi takes a long way round it?"

"Not at all," Nan assured him, and while he carefully backed his horse and began the tedious business of getting the cab turned around, she decided to have a look.

"Nasty accident" was something of an understatement. Just as she stuck her head out of the window, a horse began screaming in pain. There were several horses down in their traces that *she* could see, and at least two cabs, one of them a growler, on their sides. A delivery van and an omnibus were tangled up in the mess, and . . . an automobile. The driver of the last, identifiable by his duster, driving cap and goggles, was being interrogated by two bobbies.

"Bloody fools in them mechanical demons," the driver said to no one in particular. "That bloody demmed thing *caused* the wreck, take my word for 't! Ourta be outlawed, that they should, whizzin' about faster than God meant man t'go an' *no* respeck. *No* respeck at-all!"

And the feeling of tension inside Nan broke. She sat back in the seat, and motioned to Sarah to have a look for herself. By the time Sarah leaned back, the driver had gotten the horse and cab turned around.

Sarah turned to Nan, wide-eyed. "Do you think—"

"I don't know," Sarah admitted. "But if we had left a little earlier we might well have been in the middle of that. That's reason enough for a premonition."

"I suppose so," Sarah admitted, and licked her lips. "You know what is the worst about this? If Moriarty's people wish to do us harm, they know what *we* look like. We have no idea what they look like. They could be anyone."

"And we could equally be struck down by a disease or a perfectly accidental accident," Nan reminded her, to try and coax her out of the collywobbles. "And we wouldn't know where *that* came from either!"

"Well, aren't you cheerful," Sarah replied, with spirit. Nan smiled, having accomplished her goal.

6

"Well, that went off splendidly." Spencer did not rub his hands together in the manner of a comic villain, but he felt as if the gesture was justified. He had taken a long time to plan this, there had been several dry runs, and the result was perfect.

"It's a good thing my motor is being replaced," the man next to him on the seat of the hired carriage sighed. "She cost me a fortune." He had taken off his goggles, driving gauntlets, and cap, but still wore his duster against the chill.

"And now you'll be able to replace your machine with a better one," Spencer reminded him. "I must say, allow me to congratulate you on that bout of excellent driving. I really did believe your motorcar was out of control."

"That's why the Boss always used me to stage accidents. I was good with a horse. I'm better with a motor." He smirked. "That's one cabby that'll never pick up a fare again."

"He shouldn't have been so friendly with Sherlock Holmes." Spencer smiled thinly. "And that is one less ally for John Watson to call on. Oh, by the way, here." He reached into his coat, and handed the fellow the envelope full of banknotes he pulled out.

"And that's how you do business. Payment on delivery. I always did like that about the Boss." The fellow gave him a sideways glance.

"And I assure you, things haven't changed. As you can see." Spencer waited while he opened the envelope and counted the notes.

"Seems right. I can get off here," the driver said, pointing to a corner ahead.

Spencer knocked on the ceiling of the carriage to tell the driver to stop, and the two parted without a word.

And that . . . bothered him. He'd hired the man to stage fatal accidents before, on behalf of his employer, and the driver had always been very chatty. This time. . . .

Well, perhaps it had been the loss of an extremely expensive motorcar. In the past, when he'd staged accidents with horses, he'd made sure to use a broken-down old nag. He'd drug them to give them "pep," knowing the drug would finish them off, but that they'd be put down for broken legs when he was finished with them anyway. But there was no way to do that with a motorcar. They were either in working order, or they were not.

And it had to be an out-of-control motorcar at that spot. It was the only way he could give a glancing blow to the hansom cab that would send it over in such a way that the driver would be thrown and killed.

Still . . .

This time their clever driver hadn't wanted to talk over how he'd done the trick, the satisfying *crack* of the cabby's head splitting open on the curb, how he'd gulled the police into believing it had all been a horrible accident. And how cleverly he'd driven, so that all the bystanders were willing to swear he was telling the truth.

This time . . . nothing.

And to Spencer, that could be an indication of trouble to come. More restiveness in what was left in the ranks. Concern over whether *he* had what it would take to keep them out of the eye of the law. Never mind that it was their own skills that kept them out of the eye of the law—and their own carelessness that drew the law's eye toward them. The eye of the pack always went to the leader.

And now he was the putative "leader," someone who had always been in the Boss's shadow. They had never seen him *do* much of anything.

He understood all of this. He just didn't know quite how to instill their confidence in him.

Well . . . perhaps in a few weeks, that would be something he no longer needed to concern himself about.

The hired carriage stopped; with a start, he realized it had reached his doorstep. He stepped out, tipped the driver, and turned to go up the stairs.

To his pleasure, the delightful scent of steak-and-kidney pie greeted him. He hung his coat and hat in the hall and headed for the kitchen.

And to his surprise, the girl was there, dressed neatly in one of the white gowns Mrs. Kelly had gotten out for him. She didn't *jump* up from her chair when he entered, but she did get up quickly, and shyly presented him with a pair of well-made stockings.

He searched his memory for her name. "Why Peg!" he said, feigning pleasure. "What a delightful surprise! I had no idea you were making these for me!"

Her pale cheeks flushed, and she cast down her eyes. "Yer've bin very kind t'me, sor," she whispered.

He quickly ran through a number of things to say, and settled on, "It is easy to be kind to you, Peg. You are sweet and good." He rather thought she'd respond to that better than compliments about her looks, which to her mind had only gotten her into trouble.

She flushed again—with pleasure, he thought, and sat down again. He took his place at the table, Mrs. Kelly brought the pie, bread, butter and plates, and they ate mostly in silence. Peg said nothing. Mrs. Kelly mentioned a few trivial matters, such as what he wanted for dinner and supper the next few nights. It occurred to Spencer that this was quite the most pleasant dinner he'd ever had with a girl present. She was coming along nicely.

"Yew c'n run along, ducks," Mrs. Kelly said, when the girl had finished and didn't ask for more servings. "Yew needs t'git yer strenth back."

"Thenkee, Miz Kelly," Peg said in her near-whisper, and left the table, presumably to go back to her room.

When she was gone, Spencer lifted an eyebrow at his confederate. "At least she's no longer licking plates."

Kelly barked a laugh. "Give 'er 'nother two days. Get yer fake parson ready t'come over th' day arter. When yew ain't 'ere, all she c'n talk about is yew. So 'andsome! So nice! Loverly voice!" She snickered. "Fair besotted."

"Do you think my line of *Jesus sent me to protect you* will work?" he asked.

"Like honey fer a fly." Kelly nodded her head wisely, then clapped her hand to her forehead. "Oh! That 'minds me. That poet-feller come round and left a note fer ye."

She jumped up from her chair and came back with a sealed envelope. He scanned it quickly, and smiled. "My contact has another possibility. I'm to meet him tomorrow night at his salon. We'll have supper early; these artists drink like fish, and I'll need something to soak up all the liquor I can't avoid drinking."

"Hrrm. Welsh Rabbit, then," Kelly replied. "An' tea 'stead of wine. Don' think the gel likes wine anyways, but give 'er tea with plenty 'f sugar an' she's 'appy as a lamb in clover."

He laughed, thinking how one of his favorite dishes was a nice leg of lamb. . . .

The "salon," as Hugo Werlicke styled his evening gatherings, was every bit as boring and pretentious as Spencer had thought it would be. This would be a "non-occult" night, so none of Werlicke's hangers-on with pretensions of "powers" were present. Instead it was mostly poets and novelists who spoke more about poetry and books than they actually wrote, artists who were indifferently talented but belonged to families more than wealthy enough to indulge them, and a scattering of "models," who generally did not hold still when they were naked. However, Spencer had to admit that Werlicke's accommodations were superior and luxurious, and his taste in wines and brandies was second to none.

Spencer surveyed the crowd, indolently lounging about a sitting room in which virtually everything upholstered had been done in calfskin or red velvet and everything that could be gilded had been, and spotted Werlicke just as his host spotted him. Werlicke said something to the two people who had been leaning over the arms of their chairs to speak with him and got up languidly.

Werlicke always did everything languidly.

He was a very beautiful young man, and although he encouraged the dissipations of others, he himself was surprisingly controlled in his indulgences. "I don't have a portrait to absorb my sins," he had once told Spencer, laughing, when Spencer remarked on his habits. What *that* was supposed to mean, Spencer had no idea. Some fantastic novel or other, he supposed. He seldom read outside of his occult interests.

From his appearance and the sinuous way he had of walking, although Spencer had more than once found him enjoying the embraces of one of the many "models" that seemed to spend a great deal of time in his house, Spencer suspected he enjoyed the embraces of young men as well. Not that it mattered to Spencer. What *did* matter that he was utterly reliable, trading contact with potential . . . *prospects* . . . for certain genuine occult secrets. Werlicke had ambition. He was the sort that Spencer would *never* have as an apprentice even if he'd a need to take one, but had no problem with giving the odd bit of information to.

"He's over there," Werlicke said, indicating the darkest corner of the opulent drawing room with his eyes. "Peter Hughs. He's heartbroken. His little dolly flew off to the embraces of an officer of the King's Guard, his book of poetry has had nothing but bad reviews, and . . . well he's always been brooding and melancholy, but . . ." He shrugged. "Let's just say he's indulged in my opium for the first time, and found it very much to his taste. I think he'll do."

"Family?" Spencer asked.

"None. Dear Papa disinherited him and threw him out. Well, Mama keeps his bank account full, but only on condition he stays away, stays out of the newspapers, and doesn't ruin their daughters' prospects for marriage, or corrupt the morals of his brother."

Spencer smiled thinly. If this fellow worked out, he'd become so anonymous he might just as well have journeyed off to live in Tahiti amongst the natives. Presumably Mama and Papa would be pleased with such a result. Very probably they were hoping he'd catch pneumonia this winter and have the courtesy to die. He'd seen more than enough parents like that, for whom children were mere commodities; cared for according to their worth for as long as they were useful and discarded as soon as they were not.

Most of his brides, for instance.

He helped himself to a bottle of brandy and a pair of glasses from the sideboard and headed straight for the young man, who had driven off the last of his companions with his melancholy.

"You look like a man who could use a drink," he said, thrusting one of the glasses at Hughs, virtually forcing him to take it, lest he be considered impolite. Spencer deftly extracted the stopper from the decanter of brandy with one hand and poured a generous portion into both their glasses. "Why don't you tell me your troubles?" he continued. "The worst that will happen is that I'll get bored and find a girl."

Peter stared at him for a moment, then committed sacrilege by downing half the glass of brandy without tasting it and uttered a bleak-sounding laugh. "Why not? I've driven off everyone else here tonight."

Hughs essentially repeated everything Werlicke had related, but with more detail. If Peter's family despised him, well, he despised them even more as crass money-grubbers and society-climbers. He had invented an entirely new system of symbolism for his poems, where scents expressed emotions, and none of the fool critics had even *tried* to understand it. And as for women! He did not have enough negative things to say about them. They passed over intellectuals in favor of muscles, a uniform, and a moustache. They thought they were owed everything, yet gave nothing. They played at being helpless, when all the time *they* were the ones in control. And whenever *they* broke things off with a fellow, everyone wondered what was wrong with *him,* and didn't bother to consider that the one in the wrong could have been *her.* And then there was the way they'd lead a fellow on, just using him as a placeholder until a muscle-bound handsome face came along.

There was more, much more, in this same vein. It barely registered on Spencer. He'd heard it all before, many times. He didn't care one way or another. All that he cared about was that Hughs was appropriately despondent, easily manipulated, and in good health.

His health would suffer slightly from the opium Spencer was going to supply him, but that was nothing that couldn't be taken care of later.

When Hughs finally wandered out of the usual diatribes of life and its heavy burden, his tone darkened, to a point that greatly surprised Spencer. "I'm tired of it all," he said, heavily, and with none of the elaborate language he had used before this. "No, I really, really am. I don't know why I was even born. My mother practically threw me at a wet nurse and then to a nanny so she could resume her social life as quickly as possible. My father never saw me except to ask why I wasn't exceeding his expectations. My brother is everything he wants, so I was always useless in his eyes. I failed at University. I've failed at poetry. If I died tomorrow, no one would even miss me. I'd try doing myself in, except I am sure I would botch that too—" he gave a bitter laugh "—and so prove a further disappointment to my father."

Spencer could scarcely conceal his glee. Here was someone, at last, with such a low will to live he should scarcely put up a battle at all! "Well," he said, in a consoling tone of voice. "I'm not a doctor, but I can certainly recommend opium-eating. It cures nothing except the pain of living."

"I have tried it," Hughs admitted. "I must say that I found it pleasant, and it did take me away from myself. I would probably indulge—" he made a face "—but the creatures one has to deal with are so repugnant. Greasy little Chinee. . . ."

"Leave that to me," Spencer said, soothingly. "I have taken a liking to you, Hughs. I'll get you the opium. And if you'd rather not indulge at your home, allow me to offer you the comforts of mine. It's not opulent, but it's pleasant." He wouldn't actually allow Hughs in his real home, of course. He had a cozy little apartment here in Chelsea for purposes of this sort. Here he could make sure Hughs got carefully measured doses and came to no harm.

Hughs brightened. "You'd do that for me, old chap? Really?"

"Of course," Spencer smiled. "I'm not a poet myself, but I certain admire your sort. And who knows? You might find your muse in opium. Plenty have, or so I hear."

In fact, the only person he'd ever heard of bringing *anything* out of an opium dream was that chap Coleridge, and even then it had only been a maddeningly short fragment, but telling Hughs that only made him more eager. "Here's my card," he said, handing the young man the card with his alternate address on it. "Turn up about teatime tomorrow, I'll have what you need, and make up a comfortable place for you to enjoy it. Who knows? You might awaken in the morning with fresh inspiration."

Hughs seized the card with alacrity. "By Jove, you are a capital friend, old chap!" he exclaimed, with the first indication of enthusiasm he had shown yet.

Spencer smiled as he stood up. "I do try to be," he said, modestly. "Now, if I am to have what you need by teatime, I need to take my leave now." This was a lie, of course. He had enough opium stockpiled to kill a regiment. But he wanted to give the impression that he was going to considerable effort for this young man. The more beholden Hughs felt, the more submissive he would become. Spencer knew his type well. They longed to be the captains of the ship, the masters of their universe—but if they ever got that position, they wouldn't know what to do with it.

He returned the now-empty decanter of brandy to its place and took his leave of Werlicke. "I trust you found my little rabbit satisfactory?" Werlicke smirked.

"Very," Spencer replied. Werlicke, of course, had no idea what Spencer really intended. He was under the mistaken impression that Spencer's game was to befriend men like this, pander to their vices until they were addicted, and exploit them. Hughs was certainly an easy mark for that sort of thing, given he had access to his mother's money. Hughs was not the sort that Werlicke would allow to be a hanger-on for long. For all his faults, Werlicke was a collector of genuine talent, and possessed some of that himself.

"I'll send you that book in the morning," Spencer promised, making Werlicke's eyes light up. And with that, he took his leave.

Mrs. Kelly had gone to her own bed by the time he arrived home, and when he looked in on Peg, she was soundly asleep, with her knitting laid by on the table beside her. He thought about visiting his workroom, but decided against it. He wanted to be sure of Hughs first.

Instead, he selected the book he intended to send to Werlicke, wrapped it neatly in brown paper, and addressed it, leaving it on the kitchen table with the money for postage for Mrs. Kelly to send out with the morning post. He went to his solitary bed, reflecting rather sardonically that tomorrow would be full of the tedious business of courting. First, it was time to accelerate the courting of that girl. And then, another sort of courting, that of Hughs. Very different, and yet with the same goal.

To make them his, to bend to his will, forever.

* * *

"Good morning, Peg," he said, coming into the kitchen. And now, at last, he was rewarded with a bright smile. It was bright enough that he decided to press his luck. He sat down, but did not touch his breakfast. Instead he gazed intently at her, until she blushed and dropped her eyes, but looked pleased. And almost pretty, although most of that was merely youth. He could see why her former master had forced his attentions on her, however.

"Peg," he said, earnestly, although he did not move to take her hand. "I have been thinking about this for some time since you came into my service—"

"I'm ready to start work, master!" she said, looking up with anxiety painted all over her features. "Right now, this minute!"

He shook his head. "No, dear child, that was not what I have been thinking. It has occurred to me that I live a very lonely life. And that God may have placed you in my path for a greater purpose than for you to scrub my floors and help Mrs. Kelly. I believe that God wishes for me to make an honorable woman of you, and it is His Will that we wed."

He made this a statement, knowing that she would be unable to say "no" to it. And Kelly chimed right in from the sink, as if he had coached her.

"House needs a missus," she grunted. "You're cleanly and respeckful. You'll do." Which was perfect, the sort of endorsement she would have expected out of someone who a few moments before had been her superior.

Peg went red, and white, and red again. Opened her mouth and closed it several times.

"It is God's gift to both of us, Peg," he reiterated, again, making it a statement.

Finally she got up the courage to say something. "Yus, sor," she whispered. "I 'opes I makes yer 'appy, sor. I don't rightly d'serve sich kindness."

Now he reached out, and patted one of the hands clenched on the tabletop. The hand relaxed, and turned palm up, taking his. He smiled triumphantly. "Then will you be my wife, and obey me forever, Peg?"

"Yus, sor," she said, fervently. He clasped her hand, and felt the magic binding them properly.

He allowed her to hold his hand for a moment longer, then gently extracted it. "It will take me a few days to make arrangements. We'll be wedded here by my priest friend, all neat and tidy. In the meantime, we'll just keep on as we have been, you getting stronger and healthier. All right?"

"Yus, sor." She seemed dazzled, and clearly still did not believe this reversal of fortune. He finished his breakfast, and went up to his workroom, using the key on his watch chain. He had hidden the other in the locked drawer of his desk. Although he didn't expect Peg to have the spirit to go wandering and investigating, there was no point in taking chances.

He closed the door and, with satisfaction, felt the power and the despair of all his trapped brides. He lit the overhead gas lamp and went to the focus table. Without something to worship, it could not properly be called an "altar," but it served the same purpose of focusing power that an altar did.

He removed the silk drape from the sealed vial of old blood in its special holder in the center of the table, and immediately felt it. The force. The presence. The spirit that *refused* to die, *refused* to give in to anything, gods, fate, or destiny. The revenant that was Professor Moriarty.

He moved his vision from the material world into the space that lay between the material and whatever afterworlds there might be, the space that was inhabited by ghosts, spirits, and revenants.

Behind him, in a semicircle, were his brides, faces contorted with suffering, chained together by his magic and his power. When they realized he could see and hear them, they began to wail, but he silenced them with a gesture. All his attention was for the revenant of the Professor—who here was a somehow more sinister version of the man he had been in life. Thinner, taller—in fact, he towered over Spencer. All of the strength and menace he had hidden from the world were revealed here where he could hide nothing.

"*Well?*" Moriarty asked. It was not quite a snarl.

"I believe I have the perfect vessel for you," Spencer said calmly. "It is a poet in his twenties. He lives his life in despair, and

I believe he will not attempt to contest you when you possess his body. I need only weaken his will further with opium—"

"Opium! And then I will be forced to suffer through the effects of weaning myself off that pernicious substance! Why is it you insist on this? Why could you not bring him here, now, if he is all you say?"

"May I remind you," Spencer said, fighting down anger, "We did things your way three times. The first time, I brought you a vessel that was physically weak as well as weak-willed, and your attempt to possess him killed his body as soon as you drove out his spirit. The second time, I brought you someone who successfully fought you, and I was forced to kill him and dispose of the body, at *much* inconvenience to myself. And we both know how the third time went." He turned his gaze into a glare. *"You* thought it would be sufficient for the victim to be mad. I brought you a madman, and he nearly subsumed you, and I was forced to kill him on the spot before he infected you with his madness."

Moriarty shrank—literally shrank—in acknowledgement of Spencer's rebukes, although he did not acknowledge them in any other way.

"Professor," Spencer said, giving the man the title of respect. "You took me on as your advisor in all things magical because I have not just the learning, but the true Gift that grants such power, and the Mastery of my Gift. While you knew you could easily conquer the learning, without the Gift and the Mastery you would be operating blindly, as if you were trying to create delicate clockwork with your hands and tools encased in a box. And you permitted me to operate independently because you knew you could trust me to work to your interests. When I told you that we needed to make this talisman with your blood to ensure that I could bring you back to life at need, you agreed, because you knew you could trust that this was in your best interest. It would be illogical to lose that trust now, especially after you have proved to yourself that this is not just the best way, but indeed, the only way, to give you life again."

Something like a growl or a grumble emerged from the spirit. *"Damn you, Spencer, for being right."*

When he had been alive, Moriarty had been skeptical, even

slightly dismissive, when Spencer had first urged him to make that talisman. True, he had been convinced that magic existed, and Spencer could do and know things it was not possible to explain by any other way. But he had not been convinced that there was any way to beat death.

But Spencer was no ordinary Elemental Master. He was a Master of the fifth Element, that of the Spirit. There were, of course, two ways one could take that Mastery, but only one that led to true power. And so, he was a Master Necromancer. So eventually, Moriarty had agreed, for he had come to realize that if there was a way to control, coerce, drain, bind, or otherwise manipulate spirits, Spencer knew it, and he had conquered it.

All the Elementals were, to some extent, Spirits. That meant he could conjure and bind *all* of them, in theory at least. In practice, he generally kept to the most tractable. The Elementals of Earth and Air, for instance, and then only the lesser creatures of those Elements. It was not wise to attract the attention of the Greater Elementals. which were not only impossible to bind, but would work their wrath on any mere human who attempted to bind them. And it was just best to steer clear of Fire Elementals altogether.

But when it came to human spirits—once they were in the halfway realm, there was nothing he could not do with them, and that included finding them a new body. It had taken a while to persuade Moriarty—in fact, it had taken actually doing so with a trusted lieutenant who needed more than just a new identity. Spencer knew his own limits, and he knew that while he could control the dead, he could not do the same with the living. And he had known that when Moriarty died, the Organization would fall apart, and he would lose far more than he was willing to give up.

So this had been in *his* best interests . . . of course. The one thing that Moriarty must never be allowed to know was that Spencer would always, *always*, work only in his own best interests. It just so happened that those coincided with Moriarty's.

"*How long?*" Moriarty growled.

"Not long," Spencer replied, knowing that Moriarty had no way of keeping track of time here. There was no use, of course, in suggesting the Professor attempt to learn anything while in this state. He was more than merely trapped, he literally could not see anything that Spencer did not illuminate with his magic, such was Spencer's power over the spirits he bound. He knew better than to attempt to bind the Professor, or directly control him in any way, so he controlled Moriarty's access to just about everything. He didn't want Moriarty spying on him, for one thing, and even a ghost bound to a talisman would be able to move about the house and listen to and observe the living, unless restrictions were placed on it. And for another, he wanted Moriarty to understand at a visceral level *how much power Spencer held over him* without Spencer coming out and telling him. The best way to do that was to keep him isolated and alone with his own thoughts.

"I have nothing more to report, Professor," he said, with outward humility. "I will come to you again when I do. You will probably see another girl or even two added to the chain before then. Remember that this, too, is in pursuit of our goal. The more power there is in the chain, the more power there will be available to you to assist in your possession of the new body."

Moriarty merely waved dismissively at him, and he removed himself and shut off his vision into the half-world. Once back in the silence of his workroom, he took a deep breath and composed himself. He had not felt this uncertain since the day he had realized that his own Master intended to give him just enough education in his powers to be useful without allowing him to reach his true potential, and that he was going to have to kill the man in order to achieve that potential. That had been the day that he had first learned there *was* such a thing as a Spirit Master, by overhearing a conversation between his Master and another Earth Master. Until then, he had thought his true gift was Earth Mastery, and he had a minor talent as a medium. His mentor had known better.

He checked the time on his watch, and decided to lunch on the way to his other flat. He obtained a quantity of opium sufficient for several sessions from his supplies as his brides looked on, secreted the box in a special pocket in his coat, and left.

He wanted to avoid Peg for now; fortunately he heard her chattering excitedly to Mrs. Kelly, and he gathered they were altering a gown, probably for her wedding dress. He slipped out the front without either of them noticing.

In the cab on the way to his flat—there was a decent pub

conveniently near it where he could lunch—his thoughts returned to the discussion with Moriarty. Had there been a touch more of anger than usual? And a little less of the cold rationality that was the Professor's hallmark?

That was a problem, both with ghosts and with bound spirits. The longer they remained in the half-world, the more they lost of themselves, and the more irrational they became. There was no "normal" span of time for this to happen in; his brides were insane almost immediately, while he had known ghosts as ancient as Romans to cling to a sense of self and duty, though they might not retain much more than that. And Moriarty had a powerful will; that should keep him together longer than most. Still, his hold on sanity should be factored into any equations.

His previous mentor's sanity certainly had not lasted long. It had been with considerable regret that he'd released what had been a formidable source of power that had ceased to be useful when despair turned to mindlessness. And at that time he had not had the resources of a Moriarty at his disposal. He'd been forced to capture existing ghosts and bind them, which had been tedious, or make off with vagrants, bind their spirits, and murder them, which had been dangerous. He had not been able to afford a house, or a helper like Mrs. Kelly. He had been forced to use his flat, and take the risk that a nosy landlady could discover evidence of his murders, or poke about amidst his ritual equipment and undo everything he had accomplished by stupid curiosity. It wouldn't take much: breaking a talisman, erasing a diagram, crushing a vessel. . . .

He did not want to go back to that. It was imperative to get Moriarty a new body.

There would be a great advantage to this; provided Moriarty would leave this reckless chasing of Holmes to his underlings, Hugh's body should last him for thirty, forty, even fifty more years. Meanwhile, with the source of his income restored and secure, *he* would be able to complete the considerably more complicated procedure to procure *himself* a much younger body. There was no reason why this could not go on for as long as both of them exercised due caution, and made sure all dangerous activities were left to expendable underlings.

Perhaps I should point this out to Moriarty once he has

possessed Hugh's body. He can simply beat Holmes by outliving him. Moriarty's Organization can go on and on into the future, while Holmes becomes a quaint footnote in the annals of those who collect sensationalist stories.

The sooner he made that point to the Professor, the better. It might make him concentrate more on future plans, and less on his frustration. The longer Moriarty was able to keep himself calm and concentrate on intellectual things, the likelier it was he would stay sane and close to his pre-deceased self.

It was at this point that the cab arrived at the pub near his "convenience" flat. Having paid the driver, he entered and made a satisfactory lunch, and arrived at his flat with a good two hours to spare before Hughs arrived.

He spent that time airing the place out, lighting a small fire and scattered a few belongings about to give the flat the appearance of being lived in, and made up a comfortable bedlike arrangement on a wide sofa in the sitting room. And he rolled a carefully measured quantity of the sticky, raw opium gum inside a bit of marchpane.

Hughs arrived right on time, looking pathetic, yet eager. As soon as Spencer had closed the door and drawn him into the sitting room, he answered the unspoken question with a slight smile and soothing tone. "Yes, it was no problem. I have what you need. Would you prefer to relax with a cup of tea first or—"

Hughs was clearly torn between appearing to be a civilized, controlled man and having the release he desperately craved. Before he could say anything, Spencer directed him to sit on the couch, still wearing that faint smile. "Well, why not both? Make yourself comfortable." He went to the small kitchen and returned with a cup of tea and the opium sweet on a little plate. He handed the latter to Hughs.

"It will take some little time before the opium takes effect, taken this way," he said. "Smoking is faster, but—" he made a little face. "I cannot rid myself of the image of scrawny Chinese and stinking opium dens."

Hughs had lost no time in devouring the morsel, and Spencer handed him his cup, taking his own place in a chair where a second cup waited on the table. "Have your circumstances improved at all since yesterday?"

Hughs shook his head dolefully and said nothing. Spencer did not attempt to coax him into further speech. Instead, he took over the conversation and turned it into a sort of monologue that Hughs was not required to respond to except in a very general way. All the while he kept a sharp watch on his guest for the signs that the opium had begun to have its way with him.

And eventually, Hughs began to nod, then slowly sink back into the cushions of the sofa, his head lolling to one side. His eyes closed.

Spencer carefully lifted his feet from the floor and tucked them up on the sofa. Hughs stirred a little more and arranged himself on his side, slightly curled, completely in the thrall of the drug.

With a smile of triumph, Spencer fetched what he would need from the seldom-used bedroom and began the first of the binding magics that would eventually have Hughs completely in his thrall.

7

Nan was engaged in the homely task of ironing when she heard the doorbell at the street door, shortly followed by that good lady's steps on the stairs leading up to their flat. Carefully putting the heated flatiron on the stone tile on the end of the ironing board where it wouldn't burn anything, she hurried to the door. Mrs. Horace gave her usual discreet tap as she was four or five steps away.

"I wouldn't be botherin' you on ironing day," their landlady said, telegram in hand, "But . . ." She waved the telegram helplessly.

"Quite right, Mrs. Horace," Nan agreed, taking it from her with that sense of trepidation every telegram engendered in everyone she knew. The mail came twice daily after all, and ordinary communications could certainly stand a wait of twelve hours. But a telegram! That meant urgency, and urgency implied bad news.

But when she opened it, as Mrs. Horace hovered anxiously, she breathed a sigh of relief, a sigh that was echoed by Mrs. Horace, who turned around without a word and trotted back downstairs. *Meet lunch club. Alderscroft.* At least no one had died!

At least this is not a warning that Moriarty's men are on to us, or that Watson or Mary have been hurt . . .

"Sarah!" she called. "Alderscroft summons us to lunch! We should have just enough time to get there."

"What now?" Sarah asked, popping out of her room in her

waist and bloomers and snatching the newly ironed walking skirt from the ironing board.

"Telegram, just three words. Where's my hat?"

"On the bust of Athena." Sara slipped on the skirt without a petticoat. "Can I—oh, it's Alderscroft. Better not." She darted back into her room and returned, shaking her skirt down over her petticoat. "I hope we can get a—"

Just then the sound of wheels stopping in front of the building made Nan run to the window, still pinning her hat in place. "He's sent his carriage," she said, half-amused, half-grim.

"Oh dear. Not the—"

"No, the little one without the crest. But it means he wants us very badly." She picked up Neville's carrier and whistled, and the raven flew into the sitting room, followed by Grey. The parrot opened the door of her carrier with her clever beak and hopped inside; Neville waited for Nan to open his.

She shut and fastened both carriers as Sarah snatched her hat off the hook, pinned it in place anyhow, and snatched up Grey's carrier in the hand that wasn't holding her gloves. She flew out the door, followed by Nan, who carefully locked it behind her.

The coachman was already off the box and getting ready to open the door for them as they appeared on the doorstep. He said nothing to them except to pull on his top hat and give the customary salute of "Afternoon, miss," so evidently whatever was so urgent, the news had not percolated down to the stables.

At least in the privacy and space of the coach, they were able to make themselves tidier on the way to Alderscroft's club, the Exeter. The Exeter Club had only just recovered from the shock of allowing women past the public dining rooms; Nan didn't think it would survive the appearance of women without gloves and their hats hanging off the sides of their heads. Unless said hat was designed to perch at that precarious angle. The Club might not know a great deal about women's fashions, but it was perfectly capable of telling when a woman was transgressing in that area.

They were known to the doorman at this point, and while he did not give them the friendly greeting he would have given a member, or even the male acquaintance of a member, he did smile slightly and touch his hat. Nan was very glad the two of them had made themselves look *impeccably* tidy in the carriage. The freezing glance the doorman would have given them would have chilled the spirits of stronger souls than theirs.

They no longer needed an escort to penetrate the sacred halls of the clubroom, and the fellow who served the same function as a butler within that hallowed place was evidently on the lookout for them. It would have been unthinkably rude, not to mention acting above his place, if he had waved at them from across the room. But a brief inclination of his head and neck in their direction and a discretely raised eyebrow told Nan he wished to speak to them.

They crossed the room without occasioning more than a couple of coughs and a slightly disgruntled *hrrmph* from any of the otherwise fossilized Members. Poor things. Most of them had no idea they were there mostly as stage dressing, to obscure the fact that the Exeter was home to Alderscroft's Hunting Lodge, a circle of some of the most powerful Elemental Masters in the country. All they knew was that the Exeter was their home, and had been a bastion of exclusively male company until very recently. They still smarted from the invasion of mere women—and were terribly afraid that this invasion presaged an invasion of another sort, one in which women would (horrors!) be permitted to become *Members*.

"His Lordship has directed me to escort you to the Lodge Rooms, where a cold luncheon has been prepared." The words were barely above a whisper, and Nan and Sarah had to lean closely to hear them. The birds, thankfully, did not so much as stir; probably they understood the need for silence. A single word issuing from either of the carriers would probably have caused several strokes.

"Thank you, Williams," said Sarah, "We know the way."

The appropriate way was to take the servant's stair—encountering any of the venerable gentlemen who lived here on the guest stair would be worse than the birds saying something. Williams nodded and turned his attention back to his charges. Being here was a continual dance around the tender sensibilities of the old gents, who were encased in stone armor of hardened attitudes which could shatter disastrously at the faintest hint of change. Nan felt sorry for them rather than resentful. They labored under the illusion that *they* were the strong, stalwart defenders of

God and Empire and all that was Good and Noble, when in fact, their rigidity and their age doomed them. With every passing day they grew closer to death, while the reins of power slipped from their fingers and, imperceptibly, the young and flexible took those reins away from them. And the irony was, if they had just been willing to bend and learn and change with the times, those reins would still be theirs, and the "upstarts" would be looking to them as sterling examples.

Meanwhile, there was enough pity in her to cause her to grit her teeth a little and dance around them.

The servants' stairs were narrow and steep, and poorly lit. Had the girls been dressed in fashionable attire rather than sensible walking skirts, they'd probably have broken their necks.

Reaching Alderscroft's rooms was a relief, although they had to come in through the tiny kitchen—good mainly for reheating cold food and making tea. Alderscroft was waiting in the dining room—and so were Mary and John Watson.

Lord Alderscroft was a great lion of a man. In defiance of fashion, he wore his mane of reddish blond hair longer than anyone who was not an artist or an eccentric generally did, and strikingly intelligent blue-gray eyes gazed at Nan and Sarah with a directness that might have seemed rude in anyone else. He was tall and strongly built, currently wearing a smoking jacket of his favorite crimson—favorite, because he was a Fire Master, and both his clothing and the decor of his rooms, such as this crimson-painted dining room, reflected his Element.

They released the birds immediately. Alderscroft must have expected them, since he had a couple of tobacco-stands fitted out with food and water cups and newspapers spread beneath, which Grey and Neville flew to. The only other furnishings in the room were a mahogany sideboard, laden with a modest spread of food, and the matching dining table and red-brocade-upholstered chairs.

"Help yourself from the sideboard," his Lordship rumbled. "Now that we are all here, we can get started."

It was only then that Nan realized there was a third guest already at Alderscroft's table: Mycroft Holmes.

Mycroft was clearly the elder of the two brothers. He was as tall as Sherlock, but much fatter, and it was clear he preferred the sedentary life to the active one his brother pursued. But the moment you looked into his steel-grey eyes, you forgot he was fat, you forgot anything except the incredible intellect that high-browed head housed. His was a personality that could, when he chose, fill the room and dominate anyone and anything in it, save, perhaps, his brother. Beside him, Alderscroft seemed . . . ordinary. When Mycroft Holmes chose, he *was* the British government, or so his brother claimed. Looking at him now, Nan saw no reason to doubt this assertion.

She felt her eyes widening a little, but she put Neville's carrier down on the floor and followed Sarah to collect some luncheon. Mary Watson poured out tea for them both, suggesting that this was a very serious occasion indeed, and one at which Alderscroft wanted no outsiders.

"Well, Mycroft?" his Lordship said, when they were seated. Mycroft cleared his throat, but did not stand.

"Alderscroft and I want you to assist Lestrade with these hideous murders of young girls," he said bluntly.

Nan and John exchanged a startled glance. Nan nodded, and John spoke up. "We've done as much as we *can* do," he explained patiently. "We're good, but we're only human. You either need to find a way to bring Sherlock out of hiding, or you, sir, need to bend *your* formidable intellect to this task." He nodded here at Mycroft Holmes. "We are all out of our depth."

"Nevertheless," Mycroft replied, "His Lordship and I require you. There is more to this than you are aware."

"Indeed," Alderscroft said, taking up the thread. "To make a very long story short . . . the Hunting Lodge has detected the activity of a necromancer in London, and we believe these murders might possibly be his work."

John and Mary looked both startled and aghast. Nan was only puzzled. "What, precisely, is a necromancer?" she asked.

"You are aware of the Masters and magicians of the four Elements—Earth, Air, Fire and Water," Alderscroft said. "And you know that some of these have gone to the bad, and done terrible things. But there is a fifth Element, and very, very rare magicians and Masters of that Element—the Element of the Spirit. And Masters of the Spirit are as rare among Elemental Masters as the

MERCEDES LACKEY

Elemental Masters themselves are rare in the general population. Spirit Masters can see, interact with, and use the magic of *all* Elementals, because all Elementals are, to a greater or lesser degree, spirits. But most importantly of all, Spirit Masters can see, interact with, and control human spirits, or ghosts."

It was Sarah who understood what he was talking about first, and gasped, *"Sarasate!"*

"Indeed," said Alderscroft. "Sarasate is at the least an Elemental Magician of Spirit, if not a Master. His medium of interaction is music. He seems to be completely untaught, but because he uses his power for good, and has tremendous control, we have not meddled with him. But the converse of a Sarasate is a necromancer—one who wakes or invokes spirits, binds them, controls them, and exploits them for his own power and purposes." He took a deep breath. "And the Lodge believes we have uncovered evidence of such a necromancer in London. This necromancer may be connected to the murders. We need you to discover him, and determine whether or not he is."

"If there is anyone who is likely to be able to find such a necromancer, it is Miss Sarah," Mycroft said into the silence. "Or rather, Miss Sarah, working with John Watson, my brother's chief and best pupil."

"I am not—" John began, flushing a little. "Not nearly—"

Mycroft cut him off with a wave of his hand. "You know my brother, Watson. You know he does not suffer fools at all, nor the incompetent, nor the willfully blind. He has compassion, which was why he took the time to telegraph you young ladies at a perilous moment, but very little sentiment. Do you think, John Watson, that he would have tolerated you at his side for more than a month, if you had not had a first-class intellect not only capable of understanding his methods, but still, at an adult age, willing and able to *learn,* and to *master* them?"

John Watson looked like a man who had just been poleaxed. Mary, however, looked triumphant, vindicated.

"Now, Miss Sarah," said Alderscroft, taking over the conversation again. "I am going to ask you to try new things, things that may not have occurred to you that you could do. To begin with, I am going to ask you to learn how to extend your

102

vision into that half-world that spirits inhabit, and learn to call that vision up whenever you need it. Beatrice Leek may be of some small help there; I believe many in her family were mediumistic."

"I can certainly try," Sarah said cautiously. "But what difference will that make?"

"Once Watson has established a likely place where these unfortunates went into the Thames, instead of waiting for possibly insane spirits to come to you, *you* can venture into their world, find ones worth talking to, and interrogate them." Nan sensed Sarah's skepticism; Nan shared it, bur Alderscroft seemed very certain this was something she could do.

"This is of paramount importance," Alderscroft went on, in a tone that brooked no argument. "There have been more bodies than just the ones Lestrade has been burdened with. For a necromancer to undertake something of this nature suggests he is not just murdering random young girls for the pleasure of it. Clothing them as brides, the specific method of death, the fact that all are identical—it suggests that he is binding their spirits for a specific purpose, creating a kind of reservoir of power he can draw on that will be stronger and more reliable than hunting and binding random ghosts. We don't know what that purpose is, but it will be terrible."

"As terrible as that other-world we once ventured into? As terrible as bringing over the hideous ruler of that place into our world?" Nan asked.

Both Alderscroft and Holmes nodded.

"Terrible in some new and unforeseen fashion," Mycroft added. He pinched the bridge of his nose with his thumb and forefinger as if his head pained him. It probably did. "Bother all this occult business. It is nothing a rational man can predict."

"It is as predictable as any other threat to the Empire," Alderscroft replied dryly. "It is all down to men craving power. It is only the means of obtaining that power that appears unpredictable to you."

"I am willing to cede that to you, my lord," Holmes replied. "So long as your little band of unlikely warriors is willing to fling themselves into the battle on my behalf."

Mary looked rebellious for a moment. And before John could reply, she spoke.

"I don't want my husband to find himself chasing after chimeras every hour of the day and night," she said, firmly. "He has patients. He has a family. He is *not* like your brother, Mycroft Holmes, or like you. He doesn't find all of his joy in the chase, or fulfillment in the conclusion. We will do this, but this does *not* mean he is at your beck and call whenever you have some stupid problem you cannot solve!"

A tiny smile flitted across the firm lips of the elder Holmes. "I see I have challenged the lioness and she has shown her fangs," he said, mildly. "No, my dear lady. I promise you that I will not fling you and your husband willy-nilly at whatever perplexing occult problem rears its ugly head. Alderscroft has an entire Hunting Lodge for that sort of thing. I will come to you and ask, *ask,* I repeat, for your aid only when it is clear that only your peculiar combination of talents will do. Does that satisfy you?"

Mary relaxed a little. "Yes, Mycroft, it does."

"And we will serve Her Majesty to the best of our abilities," added John. Nan thought he might be both a bit aghast at Mary's boldness, and a bit grateful for it.

Mycroft just looked like a satisfied cat.

Instead of going straight home, Nan and Sarah and the birds hailed a hansom and went on to Chelsea, but not to the strange little tea shop where Beatrice and her artist friends usually were in winter time. This was summer, and if Nan knew anything about artists, she knew they would all be outside, painting, taking advantage of the weather and the light until it was too dark to tell one color from another. The poets would be searching for some small scrap of nature to commune with. The musicians would either be performing in outdoor concerts, busking for pennies, or practicing with all their doors and windows flung open. Only the actors were likely to be in the tea shop . . . and then, not so many as you might think. This was the holiday season, and plenty of them had thrown their aspirations of High Art and Drama aside to pick up much needed money in seaside pierrot or concert-party groups, or touring companies providing resorts with something like thespian entertainment. So Beatrice would not be there either.

So they had the cabby take them to Beatrice's home, one of a row of identical, white terraced houses, where Nan hopped down and knocked on Beatrice's door. Something like this ordinary, middle-class terraced house could not have been more unlike Beatrice Leek, and yet, here she was, and not in some witchy little thatched cottage nestled among trees.

The door opened immediately, and Beatrice greeted Nan with "I've been expecting you, ducks. Come in, and bring the birdies with you." Nan turned and waved to Sarah, who paid the cabby and jumped out herself, bringing the birds' carriers with her.

Beatrice was a plump, comfortable looking woman of late middle age, with a round face, pink cheeks that owed nothing to rouge, a mad mop of gray hair, and eyes that seemed to look right into your soul. When she visited the tea shop she habitually dressed in Artistic Reform style, but today she really looked like the witch she claimed she was, in a colorful, patchwork skirt, flowing blouse of bright green, and a shawl as colorful as her skirt. The house they walked into was just as colorful. The hall was not fashionably papered; it had been hand-painted, possibly by one of Beatrice's artist friends, in an imitation of a medieval tapestry. The scene was of a forest meadow, dotted with flowers and full of animals and birds both real and mythical, the centerpiece of which was a unicorn. There were three coatracks, all of them burdened by shawls, coats, and hats. There were two umbrella stands, full of walking sticks and staffs, all of them fancifully carved. Some of the staffs were surmounted by glass globes or odd little sculptures.

Beatrice's enormous black cat, Caprice—or "Cappy"—met them at the door, and sniffed curiously at the carriers.

"Hallo ducks," Neville said, from inside.

Grey growled a little warning.

Beatrice ignored it all and led them into the parlor.

The theme of the walls of the parlor was more of the same as in the hall. Here, tall, elegant women in flowing gowns danced, disported, or dozed amid the flowers and the animals. There were no pictures on the walls, but pictures would have been superfluous. The floor was covered in thick rugs layered on top of one another. The one nearest the hearth had a circle woven into it, and what appeared to be flowers were actually symbols, as Nan knew from previous visits.

The parlor was small, just big enough for three comfortable chairs and a couple of tables. Nan took the chair that showed the least wear, assuming the one with the most wear was Beatrice's favorite. Sarah took the one next to it.

"Let your birdies out, the raven first, and let them make their peace with Cappy," Beatrice directed. Nan flipped the clasp on the door to the carrier, and Neville stalked out, neck feathers slightly, aggressively ruffed.

But Cappy regarded him calmly, approached slowly, and carefully extended his neck until he had bumped Neville's beak with his nose. They stood there like that for several moments, until Neville raised his head, roused his feathers, and pronounced, *"You're a bit of all right."*

Then it was Grey's turn. Grey emerged with all her feathers up, looking a lot like an enormous pinecone. This time Cappy moved even slower, as if he understood that Grey was seriously alarmed and completely uncertain of all of this. But once they were beak-to-nose, Grey smoothed her feathers down, stopped pinning her eyes, and finally, reached out herself and gave a little bit of a groom to Cappy's right ear.

Then both birds went to the backs of their respective chairs, as Cappy settled down on the hearthrug, purring like a clockwork.

Beatrice listened carefully to everything they told her, starting from the moment when Lestrade had called them in to examine the first body to when they had left the Exeter Club. When they finished, she *tsk*ed and sat there thinking for a moment.

"Well, I think the Lion's right, ducks," she said. "There's been something dark a-stirring and it matches a necromancer, right enough. But Sarah, deary, do you really think you're *ready* for what the Lion wants you to do?"

"You think I can do such a thing?" Sarah asked in return. "Memsa'b never mentioned any such possibility when she was teaching me."

"Your Memsa'b is a canny wench, but she doesn't know everything, ducks," Beatrice admonished. "Particularly not about mediums. My family has had this sort of talent in it since Hector was a pup. It's not something *I* do, but I know how to teach you. But it's not for the faint-hearted."

Now Sarah raised an eyebrow at the old woman. "Whatever gave you the notion that I was faint-hearted?" she demanded.

Beatrice regarded her soberly for a moment more. "All right, then. Now . . . the Lion got something wrong, and you should know about this before you go any further. You can't just *see* into the spirit plane, my love. It doesn't work that way. The only way the living can interact with the spirit plane is for your soul to leave your body and go there."

"Oh . . . like astral travel?" Sarah asked. "Memsa'b told us about that, but she said unless it was a dire emergency, it wasn't worth the risk."

"Memsa'b was right. There's things waiting for the unwary once you leave your body, things that'll gobble you right up. And travel on the spirit plane is something like astral travel. Except instead of traveling in the real world, you cross the border, into the plane where ghosts that haven't crossed over lurk. And I wouldn't advise you do anything *but* cross the border, at least at first. It's very easy to lose your head, and when you lose your head, you'll lose your way."

Sarah nodded.

"Now . . . some people do this with drugs. It's *easier* with drugs, but I don't hold with drugs," Beatrice continued.

"I don't either," Sarah and Nan said together, then looked at each other, and smiled a little. "The easy way is seldom the best way," Sarah added. "I'd rather do this the best way."

"All right then." She glanced at Nan. "You could learn this too."

"I can?" She blinked a little at that.

"No reason why not. You two are practically twinned souls, and—"

But just then, Cappy raised his head, and made a little *mrrow?* of inquiry, as a soft whisper asked, *"Can I help?"*

Beatrice jumped, then peered just past Sarah's right shoulder. "Bless my soul!" she exclaimed. "You have a spirit guide, Sarah?"

"I forgot I was wearing the locket!" Sarah replied, with a start. "Beatrice, this is Caro. I don't know if she's a *spirit guide,* exactly, but she says she's not ready to move on until she's actually accomplished something in the world."

That led to an explanation, half by Caro, half by Sarah, of who the spirit was, and why she was with Sarah now. As for how Caro had managed to manifest by daylight, well—

"My house is guarded and warded and as full of energies as that teapot is of tea," Beatrice explained. "A simple old witch like me welcomes *any* creature of good intent, and the power here lets them manifest. More or less . . ."

She said *that,* because Caro was scarcely more than a whisper and a shimmer in the air next to Sarah.

"But now that we've got all that settled, aye, Missy, you can be of great help. Having a guide like you is exactly what we need to speed things up. Do you want to try right now?"

Nan and Sarah looked at each other. "I'm ready enough," Nan declared.

"Did either of you indulge in anything stronger at luncheon than tea? No? Then let's go up to my workroom proper. And take those cushions with you—" she pointed at two plump feather pillows covered in embroidery that the girls had taken out of the chairs before they sat down. The birds flew to their shoulders, and upstairs they all went.

Beatrice's house was a two-up, two-down, with the sitting room and kitchen on the ground floor, two bedrooms on the second floor, and presumably an attic and a cellar. The door to one of the bedrooms was slightly ajar, and Nan caught sight of an exceedingly comfortable-looking old-fashioned bed with a wooden canopy and bedcurtains all around. Beatrice turned to the front bedroom and opened the door.

The first thing she did was pull down the shades of the two windows and shut the drapes firmly. The second was to begin lighting candles all around. Then she gestured to the girls, who moved gingerly into the room.

There was something like an altar at one end—north, Nan thought—which had a lovely statue in the Art Nouveau style of a half-draped woman sitting in a crescent moon, with a man wearing stag's antlers and nothing else standing beside her. Nan was a little startled to see the resemblance to the Huntsman from the Wild Hunt in the man's features. Nan tried not to stare; although it wasn't as if she didn't know what a gent looked like with no clothing, it was a little disconcerting having that particular aspect so casually displayed.

She would have thought that Sarah would have been even more embarrassed, but Sarah barely gave the statue a glance before turning her attention back to Beatrice. And that was when Nan remembered—the African natives where Sarah's parents worked as doctors and missionaries were inclined to wear as little clothing as the occasion called for—and given the heat of their homeland, Nan didn't blame them. Without a doubt Sarah was much more accustomed to nude males than Nan was.

"Lie down here on the floor, ducks, with your head to the altar," Beatrice directed. "Birdies, settle down at their heads." Feeling quite grateful that she hadn't put on a corset this morning, trusting to the contours of Ladies Rational Dress to hide that little elimination, Nan obeyed. She already knew that Sarah was uncorseted; Sarah generally had to be coaxed into stays with the assertion that the lines of whatever gorgeous gown Lord Alderscroft had spoiled her with demanded that particular garment.

"Now, close your eyes, and *see* your friend Caro. When you can see her, reach out with your hand, only don't use the real one."

Nan got the trick of that first, more than likely because she realized that the "Nan" that was wanted was the Celtic Warrior she once had been. When she could see herself as the Warrior, she found she could see Caro too. Only this time Caro was very much stronger, more like a living person, and not at all transparent.

She "reached" out her hand. Beside her, she sensed that Sarah was doing the same. Caro seized her hand and *pulled,* and with a feeling as if she had somehow popped out of a shell, Nan found herself standing next to Caro, Neville on her shoulder, and Sarah and Grey beside her.

"By Jove, we did it!" she "said," somehow without moving her lips. And then she realized that she was projecting telepathically.

Sarah grinned at her. *"We did, didn't we?"* And they both looked about themselves.

The first thing that Nan noticed was the dome of light that covered them all; it was slightly smaller than the room itself. The second was the altar and the statues; they glowed with a gentle golden light, not unlike that of a full Harvest Moon.

The third was that where they were was a sort of grayed-out version of the real world. Certain things, like the altar and the tools on it, looked solid and even more "real" than they had in the physical world. Others had scarcely a hint of color, and seemed insubstantial.

Their bodies lay peacefully beside them, the "silver cords" Nan had heard so much about connecting them to their bodies at the navels. She tugged on it experimentally. It seemed elastic, but incredibly strong, as if one could suspend an entire building from it easily.

Standing next to Sarah was Beatrice; curiously while Beatrice was as grayed-out as the rest of the room, she seemed to have a pulsing core of golden light in the middle of her. And as Nan peered at her, she saw Beatrice's lips were moving.

She concentrated hard on trying to hear her.

Finally she made it out, as if Beatrice spoke from a vast distance away. *"Come back and try again,"*

"Beatrice wants us to come back and do it again," she told Sarah, who nodded.

They let go of Caro's hands and laid back down again. Nan *felt* her body this time, as if it was a suit of clothing she was trying to put on again. *All right,* she told herself, willing herself to do exactly that. *Time to wake up.*

There was a moment of resistance, and then—she opened her eyes on Beatrice's workroom. Beatrice nodded in satisfaction. "I thought you girls would take to this," she said.

Nan lifted her hand to her forehead and rubbed it. "I feel all heavy and clumsy," she complained.

"Well, you will," Beatrice said, with sympathy. "You can see why larking off like this is tempting."

"Except for the fact that nothing looks real," Sarah complained. "I have the funny feeling I've done this before, though."

"You might have done, you might have done," Beatrice agreed. "In another life, maybe or when you were a wee one, instead of dreaming. Or both! You'd have had your African magic man looking out after you if you had gone spirit-walking as a child, no doubt."

"And me," said Grey.

"I'm not forgetting you, ducks," Beatrice chuckled. "But back to work! Let's try this twice more with Caro helping, for three times is luck, and then three times without."

The second time went as well as the first, and the third better than the second.

Beatrice called for a rest before they tried it without any help, and Nan had to agree that she was feeling as if she had walked a brisk five miles or more. "Beatrice," she asked, as she sat up with her legs curled under her, while Neville picked at the edge of her sleeve, amusing himself. "Why does the spirit plane look like a washed-out version of the physical world?"

"Because that's our world bleeding through into theirs," Beatrice replied. "Their world is like a sheet of tracing paper laid over ours, which is a good, bright picture. They're not meant to *stay* there. It's a halfway place. All the other, spirits, the Elemental ones, have their own homes too. The spirit plane is meant to be like a—a railway station. You either get *on* your train and get to where you're going, or you come out into the material plane, as if you were coming out of the station into the city. Nobody stays in a railway station. Nobody is meant to stay in the spirit plane. That's why spirits that *do* overstay there often grow mad."

"Caro's not," Sarah observed, lying flat with her hands under her head.

"Caro's got a lot of will, and she has a purpose. Most spirits that overstay have neither. They're either afraid to go on, desperately want to be alive again, or don't know what happened to them." Beatrice nodded as Sarah agreed. "Or so my grand-mam told me. She was the medium. I've only seen ghosts when they've come across into the physical world. That's not often, here. These are new houses, and haven't anything to haunt them." She chucked. "That's why I bought one. The auld cottage might have been in the family for centuries, but it was on land that was thick with unquiet spirits, and they'll seek out a witch just like they seek you out, ducks. I like my peace and quiet o'nights, and now the only thing that disturbs my rest is when Cappy goes courting on the tiles." She flexed her fingers. "Now, let's try it three times without your guide helping, and I'll say you're ready to venture out on your own."

They took their leave of Beatrice just as the sun was nearing the horizon, but not before all three of them, birds in their carriers, walked down to the tea room and replenished their strength with a good supper. The tea room had seen odder things than a raven and a grey parrot, so the birds came out long enough to have treats themselves—Neville's look of ecstasy at his first taste of clotted cream had them all in stitches—and they caught a cab just as the artists began trickling in, sunburnt and disheveled and dreamy-eyed.

Beatrice hadn't let them go empty-handed either; she'd given them her grandmother's handwritten guide for "walking the spirit plane," and as soon as they turned the birds loose, they both put their heads together to read it on the sofa.

"I don't think Beatrice ever read this," Sarah said, after the first dozen pages. She pursed her lips.

"Oh I think she *did*. Remember, she said it's dangerous to do this. But I think she wanted us to have the words on it all firsthand." Nan tapped the pages of the book, where it described some of the kinds of half-mad spirits that Sarah had told her of as well. "The main difference between what you have encountered as a medium in the past, and what we'll encounter in the spirit plane, is that in the spirit plane these crazed ghosts actually *can* harm us. But!" she held up a finger. "We can do just as much harm to *them*. Maureen Leek went spirit-walking without a Caro, without a Neville or a Grey, and without weapons. The next time we try this, I think we should try making ourselves into our fighting selves. I suspect the sight of a sword in my hand will give pause even to the maddest of spirits."

"That's . . . a very good idea," Sarah replied slowly. "A very good idea indeed."

"Of course it is," Nan replied with a smirk. "I'm the one who had it, after all."

8

Spencer reclined in his very comfortable overstuffed armchair, a glass of excellent brandy in hand. Today had been most satisfactory in every possible way. He had added that pathetic little creature whose name he did not even recall to his collection. The memory of her stricken face still amused him, the expression not unlike that of a rabbit who has suddenly discovered that the wolf that was "protecting" it has finally decided to eat it. One of Moriarty's minions who rejoiced in the moniker of "Geoff the Elf" had made the salubrious suggestion that "If it's girls ye want, old Don, what runs th' Splendid 'otel in Cheapside c'n get ye all the Chinee gels ye want. An' 'e don' care wut 'appens to 'em. Just tell 'im yer gonna use 'em up."

He was appalled that he had not thought of this before—but then again, his tastes did not run to cheap Chinese whores, and he really had no notion of where to find their procurers until Geoff told him. There would, of course, be the matter of getting them to understand that they were going to be married to him, but that should only require learning a rote phrase or two in Chinese. And what a relief that was going to be! No more hunting in filthy taverns for men willing to sell their daughters, no more coaxing and courting those dreadfully dull wenches from the workhouse! Just a simple transaction: pay the man, convince the girl with a charming demeanor and the right sentence that she was going to be his actual wife, the quick ceremony, and the

113

dispatch. It could all be done in an afternoon.

And Hughs was coming along well. He was dreaming away at this very moment on what was technically Spencer's own bed, although Spencer rarely used it himself, which meant he was indifferent about having a stranger in it. Before he had taken to opium to the point of now eating it daily, he had been strong and athletic, and if he left off the drug this moment, he would not have lost much of that strength. He could probably go six months, or even a year at this rate before he was in the shape that the last candidate of Spencer's choice had been. But of course that would not be necessary. It would not be long now until he had enough brides to provide him with the power to do anything at all that he cared to do, and certainly enough power to ensure that even if Hughs suddenly developed unexpected backbone, Moriarty would be able to force him out of his body and inhabit it.

Not that he expected this. Hughs now considered him enough of a friend to emote in Spencer's presence. And oh, what a wet mess Hughs was . . . really. depriving him of a body he got no pleasure out of and was not putting to any good use was doing him a real, genuine favor. He wouldn't even go to hell for committing suicide, which surely would have been his fate if Spencer hadn't run into him. How someone who had as many advantages as Hughs had could manage to so thoroughly muck up his life was totally beyond Spencer's understanding. Literally *all* he had needed to do was to go into some respectable line, and just dabble in his stupid poetry on the side, and he'd have had a life any man of any sense would envy.

On the other hand, Hughs' family was wealthier than Spencer had suspected; no breeding, of course, but quite a bit of manufacturing money—which was why dear Mama could supply her wayward son with enough to live on out of her own pocket. This situation actually had some promise.

He planned to discuss this with Moriarty this evening, after sundown, when it was easier for the living to enter the spirit plane. Meanwhile, he would watch over Hughs until the opium wore off, then send him home in a hansom driven by one of Moriarty's minions to ensure he came to no harm. Not Geoff; Geoff would rob his own mother if he thought he could get away with it. No, this was just a reliable cabby who rarely had to do anything more sinister than take someone like Hughs home, though he did keep a cosh in his pocket in case of trouble.

And meanwhile, he had the company of a good book from his own small library here, and a truly excellent brandy.

"Chinee gels?" said old Don. The man lounged against the front desk of his "hotel," an establishment in which rooms were rented by the hour rather than by the night. The front looked like every other cheap hotel in Cheapside; faded, paint chipping, sign barely legible. The inside was more of the same. The front desk was little more than a tiny counter with a dim gaslight over it, behind which was a rack of keys. There was no book to sign in. Spencer tried not to show his contempt.

"Old Don" wore an ill-fitting suit that had never seen the hand of a tailor over a body that bulged beneath it and strained it at the seams, a tie in school colors he had no right to wear, the entire ensemble spotted with grease stains. Beneath this travesty of a suit was a shirt that was indifferently clean. He was clearly half-bald, but had contorted his remaining hair into a bizarre pompadour, so stiff with pomade it looked like an arrangement of brass wire, in an attempt to conceal that fact. He had teeth like a horse, a voice like a mule, and to top it all off, his skin was a strange shade of orange. Spencer suspected him of taking some outré patent medicine in an attempt to maintain his virility, but could not imagine what quack nostrum would have the side effect of coloring someone like a carrot.

"I was told by Geoff the Elf you could put me in the way of some," Spencer said casually. Why Geoff went by the moniker of "the Elf," Spencer had no idea. Perhaps it had something to do with the fact that he looked like one of St. Nicholas's helpers—a cheerful, harmless face that had conned many into thinking he was friendly and harmless. Or at least, right up until the moment when Geoff coshed them and left them half-naked and penniless in an alley.

"Oh, that'd be th' lad w' th' bettin' shop," said old Don, casually.

"No, that'd be the lad with the cosh in his back pocket," replied

Spencer, just as casually. A test, and a stupid one of course. Any undercover policeman or reported would have known the right answer. Then again, old Don certainly was not a man of intellect. He was barely a man who knew how to put two sentences together.

Having established his bona fides, old Don happily got right down to business. "Fresh or second-'and?" he wanted to know, taking out a stub of a pencil from one of his pockets and a greasy notebook from another. He licked the pencil, a habit Spencer found revolting.

"Either, it doesn't matter. But I'll be using them up," Spencer replied, with the casual manner of a man buying fresh chickens. Which in a sense, he supposed, he was.

"'Ow often?" asked Don, noting the fact.

"Every three days?" he ventured, having no hope that Don could supply girls that often, but giving his most optimistic request anyway.

"Cain't do three," Don declared. "Four's all roight, though, at least, fer th' next month. Got three ships due in wi' cargo, an' that means a pretty 'igh turnover i' th' stews. Arter that, though, cain't promise."

Spencer tried not to show his elation. One month would certainly see the completion of his battery, even if the Chinese proved to be an inferior product. "That will do for a month, and after that, we'll make another arrangement." He had to count on the fact that the girls only lasted so long before they faded and he had to release them, but as long as he had a steady supply of replacements, he could keep the battery going indefinitely.

Don did some more calculation, then flipped the page and wrote a single number on it. He turned the notebook around to display that number to Spencer. It was considerable . . . but the cost was by no means outlandish. When you added up the price to fathers, the price to workhouse supervisors, and all the time wasted in courting the wretched girls, he was going to come out ahead. "Done," he said,

"'Arf in advance," Don said shrewdly. "Then th' rest on delivery."

"Done," Spencer repeated, taking out his notecase and pulling out the exact amount by feel, without allowing Don to see how much he actually had in there. No point in exciting the blackguard's greed to the point where he'd try to hire Geoff the Elf to cosh him and steal the rest of what was in there. Geoff knew what side of his bread was buttered, of course, but he'd demand an equal amount *not* to cosh Spencer, and that would be tedious as well as expensive.

He knew he had made the right decision when he saw Don's eyes light up as he enveloped the money in his undersized hand. "Pleasure doin' business wi' ye, gov," Don said, stuffing the notes into one of his suit pockets. "Be 'ere in two days, I'll hev th' fust one for ye."

Spencer nodded with satisfaction. Two days should be sufficient to learn enough Chinese for his purposes. Moriarty was an expert in it, which was no surprise given how brilliant the Professor was, and browbeating Spencer into the precise pronunciation of the notoriously difficult language should give the Professor something to do besides concentrate on his rage.

He had taken no chances on the sort of cabs one could catch in Cheapside; another one of Moriarty's henchmen was on the box of the one waiting for him as he exited the Splendid. He snorted, observing the sign, whose red and gold had faded to pink and dun. It had better have been named "Squalid."

"Home," he said, climbing in.

Mrs. Kelly had already gone home, but she had left a note. *Dinr in ovin.* She had no real reason to linger when he didn't have a girl in residence, although he had no idea what she *did* when she wasn't taking care of his household. Some Earth witchery or other, he supposed. It wasn't as if she needed to tend to her own house; he'd bound enough brownies and other Earth Elementals to her to clean a palace. And she preferred to do her own cooking, so she didn't need Elementals for that.

There might be some way she could be making money from them—he had no idea how, but Kelly was cunning, though not exactly clever. But if there was such a way, he was sure Kelly would find it. That was no matter; Kelly could feather her nest as much as she liked as long as she kept his house clean and his meals on time.

It was bangers and jacket potatoes, which kept well enough in the warmth of the oven. Supper finished, he decided that he had enough to report that he might as well speak to Moriarty. It had been a good day, after all.

When he entered his workroom, he *felt* the despair from his girls. The new one had agitated them all. He smiled with deep satisfaction, as he sensed the power and energy flowing into the bank of obsidian spheres situated in stands beneath the jarred heads. He had hit on obsidian spheres to use as his storage device, and they performed brilliantly. He heard the girls wailing faintly in the depths of his mind.

Taking a seat facing the table, he uncovered the talisman, and moved himself into the spirit world with the ease of long practice.

The Professor was waiting for him, looking sinister and somehow spiderlike. *"Where have you been?"* Moriarty snarled.

"Doing your work," he replied mildly. "The poet is coming along nicely. He's becoming more suicidal every time he emerges from his opium haze, and more eager to return to it. And on that head, I have discovered a bit more about him. His parents are in trade, and have amassed a very tidy fortune. They have few aspirations when it comes to joining Society themselves, but they want the patina of respectability for their children. A good marriage for their daughter, and for their sons, something like the law, medicine, or—" he paused significantly "—a position as a recognized scholar, in some solid, sensible field. A Professor, perhaps, of something eminently respectable. . . ."

"Such as mathematics, perhaps?" Finally, *finally,* Moriarty smiled.

"It occurs to me that, although Professor Moriarty was not even remotely poor, it is going to take you some time to arrange matters so that the funds you once commanded are yours once again in this new body," he pointed out. "And I do not think that it will take you very long to arrange for academic credentials for your new persona." He pursed his lips. "I am not certain how one can establish one's self at a university, say, but Hughs is young, and you would not need to possess a degree yet to fulfill the familial ambitions. Then—bona fides in hand, you can easily make a reconciliation with the father and in no time you will be back in the well-padded familial bosom with access to their money."

"It will take some clever work," the Professor pointed out, but

his faint smirk told Spencer that he was already devising plans.

"It also occurred to me that tragedies can befall the best of families," he said, lowering his eyelids. "A gas leak . . . a cream soup past its prime . . . the injudicious selection of mushrooms . . . even a terrible street accident. Any of these could leave poor Hughs—that is, *you*, in sole possession of a considerable fortune."

"I do enjoy seeing the seeds of my tutelage blossom in a fine brain," the Professor purred. *"Pray forgive me for doubting you, Spencer."*

He waved a hand. "Think nothing of it, it is forgotten. But I do have a request to make of you, Professor. I need you to instruct me in Chinese."

"Mandarin or Cantonese?" The professor raised an eyebrow.

He was nonplussed for a moment. "Cantonese, I suppose? I cannot imagine that girls brought in to fill the brothels of Chinatown would speak Mandarin."

"You might be surprised. But in general, you would be correct. And I congratulate you on having hit on a faster way to staff the ranks of your brides. I shall teach you both."

As he had expected—indeed, hoped—the Professor was an exacting teacher. He learned several things that evening that he had not known before. That Chinese was a language that made use of tone and inflection as well as the sounds of a word. That the slightest change in tone or inflection could entirely change the meaning of a sentence. But by the time the evening was over, even Moriarty was satisfied with how he could say *Wǒyào jià gě nǐ, Nǐ huì chéngwéi wǒde qīzi,* and *Nǐbìxū shuō "yes."* That should cover all of his needs.

He had the feeling he was going to hear those phrases ringing through his dreams tonight, although that was not a bad thing. It would mean more practice, and practice in this case was something he could not get too much of.

He was about to leave the spirit plane, when his brides fell silent for a moment. Since weeping and wailing meant power and energy flowing to his storage spheres, he turned back to glare at them.

One of them—he never could remember their names, once he had installed them—fixed him with an imploring gaze. *"Please,"* she begged, her eyes brimming with tears. *"Let us'ns go! Please!"*

It was the first time they had directly addressed him; he took that as an extremely positive sign. It meant they were still sane enough to recognize him as the author of their captivity, and able to think enough to assume that he might grant them mercy. Of course, if they were actually thinking rationally, they would know that a man who wooed them and chopped their heads off was not someone with anything like a single particle of mercy in his entire body, but that hardly mattered.

He smirked. "No," he said, simply. "And what is more, I am about to make more of you, out of the lowliest of Chinese whores. Filthy, sluttish, ignorant, heathen Chinese peasants. You'll get to share your chains, and the honor of being my brides with them. You're all alike to me."

As he had assumed, the mere idea of having Chinese girls among them offended even the stupidest and poorest of them, girls who had never even seen a pair of shoes until he'd dressed them for their weddings. The wailing and cursing that ensued was music to his ears, and he left the spirit plane, laughing.

Old Don had his girl, all right, and she had probably been a pretty little thing before someone had beaten her black and blue and left handprints on her throat. She was small, scarcely bigger than a child, and dressed in what he would have termed "pyjamas," a baggy tunic and trousers of some faded material whose original color he could not discern. But the bruises didn't matter, and neither did the dull way she looked at him. He paid Don for her—the filthy lout smirked knowingly as Spencer handed over the money—took her by the elbow and led her, stumbling, to the cab. That was where he spoke the first of his three phrases to her.

"Wǒyào jià gěi nǐ," he said. *I am going to marry you.*

The effect on her was startling. From a dull-eyed, broken-spirited thing she transformed into a creature that was alive with hope and incredulity. A torrent of Chinese burst out of her; he silenced her with a gesture and a stern headshake. But although she did not speak for the rest of the drive, her bruised face kept turning toward him, her expression vibrating between dread and adoration. Now he smiled charmingly at her. He was very good at a charming smile. It was an infinitely useful expression.

The only conceivable thing that could go wrong would be if one of his neighbors saw him bringing a Chinese girl into his house, particularly in this condition. His neighbors were used to seeing girls turning up. He had explained to one gossipy neighbor some time ago that he was an exacting man, and that his housekeeper was even more so, and servants rarely lasted long in the household. After that, nobody cared; in this part of London, the people who lived in these houses were up-and-coming men with wives kept busy giving them perfect households they could display to superiors or clients. No one cared about the fussy man who was some sort of intellectual, and since Mrs. Kelly made it very clear to the other servants in this neighborhood that she had no time for gossip, there was no back-fence scuttlebutt about him either.

Two things aided him here; when it was he who was bringing a girl in, he could cast a spell of short duration that caused anyone in its vicinity to look elsewhere for a moment. So to outsiders, the servant turnover did not appear to be unduly high. The other was that most people never really looked at servants, even the ones in their own households. He knew for a fact that there were people who never bothered to learn a cook's name, always referring to her as merely "Cook," and addressed all girls as "Mary," regardless of what their real names were. So for all anyone else knew, the many girls they might have caught a glimpse of were all the same girl.

But the sight of a Chinese turning up might change that, especially one in the state this one was in. So along with invoking his spell, he flung the spare cloak he had brought over her, and bundled her in the front door quickly.

The defrocked, alcoholic priest who performed most of his marriages was already waiting in the hall, as was Mrs. Kelly. He handed the girl over to his housekeeper to give him time to deal with the priest. He had a suspicion he might have some trouble this time.

His instinct was right.

"Chinee now, is it?" The man's grizzled face, absent of expression most of the time, now showed suspicion and distaste.

"A girl is a girl," he said, shrugging. "These are easier to get than white girls. Why should it matter to you? It's not as if I'm actually marrying them." And to ensure that this newly awoken curiosity died again, he handed the fellow his fee—and a little more.

The man looked at the money in his hand and shrugged, putting it in his pocket, his hand trembling. Probably because he had not had a drink yet this morning. Spencer rectified that, too, taking the man into his study and pouring him a tall glass of some very inferior whiskey he kept around for just this purpose. That brought him around.

The priest was under the impression that this business of false marriages was a sexual proclivity with Spencer, an impression that would not have stood examination if the man had not been an absolutely hopeless drunk. Spencer made sure to encourage that useful impression. It was certainly much more harmless than what was actually going on.

The next issue arose when Mrs. Kelly came to fetch him. "She cleaned up jest fine, but she won't put on the clo'es." Kelly reported grimly. "She jest keeps poitin' at 'em and shakin' 'er 'ead."

He hurried to the spare room, where the girl was standing next to the bath, where she clutched her faded cotton garments, that baggy tunic and trousers, to her body. Kelly had gotten her into the knickers, the camisole, and even the petticoat, but when she saw him, she pointed at the white dress and shook her head frantically. There was something about the clothing that she did not like.

No—he narrowed his eyes, trying to see past the bruises. There was something about that dress that terrified her.

Now he used his second phrase. *Nǐ huì chéngwéi wǒde qīzi.. You will be my wife.* Still, she shook her head, and some vague memory of something he had read—that the Chinese associated white with death and funerals?—occurred to him. "Mrs. Kelly, you read popular women's magazines, do you not?" He knew she didn't exactly *read* them, but she did look at the pictures. "Can you get me some with pictures of brides in them?"

"Dunno how that'll help," she said dubiously, but obeyed, returning with an arm full of the magazines. He showed the girl the first picture that Kelly found for him, pointing to the white-clad woman and repeating, *Nǐ huì chéngwéi wǒde qīzi. You will be my wife.* This he did over and over, until she stopped clutching her old clothing to her, and really looked at the pictures, then at him, then at the pictures again. Finally some timid Chinese emerged from her. He pointed at the bride in the picture, then at her, and repeated his phrase. Now he wished that he knew what the exact word for *bride* was, because he could have pointed at the picture, said the word, pointed at her and the dress, said the word, and cleared everything right up. But he held up another couple of pictures of wedding couples to her, pointed from her to the dress, to the bride, and she finally seemed to come to the understanding that she had to be dressed this way to be married. She sighed, and let go of her clothing, which dropped to the floor.

He left, and let Kelly take care of her.

He had noticed that the rest of her body, at least the parts of it that weren't covered by underthings, was as bruised as her face. He hoped that wouldn't affect the energy he expected her to impart to his "battery." He wondered if she had been as obstinate about being prostituted as she was about not wearing a white dress. If so, that would certainly have lead to a beating, and being passed over to someone who was going to "use her up." Brothels didn't have time to waste on girls who wouldn't be broken.

Kelly brought her downstairs at last, looking very odd with her bruised face in the clean white gown, with a veil pinned to her hair. Her hair had been cut as short as a boy's, which made her look much odder, and Kelly hadn't bothered with shoes, so she was in her stockings. Still, the spell didn't require shoes, and it wasn't as if she was going to need them later.

They were married in his study rather than the parlor. The window in the study faced the blank wall of the house next door—the window in the parlor faced the street. Pure caution on his part, but he had not gotten where he was by being careless. He didn't want some snoop catching sight of an apparent wedding going on, then making inquiries about his wife.

When she saw the priest in his black garments, she appeared a little more confident and at ease. Perhaps she recognized what he was supposed to be from those pictures. He doubted very much if she had ever seen a Christian cleric—although you never knew, she might have run into a missionary at some point.

The brief, altered ceremony began. He felt the bands of the

spell closing around her, until they came to the moment when the spell settled, vibrating, waiting for the moment of closure.

Now he used his third phrase.

"*Nǐ bìxū shuō 'yes,'*" he told her, when the priest paused for her assent.

"Iss," she said, timidly. But it seemed that she meant it, because he felt the spell click into place.

The priest left, and rather than chloroform her, he had already planned on drugging her. Figuring she would recognize tea if nothing else, they shared tea and cakes in the kitchen, solemnly, half the cakes heavily laced with opium in the sugary frosting. She had the cakes with the frosting (obviously he didn't), her eyes lighting up with pleasure at the taste. This was probably the first time she had ever tasted a sugary sweet, and she gobbled them up like the child she resembled, and licked her fingers clean afterward. It was with satisfaction that he watched her succumb to the drug, catching her as she slid out of her chair. He lifted her in his arms, pleased that she weighed so little, and carried her to his workroom.

He usually enjoyed watching the horror on his brides' faces when they realized where they were and what was about to happen, but that was mostly in recompense for all the work he'd had to put into obtaining them. It felt like a reward, or vindication. But he'd had to do so little actual work for this one—apart from learning Chinese—that he didn't feel the need for her to awaken. So he simply laid her on his table without bothering to strap her down except around the waist so she wouldn't fall off when he inverted the surface. He made a quick job of the decapitation, popped her head into the waiting jar of formaldehyde, and sealed it shut, setting the last of the spell in place while the blood drained into the funnel set in the floor and down the pipe that led to the sewer.

That was one reason why he'd bought this house: indoor plumbing. The other was because it lay directly above one of London's main sewer tunnels. It had been trivial to have another pipe run from the floor of this room to join the other waste pipes. And while it had been a great deal more work to gain access to the sewer below the house that ran to the Thames, knock a hole big enough for a human body in the top of the brickwork, and install a hatch, he'd used Moriarty's hired thugs, which guaranteed silence. He'd been Moriarty's executioner for quite some time before the Professor's death, dispatching Moriarty's enemies quickly and quietly while accruing their power, but he hadn't created anything like his battery until Moriarty had met his unfortunate premature end. He'd merely strapped down the drugged victim, slit his throat, and dropped him into the sewer. From there, the victim became one more anonymous body in the Thames, with no indication of where he had come from, or who had killed him. Possibly Holmes would have recognized Spencer's work, but Spencer was never called on to dispatch anyone Holmes would have been interested in.

He used the same workmanlike procedure today.

He let himself pass briefly into the spirit world. The girl's spirit "woke" as soon as she was dead, of course. And for one long moment, as her spirit gazed about itself, and took in the weeping company of the other brides, all of them chained together in place by the bands of his spells, he thought he might have miscalculated. There was no terror, no horror, no tears. Only an expression of dull resignation, as if this was what she had expected all along.

But then the dullness shattered, and the tears and terror and wailing began. And as her shrill, nasal lamenting rose above the sobs of the others, the alien nature of her lamenting roused the others to a frenzy, and he transitioned back to the real world with a satisfied smile.

Once fully seated in his physical form, he picked up the drained body, carrying it down into the cellar, with a feeling of a job well done.

He pulled up the concealed hatch, ignoring the miasma that rose from below, and dropped the body into the darkness. It was with further satisfaction that he heard it drop into what must have been a good two feet of liquid. It would wash into the Thames quickly, then. The one time that a body had rotted right under the hatch had been . . . unpleasant. And it took a great deal of liquid to move a body along if it was stuck in this part of the sewer.

He dropped the hatch, covered it over with tarred cloth that at least helped to seal in the smell, and dropped the concealed false-brick of the floor.

Then he went upstairs for luncheon. He hoped Mrs. Kelly had made a shepherd's pie.

"So, it's to be Chinee from now on?" she asked him, as she filled a plate for him and another for herself.

"I have a dealer who can give me one every three days," he told her. "No fussing with them, and the hardest part is getting them from the cab to the door without the neighbors noticing."

She shoveled a mouthful of food into herself and chewed thoughtfully. "Don't like Chinee," she said, though from her inflection it was as if she had commented that she didn't like turnips, or something equally commonplace. "But they ain't stayin' long 'nough to sleep 'ere, eh?"

"No." He considered this a moment. "Just long enough to convince to get into the dress and be married."

"Then it's a damn sight less work than a white gel," she said decisively. "An' thet's all roight wi' me."

9

"Well, this is an improvement," Nan observed, as they all stood in the spirit plane version of their flat, next to their bodies. Sarah had suggested that they move a cot into Nan's room for her, and so they had. Grey nestled on her chest, and Neville on Nan's, both as deeply "asleep" as their humans. Grey "herself" was on Sarah's shoulder, clearly ready for an adventure.

Nan had discovered that she could call up and wear the form of the Celtic Warrior that Memsa'b assured her she once had been when they moved their spirits into the spirit plane. She brandished a bronze sword for Caro's admiration, and hefted her little circular shield with the bronze boss on her left arm.

Sarah had the feeling that if it had been an option, Nan would have dressed like this all the time. She had to admit it was an improvement over *anything* women could wear these days. The thigh-length linen tunic—at least, she supposed it was linen—and the baggy linen trousers looked very comfortable. The colors of these garments seemed to vary with Nan's whim, but they were never subtle. Right now, the tunic was striped red and yellow, and the trousers were a red and blue checkered pattern, and the tunic was held in at her waist by a wide leather belt that supported a leather scabbard. Nan's hair had been tied back in a single braid down her back, and wrapped in more red- and yellow-striped linen.

Sarah didn't have a "warrior form," at least, not as far as she had ever been able to discover. She'd compromised with a short Grecian tunic of the sort Memsa'b's spirit form wore. Her legs were bare, which was a bit distracting, but she supposed she would get used to it, particularly here, where no one lived but ghosts and people like them. There certainly was no one to be shocked by her bare legs. She'd seen ghosts in mere tattered suggestions of clothing, so she doubted anyone was going to accuse her of immodesty.

The birds had taken to this immediately. Both were larger than they were in the real world, though not so large that the girls couldn't comfortably carry them. Sarah suspected that they had already known how to slip into and out of this place long before Beatrice Leek had taught the girls how to enter it. *I wonder if Grey would have taught me, if Beatrice hadn't.* There wasn't much about Grey that surprised her anymore.

The big surprise was Caro. She had taken on an entirely new life and liveliness now that she was actively assisting. And once she had seen that Nan could change how she looked, Caro had done the same, shedding the gown she had been buried in for men's riding breeches, boots, a riding jacket, and a cap. *"I always wanted to wear something like this,"* she said with satisfaction, examining herself. *"It looked so comfortable when my brother wore it. I wish I could have a mirror and see myself."*

Well, they were in the spirit-plane version of their flat, so there *was* a mirror, but unfortunately it was fundamentally useless, because it reflected nothing. "You look dashing," Sarah told her. "And you would probably cause a scandal."

Caro giggled.

Sarah sounded normal, at least to her own ears, and so did Nan. But Caro still had an echoing, whispery quality to her voice, although they were all technically "spirits." Caro also looked just a little less "solid" than the two of the living girls did.

"You're going armed, I hope?" Nan asked her soberly. "Once we get outside the warded area of our flat, spirits will be able to interact with us. That means they can hurt us, and we don't have Puck's charm to protect us from them."

Unlike the dome of protection in Beatrice Leek's workroom, all the walls of the spirit-plane flat glowed faintly, and were written with brighter complicated signs and symbols. These were the "wards" that John, Mary, Alderscroft, and an Earth Master on a brief visit to London had placed on the flat. Sarah had felt very sorry for the Earth Master; it had been clear he was extremely uncomfortable in the city and could not wait to get back to his country home. She and Nan had been very grateful for his help, and never more so than now, because thanks to this work, nothing could enter the flat without being invited.

And this made it a secure place to retreat to—and leave their slumbering bodies.

"What sort of weapon do you suggest?" Sarah asked. "I'm not the knife-fighter you are."

"You're not bad with a staff and a singlestick. How about a spear?" Nan suggested. "That would give you a great deal of reach."

Sarah shrugged, and concentrated on her right hand. A moment later, a spear grew in it from a central point in her palm.

"Should I have a weapon too?" Caro wanted to know.

"Do you feel as if you need one?" Nan asked logically. "More to the point, do you actually know how to use one? Sarah and I were actually trained by Sahib's friends. I learned knife fighting from a Gurkha, which carries over to a sword, and Sarah learned staff and singlestick from a Buddhist who studied with warrior-monks."

Caro pondered that. *"I don't think I would be of much use with a sword or a spear,"* she admitted. *"Except—I did learn archery at one of the sanitoriums. I wasn't bad at it."*

"If you can envision yourself in new clothing, you should certainly be able to think up a bow and arrow," Sarah told her decisively. Caro frowned with concentration, and after a few moments, a misty bow appeared in her left hand, and a quiver of arrows on a belt appeared on her hip.

"All right, I think we are ready." Nan gave her sword another experimental swing and seemed satisfied with the result. "Let's make our first foray. If we do well here, we can try the Thames next. Now, how do we open a door?"

Caro laughed at them. *"You don't, you silly goose. You're a spirit. And these are your wards so you can pass through them at will. You do this, just moving right through the walls."*

And without moving her feet she drifted through the street-side wall.

It took both of them some little time to get the knack of

drifting—or "flying," as Nan called it. Sarah personally did not consider anything that had them moving at a walking pace counted as "flying."

The birds preceded them through the walls. There was a slight moment of resistance as Sarah passed the wards, then she found herself hovering above the spirit-plane version of their street.

The first thing that struck her was how silent and deserted it was. No traffic, either of foot or vehicle. No sound. But there *was* something odd, not unlike a heat-shimmer down there. She squinted at it.

"That's the real world," Caro said matter-of-factly. *"If you look at it sideways, you can make out what's going on."*

At first, Sarah could not understand what she meant, because looking at the gray, misty street out of the corner of her eye produced nothing at all.

But then it occurred to her to try to use the same mental trick that allowed her to see ghosts in the real world—and the moment she did, the street leapt to vibrant life, so much so that her heart leapt.

"By Jove!" Nan exclaimed. "It looks completely normal! Is this what you see, Caro?"

"Not so much," the ghost admitted. *"It's like a watercolor version of the world for me. But then, I don't belong there."*

"This is interesting, but the living are not what we are looking for right now," Sarah declared, and with a mental twist, the empty, silent, gray street took the place of the vibrant one. "Let's see how far away we can get from ourselves before we begin having difficulties."

"I can only get about a block away from the locket," Caro said. *"Once you go past that, I can't help you."*

Sarah nodded, and concentrated on moving. She found that if she "walked," she could go faster than if she was just hovering, and it was a distinctly novel sensation, to be walking along in midair above an empty street.

Sure enough, when they reached the intersection with the next street, Caro abruptly stopped, as if she had run into an invisible barrier. *"This is my limit,"* she said apologetically.

"Just keep an eye on us back at the flat," Nan said, and Sarah nodded. Caro saucily tipped her cap to them in farewell, and strode confidently back toward their flat at about ten feet off the "ground."

"How far out from our flat have you cleared out ghosts?" Nan asked, when Caro was gone.

"Probably about to here," Sarah told her. "If Caro is typical, that is probably as far as most spirits can travel."

"Then we can probably expect—" Nan began, when Neville uttered a harsh bark of warning, and Grey screamed.

Sarah caught the rush of movement out of the corner of her left eye just in time to intercept a tattered, frenzied looking thing flying furiously at her, clawlike hands outstretched.

And it was strange—she *should* have felt a jolt of terror at the moment. She felt fear, but it was—distant. What she felt was something like what she had once experienced when she held two wires to a battery at a demonstration of electricity—a kind of jolt, that sent her into instant action. She swung at it with the butt of her spear, like a cricket batsman swinging at the ball, and knocked it into the middle distance. It tumbled over and over in midair, and finally came to a halt and stared at her in what looked like shock and surprise. Evidently it had not expected opposition.

It was as solid as Caro, but . . . very different. It looked like something that had forgotten how to be human—or never had been in the first place. It lacked legs and a lower torso; it was a floating mass of rags and tatters from which a pair of emaciated arms and a skull-like head emerged. The eyes were the only things recognizably alive, and they burned with insanity.

"Bloody hell," Nan murmured, and readied her sword.

But Sarah already had a plan. The fact that the revenant had fixated on her only helped that plan along. "It just seems to want me. I'll take this thing," she said with confidence, braced herself with the spear held for a two-handed swing, and held the Portal to the next world balanced in her mind.

The revenant screamed; the birds answered its shriek, and it charged again. Grey mantled her wings and Neville poised himself to intercept the thing if Sarah missed, giving her more confidence in what she was about to do. Sarah had just enough time to judge where it was going to go when she struck it, and place the open Portal there, when it reached her.

The spear struck true. The revenant went flying again—

—through the open Portal, which Sarah closed behind it.

She relaxed and regarded the spear in her hands thoughtfully. "A cricket bat might be better," she said aloud. "Or a tennis racquet."

"Not enough reach," Nan opined. "I wonder what would have happened if I'd given it a good hit with the sword?"

"I have the feeling that you would hurt it, perhaps weaken it, but not actually damage it," said Sarah, looking anxiously around for another such spirit. "Remember, this is where *they* are at home. We're on their ground, now. It would take something or someone extremely powerful to affect a spirit here. Time—"

"Or a necromancer?" Nan hazarded.

Sarah nodded. "On the other hand, as a medium, I don't encounter nearly as many of these sorts of dangerous and insane spirits as I do the ones that are lost or have some sort of task to perform. And it would be a great deal easier to help *those* spirits when I'm on their ground."

"I hope you're right," Nan muttered, also looking around, but warily. "I'd hate to find myself with one of those things sinking its claws in my back. I couldn't even tell if it was male or female! Have you ever encountered anything like it before?"

Sarah shook her head. "It's either a ghost that has completely lost any semblance of a mind, or something that actually lives here. If they're solid enough for us to affect them, the reverse is probably true, and I don't want to find out for certain the hard way."

They eventually discovered their own limit, when both of them stopped moving at the same time, feeling an uncomfortable tugging in their chests. This, Sarah guessed, was about half a mile, which was better than she had feared. They didn't encounter any more crazed revenants, but they did find a few of the wispy, sad spirits that did not understand what had happened to them, and did not know what they should do. This was the sort of thing Sarah handled all the time, and it was with a feeling of great confidence that she set them to rights, comforted them, opened a Portal for them, and sent them on their way. And that was another thing that she noticed immediately. Opening Portals to the next world was much, much easier here.

Many of these poor little wraiths were children between the ages of about three and six. Babies and toddlers, she suspected, being too young to have anything but instinct, moved on to the next world immediately. And older children, in this part of London at least, had been indoctrinated by their Sunday Schools and the religious lessons taught in school to respond to the Portal when it opened for their deaths and they saw it. But children still in the nursery were sometimes confused and shaken, particularly if they had died suddenly, and simply didn't understand what had happened to them. Perhaps they were still so attuned to the material world that they saw it more clearly than the spirit plane. Perhaps they found the spirit plane terrifying and fixated on the material plane. And when they did that, they could see and hear their parents, friends, siblings, and were heartbroken that they could not touch them or get a response from them.

These were the easiest ghosts to help. Sarah had sent so many of these little ones on that helping them was as easy for her as breathing, and she no longer felt grief at seeing them. Instead, she experienced great pleasure in showing them the way out. But they affected Nan deeply. After the second, Nan couldn't bear it; she had to move off while Sarah tended to them. Instead she concentrated on searching for the horizon for danger. And in between they both looked for any other sort of ghost that might be able to give them information on the murdered girls.

The only ones they found were the kind that ignored them both entirely, lost in some sort of dreamy reverie, or focused on something they could not see. For now, Sarah decided to ignore them. They had a specific mission, after all.

Finally, after searching the area they could currently reach that was nearest the Thames, even Sarah had to admit they had probably done everything they could do. It was time to go "home"—and make a report to John and Mary.

They all met at 221C, over tea and cakes that Sarah had bought from her favorite bakery. All the windows were open to the breeze, but there was a hint that the dog days of summer would be approaching soon. Sarah was not looking forward to continuing this investigation in the heat. Three more bodies had been found, and she was just grateful that John Watson had been the one to determine there was nothing new to learn from them, because the growing heat was probably making the morgue unbearable. Poor Lestrade was beside himself, and Sarah suspected that it was only intervention at the highest levels of government that was keeping this out of the newspapers.

I suspect if the papers did start trumpeting stories, white dresses would suddenly go right out of fashion.

"Well, now that you both can walk about in the spirit plane, perhaps the best idea would be to go to a decent little hotel as near as we can get to the spot where that first body was found," Mary Watson suggested practically. "You can go talk to ghosts and John, I, or both of us can make sure nothing happens to your sleeping bodies."

"That was more or less what I was going to suggest," Sarah replied, as Grey nodded. She smiled thinly. "If at all possible, let's find one with a good dining room. We have discovered that we are ravenous when we awaken, and if Alderscroft is going to task us with this, the least he can do is pay for our dinners."

John Watson evidently found this highly amusing, as he snorted with laughter. Then he sobered. "Given the number of accidents and river suicides that could create hostile ghosts, not to mention that the Water and Earth Elementals along the Thames are not . . . friendly . . . I am concerned for your safety, and I won't deny this."

Sarah exchanged a look with Nan, and Nan nodded a little. "Actually, John, the really dangerous spirits are surprisingly easy to dispatch to their ends. They don't seem to be able to think and reason. All that occurs to them to do is to attack. Nan and I didn't even need to interact with the last three at all; all I did was wait for them to rush us, invoke Portals in their paths, and they were swallowed up before they could stop themselves."

John blinked. "Really?"

"We have a theory," Sarah continued. "We think the older the spirit, the madder it becomes, and the less able it is to think. It just acts on emotions, and if it is a dangerous spirit, its chief emotion is rage at the living. That would be why some of the older ghosts seem to be more of a memory than an actual being—they are just shadows of what they once were, endlessly reenacting the moments that led to their deaths."

"It's a good theory, and I will defer to the expert," John opined, eyeing first the last petit four, and then his wife, for whom they were favorite. Mary gave him tacit approval with a little nod of her head, and he helped himself to it. "And if you are quite confident that you can handle yourselves safely, then one or both of us can certainly keep an eye on you—"

"Actually, I had an idea," Mary interjected, "I wonder if our Elementals would be of any assistance? If they can move about in the spirit plane and help you there?"

Nan shrugged, and looked at Sarah, deferring to her. "I think it's an excellent thing to try," Sarah agreed. "We can certainly *see* them on the material plane, thanks to Robin Goodfellow, but we can't always understand what they mean to tell us. Perhaps on the spirit plane we will be able to speak with them as you can."

"I'll find a hotel and make the reservation," John said, and shook his head. "Though what is going to happen to my reputation if anyone discovers I am entertaining two young ladies *and* my wife in a hotel room, I shudder to think."

Grey made a rude noise, and Neville laughed. *"Chaperones,"* the raven suggested slyly, and clacked his beak.

"Well, you'd be pretty effective if you chose to be, old man," Watson agreed. *"I* certainly wouldn't want to cross you."

Nan and Sarah pretended to peruse the selection available at the tobacconist's across from the modestly named Hotel Meridian as the gentleman in charge studiously ignored them. He probably thought they were awful Modern Emancipated Women who had Loose Morals and smoked. Nan wondered what he would do if they actually tried to purchase cigarettes or—horrors!—cigars or tobacco. Would he continue to ignore them, or raise himself up to his full height and attempt to stare them into shame?

Of course, they *were* modern, emancipated women, and he'd probably have a stroke if he knew all that they were capable of.

She felt someone behind her and a hand lightly brush her skirt at the same time as she sensed John Watson's familiar presence. She put her hand behind her. "Room 302," said John Watson, passing the key to Nan discreetly. He left, and Sarah approached the tobacconist and politely asked for a packet of mints. Suddenly mollified, the man "noticed" her and supplied her with her request.

Once John had long passed into the door of the hotel, Sarah and Nan crossed the street together and followed in his wake.

The hotel had a small lounge with nobody in it and a modest front desk with a clerk busy with something behind it. The girls passed on to the staircase without him taking notice, and up to the third floor they went, bird carriers in hand, which probably looked like small hand luggage to anyone who was watching.

When they unlocked the door of 302, John and Mary had already taken up their places in the two armchairs in the tiny room, leaving the bed for them. "At least I won't fear for you catching a cab here," John said, as they closed the door behind them. "A few streets over, however. . . ."

"We could always have walked to a better neighborhood, had you taken a room there. And your reputation would not have been tarnished by having three women in your room. Plus, it would be amusing to give some purse-snatching thug a lesson if one was foolish enough to meddle with us," Sarah said demurely. Mary Watson laughed, as John winced.

They let the birds out and lay down on the bed, arranging their skirts so as not to make John even more uneasy; the birds flapped to the bed and hopped up onto their chests. "I feel like a voyeur," Watson muttered. Then said aloud, "Mary will summon her Elementals, and I will direct mine to meet you at the Thames."

"Which way *is* the Thames?" Nan asked, practically. John pointed at the blank wall at the head of the bed. As a Water Master Nan suspected he didn't ever need to actually *do* anything to know where water was.

By this point, slipping out of their bodies was easier than slipping out of their clothing. A moment, and they were standing in the spirit plane, the shadow-shrouded spirit-plane version of this hotel room around them, the walls glowing with the wards of Water and Air Masters. Caro and the birds were already waiting for them, and they walked through the warded walls of the hotel room and toward the Thames. They *could* have walked straight through rooms and buildings if they had chosen to, but that gave Nan the same queasy feeling she suspected John was feeling as he and Mary watched their still bodies. Of course, she wouldn't see anything of what was going on in those rooms unless she chose to, but the mere fact that she would be blundering through someone else's private space bothered her.

Spirits were far fewer here than they had been a few blocks from their flat, and the ones they spotted ignored them completely. But they had not gone more than a few dozen feet before a half dozen tiny, butterfly-winged girl-creatures about a foot tall came whizzing up to them and hovered in front of them, gazing at them with excitement and anticipation. Nan knew what these were— sylphs, the smallest and most delicate of the Air Elementals.

Caro stared at the little creatures in openmouthed amazement. "Pretty," said Grey. Neville made kissing sounds. The sylphs erupted into high-pitched giggles.

"What need ye, Daughters of Eve?" asked one of them, finally getting over her fit of laughter.

"Warning of anything ill-intentioned in our path," Nan replied. "Guidance to the Great River. And last of all, someone to call to the Water Spirits so that we may speak to them when we arrive there."

"Ye give us light tasks, Daughters of Eve," said the one that seemed to be the spokesbeing for the group. She was a lovely little thing, dressed in little more than a wisp of dark blue scarf, with wings that matched. *"Follow, oh follow."* She fluttered off at a pace they could easily match, while the others raced on ahead.

Suddenly they moved into a neighborhood that, even in the spirit plane, was shabbier and more sinister. Caro stopped, and sighed. *"I can't go any further,"* she said, and shrugged.

"You can keep watch back at the hotel," Nan told her. "We're only half-warded there, from Air and Water. Anything nasty from Earth or Fire could get to us, and John and Mary wouldn't know until it was too late to do anything. Just call up your bow and arrow and shoot anything that tries to get through the wards."

Caro brightened. *"So I can,"* she agreed, and turned back, guided by the pull of the locket.

Sarah stopped a half dozen more times as the sobs of a child that had long lost any hope drifted softly to them through the grayness of this strange, sad place. Nan and the birds stood vigilant watch as she followed the sounds of weeping to small children, called to them, and sent them quickly through a Portal.

And then they saw it, in the distance, a place that immediately caught their attention by the movement around it. A ramshackle building, differentiated chiefly by the ragged *things* that drifted in and out of its walls. Although not identical, they were not unlike the skeletal, crazed things that Sarah had dispatched near their flat. And just then, one of the sylphs came speeding back to them,

"Around you must go, and still, still, still," she said, as their guide nodded.

"What *are* those things?" Nan asked.

"Nightmares," said the new sylph.

Their guide elaborated. *"When the Sons of Adam and Daughters of Eve have black hearts, these things are born of their thoughts and dreams. They feast on the evil,"* she said. *"They, too, are creatures of Air, but . . ."* she shivered visibly.

Sarah eyed them speculatively. Nan knew exactly what she was thinking. She wanted to destroy them. "We can't take on that many, just us and the birds," she said. "And what good would it do? There would be more tomorrow. We *have* a job to do, and this isn't it."

Sarah sighed, but nodded. Descending to street level, they slunk along under cover of the buildings as directed by their guide. It seemed that either the sylphs could partially conceal their presence from the things, or that if they were not in direct line-of-sight the creatures could not sense their presence.

At last, they reached the waterfront, and drifted down to the muddy verge. There were the rest of the sylphs, and with them, humanoid creatures with scaled skin and huge golden eyes, webbed fingers, and presumably webbed feet.

"Greetings, friends," Sarah saluted them, with a little bow.

That seemed to please them. *"Greetings, Daughters of Eve,"* one said. *"The Master tasks us to aid you."*

"We know that you have not been able to find where the dead one the Master told you of first entered the Great River," said Sarah, as Nan noted she seemed to have a natural knack for communicating with these Elemental creatures. "So we wish to find the spirits of those who met their end in its waters and speak with them."

"We cannot go in that direction," the Water Elemental replied,

pointing upstream. *"But there are many such there, in the place where the Earth crosses the Water."* It looked at her with doubt. *"Many are not sane."*

"Earth crossed the Water," Nan said aloud. "Sounds like Black-friar's Bridge."

"A logical place for people to jump—or be thrown. I don't know this part of London well enough to remember which one, but I suppose the name doesn't matter." Sarah turned toward the water creatures. "Thank you."

They didn't stand on ceremony, retreating back into the water and swimming rapidly downstream. Sarah and Nan trod the air back to the top of the embankment and moved toward the bridge.

Several suicides later, and several spirits that were so mindless that Sarah had, impatiently, opened a Portal directly behind them and *pushed* them through, they knew only that there were no ghosts associated with the headless bodies. All of the spirits capable of speaking coherently were absolutely certain of that. One and all, they expressed surprise that there *was* no ghost. The most sane of them spoke at length about it. *"I've never seen a murder that violent that did not produce one of us,"* he said eloquently. *"And surely no one would end their own lives in such a fashion—"*

His voice trailed off, and he looked at her pleadingly. After dealing with so many ghosts at this point, she knew instantly what he didn't want to ask. He was tall, homely, extremely thin. She suspected, from the shabby state of his garments, that he had died in abject poverty. And from his cultured manner of speaking, he was highly educated. Putting two and two together, she deduced that he was probably an artist and very likely a suicide. Beatrice had saved many of his kind in her life, simply by taking over their lives, feeding them until they were healthy again, and coaxing them into producing something that would sell, but at the same time didn't offend their artistic sensibilities.

"It seems to me that no God of kindness and mercy would deny someone too weary and ill to go on a swift release from pain," she said, looking off into the gray distance. "And everything I have seen when I have opened the way to the next world makes me think that is true. Is that all you can tell me?"

He sighed, and he seemed to brighten for a moment. *"That is all I know,"* he said. *"I hope you can find the monster responsible for this. He deserves to be torn to pieces."*

"Thank you," she told him, and seeing that Nan had finished her own interrogation, she opened the Portal for him. He peered at it, and suddenly his expression changed from one of melancholy to one of joy, and he all but leapt through it. As for the spirit Nan had been talking to, and three or four others nearby, once the brightness of the Portal in the sullen gray of the spirit plane caught their attention, they flew to it like moths to a flame.

Their faithful little sylph had been waiting patiently all this time. *"Ready to return?"* she asked plaintively, looking like a child who is very weary of all the tedious things the adults have been doing.

"Yes, please," Sarah replied. And she looked at Nan. "In fact— let's run."

She had noticed that despite all the "walking" they had been doing, she was not in the least tired. So why not try running?

Before Nan could reply, the sylph shot off, with Sarah following, Grey flying happily at her shoulder, running as fast as she was flying. A moment later, Nan caught up with her, with Neville preceding her.

"What—"

"Are you getting winded?" Sarah asked her, feeling very much as if she was like fleet-footed Diana and could run forever, outracing a deer.

"No—" Nan looked startled. "I might as well be walking!"

"Come on then!" Sarah increased her pace, and since they were coming back a by a different path, they didn't even have to slow down to sneak past that house of sinister "nightmares."

Caro must have been able to sense them nearing, for she met them at the edge or her range, and joined them running. "All quiet," she reported. "Your friends are getting anxious, though. It's well past midnight."

"It is?" Sarah almost stopped, she was so surprised. "That can't be!"

"Time passes differently here," was all Caro said. And then

they were running on the air, up to the third story of the Hotel Meridian, and the next thing Sarah knew, she was sitting up, Grey had flown to the bedstead—and she ached in every limb, exactly as if she had just run a mile.

10

This time Spencer arranged to take delivery of his property by night, so as not to arouse any curiosity in the neighbors. The less magic he had to use, he reasoned, the better—and why waste precious power on a spell when the cover of darkness would do just as well? He had replaced the defrocked priest with a street preacher who, besides being completely insane, conveniently proclaimed from his soapbox that all men should have as many wives as Solomon. When Spencer suggested he wanted to do exactly that, and would pay the man to officiate, the fellow had literally danced with glee. All he had asked was that he be allowed to preach a short sermon.

And he'd had no difficulty over using Spencer's altered ceremony, nor with performing a wedding after sunset. Spencer gave him directions and a time, and the man promised he would show up.

And if he didn't, well, Spencer figured he could lock the girl in the guest room and find someone quickly enough. There were street preachers out every night at Covent Garden for instance, badgering the crowds of opera and ballet attendees—and a lot more of them outside music halls and pubs and gin palaces. None of them ever bothered the brothels, however. They were lucky to get away with broken bones if they tried.

The second Chinese girl was as cooperative as the first, although it seemed to Spencer that she was very sluggish. Even his assertions that he was going to marry her didn't seem to lift her out of her lethargy. It was not until after he had put her in Kelly's hands and was having quite a lively—and entertaining—discussion with the preacher in his study about the nature of angels, that he learned the reason for her behavior.

"Marster," Kelly said from the door. "Need t' talk t'ye."

He made an excuse to the preacher and poured him another tumbler of cheap brandy before retreating into the hall with Kelly. "Marry 'er and do 'er quick," Kelly told him urgently. "She's been 'ard used, an' she's all tore up inside. I 'ope that won't make difference t' th' magic."

Well that explained a lot. Why Old Don was so anxious he get her off his property, for one. The old fraud didn't want her to die on the spot. Serve him right for not specifying the limits of abuse he'd tolerate in his purchases. "It won't," he said briefly. "Can she stand?"

"Fer a while. These Chinee are like old work 'orses. Pull till they drops dead i' the traces. I'll git 'er fixed up an' downstairs. You 'eard the preacher."

Within five minutes, Kelly had the girl neatly gowned, with no sign that she was probably bleeding to death at that moment. At least that meant she didn't make a fuss about wearing white. The preacher seemed to mistake the girl's dazed condition for modesty or shyness, which was all to the good. It took some prodding to get her to whisper "iss," but the spell melded into place just as it always did. He escorted the preacher out, as the man exclaimed gleefully, "Populate the earth with your seed, my boy! A man with a quiver full of arrows is a blessed man!" And when he returned to the study, the girl had collapsed, semiconscious, in the nearest chair.

Conscious now that the clock was ticking, he scooped her up and took the stairs to his workroom. Being inverted on his killing table brought her back to consciousness briefly, but of course he had taken the precaution of strapping her down, just in case. She didn't even recover enough to do more than try to sit up before he dispatched her.

He had not expected the power of the wail of despair from her spirit after seeing the sluggish creature she had been when alive. "Gratifying" was too mild a word for how he felt about it, since he sensed it without even slipping himself into the spirit plane.

And as with the last Chinese girl, her mere presence woke anger and resentment from the other girls. This was utterly delicious. Another half dozen and he'd have enough power at his command to do anything.

As he racked the jar containing her head with the rest, out of nowhere, with a thrill of excitement, a thought occurred to him . . . he could probably get a personal interview with the Queen with that much power. It would merely take time, working his way up through those in power as a spiritualist. What would the Queen give him for a few words with her beloved Albert?

It wouldn't be the real Albert, of course. Once a spirit crossed to the next world, he couldn't touch it unless it came back on its own. But it was child's play to take a ghost lodged in the spirit plane, make it look the way he wanted, and coerce it into saying what he told it to do. So what *would* the Queen do if her dearest, dead husband told her to make Spencer her confidant and advisor?

He'd have to be extremely clever not to come to the attention of Alderscroft, of course. One on one, he could probably defeat the Lodgemaster, but it wouldn't be one-on-one; when it came to necromancy, Hunting Lodges threw gentlemanly conduct and fair play out the nearest window. The full strength of the Lodge would come to bear on him, and possibly even the strength of whatever Continental Lodges Alderscroft could contact.

And on reflection, he could not see any way of hiding his activities from Alderscroft once he reached the Queen's outer circles, much less the inner ones.

Probably not worth it.

Not when he could accomplish nearly as much by staying out of Alderscroft's purview.

He did briefly amuse himself with the fantasy of the Queen knighting him, gifting him with a small manor house (he wasn't greedy, after all), in Wales, perhaps, or Devon (not Scotland, good gods no!). And seeing Alderscroft's Hunting Lodge broken up, Alderscroft himself led away in chains on charges of treason—

And there his imagination failed him, because he didn't actually know what Alderscroft looked like.

Still. Once Moriarty was back, it all wasn't out of the realm of possibility that between them, he and the Professor could put an end to Alderscroft and his Hunting Lodge. Minds could be influenced. Evidence could be manufactured and planted. Witnesses could be created. Not even a peer of the realm was immune from the courts, if the evidence was strong enough. Then he actually *would* be able to influence the Queen if he chose. Something to think about. With this much power, and Moriarty beholden to him, many things were possible.

Hughs had been asking to arrive earlier and earlier, then spending most of the long daylight hours in dreams, so in the morning Spencer was in his alternate flat, just finishing his second pot of tea of the day, when he heard the young man's knock. When he answered the door, he found Hughs leaning against the doorframe, dark circles under his eyes. He obviously had not slept well last night.

"I don't mean to complain, Spencer, because you've been an absolute brick," he said without preamble, "But it's a long way to your flat."

"We could do this at yours," Spencer offered, although he already knew from things Hughs had let slip that this wasn't possible.

Hughs came inside and Spencer shut the door behind him, hoping that the time had come for the next stage of the young man's conversion. "That would be a disaster," Hughs said, with a grimace. "Mater has the landlady in her pay. Mostly so I don't set up a mistress there, since she knows I haven't got the ready to set up a mistress in her own establishment and she knows I haven't enough for a decent girl in a good brothel either. Not that she'd admit to knowing such things exist. If she got wind of this, it would be all over, and I don't know which would be worse, her finding out about my opium-eating, or suspecting us of 'the love that dare not speak its name.'"

Spencer laughed, partly because that was funny, and partly because the day that he first spoke to Hughs, the fact that his mother might think they were homosexual lovers would never have entered his mind, and a few weeks ago, he never would have voiced that openly. The weakening of his inhibitions was a sign of the weakening of his will.

"Well, I have a proposition, then," he said. "This isn't my only property. I have a house elsewhere with plenty of spare rooms and a housekeeper to look after the place and cook. Pay your rent in advance, tell your landlady you are going on a walking tour of the Lake District, shut the place up and move in."

Hughs stopped in his tracks, hope warring with suspicion. "Won't that inconvenience you?"

Spencer shrugged. "I have my own chemical experiments I perform there, and I'm just about to start a new series. Such things are a matter of short bursts of work and long periods of waiting. It will be no trouble to look in on you, and you're not exactly going to make a great deal of work for my housekeeper. I merely offer," he added, "Because it will be a great deal more convenient to *me* not to have to shuttle back and forth."

Hughs caved in. "In that case, I'll do it, and thanks, old man. I have the feeling old Coleridge was onto something. I'm so close to a breakthrough, I can feel it."

Spencer had read the incoherent fragments and ramblings in Hughs' notebook when the man was deep in the throes of his opium dreams, so he very much doubted that Hughs was close to anything but the same suicide he'd been flirting with when Spencer first met him. But the last thing he wanted to do was break *any* of Hughs' delusions just now. So he nodded. "Do you want to have your usual session and handle things after you wake, or a smaller dose so you can avoid unpleasantness, go deal with your landlady, and come back here? I can have a cab waiting to take both of us to my house. We'll get you settled, and you can doze off by luncheon."

"The latter, old man." Hughs clapped him on the shoulder with an unsteady hand. "That will suit me down to the ground."

Spencer smiled. The bait was taken. Now for the trap to close.

Hughs left after his quarter dose, acting very like his former self. As with alcoholics, there was a level of intoxication in opium-eaters where only the effects of addiction were alleviated, and the addict could speak, act, and reason effectively. After so much experience with his other candidates, Spencer rather thought he was good at judging just how small a dose would provide control without intoxication. Hughs proved he was still sharp insofar as his intellect was concerned by turning up just before luncheon with a heavy rucksack loaded with some personal goods and a hiking staff. Spencer had taken the opportunity to get luncheon for two from the pub, and greeted him at the door.

"I paid the old harridan for three months—she was damned happy to see it, too," he said, as Spencer let him in and took him to the kitchen. "I told her I was going on a walking tour while the weather was fine, and not to expect to hear from me until September at the earliest. Sent a note off to Mater by post." He laughed, although it was sardonic. "She'll fret, but she'll know I've already gone by the time she reads it, and short of hiring one of those investigator johnnies to try and find me, there won't be anything she can do. And Pater will want to know *why* she's hiring such a fellow, and put his foot down, and she knows it." He shook his head. "Pater would probably be just as happy to get word the black sheep of the family tumbled down a mineshaft on the moors and broke his fool neck."

Spencer politely ignored that last, but he took it as a good sign that death was still very much on Hughs' mind. "I have a cab turning up at one, so we might as well have our luncheon." He waved at the other chair, sat down at the table, and urged the young man to partake of the food, though as he well knew opium suppresses the appetite. Still Hughs ate, more than he expected. A good sign that his body was still strong.

The young man's energy was wearing off, though, and the cab ride to the house took place mostly in silence. By the time they arrived, he was looking haggard, and Spencer carried his rucksack and stick for him into the house.

But the little bedroom the girls used was clean and ready, it was right beneath the workroom, and Spencer had no expectation of needing it again now that he had found such a convenient alternate supply. In short order, Hughs had had his usual dose, his things were stored in the wardrobe, and he was dreaming in the unfamiliar bed, shades drawn, curtains closed.

Spencer went downstairs to consult with Mrs. Kelly.

"Reckon Marster'll like this 'un," the old woman said from her comfortable perch on the sofa in the sitting room, as half a dozen unhappy-looking brownies cleaned industriously at her direction. "'E's a 'andsome bloke, or 'e'll be once the devil's outa 'is system. An' 'e's young." And she looked at him shrewdly, and added, "What's th' price uv doin' that fer me?"

This was the first time, ever, that the old woman had expressed any personal interest in the procedure. He regarded her thoughtfully for a moment.

"High," he said, finally. "I'm sure you have a strong enough will to triumph in evicting the soul of the body you take, but I've no guarantee that your magic would survive the transition. I've never tried transferring a magician."

She sucked on her lower lip. "Yer gonna do it yersel' though."

Shrewd guess on her part! "I intend to. It's clear from all I have read that Spirit Masters can bring their magic and power along to the new vessel."

She thought about that some more. "Not sure I'd need magic, wi' a pretty 'nuff face. An' ye reckon I can do this thing?"

He nodded. "Success lies within *you*, for the most part. You have to overcome the will of the soul you want to replace, and expel it from the body. Mrs. Kelly, everything I know about you tells me you have a will of iron."

She nodded, as if this was something she had expected to hear. "Somethin' t' think about," she said. "Th' kind o' pretty gel I'd wanta look loike ain't gonna be easy t'get. Pretty gels go missin', some'un's gonna *be* missin' 'em. Even a hoor is gonna be missed, by 'er keeper if naught else."

Intrigued that she had thought this through, he pursed his lips. "I could—" he suggested "—go into the countryside, at hiring-fair time, and hire some passably pretty thing as a maid of all work in London."

She shook her head. "Nobuddy'd believe thet. Gels ain't that stupid. But *I* could. I look respektuble."

"So you do," he agreed. "And I am not opposed to this." He smiled. "You've been an excellent partner, Mrs. Kelly. You knew exactly what to do with the parcel last night, for instance. I can see us coming to an equitable arrangement—once the Master is taken care of, of course."

Kelly nodded. "O' course. Well, that lad don' look loike much trouble. Less'n them gels, for certain." She stopped talking long enough to send a glare at a brownie she probably suspected of slacking. The Elemental whimpered, and began polishing the bookcase at a furious rate.

"One think at a time," she said, as if to herself. Then louder, "'Ow much longer t'get th' Marster where 'e needs t'be?"

"Six more girls. That way I'll have not just *enough* power, but enough and to spare." He waited for her reaction.

She pursed her lips. "Two days t'git th' next 'un? I'll need ten pounds. I wants t' lay in what's needed i'case 'nother one's tore up inside as bad or wuss than th' last one. We got lucky; she were all in a maze like, an' not feelin' pain. If'n th' next one's 'urtin', I'll need t'fix thet afore ye c'n marry 'er wi'out thet preacher coppin' there's summat wrong."

His eyebrows rose. "Why, Mrs. Kelly, I never suspected you of having medical knowledge!"

She laughed. "There's a lot ye don' know 'bout me, m'lad. 'Appen's a Earth Magician's fair 'andy as a midwife, an' 'specially a cuttin' midwife. Reckon I ended more bebbies than I birthed, I fixed up gels as been 'andled 'ard, an' 'ere in London, plenny of call for setch i' hoor'ouses."

This was more information that Mrs, Kelly had given about her past than in all the time he had known her combined. Her value had now nearly doubled in his eyes, given this. To signify this, he gave her a slight bow. Her mouth quirked up in a wry smile. "You ain't t'on'y one wi' secrets, Spencer."

"So I see, Mrs. Kelly," he replied, amused. "And speaking of the Master, I need to go see how he feels about our guest. Oh, and here's that ten pounds you mentioned, and a little more for your trouble." He handed over the money, and left her to supervise the brownies.

The wards confining Moriarty within a rough sphere extended down into a guest bedroom, although obviously the girls that were destined to become part of the battery were of no interest to him whatsoever and he never ventured there when Spencer was grooming his little chickens. Now, however, it was time for Spencer to inform the Professor that the room contained something he would be greatly interested in.

He went up to his workroom, uncovered the talisman, sat down, and smoothly moved himself into the spirit plane. The soft weeping of his girls behind him was the best music he had ever heard, as Moriarty faded into view and noticed his presence.

"*I have been thinking,*" the Professor said, and Spencer was pleased to see that he was showing no signs of that dangerous rage that Spencer had taken for a sign of possible degradation. "*In fact, since our last talk together, I have been doing quite a bit of thinking. I have some orders for you, but first, I assume you came here because you have news for me.*"

"Your potential vessel is in the bedroom beneath this," he said, immediately. "You may wish to inspect him."

The Professor's eyes lit up, and he stood and sank through the floor. Spencer had taken it as a very good sign that Moriarty had mastered the ability to move within the confines of the wards almost as soon as he had recovered from the shock of having his spirit suddenly transferred into the talisman. Of course, Moriarty would not have been able to go *far* in this form—if anything he was more tightly rooted to his talisman than the average ghost was to the place of its death. But Spencer had decided even before the Professor died that he had no wish to find Moriarty looming over him in the middle of the night, should the worst befall, and had warded the workroom, the attic above, and the bedroom below into a single unit out of which *no* spirit could pass and none could see. He had told Moriarty that this was for his protection, although he could not tell if the Professor believed him.

In a sense though, Spencer wasn't lying. Given Moriarty's temper, the less he saw, the better. It was the spirits that were angriest that degraded the fastest.

Spencer waited patiently, and while he waited, he looked over his storage spheres and the girls. His last conversation with them seemed to have had the salubrious effect of cowing them, but the waves of despair, mingled with resentment at the Chinese within their midst and fear, combined to form a mixture that was almost exactly what he would have wanted if he'd been concocting it to his own recipe. The two Chinese struck a slightly foreign note of fear and bewilderment. They still didn't understand what had happened to them. They didn't understand why they were enchained to a gaggle of white girls. In fact, they didn't actually understand *anything*, except that they were no longer among the living, and this was no form of afterlife they had been taught to expect.

He examined the spheres and determined that several had reached their capacity and would need to be exchanged for new ones. This was delightful news, and made him feel quite prepared for any of Moriarty's new demands.

The Professor rose up through the floor and took a seat in midair, even though he didn't really need to rest in any way. Predictably he positioned himself so that his head was higher than Spencer's. Spencer wondered if Moriarty realized how obvious a play to assert himself this was, then decided that Moriarty just didn't care if it was obvious.

"*This vessel is perfect,*" the Professor declared, to Spencer's relief. "*You are right; his will was weak and is weakening more with every day he takes the drug. His opium dreams are full of death, or at least, what he imagines death is like. You will, of course, cut off the drug as soon as I have the body.*"

"I had thought to wean you off—" Spencer began.

Moriarty interrupted him. "*A waste of time. I am certainly strong-willed enough to push my way through the effects. I will need my mind completely unimpaired once I have this new body, and it will be worth the discomfort and trouble to keep it that way. Tell me how you convinced him to come here.*"

Spencer explained the ruse of the walking tour, and Moriarty chuckled.

"*Excellent planning. The tour will give a reason for the change in personality. I have considered what you suggested, and I find it has the bones of a good plan. I do not believe it will take me much, if any, time to establish myself as a mathematical genius—since that is what I actually am. I will write and publish several papers immediately on taking this boy's body, and send copies to select dons at Oxford and Cambridge. Knowing that they would want a potential genius under close supervision, so that they control what he publishes and when, and get credit for it, I shall soon have them competing for me. That alone will impress the parents without needing to attain a degree. We can then arrange for an unfortunate accident while I am interviewing at one of those*" *institutions, which will give me an excellent alibi,* and *an excellent reason for putting off my enrollment. No one will fault me for abandoning my academic pretentions, due to excess of grief. By the time I have rebuilt and revived the Organization, everyone will have forgotten poor Hughs, who had everything and lost it all to become a recluse, shut in with his sorrow."*

Spencer nodded. This was, indeed, an excellent plan, and one with a minimum of risk. Moriarty had, without a doubt, a half dozen plans for eliminating the family, and was only pondering which was the least risky.

"Now, about the Organization—" Moriarty fastened him with a basilisk gaze. *"You have said nothing. I am sure with Sherlock Holmes free and able to act that we are losing men. How many so far?"*

Spencer could not hold his breath in the spirit plane, but he certainly gave Moriarty the number with a fair amount of apprehension.

But the Professor did not explode with rage as he had feared would be the case. Instead, he pondered.

"Bad," he said, finally. *"But not the worst case."*

"I've lost a handful to circumstances I do not think Holmes had anything to do with," Spencer told him. "One died of infected wounds, and three have deserted to join Brown's gang."

"Have the deserters killed," Moriarty ordered. *"I doubt they've gone to Scotland Yard, but we can't take the chance they've become informers, and getting rid of them will send a message to the rest that deserting the Organization is suicide."*

"I'll arrange it at once," Spencer promised. "But I haven't seen any direct evidence that Holmes is responsible for the others—"

Moriarty interrupted him again. *"That's exactly why I know he was. He will leave no trace. Our men will simply find themselves in irons, whisked out of London, with charges lodged against them that cannot be denied. They'll be tried in some provincial court in secrecy, and fly through the justice system so swiftly that within days of being taken up, they will be in Dartmoor Prison in solitary confinement. No, we need to distract him before he takes any more. I want you to have John Watson murdered."*

"What?" Spencer gasped. "But—"

"We prove to Holmes that his friends are not invulnerable, and that if we cannot reach him, we can certainly reach his friends. This may make him pause. I do not say that it will, *but it* may. *And if this does not work, we will take harsher steps."*

"But won't that tell him you still live?" Spencer asked.

"It will tell him that the Organization is capable of defending itself. That is all I need him to know." Moriarty settled back in his seat in midair with an expression of satisfaction on his face. Spencer knew from long acquaintance with the Professor that this was his signal to leave.

So he did.

When he found himself back in his body, he was breathing as heavily as if he had been running. He calmed himself by changing the charged spheres for virgin ones, and added the charged to his storage bank.

Then he went back downstairs, noting by the clock chime it was six. He had been with Moriarty longer than he had thought.

Kelly was in the kitchen, and stared hard at him when he entered. "Yer white's a sheet," she said flatly. "What'd th' Marster tell ye?"

"That our losses are probably due to Holmes," he said, "Except for the three we know deserted to another gang. He wants them killed."

"Get Geoff," she advised. "'E don' 'alf 'ate 'em already. Wut else? Thet ain't all."

"He wants us to kill John Watson." Spencer took a deep breath. "He's hoping this will make Holmes pause, at least for a while."

"'E ain't thinkin' roight if 'e thinks thet," Kelly observed. "Thet's more like t'make 'im mad."

"I'm more concerned with the fact that it's going to be impossible to get anywhere near Watson," Spencer replied, annoyance now beginning to gain ascendancy over other emotions. It was all very well for Moriarty to issue instructions, but it was *Spencer* who was going to have to carry them out! "He lives and works in a highly respectable neighborhood." He sat and thought for a moment. "Moriarty didn't give me a time limit. Very well, I shall take my time. I'll have him followed by a team looking for an opportunity. If that doesn't work, I'll arrange for one of his regular patients to be poisoned; nothing lethal, but something that will give painful symptoms after night falls. They'll send for him when they feel ill, and he will certainly come. We'll ambush him as he leaves the patient, while he is preoccupied with thoughts of his patient."

"Marster don't give ye 'alf credit fer brains," Kelly remarked.

"Well," he replied with a smile, "We both know what happens to those he thinks might challenge him. No, I'd prefer him to believe I am complete dependent on him for guidance. It's safer that way,"

Perhaps Moriarty had expected him to run out and engage the first thug he could think of to deal with Watson. Instead, the first thing he did the next day was seek out Geoff the Elf in the building that the most connected of Moriarty's henchmen used as a sort of informal headquarters. It was an outwardly respectable boarding house for working men. And indeed, the men that came and went from its doors dressed to *work,* as cabbies, as waiters, as shop-tenders, as mechanics . . . as every sort of job where a man was likely to overhear things that would be of profit to the Boss.

Well the Boss was dead, so far as any of them knew, but pay kept flowing from the man Spencer, the boarding house matron still didn't demand a weekly rent, and the meals continued to be hearty and abundant, so they kept right on as they had been.

There was a kind of informal "pub" in the basement of this boarding house. No refreshments were sold, but there was a billiard table, a blind eye was turned to card and dice games, and nobody troubled a man if he brought in bottled beer, fish and chips, and a few friends. This was where, when he wasn't sleeping or driving his cab, Spencer knew he would find Geoff the Elf.

He was, indeed, there. Observing a game of billiards, rather than playing, as the men who lived here knew better than to play anything but a strictly friendly game of billiards, cards, or dice with Geoff, with no money involved. And of course, if there was no money involved, Geoff did not want to play.

As soon as Geoff caught sight of Spencer coming down the stairs, he lost his bored expression and put on that wide, friendly smile that was partly the reason for his name.

"'Allo guv!" he greeted Spencer. "Lookin' fer a lad?"

"For you, in fact, Geoff," he replied.

"Then let's us go up t'me room," Geoff said, not wasting any time. He led Spencer up the stairs to the third floor, down a corridor, and unlocked the door to his room.

Spencer had been here before, but it always struck him how very unlike the man he knew the interior of Geoff's room was. It was as clean and neat as if Kelly's brownies had been at work there. His bed was neatly made with a patchwork counterpane. There was a small bookcase, and two chairs. The most prominent feature was a huge crucifix on the wall. The only literary works were religious ones. The first time he had come here, he hadn't even known Geoff could read. . . .

As the door closed behind him, he finally asked Geoff what he had always wanted to know. "Geoff, what is all this about?" he asked, waving his hand vaguely at the crucifix and the books.

Geoff looked at him quizzically, then sighed, divining that Spencer wasn't going to get down to business until he answered. "Well, guv'," he said. "Sez i' Bible thet if a man repents, an' b'lieves in Jesus, 'e goes t' 'Eaven. Aye?"

"Well, yes . . ."

"An' it also sez, ye obeys yer Marster. An' ye gives Caesar what Caesar's owed, aye?" Geoff persisted.

"It—"

"The Boss wuz me Marster. I guess yew are now. 'E wuz me Casesar too, an' I guess that's yew too. So, I does me dooty, loik Bible sez. An' I repents. I repents uv ev'thin' soon as I does it. I believes i' Jesus, I prays faithful, an' I gives t' th' poor, I obeys me Marster, an' I repents." He grinned. "Reckon I'm goin' t' 'Eaven."

Spencer stared at him in slack-jawed astonishment. Never in his entire life had he heard so twisted and yet so logical a view of Christianity. He had heard with his own ears many preachers claim that as long as you repented of what you did, and believed that Christ was your savior, you'd be cleansed of any and all sins. Geoff had just taken that to extremes. And Spencer would have given a very pretty penny to hear some of those preachers debate this with him.

"Well, I'm going to give you some more things to repent of,

I'm afraid," he told the white-haired, wizened man.

"Oi'm all ears, guv," came the cheerful reply.

"I need you to get rid of those three fellows that ran off to Brown's gang," he said, sternly. "We can't be having that."

"Dead roight ye cain't," Geoff agreed. "People'll think yer soft. I wuz gonna say somethin', but it weren't me place." He rubbed his hands together with glee. "Roight, Ye want 'em disappeared, or turn up as an ex-amp-ell?"

Spencer thought about that for a moment. "If we don't make sure people *know* that running off has consequences, we might as well not go to the effort at all."

Geoff made no mention of the fact that there was no "we" involved—that he and he alone was going to be making the effort and taking the blame if he got caught.

But of course, he wouldn't get caught. Geoff the Elf was named that way for another reason—his near-magical ability to be half the city away when bodies were discovered.

"Jest leave it t'me, guv," he said with glee, as Spencer handed over a triple fee. "By this time termorrow, people'll know yer the Boss now, an' ye won't be trifled with."

"I have another job for you as well," Spencer told him. "Something more difficult. I want you to put together a group, very carefully, to follow John Watson and kill him if you get an opportunity."

Geoff's eyes widened at that, but Spencer was not done. "I'm serious about how careful you need to be. You absolutely must not be caught. And Watson is a clever man and he's very likely to catch anyone following him, so you need to be able to watch him without him catching you."

Here Geoff rubbed his temple, and looked dubious. "Watson! 'E may play th' fool in 'is stories, but he's a slippery cov, 'e is. That'll take some special lads . . ."

"There's a hundred pounds in it for each man, and an extra hundred for you," Spencer replied. And Geoff's eyes widened still further. "For that, you should be able to get the best men in the city."

Now Geoff looked ready to explode, and well he should. This was a small fortune—or to men like Geoff, a large one. "Roight ye are, guv. Oi'll lecher know when I gots 'em."

"Payment for them on delivery. Here's fifty for you on account."

Spencer pulled his wallet out of the inside pocket of his coat, and counted ten five-pound notes out for Geoff, who took them with trembling hands. "I'll be at my house, not my flat, for the foreseeable future."

Geoff took the notes to the bookcase, and turned his back to Spencer so that his body hid what he was doing—although Spencer was pretty sure he had a counterfeit book-safe among his volumes and he was putting his money in it. When he turned back, his grin was as broad and innocent as ever. "We'll be 'wise as serpents, an' 'armless as doves, 'guv," he said, proving he actually knew his Bible. "Watson won't know we're there till we 'it 'im. An' 'e'll be alone when we does it."

11

"We may be going about this from literally the wrong end," Mary Watson said thoughtfully, twirling an errant curl around her finger.

Rather than 221C, they were meeting in the flat above John Watson's surgery. He'd had patients to see to today, and the summer heat made itself felt strongly, so no one really wanted to make the trek to Baker Street—especially not when the Watson's flat was situated in such a way that it was catching all of the breeze, such as it was. "Sultry" was a kind way to describe the heat. It made Sarah long for the school, all the green, and the huge oak trees that cast such delicious shade.

The fact that the surgery flat was not lived in much helped too. A minimum of furnishings, none of the clutter of everyday life, meant the place felt light and airy, not hot and stuffy. It even looked cool: the furnishings were all in gray and pale blue, the walls were papered in gray and white stripes, the draperies were pale blue, and the rugs were all in blues. Visually, it was like being in a snow scene, which was where Sarah wished she was.

Sarah felt she needed someplace cool where she could *think*. They seemed to have come to another impasse, and the heat was not helping her at all. She felt as if her thoughts were trying to swim through treacle. Fanning herself didn't help much. But at least it sounded as if Mary had an idea.

"What do you mean?" Sarah asked.

"Well, we've been asking John's Elementals about the bodies in the area of the river where they were found—which of course, is a place where they don't like to go. But we haven't asked the ones *above* the most fouled part of the river." Mary tapped the map of London in the area between the Putney and Hammersmith Bridges. "This is about the last place where they'll go. Then the water turns too foul for them."

"That's a possibility," John replied, but he sounded doubtful. "But I don't think we'll learn anything." He paused, then added reluctantly, "There's something else I haven't tried, and to be honest I have been trying *not* to do it. But I think I'll have to summon one. I don't think I have a choice."

Mary put her hand to her mouth. "Oh no. Not Jenny Greenteeth—"

"I'm afraid so." John sighed. "At least I'm not a child."

Sarah was lost; so, obviously, was Nan. Grey shook her head. But Neville made an unhappy clacking sound and said, *"Rrrr bad."*

"Who exactly is Jenny Greenteeth?" Nan wanted to know. She looked behind her at Neville. *"You* obviously know."

Neville just repeated, *"Bad!"*

John ran his hand over his hair. "I suppose the easiest thing to say is that there are good and evil Elementals. Now, that's oversimplifying things by a very great deal, but the point is that there are Elementals that are willing to work with humans and there are those who are not—and there are those who would be happiest if they could sink their fangs or claws into our throats and devour us. A Jenny Greenteeth is one of those. A Jenny mostly preys on children . . . and the only reason Jennys don't take many children these days is that they have to take them secretly."

Sarah nodded. "And these days not even country children are alone much."

John continued patiently. "The hostile Elementals are often attracted to poisoned or polluted places. A Jenny is generally a creature of stagnant ponds and swamps, but there is, without a doubt, at least one of them living in the nastier parts of the Thames. It's the sort of place a Jenny would love."

"They're dangerous, John," Mary said, frowning fiercely. "And not just to children. If you lose your control over her, she'll attack, and she's more than strong enough to drag you under before any of us could react."

"What do you mean by 'lose control over her'?" Nan demanded, her voice a little sharp with worry.

John shrugged. "An Elemental Master normally doesn't coerce Elementals, because we only work with the ones that are 'good,' although that is a crude way to put it. But sometimes we've got no choice but to interrogate or force something out of the others, the neutral or hostile ones. So . . . we cast coercive magic over them to force them to do what we want. And if that spell is broken, or the creature fights free of it—"

"But you won't be there by yourself," Nan pointed out. "You'll have me and Sarah. If you can do this by daylight, you'll have the birds. And by night, even possibly Caro can help, if these things are half in the spirit plane and half in the material plane the way the sylphs are."

John opened his mouth to say something, then blinked, and closed it again. He pondered for a moment. "By Jove," he said, finally. "You're right, actually." He turned to his wife. "What do *you* think?"

Mary wore an expression of intense relief. "That this is the best suggestion I have heard so far. If you'll take all three of us along, while my Elementals may not actually be able to intimidate or hurt a Jenny, they can certainly distract her. Meanwhile Nan, Sarah and Caro can be right there, with weapons drawn, making it quite clear you'll tolerate no nonsense from the hag."

Sarah laughed suddenly, realizing the sheer absurdity of all this from the point of view of someone who knew nothing about magic and wouldn't believe in it if you told him about it. "Can you imagine poor Lestrade listening to us? He'd be certain we were all lunatics!"

Mary blinked, then began to laugh. "I can just see his face!"

Grey flapped her wings a little to get their attention, then, in a perfect imitation of Lestrade's voice, said, "*Wut—wut—wut—*" and spluttered in an imitation of his indignation.

That sent them all into peals of laughter, and if the laughter was a little hysterical, well, they had been at this with no tangible results for quite some time. Hearing about bodies turning up was not helping their spirits any.

Mary recovered first, wiping her eyes. "All right, now the question is, how are we going to do this without attracting attention we don't want and *looking* like a lot of lunatics. I don't want to do this by night."

Sarah and Nan nodded; they already knew such creatures were strongest in the dark. They'd had plenty of experience at this point. Sarah made her suggestion. "What about hiring a boat? We'd just be a party of people cooling off on the Thames. I think we can all row."

But John shook his head. "I'll never get a Jenny out on the open water. They're creatures of shorelines and stagnant backwaters." He chewed on his lower lip unhappily. "And we need to be someplace on the shore where we aren't going to attract attention. I hate to say this to you, my love. We might actually *have* to do this by night."

"But *where?* That could make a big difference to your safety. The docks where the river excursions launch?" Mary asked dubiously. "Even at night, that might be too public."

But then Nan's face brightened. "No! Execution Dock! Down at Wapping, where all the pirates and mutineers used to be hung!"

John snapped his fingers. "The very place!" he exclaimed. "No one will be anywhere around the stairs or the passage that leads to the stairs after dark, and I cannot imagine a place more attractive to a Jenny." But then his face dropped. "My love—that is no place for someone like you, not at night. Wapping is a rough area even by day. By night—well, rough men become even rougher with a few drinks in them."

Mary grimaced. "I would like to argue with you, but I cannot. I would only be a liability. My Elementals do not like to fly at night—"

"Neither do the birds, but you would be able to help Sarah and me there. Would you watch them for us?" Nan asked. "What with the dangers Sherlock warned us about, we don't like leaving them alone at night."

"*I* don't like putting them anywhere near the clutches of a Jenny in the dark," Watson added. "Not when I know the Jennies have got some equally nasty allies of Air. I'd rather they did not come on this expedition, myself."

"I'd be very happy to watch them. We can all worry about you together," Mary replied, then grimaced. "And the sooner we do this, the better, so it might as well be tonight. At least it's a full moon."

Nan and Sarah left the birds in Mary's charge and went home to change. They were not about to attempt this in dresses, even Ladies' Rational Dress. Instead, they both changed into the clothing they wore when practicing with their instructors—outfits based on traditional Gurkha men's clothing. Baggy cotton trousers and a knee-length cotton tunic held in at the waist with a wrapped sash, all in a dark charcoal color, the better to fade into the shadows. The trousers were at least as full as the ones worn under a bloomer suit—in dim light, if they moved carefully, these could be taken for unfashionable skirts, which was exactly what they were counting on, because they were going to have to get cabs to and from Execution Dock.

Fortunately they didn't excite any attention on the street, and managed to get a cab to pick them up. They had the cabby leave them in front of a cottage in Wapping, waited for him to drive off, then carefully made their way to The Prospect of Whitby. This was a public house . . . but not just any public house. Squeezed in a narrow passage between it and the building next door were the Wapping Stairs, that once led to Execution Dock.

Nan had been reading about Execution Dock in regards to the age of piracy not more than a couple of weeks ago, which was why the site was so fresh in her mind. Before The Prospect of Whitby and the warehouse next door had been built, this part of the river had been more open. Pirates had been tried at the Admiralty Court and brought here, to the river's edge at low tide, to be hung. Then they were left there until the high tide had covered them completely over three times. *Why* they did this, she had no idea, but then, in those days it was not uncommon to keep a dead man hanging on display for some time while the flesh rotted from his bones. That was no longer done, but the Wapping Stairs and the brick platform the gallows had stood on were still in place.

I wonder how many ghosts we're likely to run into.

But right now, it wasn't ghosts that concerned her. While this was by no means the worst part of London, it *was* the East End, and full of sailors and dockworkers, and they were two young women out alone. Nan really did not want to get into a battle. Not when they had a job to do.

As they neared the Wapping Stairs, a figure stepped out of the shadows and into the light from the pub's windows. Although he wore the clothing and cap of a dockside worker, Nan immediately recognized John Watson's features with immense relief.

"You're in good time," he said in a low voice. "The tide's out, we can go right down to the water without anyone in the pub seeing or hearing us."

The stairs were barely wide enough for two of them; they had to go single file, and Nan was relieved when they stepped out onto an ancient bit of brickwork that led down to the water's edge that was big enough for all of them. The rear porch of the pub was a good two stories above their heads—that was how high the river got here at high tide. There was just enough light from the pub above them and from the full moon to see by. The mud of the bank glistened and stank. The brickwork was slippery with algae and things Nan didn't want to think about. Permeating everything was the greeny-fishy odor of the Thames, with an undertone of rot and raw sewage.

Sarah carried an umbrella—an incongruous weapon, unless you knew that it had a solid steel core and the ferrule at the end was sharp enough to pierce heavy leather. Nan had her Gurkha knives. And as both of them readied their weapons, Caro faded into view with her ectoplasmic bow and arrows. Dressed in her now-favored riding breeches, cap, boots, and jacket, Caro hovered above John's head, Sarah stood at his right and Nan at his left.

Nan really didn't know what to expect. John had never performed magic in front of them before, at least not in the sense of spells and incantations. As noise from the pub above drifted down toward them and the water lapped at their feet, she heard him muttering under his breath and watched him sketch signs in the air in front of him.

And a part of her was giggling with nervous hysteria at the thought that at any moment, some drunk from the pub above could come staggering out to the porch, whip out his tackle and take a piss over the railing. Or hike down his trousers and deliver a load. Because that was basically what that porch was *there* for in the first place, since drunken dockworkers and sailors are not thinking about modesty when its dark and they need to relieve themselves.

At least they weren't standing under the porch, but off to the side.

But no one did, and after many minutes of mumbling and gesturing, John called out softly over the water, "Jenny Greenteeth, by my power as a Master and my rights over all Creatures of Water, I summon ye!"

Nan got very little warning; something in the river at her feet erupted out of the water, splashing them all with a noisome spray.

And standing on the water before them, glowing with sickly yellow power and moonlight, was the ugliest creature Nan had ever seen.

Naked, with sagging breasts hanging down to her waist and long, wet, matted hair hanging down her back and in her face, Jenny Greenteeth not only had green teeth, she was green all over. The aged hag sported a long nose, thin lips, a pointed chin, emaciated limbs and a pot belly. Her hands were more "claw" than "hand," and there was a suggestion of scales about her skin.

"What d'ye want, Son of Adam?" the creature snarled. *"Why d'ye disturb my rest and conjure me?"*

Her voice was like the tearing of canvas, and it sent chills running down Nan's spine. Every word held a world of menace, and Nan had absolutely no doubt whatsoever that if John wasn't keeping her under tight control, she'd have torn their hearts out. Or tried, at least. Despite her determination, Nan felt sick with fear.

"What do you know about the headless girls, Jenny Greenteeth?" John asked through clenched teeth. "The headless girls sent floating down the Great River?"

"Oh the headless girls! No taste to them, no taste at all. Give Jenny a sad, sad suicide, or a fool afoul of his comrades! Jenny knows them, right enough. What will ye give Jenny to hear what she knows?" Jenny's words might have been playful under other

circumstances, but all Nan could hear was threat.

"I'll give Jenny her freedom, and naught else," John replied. Nan gripped the hilts of her knives as Jenny's eyes literally flashed with rage. "Otherwise I'll bind you right here, right now, and let the ghost above me fill you full of arrows. You can die, Jenny Greenteeth, and we both know it. Now, where do those girls enter into the river?"

Jenny threw back her head and screamed her rage, and Nan glanced reflexively up at the pub, sure that people were going to come piling out in response to the noise.

But no one did, and after a moment, she realized that the only reason *she* could hear it was because of Robin Goodfellow's blessing on her. Jenny's scream had not been in her ears, but in her head.

Nan braced herself as Jenny leapt out of the river, claws outstretched. She felt afire with anticipation for the fight. But she wasn't the one that got in the first blow.

Sarah was.

Using the umbrella like a spear, Sarah stabbed Jenny in the throat as Caro struck her with an ethereal arrow from above. Nan fended off the scrabbling claws with an upward slash of her right-hand knife, then cut at Jenny's belly with the left. Both strikes were solid hits that jarred the hilts in her hands, and she smelled the foul green ichor that served Jenny for blood.

Then John made an abrupt gesture with both his hands, throwing the hag back into the river. She emerged again, but much worse for wear, bleeding from the wounds they'd inflicted. She pulled out the arrow from her shoulder and screamed again as she cast it aside.

She launched herself at them, still not deterred; this time Caro feathered her with three arrows before John cast her back. She pulled out the arrows and dove under the water. But Nan was not taken by surprise when she erupted at Nan's feet. This time Sarah stabbed her in the back as Nan slashed both knives across her face, and John flung her back for a third time.

She emerged from the water halfway and screeched at them.

"You can scream all you want, Jenny Greenteeth," John barked. "But I shan't release you till you tell me what I want to know."

But sweat stood out on John's forehead, and Nan could tell that holding Jenny back was costing him.

Jenny's head dropped back down as her wounds sealed over, and she glared at him from under her dripping hair. *"Jenny can't tell you, Son of Adam. Jenny can only show you."* She grinned, showing two rows of pointed teeth. *"Come into the river, Water Master. Jenny will show you."*

Before John could answer, Caro spoke up. *"I can follow you, Jenny Greenteeth. Show me. But one sign of betrayal, and my arrows will fly. You can't harm me, but I can make you hurt."*

Jenny snarled up at Caro, who shot another arrow into the water at her feet as a warning.

"I agree," John said quickly, before Jenny could object. "When Caro says 'I release you, Jenny Greenteeth,' the spell will be broken and you will swim free." He looked up at Caro. "We'll meet you at the Passage at the top of the stairs."

That was a smart idea, Nan thought, admiring how well John Watson and Caro both thought on their feet. She had no doubt that Jenny would swim back here to attack them the moment she was free—but hopefully, she couldn't leave the water. So they wouldn't be here to attack.

"Follow then, feckless boy," snarled the Water Elemental, who took off swimming as fast as she could go. But as fast as Jenny swam, Caro kept up with her, until the two were out of sight.

"Better get up the stairs," John said, taking a handkerchief from his pocket and wiping the sweat and the fetid river water from his face. "I'd rather not be here when she's freed."

When they reached the Passage, they all leaned back against the damp brick walls. John looked exhausted. Nan wasn't sure how the others felt, but she wanted to be out of here so badly she could taste it. The bottoms of her trousers were soaked, and she was pretty sure Sarah's and John's were too. *Ugh. I'm going to have to soak these things to get the river-stink out of them.* And when Caro materialized suddenly at the top of the stairs, Nan jumped and had to suppress a yelp.

"The bodies entered the river from a big sewer," Caro reported. *"Jenny said she couldn't swim up it to tell exactly where they came from. I didn't want to push her any harder, and I wasn't*

sure she actually could *determine where they entered the sewer, so I let her go."*

"I can't argue with your reasoning," Watson said. "Can you show us on a map where that opening is?"

"Oh definitely," Caro said cheerfully. *"I came back slowly, by way of the riverbank, and I took note of all of the landmarks. Oh, she hates you, John. She hates all of us, but it's you she cursed under her breath the entire time. You'd better do something specific to protect yourself from her, or the next time you're on the water she'll make a try for you."*

"That's the hazard of being a Master." John sighed. "All right, this is all we can do for one night. I'll have to get a borough map of Wapping tomorrow, and a find out if there is a map of the sewer system here. Maybe we can find out where it goes. If not, at least we have a start, and I might be able to use Water Magic to trace the path. Ladies, I will find you a cab, then see you tomorrow at 221C. Right now all I want is to wash. Faugh!"

But from the way he held himself, Nan was pretty sure he was close to exhausted.

"Go home, John," she said. "We'll find a cab on our own."

It was a measure of his exhaustion that he didn't even argue with them. Instead, he trudged off downstream—since the road ran alongside the Thames. They turned and went upstream, passing the door of the Prospect of Whitby. Merry, raucous voices came from inside, but it sounded as if the inhabitants of the pub had settled in for the next couple of hours. At this point, the excitement of the fight wore off, and Nan found herself wishing that it was a coffeehouse and not a pub. *I could do with a pot of something hot, and some food.*

"I think if we find a cab, we should send it after him," Sarah said, in a worried tone of voice. "We can squeeze in three until we get to a part of town with more cabs."

"I agree." Nan was worried too. She'd never seen John Watson look so tired after working magic, and she had the shrewd suspicion that a lot more had been going on than appeared on the surface. He'd spoken of *binding* the Jenny Greenteeth, and perhaps that was what had exhausted him so much. "I don't think he does this sort of magic often."

"Nan! Sarah!" They were about fifty yards up the road from *The* Prospect of Whitby when Caro materialized in front of them. *"Help! John is being attacked!"*

Nan felt another jolt of energy, turned and ran back down the road, Sarah at her side, her wet trouser-bottoms flapping against her legs. They raced past the pub—there was so much noise from inside that no one even noticed them running past—and spotted John in the distance by the light of the moon.

Or rather, she spotted a clot of men scrumming, moving in and out of the shadows, and figured John was in the middle of them. At least four, certainly not more than six . . . her heart pounded like a railway engine.

The two of them hit the clot of fighting before anyone realized they were there. Nan smacked the back of the head of the nearest with the hilt of her right-hand blade at the same time that Sarah hit the kidneys of the one next to him with a two-handed blow from her umbrella.

The solid hit jarred her arm up to the shoulder, and she jigged back out of retaliatory range. Nan expected a shout or a scream, but all the two thugs uttered were grunts. But the attacks certainly got their attention. Four of the men turned toward the girls, leaving two still fighting with John.

Immediately, the two girls went back-to-back. The thugs that turned to face them were armed only with cudgels and sticks; they didn't have the length of Sarah's umbrella nor its point, and they certainly didn't have Nan's blades. Now Nan concentrated on two things and two only—the men in front of her, and keeping her back pressed against Sarah's.

She felt the Celtic Warrior in her pressing on her, trying to come through, and she opened the mental door and let that long-ago self charge through.

It was like dropping a shot of whiskey, neat, into her stomach. Fire ran through her limbs, and she felt a fierce and angry grin split her face. The reasoning part of her, the part that would have urged caution, got shoved to the side, and the wild Celt took over.

It almost felt as if she had eyes in the back of her head; she didn't need to see to know when a blow was coming and from where. She *felt* the attacks before they landed, and one of her knives was there to counter every blow. She maintained enough control to use the flats of the blades, and the hilts, rather than the edges—if she'd gone all out, the fight would have been over in seconds, and there'd have been four men with severed hands or throats on the ground. The Celt in her wanted blood, but dead and severely wounded thugs were going to be very difficult to explain to the police, and while this was a rough neighborhood, it wasn't as lawless as Whitechapel.

They didn't seem to realize this, however.

The one thing that was *incredibly* strange was that the fight took place in almost complete silence—the most noise these men made were grunts or wheezes when the girls or John Watson connected with a blow.

And for several minutes it was an even match.

Then things rapidly began to fall apart, and not for the girls and John.

Behind her, Nan heard the *crack* of breaking ribs, and one of Sarah's opponents fell to the street, gasping in pain. Taking advantage of the momentary distraction, Nan seized one of *her* opponents' arms and dragged him toward her. The second thug smacked him across the shoulders with his cudgel before he realized he had hit his own man, just as Nan hit the man she'd dragged toward her in the back of the skull with the hilt of her knife. *He* went down, falling into his partner, bringing the uninjured man down. Nan lashed out and kicked the first one in the side as he went down. If she hadn't been covering Sarah's back, she would have whirled and kicked the second man under the chin, but she didn't want to leave Sarah undefended.

Instead, she concentrated on the second man, who had gotten back to his feet, looking for an opening to take him down as well. She got one; he was unwary enough to let his left hand drift within range and she slashed the back of it with her right-hand knife, this time using the edge.

Now he made a sound; a curse, as he realized what she was armed with. And at that moment, a flicker of movement out of the corner of her eye showed her that John Watson had landed a haymaker punch right on the chin of one of his attackers, sending the man staggering backward until he fell into the street.

That seemed to decide the man Nan had slashed. "Bugger it!" he shouted. "I'm orf!" And he took to his heels.

The man whose ribs Sarah had broken staggered after him, and after a moment, so did his—thus far—uninjured partner. The man Nan had put on the ground got groggily to *his* feet and made his escape, and John Watson's final assailant stumbled away, grabbed the man John had punched by the collar, hauled him up and together they made their escape.

"Chase them?" Nan asked, perfectly ready to do just that.

John bent over his knees, panting. "No," he gasped. "There might be more of them. Besides, we know who this is. Sherlock warned us."

"Moriarty's men," Sarah replied, grimly. "Of course it is."

John stood up abruptly, but Nan already knew what he was thinking. "Wait—I can make sure Mary is all right," she said, and closed her eyes, leaning on Sarah.

It took no time at all to find Neville's mind; he drowsed next to Grey, but came completely alert when she touched him. Within moments, he and Grey knew what had just happened, and the rage that filled him took her a little time to calm. *Warn Mary,* she said, when he had finally regained his composure, and withdrew her mind from his to let him and Grey get on with just that.

"Mary's fine, the birds are fine, and they are warning her," she said, opening her eyes.

But there was panic in John's eyes. "I have to—" he began, then stopped himself. "No . . . no. She's been warned. And no one knows about 221C but us and Mrs. Hudson. Mary knows where my revolver is, and she's a decent shot."

"Yes, and yes, and yes," Sarah told him, one hand on his arm. "John, she's all right for now. What *we* need to do is be extremely careful about getting back to her. The last thing we want to do is lead anyone back to her."

"We should split up again," Nan said, her brows creased with worry. "But I don't want you alone, Watson—"

"*Sarah, give him the locket.*" Caro appeared again; Nan suspected she had followed the fleeing thugs to make sure they weren't doubling back. "*I can go with him and watch for trouble and warn him before it reaches him. He can give the locket back to you once we're all at the flat."*

Sarah snapped her fingers. "Of course! Thank you, Caro! That's brilliant!" She reached up around her neck and unfastened the strong chain she had bought to wear it on.

Watson obediently bent his head so she could fasten it around his neck. "For right now, we all stick together," he said. "It was daft to separate in the first place. Once we find a cab we can all squeeze into it until we encounter another. Then we'll split up and follow Holmes' standard instructions for evading followers and meet back at 221C."

They managed to find a cab in front of the City of Ramsgate pub, and thankfully it was a growler, not a hansom. It wasn't long before the driver intercepted a hansom, which Watson took, leaving the girls with the growler. Nan took Sarah's umbrella and knocked on the roof of the growler. The driver opened the hatch and peered down at them.

"Sir," Nan said. "We think we may be being followed. We would like you to go to 221 Baker Street, but by as random a path as you can contrive—and keep an eye out around you—"

But in the dark, Nan saw a sudden gleam of teeth. "Bless you, miss, I useta drive fer Master 'Olmes, Gawd rest 'is soul. No worries. Oi'll git ye there safe'n'sound."

Suspicion bloomed in her. She dropped her mental shields and quickly touched his mind.

Only to discover to her vast relief that he was exactly what he claimed to be—one of Sherlock's regular drivers: in effect, part of an adult version of the Irregulars.

"Thank you," she said simply, with a nod to Sarah to indicate that everything was all right. "That is the best thing I have heard all night."

And with that, she leaned back and relaxed as best she could over what was surely going to turn into a very long journey.

12

Spencer looked in on Hughs. The morning dose had been sufficient and everything was satisfactory with the young man. He was pleased to have so easily persuaded Hughs to move in here; it made it much easier to keep him healthy. As long as he insisted that the fellow eat a good, hearty breakfast on condition of getting his opium after, and an equally hearty supper on condition of getting another afterward, he wasn't wasting away as so many opium-eaters did.

And tomorrow he would take possession of another girl from old Don; this time Mrs. Kelly was ready for anything, and he had gotten his hands on some cocaine, which would, judiciously applied, keep even a badly injured girl on her feet long enough to be prepared and get through the ceremony.

Pounding on his back door made him frown—but the back door was Mrs. Kelly's to answer, and perhaps it was just some early tradesman. He retired to his study—but had not even had a chance to sit down when Mrs. Kelly hurried up from the kitchen. "It's them men ye sent on yer errand larst night," she said. "They didn' do it, an' they got beat up."

He swore under his breath, but what could he do? Moriarty had made it a practice never to punish anyone unless they had actually proven incompetent or stupid, so he was going to have to tend to these fellows and find out how it was that six men could not manage to kill one man alone.

"Get my medical kit," he told her, "Are they in the kitchen?"

"I ain't lettin' them in me clean parlor!" she said indignantly. "An' them all over muck an' bleedin'!"

"Good, I'll tend to them there then." He trudged down the hall while Mrs. Kelly went in search of the doctor's bag where he kept the supplies he used to occasionally patch up Moriarty's minions.

They were a sad sight, crowded into the kitchen, all wearing hangdog expressions. They were bruised, battered, cut, and bleeding. Of course, the fact that they had missed out on a big payday probably accounted for that expression on the faces of the two who were uninjured. They already knew he wasn't going to pay them for work they'd botched.

"Not a word," he said sternly, as Kelly brought in his bag. "Not one solitary word out of you until I've put you back together. Then you can try, *try*, to give me an explanation I'll believe for why six men were unable to take down one."

The lightest injury belonged to a man with a nasty slash across the back of his hand, or rather, wrist. If it had been his *hand* he'd likely have bled to death. The worst was something of a tie between a fellow with a cracked skull and one with broken ribs. There wasn't much he could do for the cracked skull, but he got the man with the broken ribs bandaged up so with luck, and if he wasn't an idiot, he wouldn't pierce a lung and die. When he got them all sorted out, he looked them up and down for a moment, and said, "All right, which one of you idiots is supposed to be the leader?"

The man with the slashed wrist sheepishly nodded.

He sat down in the kitchen chair and looked at the thug sternly. "I'm waiting."

"'E wuz in Wappin', sor," the man said, clutching his greasy cap in his uninjured hand. "We follered 'im there, lost 'im fer a bit, then found 'im again. Dunno wut 'e was doin' but when we found 'im, 'e wuz alone, loik yew wanted. So we jumped 'im. An' then outa nowhere comes a gang of 'Indoos, wut starts beatin' on *us*."

Spencer gave the man an incredulous stare. *"Hindus?* In *Wapping?* Are you out of your mind?"

"Oi swear, guv, they was 'Indoos. Them long shirts and bloomers an' all. They 'ad sticks an' knives, an' they fought loik devils, must've been five or six uv 'em! It was loik they came outa thin air, loik some sorta conjurin' trick. They 'ad four uv us down afore ye could say 'knife.' I figgered we was gonna get pinched fer sure, so we bolted outa there." The man didn't seem to be lying. He had none of the aspect of someone who was lying. And besides—Hindus? If he had been lying, surely he would have come up with a better story!

Then it occurred to him. The Hartons had Hindus and Sikhs and god only knew what all else working for them. And he knew they were friendly with Alderscroft, the old man gave them his estate for their damned school. Could they have sent their servants to protect Watson on Alderscroft's orders? It was certainly possible. More than possible, actually. Sherlock had probably said something to Watson, Watson had said something to Alderscroft, and the old man had called in the Hartons.

He cursed mentally, although he let none of his irritation show. He simply could not have anticipated this. But it definitely complicated matters. He didn't know *why* Watson was in Wapping, but Wapping was much too close to this house for comfort.

Was it possible that some of the headless bodies had been found? Possible that wretched Lestrade had been put in charge of the case, and enlisted Watson to help? Yes, yes it was possible; it was even probable. He'd thought by dumping them in the sewer they'd be carried out to sea, but he really should have known better.

He looked up at the six sheepish, groggy men crowding his kitchen. "Well," he said aloud. "I am not happy with you. You are certainly not going to be paid. But I am not going to punish you either. Go on, get out of here. And leave Watson alone; he's clearly got protection *you* didn't see until it was too late."

"Yessir," said the self-appointed spokesman, the hand holding his cap white at the knuckles. "Thenkee, sir."

They filed out, with Kelly watching from the doorway, her face a mask of disapproval.

"Yew b'lieve 'em?" she demanded, when they were gone.

"I do, actually," he replied. "The Hartons have Indian servants, several of whom are seasoned fighters, and the Hartons are friends of Lord Alderscroft."

"Ah . . . so ye reckon arter 'Olmes faked 'is death, th' old man 'ad 'is friends put their men t' guard Watson?" Kelly surmised.

"I'd have done the same in his place," Spencer admitted. "Some of these Indian chaps are the very devil for being able to slip about unseen. Dammit. This is a complication I did not anticipate, and I am afraid that Doctor Watson may be a serious threat to our plans."

Kelly sucked on her lower lip. "Wappin' is too close to us fer my likin'."

"My thought exactly." He considered consulting Moriarty, then decided against it. "I'll be in my study," he said instead, and got up. "I need to think in peace and quiet."

Once safely in his study, he sat and stared at the bookcase on the wall opposite while he pondered.

So far, except for eliminating Watson, everything had been going according to plan. When Moriarty perished, the anchor Spencer had constructed had drawn his soul *here,* and the talisman he had made had contained it. As for the Professor himself, Moriarty could only see what Spencer allowed him to see, and move in the limited space Spencer gave him. Moriarty had supplied Spencer with enough details that he had been able to keep the Organization mostly running. Spencer's battery would soon be completed, and Moriarty would soon be in a vessel everyone was happy with and running the Organization himself, taking that work out of Spencer's hands. Perhaps things had been going too well. Whenever things seemed to be ticking along like clockwork, somewhere under the surface there were always gears slipping.

So now he knew things were not going as well as they had seemed, and Watson's presence in Wapping alarmed him. And that presence suggested something else. Just because Watson was a Hunting Lodge Master, it didn't follow that he *wouldn't* bind an Elemental if he thought he had to. Would Watson have dared to try and bind one of the darker Water Elementals in order to get information?

. . . very probably. There didn't seem to be much that Watson *wouldn't* dare. He was a great deal more like Holmes than his writing would have suggested.

Bad enough that the attempt to kill him had failed. Worse that now—perhaps—he had been warned. Or at least, he was warned against the ordinary sort of attack.

But what about a magic attack?

Watson *couldn't* know about Spencer, couldn't know he

worked for Moriarty. Alderscroft might suspect a necromancer was to blame for the headless corpses—in fact, it was entirely possible that despite his best efforts, some signs of Necromantic activity had leaked past Spencer's carefully built shields. And that was probably what Watson was looking for. Bad . . . but not a disaster.

But he also *must* have attributed the purely physical attack on himself as something unconnected to that search; that it was Moriarty's men trying to get revenge for all the times Holmes and Watson had put them behind bars. He couldn't know Moriarty was still—in a sense—alive. He had no way to know that Spencer and Moriarty were working together. He had no reason to think that Moriarty, a man of science and logic, would give credence to the existence of magic. Which meant he had no reason to think it was Spencer, rather than Moriarty (or rather, Moriarty's men) who was responsible for the attack.

Which meant he probably thought the necromancer he was hunting for had no idea he was being hunted, and would not in his turn launch an attack against Watson.

So . . . bad, but not a disaster. Because Watson was probably not going to expect a magical attack. And Spencer had no intention of doing that. It would be some other attack. A plain old assault hadn't worked, so he wouldn't be trying that again.

Now . . . the question was, what *kind* of attack? This was going to require some extremely careful planning. It had to be nothing Watson would anticipate coming from a necromancer. No dark Elementals. No undead. This was going to take some bloody clever planning.

He sighed. Just one more damned thing on top of everything else he needed to think about.

But first things first. If Watson had invoked one of the dark Water Elementals, then he probably knew approximately where the bodies had entered the river—but there was a lot of sewer between this house and the river.

So the best thing he could do right now was to strengthen his shields. That was going to deplete his stored energies, but that was all right. There would be a lot more coming from the girls, especially if he spent some time taunting and tormenting them.

He stood up. He was going to have a lot of work to do today. The sooner he got to it, the better.

The killing table was, fortunately, easily pushed aside by someone as strong as he was. And as long as the talisman remained shrouded in silk, Moriarty was unlikely to notice his presence. He went to the storage chest under the shelves of heads and brought out a small floorcloth, just large enough to cover the center of the room. It had cost him a lot of hard-earned money to have it embroidered exactly the way he wanted it, but the result was worth it. No painting the circles and glyphs and sigils. No worries about stepping wrong and breaking lines chalked on the floor. He inspected it closely every time he took it out of storage or got ready to put it back in. Kelly was capable of mending anything that was damaged; she just wasn't good enough to have done the initial work.

He placed the floorcloth in the center of the room and drew on the power in his obsidian spheres until he could take in nothing more. Then he stepped into the innermost circle on the cloth and bent his will on the sigil of the west. He smiled to himself a little, as he reflected that he was beginning with Water—John Watson's power.

Within moments, he had a struggling, dripping wet nixie inside the circle holding the sigil. The creature was about knee-high and looked like a naked, green-haired woman with scaled skin. She looked up at him with angry, bulging green eyes, but he ignored her for the moment. He turned a quarter circle and moved on to the south, and Fire.

He was always very careful with Fire . . . even a necromancer as powerful as he was needed to make sure he did not catch the attentions of the Greater Fire Elementals, creatures which could end him with a thought. So he merely summoned and bound a common salamander. Nothing they would take note of. The salamander, a fire-sheathed lizard the same size as the nixie, hissed angrily at him and writhed in its invisible bonds.

He turned another quarter circle.

For Air, he was very happy to entrap one of Mary Watson's

cherished sylphs, a delicate little thing with dragonfly wings clothed in a wisp of blue mist that looked up at him out of enormous, terrified silver eyes, shedding tears like pearls. And finishing up in the north and Earth, he dragged in a struggling brownie, who spat curses at him in language suited to a dockworker.

With all four creatures bound and held, he began the spell that would strengthen his wards and shields against *all* of them, until even the Greater Elementals would have a difficult, possibly even impossible, task penetrating them.

A shrill keening arose from all of the bound creatures, a wail of pain as their very substance was drawn from their bodies and incorporated into the shields. This took more of his power and concentration than summoning and binding the Elementals themselves. He had to keep them from breaking their bonds, spin out threads of power from their bodies, and weave it all into his shields.

The Elementals wailed with pain as he did this, the sound of their cries penetrating his skull and sending lightning bolts of agony from his eyes to the nape of his neck. But that was part of the price to be paid, and he gritted his teeth and went on with the work. The first time he'd done this, he'd tried using earplugs of wax, which had been completely ineffective. Now he just worked through the pain, knowing a very, very small, carefully measured dose of opium would ease his agony until the pain faded on its own. This was just about the only time he ever resorted to drugs. He'd seen the deleterious effects on others too much to want to hazard them himself.

The Elementals began to fade, growing more and more transparent as he literally spun them into his shields, their cries growing thinner and weaker, until they faded into nothing, and were gone.

He took a long, deep breath and regarded his handiwork with satisfaction. *Nothing,* not a Master, not a full Hunting Lodge, nothing short of a Greater Elemental was going to get through those shields *or* realize he was there. He had learned well from his former Master, whose specialty had been shields. His protections were also camouflage. From outside, there was literally nothing to see.

With a suppressed groan of pain, he dismissed his protections, then bent to pick up the dropcloth. And had to catch himself on the side of the killing table as a wave of dizziness overcame him.

This had taken even more out of him than he had anticipated. But it was so very worth it.

Too bad he had one more task in front of him before he could count himself safe.

"Blimey," Kelly said mildly, as he dragged himself to the supper table. "Yew look like ye run ten mile in yer stockin' feet."

Should he tell her? Well, why not. She ought to know what he suspected so that she could take her own precautions. Their interests were exactly aligned on this point.

"The men I commissioned failed to kill John Watson," he told her, "And I have reason to think Scotland Yard has recruited him to discover where my leftovers are coming from. I believe he invoked a Water Elemental in Wapping to determine just that. And I believe the Hartons have loaned him some of their servants to guard him, at least when he undertakes excursions away from home."

Kelly's chin hardened. "Thet ain't good."

"No, it's not," he agreed. "So I just strengthened the shields to the point where an entire Hunting Lodge will neither be able to see them nor break them. And I am going to try and find out what, if anything, Watson learned. If there are any preparations or moves you need to make to protect yourself, I suggest you make them."

"Closin' me 'ouse down an' movin' 'ere," she said immediately.

He had anticipated this. "Clear the rubbish out of the upstairs bedrooms into the attic and take however many you need," he replied. "It's in my best interests that neither of us get pinched by these people. Once we get the Boss back in place and running the show, we won't have to worry about them anymore."

"Too roight." She licked her lips. "Oi'll git on cleanin' out the rooms then. Oi c'an move termorrer."

"Meanwhile I need to have a bit of a lay-down." He ate soup he had no appetite for, drank half a pot of tea at a go, and swallowed his tiny ball of opium. Once in the cool and dark of his bedroom, he sighed, and slowly felt the lightning bolts of pain behind his eyes fade.

At least he had warning to get his protections in place. If those men *had* killed Watson . . . he might not have had that. They wouldn't necessarily have told him *where* they had ambushed the doctor. He'd never have been able to put two and two together and come up with "Alderscroft is interested."

So . . . perhaps this wasn't a disaster after all. . . .

He felt the opium take the last of his pain and drifted into sleep.

One of the few benefits of opium in his opinion was that it tended to allow the imagination complete free rein. He knew that he was not an imaginative man—or rather, he was a methodical man, not given to leaps of intuition. Opium freed his mind from those inhibitions.

He emerged from his short rest with the germ of a plan uppermost in his mind. Moriarty had wanted to use the death of Watson as a means of making Holmes more cautious.

But something that would serve just as well would be striking indirectly, rather than directly, at Watson. And what would take Watson *right* out of the game, thus proving to Holmes that his friends and allies were all potential targets?

Killing Mary Watson.

The only question was, how to accomplish this? After the attack on John Watson, the couple would be alert and ready for anything like another straightforward attack or an ambush. No, this would have to be subtle, and require finesse.

Finesse meant he would have to use magic. But fortunately, Spencer had experience with much more than just necromancy. He had always been interested in things that granted mental control of others. Compulsions, especially; modifications of the old-fashioned "love" or "lust" spell or the "geas" that would compel someone to a particular action. He thought he had a good idea, but there was one aspect that was not in his area of expertise.

Although he was loath to do so, it was time to inform Moriarty of developments, and consult him.

It was night when he awoke, but night or day meant little to him for this purpose. It wasn't as if he was going to wake the Professor, after all.

Once again he went to his workroom, sat down in front of the talisman and removed the silk covering, then closed his eyes and slipped into the spirit plane.

Before Moriarty could say anything, he spoke up. "I followed your instructions about John Watson," he said plainly. "I sent six of our best men to follow him and ambush him when he was alone. They followed my instructions to the letter. Unfortunately, someone else must have been watching Watson, because the attack was foiled. By Hindus, the men claimed, and I have reason to believe they were not gammoning me."

Moriarty looked at him sharply. *"Hindus? That sounds highly unlikely."*

"It would take too long an explanation; let me just summarize by saying I think Lord Alderscroft is at the bottom of it." The Professor had not, in life, had the time nor the patience to hear the details of occult life and practices in Britain, but Spencer *had* told him about Alderscroft and the Hunting Lodge.

"Why would Alderscroft—oh. Yes, I see. But why Hindus?"

"Because these are not just any random Indian servants. These are highly trained fighters." He shook his head. "The point is that John Watson is protected from a direct assault. I think we need to try an indirect one."

"Go on," the Professor told him. *"I'm listening."*

Spencer told him the plan, and halfway through, the Professor stopped frowning and started smiling.

"That's not bad, not bad at all," Moriarty admitted. *"But how do you propose to make sure this works?"*

"Well . . . that's where I need your help," he replied. "Did you, by any chance, ever get your hands on photographs of John Watson, or his wife Mary?"

"Now that you mention it . . ."

Spencer smiled, thinly.

Magicians are supremely careful about their belongings and about anything personal of theirs. Such things can be used against them, after all; although Elemental Masters rarely dabbled in the crude spells of witches of old and the like, they all knew there was truth in such things, and that great harm could come to them should anything connected to them fall into the wrong hands. Spencer himself routinely burned hair trimmings, nail clippings, and old bandages, and laundered his own handkerchiefs.

But images can be as potent as personal items in the right—or wrong—hands. And Moriarty not only had photographs of the Watsons, he had something better.

He had the photographic plates.

Moriarty sent him to a particular vacant home that the Professor used for storage. And there he found, neatly categorized and alphabetized, box after box of developed photographs, cross-referenced with the box after box of their corresponding photographic plates. The Professor evidently had several photographers on his payroll whose only job seemed to be to find ways of getting pictures of his enemies and future targets.

Well, he supposed that would be very useful. If you were sending a trio of thugs to eliminate someone, it would be wise to have a picture of them on hand.

Spencer would never have dared to hope for this. A photographic plate, with the image etched on it by light that had *directly touched* the subject, was as good as a lock of hair to him. He picked one in which the Watsons appeared in a scene along the Serpentine, sitting on a bench, on what seemed to be a lovely spring day. It was clear from the composition of the picture that the photographer had been feigning to take a general "day in the park" picture—but he had very carefully used the Watsons as the focal point of the picture.

He brought the plate back to his workshop and assembled what he needed. The killing table made an excellent workbench, once he leveled it off with the crank, and there was plenty of light to work by.

It had been a very, very long time since he had performed this sort of primitive witchcraft, but it all came back to him quickly enough. It amused him that he was literally playing the role of the Wicked Queen in Snow White, as if this was a panto.

Using a glass cutter, he carefully excised the part of the plate holding the Watsons' faces. Making a circle on his table with thirteen black candles, he put the glass plate fragment in the center of the circle and began lighting the candles, moving in a counterclockwise direction and muttering the words of the first part of the incantation under his breath.

When the candles were all lit, he began the second part of the incantation, dripping three drops of wax from each of the candles in turn onto the plate.

In the third part of the incantation, he muttered two words while dropping three drops of his own blood on the plate. Then he blew out the candles, again moving counterclockwise, wrapped the wax-covered plate in clean parchment, tied it with a scarlet string, and set fire to it, all the while concentrating on what he wanted the Watsons to do.

When the fire had burned out, he scooped up the plate and the ashes, placed them in his mortar and ground them to powder. He mixed the powder carefully with a quick-drying lacquer, and used the lacquer to coat the inside and outside of the sort of common basket made with long wood shavings used by grocers to hold fruit.

When he was finished, he knew he had succeeded in properly setting the spell because he felt as tired as if he had walked ten miles. But his work wasn't done yet; he needed to consult Moriarty's notes on the Watsons.

The Professor had also sent him to a series of file cabinets stored in the same vacant house. The details of peoples' lives housed within those cabinet had left him flabbergasted. There was nothing—nothing mundane anyway—that the Professor did not know about the lives of his targets or potential targets. Small wonder Holmes had considered him the most dangerous man in the Eastern Hemisphere. Everything imaginable was there—potential blackmail material, commonplace details of their lives, right down to the number and kinds of servants that were employed, and even details on the servants' lives. The *only* thing that Moriarty had missed about the Watsons was their mastery of magic—and there was a note left in the file written in red ink that said "Spencer claims magicians are associated with Alderscroft and the so-called 'Hunting Lodge.' Get details if needed."

There in the file was exactly what he needed; the name of the grocer the Watsons used.

He noted the name and address and set the file aside to be replaced later. For now, he had done all that he could.

Once his basket had dried, around three the next morning, he turned his attention to the contents of his basket.

He left a small pot of beeswax melting over a candle, and looked over his selections of fresh fruit critically. Selecting the juiciest of pears, plums and grapes, he filled a syringe full of arsenic solution, a syringe with the finest needle he had been able to procure.

One by one, he injected the fruits with a lethal dose, then covered the injection hole with a dot of wax, carefully polishing the surface with a soft cloth so neither the wax nor the holes were obvious.

Now time was of the essence. From the file, he knew that Mary Watson habitually placed orders every day with the grocer in the summer, to ensure nothing spoiled. He'd ordered Geoff the Elf to bring a hansom around by five; by six, he was at the grocer's.

He waited while the grocer made up boxes of food for the day's deliveries; steady customers had their very own boxes labeled with their names. Sure enough, there was one saying "Watson." Having assured himself that the Watsons had placed an order for the day, he entered the store, getting the proprietor's prompt attention.

Very prompt attention. . . .

Once he caught the man's eyes, he had him; the grocer stared helplessly into his gaze as he softly issued orders.

"The Watsons ordered these fruits," he said, placing the basket on the counter between them. "You will put them in the order box now."

Dumbly the grocer took the basket and placed it on top of the rest of the order, still entrapped by Spencer's gaze.

"You will not remember me. You will not remember that I gave you these fruits. You will remember only that the fruits were on the order for today," he said. "You will stand quietly until I am completely out of the shop and looking idly in the window. When you see me looking at the plums, you will awaken, and call to your delivery boy to make the delivery to the Watsons. Do you understand?"

"Yessir," the grocer mumbled.

Satisfied, Spencer left the shop and spent a minute looking at the contents of the boxes displayed on the pavement, keeping watch on the grocer out of the corner of his eye. When he looked up at the plums, which were at the top of the display, he saw the grocer shake himself as if awakening from a trance, then sharply call to his delivery boy and thrust the Watsons' box into his hands.

Then the grocer hurried outside. "Is there anythin' I can get for you, sir?" the man asked.

"Yes," Spencer replied casually. "Those are uncommonly fine plums."

"Best in London," said the grocer automatically.

"I will have two pounds." He waited while the grocer weighed out the required amount, paid him, and made his leisurely way to Geoff's hansom, paper bag cradled in the crook of his arm.

"Do you like plums, Geoff?" he asked, as he climbed inside.

"Oi'm partial to 'em," the thug said, then laughed. "Long as yew ain't been meddlin' wi' 'em that is."

"Oh, you caught on to that, did you?" Spencer laughed, and handed up the bag. "Here you go. Fresh from the hands of the grocer. Should be safe enough. Home, please."

He relaxed back against the seat of the cab, pondering his plan, and on the whole, pleased with it. He didn't think much of Mary Watson's abilities, no matter that she had been rated as a Master. It was his experience that women didn't have the strength of will to impose their control on Elementals, and thus bargained with them rather than controlling them. She would never be able to resist or break his spell of coercion. The moment her hand touched the basket, she was doomed.

And that would be all that he—and Moriarty—needed. Watson would be broken, shattered, by the death of his wife. He'd be utterly useless to Holmes, and even more important, be utterly worthless to Alderscroft. Watson was too sentimental, too soft, to look for revenge until it was far, far too late for him to do anything about the matters Spencer had in hand.

And if Watson also fell prey to the coercion? All the better. They would both be dead, Alderscroft would be out his chief investigator, and by the time he organized another, Moriarty would be in his new body, and Spencer would be—where?

Somewhere quiet, and cool. Scotland, perhaps. Although living conditions in Scotland left a great deal to be desired. Northern France?

No, Germany. Germany was up-to-date, efficient. First-class hotels. First-class food. First-class drink. He preferred German wines to French, and German beer to English. A nice holiday in Germany was in order, he thought, and chuckled to himself at the idea of taking a side excursion to the site of Moriarty's death at the Reichenbach Falls. That would be highly amusing, actually.

Even more amusing if he could, by some wild chance, manage to acquire a bit of Moriarty's body. A fragment of bone, perhaps, or a tooth.

He'd have the means to completely control the mastermind in his own two hands if that happened.

He was so engrossed in these musings that the horse pulled right up to his house without him noticing until Geoff knocked on the roof of the cab. "We're 'ere, guv!" the man called out, and Spencer climbed out.

On impulse, he turned to the man rather than going back in the house. "Geoff, if you could go anywhere on earth for a holiday, where would you go?"

"Blackpool, guv," the man replied without hesitation. "They got music 'all's there wi' gels wut dance th' can-can wi'out bloomers. Aye, Blackpool. And nivver let Mother know where I was goin'."

Spencer blinked. It had never occurred to him that Geoff had a parent. He seemed to have sprung forth fully grown, possibly spontaneously generated from a heap of rags in the back of a betting parlour in the East End. "I didn't know you lived with your mother," he said.

"Mother's me missus," Geoff said, and frowned. "Ol' ball-an-chain she is, too. If I 'ad me a 'oliday, it'd be far away from 'er."

Astonished by the revelation that Geoff the Elf was married to *anyone,* Spencer passed over a handful of coins without bothering to count how many there were. Probably too much; Geoff grinned fit to split his face in half and pocketed the lot.

And with that, he went back into his house, to sleep the sleep of the well satisfied, certain that when he woke, the papers would be full of the news of the Watsons' deaths.

13

The grocer's boy tapped on the door to the flat above John's surgery, and Mary Watson let him in. They had decided to move to the flat temporarily, to let Mrs. Hudson and the two girls she had hired for a few weeks give it a good clean. It was too hot . . . and there were lingering smells that Mary wanted to be rid of.

Being here was a little like being on holiday, and it was so much cooler that she could scarcely believe it. And if she was doing the cooking herself for a change, instead of Mrs. Hudson, well, the "cooking" consisted largely of things she associated with being on holiday. Meals from the pub two doors down. Fish and chips from the shop on the corner. Sandwiches. All the sweets were from the bakery. In fact the only "cooking" she was doing was to light the stove to heat water for tea.

She was expecting Nan and Sarah and the birds shortly. They needed to have a serious discussion about the attack on John, and what it meant.

If they hadn't all been so anxious and keyed up about the necromancer, and the attack on John, living here would have been lovely. Or at least, as lovely as things could be in the middle of London in the heat of summer. She knew in a week or two she would start to miss things that were back at Baker Street, and not having them would be infuriating, but for right now the making-do was amusing.

She heard the boy put the box on the kitchen table in the flat's relatively small kitchen and leave, and she went to make sure everything she had ordered was in there. That was when she noticed the basket of fruit she *hadn't* ordered, right on the top of the box.

That's odd. She frowned. Not that she'd mind fruit; she could make a lovely fruit soup or salad or a nice trifle out of it—but she definitely hadn't ordered it. It was in an unusually nice basket too, not the usual wood-chip thing, but something that had been lacquered. The silky finish made her reach out, wanting to touch it.

She put out her hand, and the moment her fingertips contacted the basket, she was seized with an uncontrollable desire to fill her hands with plums and pears and devour them like a starving animal. It was like a fire in her—she *had* to have them, now, this very instant!

Mental alarms were going off in her head, but she ignored them. The fruit . . . it was beautiful, so lovely it made her mouth water just to look at it. She wanted to taste it—to devour every scrap. Her mouth was dry as sand, and only that beautiful fruit would slake her thirst.

And a dozen screaming sylphs flew up into her face, driving her away from the table. They attacked her hysterically, screeching at the tops of their tiny lungs, pummeling her with their little fists, scratching her with miniscule nails. *"No!"* they screamed. *"No! Danger! Bad!"*

She tried to brush them aside to get at the fruit, the luscious, tempting fruit, but more of them intercepted her, blinding her with their wings. "Let me alone!" she ordered, but they wouldn't obey. Instead they closed around her, hemming her into a corner, and she was afraid to strike at them for fear of hurting them.

Behind her, she heard John running through the sitting room, into the kitchen—and then he, too, was swarmed. The room seemed full of butterfly-winged sylphs, all of them trying to keep her, and now John, away from the fruit.

Finally she lost her temper. She gathered her magic and shouted at them, "Begone!" putting all of the force of her will behind the command. The sylphs wailed and vanished—

But before she could move, Neville flew through the kitchen

189

window and straight at her, hooking his claws in her bodice, and flapping his wings in her face. A moment later, the raven was followed by the parrot, and beside her, John fought a similar battle with Grey—

The girls had taken the 'bus as far as the street where John's surgery lay. The birds flew free today, since there was no good reason to confine them to their carriers, and *every* good reason to keep them out where they could watch for danger. They were about halfway down the block when the birds both gave alarm calls and shot like a pair of bullets for the open windows of the flat.

At the same time, a cloud of frantic sylphs boiled up out of nowhere and assailed the two of them, tugging on their clothing, flying in dizzying circles around their heads, shrilling something about . . . fruit?

It didn't matter what they were saying, it was clear that Mary, and perhaps John too, were in danger; Nan picked up her skirts and ran with Sarah right behind her, bursting in through the door of the surgery, pelting up the stairs at the rear to the flat, flying in through the open door. That was where they heard the struggle going on in the kitchen—Neville shouting *"No! No! No!"* and Grey screaming *"Bad fruit! Bad fruit!"*

Nan shoved her way into the tiny kitchen and took in everything in a glance. Neville attached to the front of Mary's bodice like a brooch from hell, flapping his wings in her face as she flailed at him. Grey dancing on the table between John and a basket of fruit, snapping at his fingers as he tried to reach for it.

Dear god—his eyes!

John's eyes were wide and maddened, and he paid absolutely no attention to the fact that his wife was locked in a struggle with a large and dangerous bird. Clearly all he wanted was the basket Grey was keeping him from. Sarah interposed herself between John and her parrot, shouting at him, grabbing his lapels in both hands and shaking him.

Nan didn't even think. She pushed past him, snatched up the basket, and threw it in the stove, ignoring John's wail of anguish. Someone had lit it already, and there was a merry little fire going.

She looked around, saw a pan that still had some bacon grease in it, and poured it over the fruit, basket and all, then slammed the firebox door shut as it all went merrily up in flames.

They had all moved to the sitting room, sparsely furnished in white wicker with cushions of blue chintz. Mary reclined on a lounge, while Nan carefully applied witch hazel to the scratches on Mary's face and hands, as Neville sat on her shoulder, occasionally muttering *"Sorry."*

"I don't think you're going to have a black eye," Nan said, finally. "Which is a wonder, given how he was buffeting you with his wings."

"He saved my life, and Grey saved John's," Mary Watson replied. "A few scratches and a black eye would be a small price to pay. I don't even mind that he made rags out of my shirtwaist." Nan winced a little. Neville *had* destroyed the front of her shirtwaist past mending; for modesty's sake she'd gone and put on a new one before she let Nan tend her injuries.

"Sorry," Neville croaked, his head down, and his neck feathers ruffled.

Mary put up a hand to caress his head. "Don't be, Master Mischief," she said. "You did what you had to do to save us."

"Do you suppose you can tell us now just what was going on?" Sarah demanded, looking from Mary to John and back again.

"I'd like to know that myself," John added. "Mary's sylphs came boiling up at me as I was cleaning some instruments in the surgery, yelling something about danger. I ran for the stairs and into the kitchen. Mary was beset with sylphs and there was something on the kitchen table she was trying to get to. And then . . . I stopped thinking entirely. All I remember is being overcome with an irresistible compulsion to cram fruit into my mouth, while Mary's sylphs tried to keep me away from it. Then she banished the sylphs, and just as I was about to get my heart's desire, Grey drove me away from it."

"That was exactly what happened to me!" Mary exclaimed. "The grocer's boy delivered what I had ordered, and I came in here to make sure it was all there. And there was that basket of fruit that I knew I hadn't ordered—I touched it, and all I could think about was eating it—"

"Sounds like the 'Goblin Market' poem," Nan said, dubiously.

Sarah's head came up. "Or Snow White!" she exclaimed.

"I was just thinking the same thing," John replied, frowning fiercely. "There was a compulsion on that basket, and I will wager the fruit in it was poisoned. Why else would there be a compulsion on it?"

"But why didn't it affect me?" Nan demanded, corking the witch hazel.

"It had to be specific to John and me." Mary put her hand to her forehead, as if her head suddenly pained her. "This isn't Elemental Magic. It's—"

"Old-fashioned black witchcraft," John said, angrily. "Curse it, we are being attacked on all sides, we have *no* idea who is doing the attacking, and they are actually able to come at us *in our own home!*" His fist came down on the arm of the chair so hard Nan heard the wood crack. *"They nearly murdered my wife!"* he cried brokenly.

Mary instantly left her lounge and went to him, gathering him in her arms, murmuring to him soothingly. Nan looked away, feeling very uncomfortable at witnessing such a moment of personal weakness on John Watson's part.

"I've half a mind to tell Alderscroft he can find someone else to hunt his necromancer," John murmured, his face against Mary's shoulder.

"That's exactly what the necromancer wants you to do," Mary replied, absently. "He must have discovered that we are hunting him. I can't think of anyone else who would have the sheer ability to put such a powerful compulsion on an object."

Nan snapped her fingers. "Mary, you're right. That *is* exactly what he wants you to do, John. And maybe if you do just that, he'll become overconfident, or at the least drop his guard, and make a mistake."

John raised his head. "I—I can't think," he said thickly.

"I've already got an idea, and most of a plan," Nan replied. "And if *nothing* else, it will buy you some peace. It starts with us faking Mary's death."

"I'll send a telegraph to Alderscroft, telling him to come here, that it's an emergency." Sarah snatched up her purse, and ran out the door.

"And I'll go downstairs and lock up the surgery," Nan said. "Thank goodness this happened *here*. You'll be able to move back into 221C without the necromancer even knowing you are there. Hopefully Mrs. Hudson has finished her cleaning."

The next couple of hours were a whirlwind of activity. Alderscroft arrived, was given the explanation of what had happened, and for the first time, Nan saw the man in a towering rage.

Alderscroft's eyes literally blazed. There was a fire in the bottom of them, and he seemed a good foot taller. His jaw tightened, and his hands clenched at his side, the knuckles white.

It terrified her. It was like being in the same room as an erupting volcano. For a moment she was afraid to breathe.

When he had calmed himself, he proceeded to move mountains. An ambulance was summoned, and Mary taken off under a shroud. John rode in the ambulance with her, in case anyone was watching.

Meanwhile Alderscroft summoned Scotland Yard, who proceeded as if this had been a murder scene. They collected the half-burnt fruits from the stove (without asking why they had been flung in there in the first place). They questioned Nan and Sarah, who, following the story Nan had concocted, told them that they had arrived to find John cradling his wife's body, a half-eaten pear in one of her hands. They took notes, they took measurements, they went down to the surgery and presumably took more notes and measurements. They then went to question the grocer, and presumably the grocer's boy. Alderscroft saw to the locking up of the surgery and sent Nan and Sarah to Baker Street.

Meanwhile according to Nan's plan as enhanced and enlarged by His Lordship, the coroner was given most of the real story by Alderscroft, John, and Mary at the hospital. "Most" of the real story, because he was not told about the compulsion to devour the fruits, only that the fruit had arrived without being ordered, slipped in with the rest of the order, and that Mary had gotten suspicious. He agreed to create a false death certificate at the behest of Alderscroft, and once the results of testing on the fruit was complete, would fake autopsy results that would corroborate the tests.

Alderscroft smuggled Mary back to 221 Baker Street, where Nan and Sarah had given Mrs. Hudson all the details except the magical ones.

"Well," said Mrs. Hudson when they had finished. "It's a mercy we just finished cleaning, at least."

The newly cleaned sitting room now held the five of them. Alderscroft sat there calmly enough, but it was clear to Nan there was a still-smoldering fire of anger in the man. Watson had waited with the coroner to get the results of the chemical testing on the fruit. Uncharacteristically, the men had removed their coats and were sitting in rolled-up shirtsleeves at Mary's suggestion.

". . . and there was enough arsenic in just one grape to have killed two men my size," Watson said, wearily. It had been a very long day for the Doctor, and a trying one, but at least now everything was over but making arrangements for the "funeral." "There was probably enough in the whole basket to have murdered three dozen."

"He wasn't taking any chances, was he?" Sarah asked.

"It might not be a *he*," Watson reminded her. "Poison is a woman's weapon."

"Don't tell the Borgias that," Nan murmured, then spoke up. "Not true. Poison is the weapon of someone who has no intention of getting caught. And the only reason most poisoners get caught in the first place is because they murder someone close to them." She didn't mention that if Mary were *really* dead, John would certainly be a suspect at this point. He was already shaken and heartsick enough.

But John said it for her. "It's a good thing I can produce Mary at any moment, then," he replied grimly, holding her hand tightly. "The coroner was nothing short of wonderful with Scotland Yard. I'm sure they'll investigate me, but thank the good Lord there is no arsenic in my surgery, and I haven't bought any in—"

He looked at Mary, who shook her head. "I don't remember you *ever* buying any, after Sherlock once pointed out that arsenic, strychnine, and cyanide are very dangerous substances to keep on hand, because one never knows when one is going to be framed for murder by a *real* murderer."

"I wish Sherlock was here," John sighed mournfully.

"Chin up," Nan said, as Mrs. Hudson tapped on the door and brought in a loaded tea tray.

Wisely, Mrs. Hudson had included no fruit in what was a very substantial and heartening spread of food. There was some silence as they sorted out who was taking what, then more silence as they ate. John Watson and Alderscroft devoured ham sandwiches with single-minded doggedness that suggested they were trying to get as much energy in the shortest possible time as they could.

Nan, Sarah, and Mary, to whom Mrs. Hudson had supplied food by way of comfort, let them have the lion's share. Finally, when the edge was off the masculine hunger, Alderscroft turned to Nan.

"You have had the plan so far," he said bluntly. "Did it go past this point?"

"Actually, it did," she replied. "John will have a funeral as soon as humanly possible—no one will blame him for hurrying things in this heat. He'll then close up the surgery and—"

"Ah, I have a better idea," said Alderscroft. "I have a gifted young Earth Mage physician who would be happy to take over your practice and your patients, John. He's here for the summer at least, and if our investigation goes half that long, I'm saying be damned to it all and bringing the full force of the Hunting Lodge down on this blackguard."

John looked very much relieved. "I'd hate to leave my patients in the lurch," he said. "Especially in summer, when so many physicians are on holiday. He might as well take the flat, too, as well as the practice."

"That's perfect," said Nan. "All right, John. You will announce that you are leaving London—losing your wife and Holmes so closely together has shaken your nerves. You might as well go through with the ruse of leaving—if this fiend was able to discover what grocer you use, who knows what else he can do."

"That's probably wise, John," Alderscroft said after a moment. "In a moment of grief like this, if you put up shields that are so good he can't scry you, that would be suspicious. And he used poison as his primary weapon, not magic; I believe we're meant to think it's not the necromancer, but a lesser practitioner gone to the bad."

John rubbed his temples. "All right. It's not as if Sherlock didn't teach me more than enough to shake off pursuit, whether it's someone actually following me or someone scrying me. I'll say I'm going on a walking tour; I can take the train to Devon, start off, double back and take the train home in disguise."

"I've also got an alternate, if you'd rather not leave London," Nan continued. "You still give over your flat and the practice to this protégé of His Lordship's, but instead of leaving town, you tell people that you are going to 221B to be tended by Mrs. Hudson."

The rest of them sat quietly, considering both options.

"I like the second choice," Alderscroft said, breaking the silence. "Less to go wrong."

"And a great deal less suspicious," Watson agreed. "Plus, it means I won't leave Mary alone."

Nan bit her tongue on retorting that Mary was not going to be *alone*. John was probably feeling both protective and very fragile right now.

"All right. Does your plan go past the point of John coming here?" Alderscroft asked.

"Well . . . after that it gets rather nebulous," Nan admitted. "Obviously we need to discover who this necromancer is, and where he is, but I don't know that much about magic, so I don't know how you would go about that. My main idea was to get John and Mary some peace from this monster."

"It's a good plan," Alderscroft told her.

"Really, you gave us something to throw the blackguard off the trail initially, which is the most important thing," John agreed, managing a wan smile. "If you hadn't done that, he might be planning his follow-up attack on us at this very moment."

Nan shrugged. "It's not pulling victory from the jaws of defeat, but it's better than pulling defeat from the jaws of defeat."

The girls finally went back to their own flat just before sundown. Neither of them wanted to travel at night, and both of them kept a sharp lookout for anyone who might have been following them.

"It's a mistake to assume this fellow hasn't got perfectly

ordinary minions at his disposal," Nan pointed out, as they sent the birds to their perches for the night.

"I don't think John or his Lordship are making that mistake." Sarah replied, and went to her room to change into a light wrapper. Nan evidently had the same idea, as she was sprawled in the sitting room in a cotton kimono fanning herself, with two glasses of lemonade waiting, when Sarah came out.

"It's my turn to have an idea," Sarah said. "The one person I can think of who would have the best idea of how that compulsion was done and what it would take is Beatrice Leek."

"True, but what would that tell us?" Nan asked.

"I don't know, but Beatrice might. We simply don't know that much about magic, you and I." Sarah sighed. "It's hard to be useful."

"Then let's visit her first thing in the morning." Nan agreed. "Alderscroft can take care of the Watsons. We might as well see if there's anything Beatrice can add."

Nan didn't even get a chance to knock on Beatrice's door. The self-described witch was waiting for them as they got down from the cab. It made Nan wonder, not for the first time, how Beatrice always seemed to know they wanted to talk to her. And from her sober face, Nan had the feeling that the old woman had *some* idea that there had been serious nastiness afoot.

She hurried them inside her house and shut the door quickly. "*What* is all the hue and cry in the papers this morning about Mary Watson murdered?" she asked anxiously.

"She's fine," Nan assured her. "But someone did try to murder her with the help of magic. That's why we're here."

Relief spread over the old woman's face. "Then come in and have some tea and toast and tell me all about it."

With the birds perched on the backs of their chairs, and the cat in Beatrice's lap, Nan explained everything that had happened— at least, as far as she knew. "So we came here to find out if there is anything you can tell us about magic that works like that," she concluded. "And anything else that occurs to you, for that matter."

"Well, ducks, I can tell you one thing. That's the blackest of black magic." She shook her head. "The important thing is that *traditionally*, you need something very personal from the victim. Hair, blood, that sort of thing."

"I would think that John and Mary would be too careful to leave that sort of thing where anyone could get their hands on it," Sarah replied, her brows furrowed.

"Well I did say *traditionally*. And His Lordship and John and Mary, not having to trouble their powerful little heads with old-fashioned witchcraft, probably haven't paid any attention to what us simple folk have been experimenting with." Beatrice smiled slightly. "We've found you can use a photograph, and it works just as well."

The implications of that staggered Nan. "How—there are photographers *everywhere*. I'm sure John has had his picture in the papers because of Sherlock. And there may be wedding photographs of John and Mary as well, for the same reason."

"Or someone could have caught them in one of those scenes of Hyde Park that people are always taking, or something else," Beatrice agreed. "All the magician needed to do was *find* one, and there are clipping agencies for that."

"Bloody hell," Nan swore. "Well, that solves that question. Is there any way we could trace this back to someone?"

"Not once you threw it in the fire, ducks," Beatrice said. "Fire breaks those connections." She shook her head. "All I can tell you is this is a nasty business. I think John was quite right to feign that Mary is dead. This kind of magic is vicious enough in the hands of a plain old witch like me. In the hands of a necromancer . . . I don't like to think how powerful it must have been."

"Does that sort of thing happen often?" Sarah asked. "A necromancer using . . . well . . . "lesser" magic?"

"Well, you likely would never see the likes of Milord and his Lodge resorting to it, but that's just why it would be so effective on them, you know." Beatrice smirked, ever so slightly. "They just wouldn't be looking for it."

Nan sighed. Here, she'd had some hopes of getting some help from Beatrice, but it seemed they were at yet another dead end.

"Bloody hell," she muttered, and throttled back the sudden urge to cry. It had been a very long couple of days, and not only had they made no progress, it seemed they were now several steps behind. "Dammitall," she added, and to her horror, felt a tear running down her cheek.

"There, there, ducks," Beatrice said, handing her a napkin to use in lieu of a handkerchief. "It's always darkest before the dawn."

"I could use one of those too," Sarah said, thickly.

They didn't break down into sobs, but both of them had to set aside their teacups and wipe fiercely at their eyes for about fifteen minutes while Beatrice politely pretended not to notice.

"It's just wretched to feel so damned helpless," Nan managed after she got her eyes to stop leaking tears. "I'm tired, and Sarah's tired, and God knows John and Mary are tired, and we just can't get anywhere with this. And this . . . madman goes right on murdering poor girls and we can't stop him."

"What's he murdering 'em for though?" Beatrice wondered aloud. "I've not sensed any great conjurings going on. And there's only so much death energy one magician can use at any one time. That's why usually the most you see is the murdering blackguards killing something once a month."

"Could he be . . . storing it somehow?" Sarah wondered.

Beatrice frowned. "Well, now that would be right outside of anything I know," she admitted. "I know how to store spells in talismans, but . . . well no. I have no idea how, or even if, you could do that."

They fell into a glum silence.

"And even if he is, what's he doing it *for?*" cried Sarah, in an outburst. "Why would he need that much power?"

"Whatever it is, it can't be good for the likes of you and me," the old woman said shrewdly. "But you'd know better about that than I would, I reckon."

"Not really," Nan admitted. "I'm not very good at imagining what people want with a great deal of power. Horrid monsters, yes, they generally want to make everything go smash."

"There are people who want to make everything go smash too," Sarah reminded her. "But I've never understood them, either."

"In my experience, the ones that want to smash everything up are the same ones who think they won't go up in flames with the rest of us," Beatrice opined. "And they're the first to be shocked when the flames are licking at their toes."

"So what are we to do?" Nan asked rhetorically. "Advise everyone to invest in asbestos gowns and watch for the fires to be set off?"

"No . . ." Beatrice got a thoughtful look on her face. "Now that you mention fires being set off . . . it reminds me of when we had a rash of fire-setting when I was a girl, back in my village. There was a lot of nonsense about curses, and then a lot of finger-pointing when half-burned rags soaked in oil turned up, but eventually me old Gram said to the mayor, 'You watch and see who turns up first at every fire, and that'll be your lad.' And sure enough, there *was* a fellow who turned up first at every fire, and eventually they caught him dead to rights."

"I don't see how that helps us," Nan objected. "Whoever this is, he's not lingering about the Thames, watching for bodies to be pulled out."

"No, but he might well turn up at the funeral—just to be sure Mary's dead," Beatrice pointed out. "Even if it's all private like, he'll be lurking about the graveyard, maybe."

Sarah and Nan both nodded, slowly. "All right, we'll take that back to John and His Lordship," Nan agreed.

"And you know who'd make the best fellow in the world to keep an eye out for a lurker—" Beatrice said.

"Me!" shouted Neville.

The day of the "funeral" certainly turned out to be perfect for discouraging all but the most dedicated of lurkers. The morning dawned without any sun at all, only heavy, lowering clouds. And the threatening storm made good on its threat as the very small funeral party arrived at the equally small chapel where the funeral was being held.

John Watson in full mourning was supported by Mrs. Hudson, Inspector Lestrade, and some of his medical colleagues. Nan and Sarah had wanted to attend, but Alderscroft *and* John had warned them off. "We don't what to alert whoever this is to the fact that you two are working with us," John had said, grimly. "There have been enough victims already. I'd rather not add you two to their ranks."

Mary, of course, could not be seen either, not even in the thickest of black veils—John had no sister, not even a female cousin, so who could she impersonate? "I think it's very hard that I cannot attend my own funeral," she said, trying to extract some humor from the situation.

So only Nan could watch the procession into the chapel, and then to the graveyard nearby, through Neville's eyes. And Neville was not at all happy about having to sit and fly in the downpour.

Alas, the only lurkers about proved to be members of the press, who had their hopes of interviews drowned under the steady rain. Neville flapped back to Baker Street in a foul mood, to be let in, dried off in a nice thick towel, and spoiled with bits of beef heart.

John followed about half an hour later, soaked to the skin and not in much of a better mood than Neville. "I'm beginning to think we should have had the damn sham of a service in Westminster Cathedral," he grumbled, after going off to change into something dry. "At least then there'd have been a chance someone would have turned up to spy on us."

"Well, I suppose I didn't miss anything then," Mary said philosophically. "I hope I got a nice eulogy."

14

Old Don was waiting for him, standing in front of his counter and gripping a girl tightly by her upper arm. She was dressed in a shapeless black tunic and trousers, and her eyes were half-closed.

There was something very wrong here.

Spencer eyed the Chinese girl old Don had for him dubiously. "What are you trying to sell me?" he demanded. The girl didn't look right. She was as pale as a ghost, and it looked as if the only thing keeping her on her feet was Don's peculiarly small hand gripping her arm so tightly that his knuckles were white. As tight as he was holding her, the girl should have been registering pain, yet she sagged in his grip.

"Ye said ye didn' mind 'em used," Don said, angrily. "'Ere!"

He thrust the girl in Spencer's direction. She staggered a single step, made a strange gurgling sound, and collapsed bonelessly at Spencer's feet.

She didn't move. And he couldn't see her breathing.

Spencer poked her with a toe. The flesh was flaccid. Literally lifeless. And literally worthless. Don had just tried pawning off another dying girl on him. Only this time, she'd dropped dead before he could make use of her.

"Bloody hell, you cheat," he snarled, looking up at old Don. "She's dead."

"She ain't dead! She's jest fagged out!" Don protested. "She jest swooned loike."

Spencer, of all people, knew "dead" when he saw it. "In your eye, she's fagged out. She's bloody dead. She couldn't get any deader if she was on a slab right this minute. I don't know how you kept her on her feet this long, but I'm not paying for a corpse and I'll be having my money back right now!"

He was glad he'd followed his instincts tonight and brought along one of Moriarty's larger thugs, a huge Italian boxer named Tony. Without prompting, Tony bent down and hauled the corpse up by an arm, shaking it like a dog shakes a rat, eliciting no response from it whatsoever. The body just flopped around limply. The bruiser flung it at old Don's feet, where it landed in a heap of arms and legs. The boxer glowered at him, fists clenched at his sides.

"I said," Spencer repeated, slowly enunciating each word, "I'll be having my money back now. Or must I tell Tony to shake you until the money falls out of your pockets?"

Old Don looked from Tony to Spencer, and back to Tony again, getting red in the face with anger. Tony grinned at him and raised his fist. Hastily, old Don dug in a pocket, pulled out some greasy notes, and flung them at Spencer's feet. Spencer bent, picked them up, and thrust them in his own pocket, turning on his heel to leave.

"'Ere! What'm I s'pposed t'do wi' this?" old Don shouted after him.

"It's your mess. You clean it up," Spencer said coldly. "Be grateful I'm not calling the law on you. I'd like to see you bluff your way out of having a dead Chinagirl on the premises. I won't be cheated again, and I expect to have better merchandise from you in three days."

And with that, he left. He and Tony crowded together into Geoff's hansom, which was waiting at the curb for them.

"Where to, gov?" asked Geoff from above.

Spencer wanted to tell him "to Perdition," but he doubted Geoff would understand the reference. "Drop Tony off first, then take me home," he said instead.

Outwardly he was calm. Inwardly he seethed. Setting up the magic defenses against Alderscroft had taken much of his stockpiled power, and he knew he was going to need every girl he could get. Now this! And he wouldn't get another for three more days—and that assumed old Don would continue dealing with him.

The cab pulled away, the horse's hooves tapping briskly on the street.

"Gov?" Tony said tentatively.

"What?" Spencer snapped.

"Nivver mind," Tony said, hastily. "Weren't nothin'."

He knew what Tony was going to offer—that he'd ask around for someone else selling Chinese girls. The trouble was the brute had no idea that he wanted something besides an exotic whore.

And Spencer didn't want any more people knowing he wanted "disposable" girls than were already in on the secret. Bad enough that Geoff and old Don knew. Many more, and word would get out and would *certainly* get into the circles where Alderscroft would hear about it. Alderscroft absolutely knew by this time that Mary Watson had been murdered with the help of magic. Right now he was looking for a common magician or even a witch, and had not put that together with the serial murderer Watson had surely been looking for. But let him put "disposable girls" together with "headless girls" and a magic murder and he'd know that the person who'd killed Mary and the murderer were the same, and that person must be a necromancer. Then the full force of the Hunting Lodge would be brought to bear—and possibly more than one Lodge. He'd heard that the Lodges in Germany were particularly ruthless when they caught who they were after.

"It's all right, Tony," he said instead, as the dark and mostly deserted streets rolled by. "He's learned his lesson, thanks to you. I'll take you with me in three days when I pick up another shipment to make sure he behaves."

"Roight yew are, gov," Tony replied, sounding relieved.

After dropping Tony off, Spencer brooded all the way back home. He wondered how he was going to explain the delay to Moriarty, because delay there certainly would be.

Still, might as well get it over with rather than drag out the inevitable.

He gave Geoff a half crown as he exited the hansom. "Wait a minute," he said. "I'm sending you another fare out. He's not to be meddled with."

Geoff chuckled. "Sutcher self, gov," he replied. "'E'll 'ave a roide loike Oi'm carryin' eggs."

As soon as he got inside, he found the preacher waiting in the hall. He acted surprised to see him.

"Good heavens!" he exclaimed, slapping his head in feigned dismay. "Did I give you the wrong day? I must have! I am so very sorry!"

The preacher lost a little of his ebullience and began to say something, but Spencer ran right over the top of him. "No, no, all my fault, father, my fault entirely. Here—" He thrust three of the bills he'd gotten from old Don into the preacher's hands. "This is for your time, and look! The cab I took home is still at the curb. If you trot you can catch him before he drives off!"

That quelled any further palaver from the preacher; anxious not to be stranded here at night, the preacher quickly hurried out and was helped inside.

Geoff drove off, and Spencer sighed. One problem solved, anyway.

Climbing up the stairs to the bedrooms, he checked on Hughs. He was pleased to see that between them, he and Kelly had arrived at the optimal mix of drug and nutrition—and that Kelly had left a selection of succulent fruits at Hughs' beside to encourage him to eat in his drowsy state. That was an excellent idea, and one he had not used with previous candidates. Hughs could probably keep on this way for as much as six months without substantial harm.

Kelly came up the stairs from the kitchen, frowning a little when she saw he was alone. "Summat go amiss?" she asked.

"Girl died," he said shortly. Kelly tsked.

"Wuz afraid th' bloody barsted 'ud try an' pass another near-deader off on yew," she said shrewdly, wiping her hands on her apron.

"It wouldn't have mattered if she'd just lasted long enough for the bloody ritual," he growled. "If I didn't need him—"

"Wall, yew don't. Thin's'll go slower wi'out 'im, but we c'n go back t' the old way." She smoothed down her apron. "One thin' we ain't tried. You go pickin' up hoors, get 'em drunk, an' make 'em thin' yer drunker. Hev' the weddin', on a dare, loike."

He sighed. "It's a complication I'd rather not put myself through. . . ." Then he brightened. "But I *can* send a couple of the boys to have a chat with him in the morning, to make it understood I won't accept inferior merchandise again."

Kelly smiled encouragingly—which on her face was a bit ghastly. "Thet's th' spirit. Don' let 'im think 'e c'n gammon yew again." She yawned, covering it with her hand. "I'm fair knackered. I'm off t'bed."

"You do that," he said. She'd made a thorough sweep of one of the rooms used for storage and had set herself up rather nicely, so far as he had been able to tell from glimpses through the open door.

Closing himself into the workroom, he made himself comfortable in his chair, then uncovered the talisman and sent himself into the spirit plane. He was immediately conscious of the level of exhaustion of his brides—he'd prodded and tormented them unmercifully to try and make up the energy expended on the spells to be rid of the Watsons, and they had not recovered. In fact, one of them was faltering so badly he feared he would have to release her, or she would actually become a drain on the system. Again, he cursed old Don. If it hadn't been for that cheating blackguard, he'd *have* a replacement.

If only he'd been able to construct a way of binding souls to his battery without all the tedious marrying! But there was no getting around it. In order to control them that powerfully, they had to bind *themselves* willingly to him before death. And the fastest and easiest way to do that was to trick women into marrying him. There just was no other ceremony where one person would bind herself specifically to *obey,* and his slight alteration of "till death do us part" into "in this life and hereafter" was subtle enough that he doubted any of them had even noticed.

"What in the name of God were you doing the other night, Spencer?"

Moriarty phased into view, seated, as usual, in midair—though looking much calmer than he had been of late. Spender took some heart at this. A calm Professor could mean this wouldn't be as difficult as he had feared.

"Following your orders, actually, Professor," he replied, and proceeded to explain his actions in eliminating Mary Watson instead of her husband, and his failure at the direct approach to killing John Watson, and his reasoning in using magic. For once, Moriarty didn't fly into a rage. In fact, it was uncannily like having the old Professor back. He listened, nodding occasionally, and said nothing until Spencer was finished. Spencer waited, holding his breath.

"*Clever,*" Moriarty said with approval. "*Very clever. Absolutely nothing the police can trace back to you, and nothing that the occultists will connect with the sort of magician you are. Really, quite clever. I commend you.*"

The Professor tilted his head to the side, as was his old habit when inviting a response.

"Praise from you is high praise indeed," Spencer replied, feeling unusually flattered.

"*Well, to use the common phrase, the proof is in the pudding. Did it work?*"

"Mary Watson is dead. The papers have quite properly reported it as a poisoning, and a presumed murder, but it is assumed she ate the fruit unknowingly. So Sherlock is sure to hear of it eventually, and he will very probably attribute it to the Organization, just as you wanted. He will know that we can strike when we wish— again, just as you wanted—and that if we care to, we can strike at anyone. She was buried yesterday. John Watson has passed his surgery on to a colleague and gone to live at Baker Street to be looked after by Sherlock's housekeeper," Spencer told him, with immense satisfaction. "He looked to me to be an utterly broken man, and frankly I don't think the old bastard is a good enough actor to feign that. He genuinely loved his wife, and losing her has shattered him. This is actually better for our purposes, *I* think, than killing him outright would have been."

Moriarty gazed at him for several long moments, then began clapping, slowly and deliberately. After a pause to make sure the Professor wasn't making the gesture ironically, Spencer felt a smile cross his face, and he gave an abbreviated bow.

"*Well done. You are correct. This is better revenge than killing him outright. He'll suffer for years, and he'll know we did this to him. He's useless to Holmes now. We've shown Holmes we can strike down his friends when and where we choose, with complete impunity. It will drive him utterly* mad, *trying to work out why the woman ate such obviously suspicious viands. Even if Watson explains the magic to him, he's unlikely to believe it. And*

Watson's patron will be haring off after a chimera, looking for a common witch. You haven't just created a red herring, Spencer, you've created an entire school of them. Now . . . am I correct in remembering that you said something about needing to conceal your presence and your magic from Alderscroft?"

Spencer blinked with astonishment. He had not expected Moriarty to remember that. "You are," he said.

"I should like you to redouble your efforts, even though I am certain this will delay my acquisition of that new body. I understand, looking at your brides, that you needed to deplete them in order to get rid of Mary Watson. You will need to replenish your energy stores, and you will probably need more girls than you had originally anticipated. I would rather we worked slowly and deliberately. We can leave nothing to chance. Just keep the boy healthy, or as healthy as possible."

Once again, Spencer blinked in tentative hope as well as surprise. "Forgive me, sir, but this is . . . very unlike you. Or rather, unlike the person you have been since your unfortunate demise."

"And this has concerned you until now." the Professor stated.

"To be candid sir, yes, it has." He decided to fling caution to the wind and explain everything to this newly rational spirit. "You see, sir, you have been understandably emotional since my spell brought you here and tied you to the spirit plane. The spirit plane is half in the physical world, and half in the spirit world, so that you can see and sometimes be seen in the physical world, although *most* ghosts cannot act in the physical world. Emotion does help hold you here, but there's a cost, you see. Now, the more a spirit concentrates on emotion, the more a spirit loses of himself *to* emotion. It's a complicated dance, you can understand. It is emotion that anchors you and keeps you in this half-and-half state on the spirit plane. But the more you concentrate on emotion, the more you begin to lose your rational, reasoning self. That is why old ghosts are always locked in a single path and a single emotion—rage, for instance, like the infamous Highwayman or Screaming Man outside of Pluckley. Or terror, as in the ghost of Catherine Howard that haunts Hampton Court Palace. They have lost everything but the memory associated with that emotion, and thus they replay the memory over and over, like a child tracing the same simple drawing over and over."

He paused, and was encouraged further to see Moriarty nodding. "*Do go on,*" the Professor said. "*I feel I am ready to listen to anything and everything you can tell me now.*"

He continued, greatly encouraged.

"You were, I feared, losing yourself to rage and the need for revenge. I was concerned that your formidable intellect would not survive for much longer beneath the heat of your anger. Hence, until this moment, I have been doing my best to speed the process of your return, sometimes at the expense of the strictest safety for both of us." He waited, a little breathlessly, for Moriarty's reply.

"*After our last discussion, I attempted to make a calculation, and I was alarmed when I could not do so. Then I became angry . . . and realized at once that I was now unable to make an even more trivial calculation. Within a short period of time I concluded for myself something of what you just described to me.*" He smiled thinly. "*So since our last meeting, I imposed strict discipline on myself. No more rages. No dwelling on revenge. Nothing must ruffle my composure. I kept myself controlled. I found my ability to reason returning. And now you have given me both corroboration of my observation and the explanation for it. There will be no more outbursts from me, Spencer. If I am to rebuild my empire quickly, I will need every iota of my reason and intelligence. And we will proceed with all due caution; indeed we will proceed with the greatest of deliberation.*"

"Professor, words cannot express how pleased I am to hear this," he said, with real sincerity.

"*I should like you to redouble your efforts at concealing this endeavor from those most likely to detect it,*" Moriarty continued. "*That will take precedence over all else, even my return to the flesh. After all, if we are discovered because of haste or not enough caution, everything you have worked for will be ruined. Now, if you will take down some mental notes, I can give you some ways of keeping my new body strong and relatively healthy. That will purchase us more time.*"

Spencer had long ago mastered the art of being able to memorize quickly and easily, and the Professor's suggestions were clever, and simple. Gavage feeding for instance: Hughs would not even notice being tube-fed if he was sufficiently stuporous.

"And now can you explain to me the details of how your— battery—works? What, exactly, do you need to do to ensure your brides can't somehow escape your control?"

Spencer did not even pause to think; he merely launched into the explanation, which the Professor listened to with every evidence of interest, leaning over in an attitude of intense listening.

From time to time, Moriarty held up a hand to get him to stop, which made him apprehensive again, until the Professor asked him to explain the theory behind Spencer's actions.

That did lengthen the explanation, but since Moriarty remained rational the entire time, Spencer was even more encouraged, rather than the opposite.

Finally he concluded his explanation. Moriarty remained bent over his knees, his expression one of deep thought, his hands clasped. Finally, he spoke.

"I believe you must teach me about magic," Moriarty said, at last.

Spencer felt his jaw going agape, and snapped it shut. "But— why? The ability to use magic is born, not learned." That wasn't . . . exactly true. Moriarty had the strength of will to manipulate magical energy even if he couldn't see it. But Spencer wasn't going to tell him that. "You never had it in life, and Hughs shows no sign of that gift either."

"I do not need to be a star to plot the course of one," the Professor said, smiling thinly. *"I do not need to see gravity to understand its influence, nor to map that influence mathematically. This magic has laws. I can learn them. I can reduce them to equations. I can assist and suggest. And—if I am to surpass Holmes, I need to have a tool he does not have. I need to understand magic, so that I can understand when and how to apply it in order to get the most out of it."*

This was entirely like the Professor of old. And Spencer felt a great burden lifted from his shoulders. Which—suddenly made him realize he was exhausted.

"Then I will teach you," he promised. "But not until I have had sleep. I think it must be three in the morning, or thereabouts, and I cannot keep my eyes open."

There was a brief flash of impatient anger in the Professor's eyes, which was instantly subdued. *"I understand,"* Moriarty replied. *"The flesh is weak, and you are still in possession of yours, which is extremely fortunate for me. I will bid you farewell until you are ready, then. Good night, Spencer."*

"Good night, Professor," he replied, and slipped out of the spirit world and into his own body again.

Total and complete exhaustion slammed him so hard he very nearly passed out, and when he checked his watch, to his astonishment he saw it was nearer five in the morning than three. Now he was exceedingly glad that Kelly had temporarily moved in; she could make sure Hughs was all right and got his opium on time if he couldn't manage to awaken.

He left the workroom and staggered downstairs, dropped his clothing on the floor as he pulled it off, and fell into bed.

When he woke again, the sun was pouring in through the windows, it was uncomfortably warm, and his clothing was still where he had dropped it.

At least he felt nearly human again.

Either Kelly had left him wash water or there still had been some in the pitcher last night; he cleaned himself up, shaved, and donned last night's clothing.

Now completely awake, he checked his watch and discovered it was just past noon. Well, he'd missed breakfast, but at least he'd be in time for luncheon.

As he had hoped, Kelly was in the kitchen, methodically slicing bread and cheese. She looked up as she stood in the kitchen doorframe. "Ploughman's," she said tersely. "Tea's in the pot."

"Ta," he replied. A ploughman's lunch would suit him very well. He sat down and poured himself a cup of tea, drinking it right down before pouring another. A few minutes later Kelly brought over a platter filled with sliced, buttered bread, cheese, sliced onions, pickles, radishes, and hard-boiled eggs. They both set to without any further conversation.

Halfway through, Kelly got up to make a second pot of tea, since he'd drunk the first pot dry. She also brought over a bowl of hulled strawberries and sugar to dip them in.

"Th' boy's set fer th' day," she said conversationally, between

211

strawberries. He was amused at how she referred to Hughs as "the boy."

Then again, the poet had about the same emotional maturity as a youth.

"Thank you," he said, simply. "I found myself in a very long conversation with the Professor last night."

"Thet good 'r bad?"

"Good." He scratched his ear and sipped his tea. He didn't care particularly for sweets, so Kelly could monopolize the berries all she liked. "He's like his old self. He wants us to go slow and careful, now John Watson's out of the way."

"Shhhh." Kelly hissed in relief. "Tha's better."

"You're damned right it is. All we need to worry about is making sure the boy stays healthy. This gives us breathing space to make *sure* Alderscroft can't find us. And if my supplier of girls isn't up to snuff—"

"*Oi* will person'lly find ye another," Kelly said firmly. "Oi'll bet that old Chinee wut sells yer opium c'an git 'is 'ands on girls, and won't care wut 'appens to 'em."

Spencer blinked. He had never thought of that. "I would bet you are right. And I am going to find out this afternoon."

Shen Li did not run an opium den. He supplied those who did with the drug. He was rumored to be able to get his hands on just about anything anyone wanted. He was, very probably, one of the richest men in London.

He also lived so modestly no one would ever have guessed this. To all intents and purposes, he was just one more ancient Chinaman running a tea-and-herb shop and living in the flat above it.

He appeared to be utterly harmless. Spencer knew he was utterly ruthless. The London Tongs all lived in fear of him, and he was very probably the only Chinese merchant in all of Chinatown who did not pay "protection" money to anyone.

Spencer suspected the old man was some sort of magician, although he had never picked up a hint of magic about him. But perhaps he wouldn't have, if Chinese magic was fundamentally different from that which the Elemental Masters practiced. What he did know for certain was that the man could get you anything you had the money to buy.

Provided, of course, you approached him with the proper respect, and obeyed the proper protocols.

So when he entered the shop, he did not in the least scruple to bow to the old man as he stood on the threshold.

"I have a need I would like to discuss," he said diffidently. "I have heard that Shen Li is wise in the way of helping one to acquire needful things."

"This may be true," the old man replied, in a flawless Cambridge accent. "Perhaps you would care to take tea."

"I would be honored to take tea," Spencer replied. And the shop assistant ushered him into a small back room he had been in before, one that could have come straight from an inn in the heart of Shanghai. There was a simple table and two spare wooden chairs, with a statue of a dragon carved in some white stone on a pedestal to one side.

The old man joined him after a few moments of waiting. He had not yet taken a seat, but waited for the shop assistant to seat Shen Li, then took the other.

Shen Li looked—to his eyes anyway—just like any other shop proprietor. Old, though who knew how old—silver hair braided tightly down his back, a little round blue cap on his head, simple blue tunic and trousers, both trimmed with red. He himself had taken care with his dress, to make certain of not offending the man.

"I have a very fine Oolong I would be honored if you would try." Shen Li said, in a mellow, soothing voice.

"And I am honored that you invite me to partake." These things could not be rushed. This was not like walking up to the counter and ordering some opium or hashish, or esoteric herb.

They bowed to each other. A girl in fine brocade tunic and trousers came from the door opposite to the one into the shop, carrying a teapot and two cups. She set the cups down in front of the two men and poured, not wasting a drop. Spencer waited until Shen Li had picked up his cup, then took his own. They sipped at the same moment.

"Extraordinary," said Spencer, for indeed, it was. "Absolutely extraordinary."

"I am pleased," Shen Li replied. He leaned over the table a trifle. "I am going to confide something in you, Mister Spencer, so that you will have a reason to trust that I will deliver what I promise. I am not Chinese."

Spencer's brows furrowed. Shen Li tapped the side of his left eye with his finger. "I am Russian. These . . . are merely the legacy of my Tartar ancestry, and the reason why I would never be permitted to prosper in Russian society. I shall not bore you with the tale of how I came here and rose to where I am. But here—I am invisible. And yet, very, very wealthy, because I can obtain anything anyone wants, at a price they are willing to pay. Whereas in Russia, I would still be working in a stable."

The two sipped until the cups were empty, and set them down almost simultaneously. "Now, Mister Spencer," said the old man, "What is it you require?"

"Something living," he said, cautiously.

"Ah. Neither fish nor fowl nor animal?" The old man did not seem in the least surprised.

"Females," Spencer ventured.

"Attractive?"

"That does not matter. What does matter is that they are . . . disposable. And that they believe I will marry them." Now he waited.

Shen Li's right eyebrow rose elegantly. "And will you?"

"Oh yes," Spencer replied.

To his surprise, Shen Li smiled broadly, and applauded, slowly. "Mister Spencer, you are a bold man. And an ambitious one. I will help you. But such items are expensive."

Now Spencer relaxed and nodded. "I see we understand each other. Let us bargain."

Spencer arrived at the Hotel Splendid in a growler driven by Geoff, accompanied by Tony and Tony's brothers, Rudolfo and Michael, or Rudi and Mike. He walked in to find old Don presiding behind the counter as usual—and, as usual, with not one other person to be seen in the little lounge.

Don looked pleased to see him . . . but not so pleased when the three huge bruisers entered the door and stood behind him, hands clasped loosely in front of them.

"I won't be doing any more business with you, Don," he said, evenly. "And I'll want the rest of my deposit back."

Old Don evidently knew better than to argue with a man who had three tough Italian thugs standing behind him. He cursed under his breath, and grumbled, and cursed some more, but eventually produced the required sum from a safe.

"Take it from him, please, Tony," Spencer said, quietly. The thug snatched the money out of Don's hands and brought it to Spencer, counting it as he walked. "It's all 'ere, guv."

"Good. I'm glad to hear that," Spencer replied. "Now to show there's no hard feelings, let's have a little drink, shall we, Don?" He nodded to Mike, who pulled a bottle out of his jacket and two glasses from his pockets. He handed the glasses to Spencer, who held them steady while Mike poured out the amber-colored liquid.

Spencer offered one to Don, who took it suspiciously. "Wut's all this, then?" the portly man asked.

Spencer sighed elaborately. "It's whiskey, Don. We're about to have a drink to show that while our business dealings are at an end, there are no hard feelings. Look—" he tossed his shot down, and held the empty glass upside down to show he'd drunk. "Surely you're not going to turn down a free drink?"

With the evidence that it was safe to drink in front of him, old Don surely was not going to turn down a free drink. He drained his glass, and held out his glass for more.

Spencer smiled thinly, and nodded to Mike to pour another.

"Leave him the bottle, Mike, and we'll be on our way," Spencer said smoothly as old Don downed the second drink as fast as the first. Mike set the bottle down on the counter next to old Don, and the four of them walked out.

Spencer smiled the entire trip home, and took the steps two at a time to report to the Professor.

"That's very good news about the girls," Moriarty told him. *"And knowing you . . . there was some ulterior motive in providing the cheat with a bottle of drink. I am eager to hear it."*

"Of course there was, Professor," Spencer replied, still smiling.

"There wasn't just whisky in that bottle. There was a potion I made up especially for him. It opens up the ability to see into the spirit plane."

Moriarty thought for a moment, and then began to laugh. *"Of course! And how many spirits are haunting that hotel of his?"*

"I didn't count . . . but a number of them are surely Don's victims." Spencer replied, with no little glee. "That last Chinese girl for one. And when they realize he can finally see them. . . ."

"Well played, my boy," the Professor said. *"Well played."*

15

Sarah and Nan were sharing breakfast with the birds when Mrs. Horace tapped on their door, then opened it.

She squinted a little against the sunlight filling the room. "There's a man to see you, ladies," said Mrs. Horace, her stiff back, careful pronunciation, and the fact that she did not use the word "gentleman" showing her disapproval of the early arrival. "He claims he is from Scotland Yard. An Inspector Lestrade, if you please. Shall I tell him to come back at a more convenient hour?"

Nan, who was merely wearing a wrapper over her nightgown, fled to her room. Sarah answered their landlady for both of them. "No, you can send him up, Mrs. Horace. It may have something to do with Doctor Watson."

At the mention of Watson's name, Mrs. Horace softened somewhat. "Oh. Well, that's all right, then," she said, and closed the door. Sarah got up and waited for Lestrade's knock and opened it again immediately.

The poor, harried man looked as if he had not slept in days. His suit was more rumpled than usual and there were dark circles under his eyes. "Beggin' yer pardon, Miss Lyon-White, but, I was hopin' you and your friend could help me."

Sarah held the door open for him, and left it open a crack for propriety's—and Mrs. Horace's—sake. "I know we will try, Inspector. Nan will be out in—"

"Nan is out this minute," replied Nan, emerging from her

room, properly clad, but still pinning her hair in place. "The only thing I can think of that would have brought you here, Inspector, is that you've found another headless body and you'd like us to have a look at it."

Lestrade had removed his bowler and was turning it in his hands, nervously. "That would be the long and the short of it, Miss. I don't like to bother poor Doctor Watson at such a time—"

"We'll do what we can for you, Inspector," Sarah assured him. "But it may not be much."

"Anythin' is better than what I got now," Lestrade replied dispiritedly, as he followed them out of the flat and down to where he had a Scotland Yard conveyance waiting.

"No shoes *or* stockings," Sarah noted as soon as the poor thing on the table had been unveiled. This time she and Nan had taken the precaution of bringing camphor balls with them, but the smell was still bad enough to make a maggot gag. "That's inconsistent. And . . . forgive me, but the skin color seems . . . off."

In answer, Lestrade rolled the body over and pulled open the back of the dress, which had been unbuttoned and left undone, then pulled down the chemise. There was a Chinese character tattooed at the base of the girl's neck. "That's a slave-mark," Lestrade said with authority.

"She was a Chinese slave?" Sarah asked in surprise. "And yet she is dressed in the same sort of garments as the last girl we saw."

Lestrade blushed a deep crimson. "And the last girl hadn't been . . . interfered with. This one was."

"Hmm." Nan leaned over the body and examined the tattoo carefully, although what she thought she could learn from it, Sarah had no idea. "This is fairly fresh, although not brand new. She hadn't been a slave for long." Nan stood up and faced Lestrade. "Her feet are used to shoes, but they're not bound, so she's peasant class, I would hazard. I believe even peasants in China are accustomed to wearing shoes. Is there a problem in London of Chinese girls being brought in as slaves for . . ." she coughed ". . . immoral purposes?"

Sarah had thought Lestrade couldn't get any redder. She had

been wrong. He turned from the color of a strawberry to the color of a beet. "Yes," he managed, although he sounded as if he was strangling.

"Let's get out of here," Sarah suggested. "Even with the camphor ball—"

"Quite." Nan led the way out, but Lestrade was right on their heels. When they finally reached the open air, Nan paused and took a deep breath. Sarah did the same. The air in London in the summer was pretty bad, but compared to the stench in the morgue, it was positively ambrosial.

"Well, let me assume that in most aspects, this corpse is identical to the others," Sarah said briskly, noting that Lestrade's color had finally faded. "Clothing, approximate age, and so forth. It is only the race, the social class, and the apparent profession in which this one differs, which actually suggests some things to me."

"Me as well," Nan agreed. "We had no idea until this moment. but it seems to me that what the girls look like means very little in terms of what sort of victim that this madman chooses."

Lestrade paused, about to say something, and shut his mouth. His brow wrinkled for a moment, then he spoke. "That's . . . not usual, in these cases, is it? Most of the time I've seen, if a bloke does in more than one girl, 'e usually does 'em all of the same type."

Sarah shrugged. "I don't know. You'd have to ask your colleagues at the Yard." She *almost* said "Watson," but decided this was not the time. "It also suggests to me that purity or lack of it is not a motivating factor in the murders. He's murdered both those girls that retained their virtue and those that did not. So this isn't someone obsessed with sin and sinners."

Lestrade pulled on his lower lip. "That's quite logical."

"What they all *do* have in common is that they are impoverished, and possibly desperate," Sarah went on. "So he was able to lure them somewhere, with promises, I'll wager, and the clothing they were found in might have something to do with what he promised. But a Chinese slave in the same clothing makes me think that either he is now having a difficult time finding impoverished girls desperate enough to be his victims, or he is concerned that the Yard is aware of his actions by now, and is looking for someone 'fishing' for girls. So he has turned to girls no one will miss. Girls he can purchase, like any other commodity."

Lestrade sighed heavily at that. "So we may never find him now. The Big Men won't care if it's only a few Chinese that are turning up dead."

"You might be surprised," Nan told him. "This also has Lord Alderscroft looking for answers, and he is going to continue to push for an answer regardless of the race and class of the victims."

"I do 'ope so, Miss," Lestrade said sadly. "It seems Downing Street don't care much about what 'appens in the East End, as long as it don't get in the papers and scare the knickers off the up-and-ups."

Sarah reached over and patted his shoulder. "You are a good man, Inspector Lestrade, and a fine officer of the law. Holmes thought very highly of your ethics. I know Doctor Watson does, too."

Now Lestrade went red again, but from a different sort of embarrassment. He mumbled something Sarah couldn't hear, but it sounded self-deprecating. "Well you ladies 'ave given me a bit more'n I 'ad, so I'll take it all back t'the Yard. Mebbe a lot of 'eads can be as good as one 'Olmes."

He parted with them; they hailed a cab.

"Baker Street?" Nan asked, once they were in it.

Sarah nodded. "But first, home, get the birds, and change. We *really* do not want anyone to connect us to Watson now."

Fortunately, before Holmes encountered Moriarty at the Reichenbach Falls, he had been instructing them in disguise. So while two young ladies entered the front door of their landlady's house, two young working-class men exited the rear with some empty produce crates. And no one was on the yard-side to notice the two birds leaving by the rear window before that happened.

The young men piled the crates at the back fence for the grocer's boy, then left the yard, taking the alley to the street, then strolled in a leisurely manner toward the nearest 'bus stop. Working-class lads would not be taking cabs . . . assuming one would even stop for them.

"This is *so* much cooler," Sarah murmured to Nan, who sauntered along beside her with her hands in her pockets and a slight slouch to her shoulders.

"I swear if it gets any hotter this summer I am going to become my own brother for the duration," Nan murmured back, tilting her head up to catch sight of Neville overhead.

"I think I'll join you."

It meant a lot of walking, but walking in masculine clothing was a positive pleasure. With so little being pleasurable these days, it was nice to find something that could bring a smile to their faces.

The birds had no difficulty keeping up with the 'bus, given how many stops it was making. The girls got down about a block from Baker Street, went around to the back entrance, and tapped on the door.

A wary Mrs. Hudson answered it, but her expression changed to one of relief when she saw who it was. She had seen them in their disguises before. "Are you girls going to keep arriving here as boys from now on?" she asked, letting them in. Sarah was unsurprised to see her putting a pistol back in the pocket of her apron.

"Probably," Sarah replied. "It seems safer."

"Aye, it does. Well, go on up, the Doctor is frettin' because he's supposed to be prostrate with grief and no one's telling him anything."

They ran up the stairs, taking them two at a time, and knocked on the door of C. John Watson opened it immediately, and he managed a smile at the sight of them. "Thank heavens, someone that can tell me something! Come in."

They entered and Nan immediately went to the flat window that overlooked the rear entrance. She opened it wide, and when she turned back to the room, she had a bird on each arm.

"Lestrade called on us this morning," Sarah said, sprawling inelegantly on a chair, clearly reveling in the freedom her trousers gave her. "He's found another body."

"Well we knew that was bound to happen," Mary Watson put in, coming from the pantry with four glasses of lemonade on a tray. She put the tray down on the sitting room table and they each took one. The birds were already on their stands, watching them all.

"Well, this one is a bit different." Sarah went on to describe exactly how different the body was, and in what ways. "I think all this is significant," she concluded.

Watson had been listening with a frown on his face. "I think you are right. It does suggest the appearance and even race of his victims are not important, but something else about them *is*. Perhaps it's just the costume?"

Mary tapped her fingernail on the side of the glass. "The costume seems to be the single commonality," she agreed. "And I cannot imagine any way those girls were obtaining clothing like that on their own. It might have been used, but it was simply too expensive for girls who were clearly going *barefoot* most of the time because they could not afford shoes."

"Well, let's concentrate on that, then," Watson decided. "What kind of meaning could it have?"

"Perhaps the sort of woman who can afford white tea gowns. He could be revenging himself over and over on some woman who jilted him, or something of the sort," Mary offered, frowning a little. "Or he is revenging himself on women like that as a class."

"It could represent a bridal gown too," Sarah put in. "If he's been rejected as a suitor."

"Or purity," Nan pointed out grimly. "In which case he's probably also doing black magic—" she pointed at Mary Watson "—which is *exactly* what nearly got you, Mary."

Watson cursed under his breath. "By Jove, you're right! It makes more logical sense to think that these are for some devilish ritual purpose than that they are the work of a madman. If this was a madman, based on our past cases, his mind and cleverness would be degrading over time—or at the least, he would become overconfident. And it makes more sense that we have one single practitioner of powerful black magic out there in London than two. And in that case, it also makes more sense to assume that he is not only aware we are in pursuit of him as the murderer, he is aware we are in pursuit of him as the magician that cursed Mary and me."

"And he is certainly also the necromancer Alderscroft wants us to find." Nan made the statement flatly. "I absolutely refuse to believe in multiple practitioners of the dark arts running in and out of doors all over the city as if we're in some kind of twisted French farce. I cannot believe some garden-variety curse nearly drove *both* of you, both Elemental Masters, into stuffing your faces full of poison. If he wanted us to think that, well, he tipped his hand by making the curse too bloody strong."

"This still gets us nowhere," Mary said dispiritedly. "We're no closer to finding the necromancer than we were before. All we know—or guess—is that the necromancer is the murderer."

"I thought you were going to look into the sewers, John," Sarah pointed out.

"Unfortunately . . . there are many complications with that," he replied grimly, then got up, secured a roll of paper from above the mantelpiece, and unrolled it. "Here is where the mouth of that sewer system emerges into the Thames," he continued, tapping the paper. "But look at what leads into that final sewer tunnel!"

Sarah gazed at it with deep dismay. It looked like some ancient tree. Branches led into the main tunnel from *everywhere*. This was another dead end.

"And I promise you, there is not one single Water Elemental, not even the worst of the worst, that will go in there to trace where the bodies are coming from," he continued glumly. "Even at high tide, what's in there is not exactly water, after all."

"I don't see any hope for it," Mary sighed. "We'll have to contact his Lordship and tell him that we've done everything we can and we're at a dead end."

"I'd rather tell him to his face," Nan said firmly. "Mary, can I have something to write a note with?"

By way of an answer, Mary pointed to a little secretary desk in the corner. Nan swiftly wrote out a note, blotted it, sealed it in an envelope, and wrote something on the outside. She went to Neville's stand, picked him up, and handed it to him. He took it politely in his massive beak.

"The club. If Alderscroft hasn't left any of his windows open, give it to the doorman, he knows you."

Neville *quorked* around the note held in his beak and launched off her arm as she held it out the rear window. She turned back to the rest. "If he's in, we should have an answer soon."

In fact, it took less time than it would have to send a human messenger for Neville to return, landing on the windowsill with a note of a different color paper in his mouth. Nan took it from him, gave him a piece of cheese as a reward, and opened it.

"He's on his way," she said, reading it.

"I'll go tell Mrs. Hudson to expect a distinguished visitor," said Watson, who went downstairs.

Mary sighed. "I don't want to complain . . . but I'm already very weary of these four walls."

"Then why don't you disguise yourself?" Nan suggested.

"As what?" She raised an eyebrow at Nan. "I don't think I could fool anyone as a young man."

"Some relative of Mrs. Hudson. Or a scullery maid. It's not as if you actually have to do the work to pass as one," Sarah suggested. "Watson could come by and wait outside for your half day off as your beau."

Mary's expression lifted a trifle, then gloom overcame her again. "It seems wrong to be joking when there are girls being horribly murdered by this awful person."

Watson entered just as she said that and sat down beside her, taking her hand in his. "My dear, whether or not we joke has no bearing on their fate. We'll do them neither good nor harm by trying to be as normal as we can."

It's one thing to say that, but quite another to accomplish it, Sarah thought sadly, as they all attempted, and failed, to keep "small talk" going while they waited for the arrival of Alderscroft. The difference in sound that carriage wheels made on the road outside—as opposed to those of hansoms or even growlers—alerted them to his arrival, which was confirmed by the bell and the sound of Mrs. Hudson showing their distinguished guest up.

Watson opened the door before anyone could knock and ushered Alderscroft inside. Even before Alderscroft could sit down, he held out one hand in a gesture of failure and said, "I'm sorry, milord, but we've run ourselves to earth. You are going to have to summon the Lodge."

Alderscroft sat down, heavily. "It's that bad, is it?" he asked, with no hint of accusation in his voice.

"It's rather worse than bad," Watson admitted, and related everything they had discovered or reasoned out.

"In all the time I have worked with Holmes, I have never known a murderer of this sort to change the race of his victims, so we are forced to conclude as you originally thought that the murderer and your necromancer are one and the same," he finished. "And as Nan pointed out, since having black magicians popping up all over London is rather too much like a twisted farce, the necromancer must be the same person who tried to murder Mary and me, and that means he knows we were on his trail. We can't do anything more. Outside of the protections of this flat, he is probably spying on us somehow. The Lodge is our only recourse."

Alderscroft bent his head for a moment. "And I am sorry to tell you that I had already come to that conclusion and summoned the Lodge after the attempt on your lives, and we . . . were able to find nothing."

Silence fell. The street noise through the windows seemed unnaturally loud.

"How?" Nan asked, finally.

Alderscroft shrugged. "Enough power at his disposal and he can effectively conceal himself from almost anything. And I need not tell you that blood and death can raise an enormous amount of power."

"Well . . . *now* what do we do?" Sarah demanded.

"I'm sorry, my dear," Alderscroft replied, sadly. "But I have no idea."

The message had arrived by a courier; Mrs. Kelly had accepted it, and brought it to Spencer as he sat eating luncheon. It was contained in a cream vellum envelope of very high quality, and sealed with a curious Chinese stamp in the wax holding it shut. He opened it.

Have something very special for you, it said. *Come at once.*

He didn't need to be able to read the pictograph at the bottom to know that it came from Shen Li.

"Som'thin' important?" Kelly asked.

"Could be. I'll be going out." But before he did—he went back to his room and changed into his best suit. The last thing he wanted to do at this point was to insult Shen Li in any way. Chinese, Tartar, whatever—the man was going to supply him with something he desperately needed, and was clearly no "old Don."

The servant was waiting outside at the shop door for him, and hurried him into the room in which he had met Shen Li the first time. This time the furniture had been removed and replaced with two comfortable chairs facing each other, with nothing else in the room. Shen Li was already in one. He gestured to the other.

Spencer gave him a slight, but respectful, bow, and only then did he take his seat.

"I have made some inquiries into your activities, Mister Spencer," said Shen Li. "And I became . . . impressed. I sense that you will go far. And so I determined to give you more assistance than merely supplying you with raw materials." He leaned forward a trifle, his face somber. "I am going to supply you with allies on the other side of death."

Spencer was startled at first . . . then it occurred to him for the first time to utilize mage-sight, and both the room and Shen Li himself lit up with the energies of Fire. This man was *at least* a Fire Mage, and possibly even a Fire Master. And *he* had not been taking precautions about concealing what he was the last time he had come here. Well, that would end—although so far as Shen Li was concerned, it was definitely closing the stable door after the horse was gone.

Spencer looked at him skeptically. "How do you propose to do that?"

Shen Li leaned back in his chair. "The Chinese live within a strictly regulated society. If one is born a peasant, it is wildly unlikely that one will ever rise above that status. A man only has the hope of passing certain examinations, and going to work for the Imperial bureaucracy. Women, of course, may not even apply to take the examinations. So rising beyond peasant status is even more unlikely for a woman, and impossible for an ugly woman."

Spencer couldn't see where this was going . . . but he was a patient man. He nodded.

"The path to status and rank for a woman is only achieved by beauty," Shen Li continued. "To catch the eye of someone in high rank. To become a cherished concubine. Or, most desired of all, to become an official wife. This path is closed to an ugly woman."

"How unfortunate for her," Spencer said, since it seemed Shen Li was waiting for a comment.

"And yet—" Shen Li held up one elegant finger. "Hope. There

is always hope. Hope that if the path is closed in life, it may be opened in death."

Spencer shook his head, finally. "I am very sorry, Shen Li. I don't know the Chinese ways well enough to have any inkling of what you are talking about."

Shen Li smiled. It reminded Spencer of a patient, but hungry, tiger. "Let us say, I have come into possession of an unattractive slave, but one with imagination and dreams. I have told her that you have seen her spirit in dreams, and you know it is beautiful, and wish to wed her—but obviously a man of your rank and power could not have a Chinese wife. I have told her that in order to become your true Chief Wife, she must shed her body as a worm sheds its skin and rise as the butterfly she is. She has agreed to this. Am I correct in thinking that this will be the first woman you have chosen who is literally willing to die for you?"

Spencer's jaw dropped.

Shen Li smiled with the deep satisfaction of the tiger who has just eaten a particularly succulent lamb.

"That would be worth . . ." he shook his head. "If I am actually going to have her cooperation . . ."

"She will quite literally willingly be your slave in the next world, and will ask nothing more," Shen Li assured him, and held out his hand, palm upward. There was no need to ask the meaning of that universal gesture.

Spencer didn't even count the money he dropped into that long hand. Whatever magic Shen Li had worked on this girl, it was going to be worth every penny. It must have been enough, because the old man's smile did not falter. He folded his hand around the money and gracefully tucked it into his sash, then rose. "Come," he said. "This must be done properly. There must be a wedding feast. Please be kind and show your deep admiration of this girl. She is about to enjoy the best day of her entire life, and any lapse on your part may put all my work in jeopardy."

Spencer followed the old man into the next room, where a table had been set up, and a young woman dressed in red brocade robes and an elaborate wig with beaded hair ornaments waited. She looked up at him with the hopeful eyes of a puppy.

Her eyes were the most attractive thing about her. The rest of her . . . well, the body beneath the expensive robes was lumpy, her face was like a ball of dough, her teeth were bad when she smiled shyly at him, and even her movements were clumsy.

But he'd had *plenty* of practice in wooing by now, and he set his face in an expression of pleasant cheer, and took her hand, which was as rough as sandpaper, and kissed it. She giggled and her big eyes grew moist. So did her hand.

He continued to hold her hand until one of Shen Li's servants appeared and began to serve a meal. Her expression of astonishment told him that she had never seen what was set before them before, much less tasted it. This was not at all unlike the rest of his brides, so he encouraged her to eat, sampling only a morsel or two himself. He didn't recognize any of the foods himself, but they were actually quite good. Thank goodness he had been supplied with a fork—he could never have managed the use of the two sticks she was eating with.

When she'd eaten enough for two—literally, she ate all of her portions and most of his—a gong sounded and servants came to clear away everything, including the table and chairs. He took her hand again, and to his surprise, it was not some Chinese priest who turned up at Shen Li's side, but his own street preacher.

The man did not seem at all nonplussed by the appearance of Spencer's new bride, nor did he show any sign that he considered her to be as monumentally unattractive as Spencer did.

"I am here to translate for Xi'er," Shen Li told them both. "You may begin."

Xi'er dutifully repeated everything she was told to in a lisping, thin voice. He held her hand the entire time, and she never stopped smiling up at him. And in the end, when the preacher asked her if she would obey him in life and after, and Shen Li translated for her, she whispered *"Yis,"* and clutched his hand desperately, He nearly reeled with the strength of the spell as it snapped home around them both, although she showed no signs of feeling it.

But Shen Li clearly did. He nodded with satisfaction.

He ushered the preacher out. When he returned, he had two small porcelain cups, and two bottles. He handed Xi'er one cup, and poured out what was in the white bottle for her. He handed Spencer another, and poured out what was in the green bottle.

"Now you must drink to your eternal bond," he instructed.

Xi'er sipped tentatively. Her eyes widened and she finished the cup of liquid, and looked as if she was contemplating licking the cup clean when Shen Li took it from her. As for Spencer, his highly educated palate could distinguish nothing but water.

"She should fall into a slumber in your cab," Shen Li said. "This should facilitate your work." He made a slight shooing motion with his hands. "Go now. It is after sunset, and no one will see you carrying her into your home."

Geoff the Elf looked as if he was going to laugh out loud at the sight of Spencer's Chinese bride, but he was smart enough to keep his mouth shut.

Sure enough, the girl fell into a coma-like slumber before the ride was half over. But not daring to ruin the promise, Spencer allowed her to pillow her head against him, only interposing his handkerchief between them so that she did not drool on his suit.

When they arrived, he picked her up and carried her into the house himself. He thought about pausing to change her into the customary white dress—but then, the white dress had never been anything more than the symbolic representation of the girl's bridal status, and for *this* girl, that was represented by the crimson brocade robes. Best to leave her in them.

Kelly held the door open for him, and raised an eyebrow as she caught sight of the girl's face when her lolling head turned toward the housekeeper. "Not 'xactly a looker, is she?" Kelly asked.

"Nevertheless, I have been assured that she is extremely special. We shall see shortly." He carried the girl all the way upstairs himself, as always.

This time, as the sharpened blade removed the head in a single blow . . . he felt a surge of power and energy unlike anything he had ever experienced from his victims before. When he took the wig from her head and placed the head in the usual glass jar full of preservative liquid, he could have sworn the head was smiling.

He seated himself, shaking with excitement, and moved himself into the spirit world—

He had not been sure what to expect. But the vision of beauty that met him left him stunned with shock.

She was exquisite. Lovelier than any of the handsome women

he chose when visiting a brothel. Lovelier than the "Professional Beauties" that frequented Prince Edward's circles. In this, her spirit form, she wore flowing robes of green and blue, with sleeves that hung down over her hands, and a long, elaborate sash. Her hair was in a more elaborate style than the wig she had worn, and it was ornamented all over with flowers, buds, and butterflies of jade. She held out her hands to him, hands from which dangled solid gold chains. *"Husband,"* she said, in perfect English.

"Wife," he replied. "You are and always will be my Chief Wife. You are a peerless pearl of radiant splendor!"

She giggled, and freed one hand to hide her face for a moment behind a dangling sleeve. *"But what is this?"* she asked, as the usual wailing and weeping arose from his other captive brides.

"My other . . . concubines," he replied. Then, in a flash of inspiration, added, "They are yours to discipline, as is proper for my Chief Wife."

She turned to face the rest as they faded into view, the two Chinese girls pulling away from the white girls, all of them chained, all of them weeping.

"How dare you! Ungrateful sows!" she scolded, gathering up her chains and using them to yank the others nearer her, dragging them off their feet and forcing them all to grovel before her. *"How dare you lament that you have been chosen by this Dragon among magicians! How dare you withhold your power from him? I will teach you to serve him, and serve him well!"*

And to his astonishment, a whip appeared in one of her hands, a whip that she used to beat the other girls mercilessly—but only the white ones. *"How many times have I been spurned and beaten by those like you?"* she scolded. *"And I thought, Oh! They are so lofty, and I am so low, this is only right! But now I see that you are spoilt, spoilt and ungrateful, and have no respect for he you pledged to serve! I shall teach you respect! I shall teach you your place!"*

The two Chinese girls watched this with eyes that seemed to take up half their faces, while the white ones cowered and screamed for mercy. At length, Xi'er seemed to think she had done enough. She turned back to face Spencer, folding her hands in her sleeves so that the golden chains lay across the skirts of her robes, and bowed to him.

"I beg my Husband's pardon, but it will take me some time before these wretched women understand what they owe to you—and to me," she said. *"But they will learn . . . they will."*

"I place them in your hands, Xi'er," he said, solemnly. "You will always be my Chief Wife, my pearl above price."

And with that, he let himself fall back to the material plane, and regarded the head of his latest victim with utter astonishment.

Finally he picked the body up off the table. He was about to dispose of it as he had all the others . . . but something made him stop. So instead, he went to one of the storage rooms and picked out a particularly nice coverlet. He wrapped the body in it, and carried it down to the basement. There, he pried up several of the flooring stones, labored for a good hour to dig a shallow grave, place the body in it, and covered it with the loose earth, and then the stones.

He looked at his watch, and saw without surprise it was nearly six in the morning. He went upstairs to discover Kelly frying eggs. Sausage and bacon was draining next to her.

"Wut was all that 'bout?" Kelly asked, as he washed his hands and face at the sink, and took his place at the kitchen table.

"Something I needed to do," he replied, and took a plate of food from her.

She looked at him sharply, but the expression on his face evidently gave her the idea that she wouldn't get any more of an answer than that.

"So, was this 'un worth it?" she asked instead, taking her own place at the table and beginning to eat. "Thet was a lot of fuss yew went to, runnin' outa 'ere and stayin' so long. An' she was powerful ugly. Was she worth what yew paid?"

"Oh no," he replied, in a voice full of astonishment. "Oh no, she wasn't worth what I paid. She was worth a hundred times more."

16

Spencer finished drawing out the last of the life force from the djinn he had entrapped in his southernmost Elemental trap, and added it to the shields on the house. Now, besides the first set of Elementals he had incorporated into his household shields, he had a second set of even more powerful Elementals; the djinn, a waterhorse, a scirocco, and a troll.

If he had not had Xi'er ruling over his brides with her tiny iron fist he never would have been able to accomplish this. But he had not only been able to strengthen the household shields, he'd had power to spare to strengthen his own personal shields.

He had been afraid at first that Xi'er would grow bored in her role, and angry that she was not getting to experience physical pleasures anymore. But she hadn't shown any sign of boredom, and she apparently didn't miss physical pleasures.

Maybe it was because she hadn't experienced many physical pleasures in her former life. She seemed perfectly contented to bask in the attentions of the two Chinese girls, who had taken on the role of her personal servants, lord it over the white girls, and invent new and more elaborate robes and jewelry to wear and ephemeral food to enjoy.

As an added, and entirely unexpected bonus, Moriarty seemed to appreciate her company as well.

"She amuses me," he had told Spencer, the first time he called the Professor up after acquiring Xi'er. "She's such a perfect little *tyrant. Her desires are so simple—to have everything that was denied her in life, and to inflict the same misery on others that she herself experienced. She's clearly happier now than she has ever been. And her will is extraordinary. Absolutely extraordinary."*

"She's not in love with me, is she?" he had asked the Professor with some apprehension. Moriarty had laughed at him.

"No more than a mongrel dog is in love with the person that gives it a warm bed and food," Moriarty had said carelessly. *"That's all she is, really. Oh, she values you highly as the author of her good fortune, and is under the impression you are a truly powerful magician, but Chinese women are bred to value themselves only as extensions of their husband's status. She won't challenge you, and she won't demand anything of you. Don't concern yourself."*

Well it was hard to not to be concerned when there had been so much improvement in the energy output of his brides, and it was absolutely clear to him that this was purely due to Xi'er's efforts. And on the one hand, he had no intention of reciprocating whatever she felt for him. On the other hand, the only gestures of affection she seemed to need were all verbal. Not that she wasn't attractive enough for him to have been interested in her carnally— oh, no, she was, if anything, highly alluring. But getting involved in that way with a ghost was dangerous. Very, very dangerous. It gave *them* power over the necromancer, and was where the legends of incubi and succubi came from. Not to mention that besides getting hooks into a necromancer's power, playing those games allowed the ghost to have access to parts of your mind and memories no wise necromancer would want them to see.

No, he was not going to allow her that kind of hold over him.

But she didn't seem at all interested in that. She was perfectly happy to have him heap praise and compliments on her and lord it over the other girls, an empress in her own tiny domain. He was now very thankful for his classical education; it gave him a lot of poets and playwrights to steal flowery phrases from, things she would never have heard and would think were original and created to praise her.

And that made him think of something else; Shen Li had informed him that he had another girl for him. *Nothing special this time*, the note had read. So he had informed the preacher there would be another wedding, and all was in readiness.

Since this girl was "nothing special," he wouldn't have to go through squabbles over who was the Chief Wife . . . but he really should inform Xi'er that she was about to get a new servant.

Shen Li had simply handed over this girl with a smile. He'd brought her home, Mrs. Kelly and the preacher were ready, and everything went off like clockwork. He slipped into the spirit world to see how the new bride was integrating with the rest, just in time to see Xi'er already in charge. The new bride didn't even make a squeak of protest.

"Xi'er," he said, when the spirit had finished loftily informing the new bride of her proper place in things. "One of the concubines has faded to the point of being nearly useless."

"I was going to tell you this, Husband," Xi'er said with a little bow. *"And ask you what you wished to do with her."* She looked utterly exquisite today, her hair braided and wrapped on the top of her head and secured by pins topped with gold butterflies with moving wings, her robes of gold and red brocade layered with silk so light it was transparent, wearing her golden chains as if it was an honor to wear them. And he noticed for the first time, as the hem of her robe moved aside, that she now had the tiniest feet he had ever seen, in red and gold shoes. Well, he presumed that she could will herself not to feel the pain that bound feet were supposed to cause.

"I will use her to bolster our defenses against our enemies," he said immediately, relieved that he wasn't going to run into an objection.

"Ah good. These white concubines are nearly useless. I think you should replace them all with Chinese." Her arrogance was actually oddly charming. He found himself smiling. *"Chinese girls will know the honor you have given them, and be as proud to serve you as am I."*

"Well, she can serve as an example to the others, as to what happens to girls who don't perform to your standards," he said, and "unhooked" the girl's chains from the others. As the wraith writhed in terror, he drew her close to him, then spun her substance out, as he had spun out the substance of the Elementals, to fit into the matrix of protections on the house. When he was done, there was nothing left of her, and her chains vanished into the aether.

"*There!*" Xi'er exclaimed to the other, cowering, whimpering white girls. *"You see? This is what your master can do if you do not give him all he needs!"* The spirits huddled together, struck dumb, he suspected, by the complete obliteration of one of their kind.

He left her giving one of her lectures to her captive audience and enjoying herself immensely.

How is this even possible? he wondered. Moriarty had said she had great willpower. She surely had an *immensely* strong will, much stronger than he would ever have given the ugly little thing she had been credit for. She'd turned herself into a stunning beauty on the other side of death, and her spirit self showed no signs of degradation. If anything, she seemed stronger than when she had first been sacrificed, as if she was feeding off something now.

It occurred to him then that this might be the case. That she might be feeding off the spirits of the other girls. But if she was, well, she was earning it. His "batteries" were filling up at a steady rate, replenishing the energy he'd spent on defenses. And soon, between the batteries and the girls, he would be able to transfer Moriarty into Hughs' body.

He went to the shelves of jars and took down the one that held the head of the girl whose spirit he had just obliterated. It wasn't difficult to tell which one it was; once the spirit was gone as a discrete entity, the head immediately started to decay, regardless of the fluid preserving it. This one was already showing the first signs; the eyes had shrunk in, and the skin around the mouth and eyes had darkened. He took the top off the jar and decanted the whole thing down the chute in the floor into the sewer below. He closed the door in the floor.

It was highly unlikely that Scotland Yard would ever recover the few heads he had disposed of; there was generally nothing left but a skull by the time rains and sewage washed a head into the Thames, and of course, being bone, it would sink to the bottom immediately. They must be wondering where the heads of the corpses they had recovered had gone. *I think not even Alderscroft can guess what use I have for them.*

Speaking of Scotland Yard . . .

He went downstairs to the kitchen, his nose telling him Kelly was baking scones. She seemed to enjoy being here, if the fact that she was making more baked treats for both of them was any indication. "Mrs. Kelly, have you heard from your urchins today?"

She turned, wiping her hands on her apron. "Th' shop-lads, y'mean? Aye, this mornin'. Nothin' t'say. Watson mopes 'bout the flat. Some toff turned up two days agone, nothin' changed. I reckon the toff was Alderscroft. Watson don't go t'the Yard, an' the Yard don't come t'him."

He smiled. No matter how many shields against scrying Watson put on his flat or Sherlock's, there was no fooling real, living eyes. And as Sherlock had proved many times over with his Baker Street Irregulars, no one pays much attention to a child. Perhaps Watson should not have chronicled that aspect of Holmes' investigations so faithfully. It allowed others to copy him.

Right after eliminating Mary Watson, he'd sent Kelly to make the rounds of the shops around 221 Baker Street, pretending she had just moved there. Every few days she would go from shop to shop, buying something small in each place, asking about Watson. It wasn't as if his address was secret, after all. He himself had posted it in every one of the adventures he had chronicled. It wasn't hard to get the boys to talk, either—Watson was their local celebrity now that Holmes was gone, and they were avid to gossip. There were at least a dozen boys, all told, and among all of them he was getting a pretty accurate description of every move Watson made. Sometimes their reports included such details as the dishes Mrs. Hudson, the landlady, was making to tempt his appetite. The only thing better than asking the shop-boys would have been to somehow recruit Mrs. Hudson or her maid, but Mrs. Hudson had proved to be a taciturn and close-mouthed Scot, and the maid was evidently her relative and absolutely incorruptible.

"I think we can count on the fact that Watson has lost his taste for detective work, Mrs. Kelly," he said with satisfaction. "How is Hughs coming along?"

Mrs. Kelly got that sly smile on her face that told him she had been up to something clever. "Oh," she said, far too casually. "He's comin' along. Didja know, Mister Spencer, the lad's *highly* suggestible?"

Kelly was every bit as useful as Xi'er, and then some. "You interest me, Mrs. Kelly," he replied. "Do say on."

"Well, I thought, it wouldn't do a bit'o harm if I talked to meself whilst I was cleanin' 'is room. I thought I'd see if 'e could 'ear me. And there yew go, 'e started talkin' in 'is dreams, and 'is dreams 'ad what I was talkin' about in 'em! So . . . I been tellin' 'im 'ow terrible 'is poesy is. 'Ow 'e's a disgrace to 'is fambly. 'Ow the people 'e thinks are 'is friends are larfin' at 'im pretendin' t'be a poet. 'Cept you, a'course, but yer losin' faith, an accounta 'e's not written one word since 'e got 'ere." She cackled evilly. "I daresay it's all makin' 'im wisht 'e was dead."

Now, such an approach would never have occurred to him. He'd always assumed that when Hughs was in his drug daze, he was deaf to the world. "Mrs. Kelly . . . that's inspired. I think I shall have to go reinforce that before I leave the house today."

And suiting his actions to his words, he went up to the guest room where Hughs lay, already deep in opium dreams.

"Oh Hughs," he murmured, standing over the young man, in tones of deepest disappointment. "When are you going to throw off your lassitude and *write*? I had such faith in you, my boy. I was sure you had the makings of another Byron in you. And what do you do? You waste your time and mine in these idle reveries. You break my heart, just as you have broken your parents' hearts. Now I see why your father cast you off. Perhaps I should, too."

And having deposited this rich ore of melancholia for Hughs to mine in his dreams, he left, smiling.

The more he infected Hughs with depression, the more Hughs would lose the will to live. The more he lost the will to live—although he would be in no position to even attempt to take his own life—the weaker the hold his spirit would have on his body. And that would make it much easier for Moriarty to push him out.

It seemed that absolutely everything was going his way. He headed out to take care of the business of the Organization with a light heart. Very soon now, it would no longer be his task to take care of these mundane details and keep a firm hold over the remnants of the gang. Very soon Moriarty's hands would be on the reins again.

And with Watson disposed of, it would not be long before they found and disposed of Holmes. This time for good.

And *he* would be able to get on with some of the other projects that had occurred to him—such as getting his own hooks into members of the Court, until he could depose Alderscroft and gain the ability to influence the Queen herself.

Nan longed desperately for something to take the two of them out of town—preferably as far away as possible. Despite the beautiful sunny day, a black gloom hung over the flat and both of them. Sometimes she wanted to run out into the street and shriek at the top of her lungs that something *horrible* was about to descend on London, like one of those crazy Hyde Park religious lunatics, screaming about the end of the world being at hand.

I don't know about the end of the world, but I do know that having a necromancer building up to some unknown goal in the middle of the most important city in the world is not a good thing!

"I feel so helpless!" Sarah exclaimed, throwing down her knitting in frustration. "But how can either of us find this fiend, much less do anything about him, if Alderscroft and his entire Hunting Lodge cannot?"

"You are reading my mind again," Nan replied, and put her book aside. "I have been reading and researching, and I can come up with *nothing*. Well, almost nothing. I could, I suppose, try walking every street in the East End and attempt to find him by sifting through thoughts—"

"Don't do that!" Sarah shuddered. "What if he has some way of sensing that you are a mind reader? What if he was ready for you? What if he could somehow trap your mind, or render you unconscious? What if he has some way of putting a curse on you like the one he put on Mary?"

"He wouldn't even have to do that. All he would have to do would be to identify me as someone looking for him, and follow me back here with more of those thugs of his. I'm not sure we could handle more than four—and fewer, if they are better fighters than we are. We can't be on the alert all the time." Nan stared down at the street outside, grimly. "I fear that we've only escaped his attentions thus far because he wasn't aware how closely we have worked with Holmes, Watson, and Scotland Yard."

Even the bright sunlight seemed to fade a little as gloom settled over them both.

"I wish we were children at the School again." Sarah sighed. "Things were so much simpler then."

"Well, we *thought* they were, anyway." Nan sighed. "I guess they were. We didn't have to hunt down horrible things, they came after us."

"I suppose we could make targets of ourselves," Sarah replied dubiously.

"*No!*" Grey exclaimed. "*Noooooooooo!*"

"My vote goes with the bird's," Nan said dryly. "Look what nearly happened to Mary Watson, and we are not nearly as prepared to defend against magic. John and Mary have learned nothing, despite their near-demise."

They stared glumly at one another for several long minutes. Then Nan glanced over at the little nook in the sitting room where Suki kept her own chair, made for her size, and her storybooks. "I miss Suki."

"So do I."

After a moment, Nan shook her head angrily. "All right. We're overheated. We're overtired. We are getting absolutely nothing done. Let's go visit the school and Memsa'b and Sahib. Perhaps they can suggest something that we have overlooked because we are too close to the problem. If nothing else, we'll get some fresh air and rest. And let's convince the Watsons to come with us."

Sarah bit her lip, then nodded. "Yes. Let's. I'll get my disguise. Time for the lads to come court Mrs. Hudson's niece."

"It's true we're doing no good here," Mary Watson said, tentatively. She had mending in her hands, but from the look of it, hadn't been getting much done before the girls arrived.

"I feel as if we would be running away." Watson stood at the

MERCEDES LACKEY

window, his back to them, staring out at the street below with his hands in his pockets. But there was no mistaking the dispirited nature of his posture.

"I feel as if there is nothing keeping us here," Mary countered. "Perhaps Mr. and Mrs. Harton have some ideas. Or their associates—" She shook her head. "I don't know. I only know that if I sit around here for much longer, I am not going to be responsible for my actions. I may be going slightly mad, and I do not believe I will do so quietly."

Watson turned away from the window. "Then in that case, if nothing else, it will do us good to get out of the flat." He turned to Sarah. "We will meet you there; it will take a little more stealth for us to leave than it will for you. But I am sure Mrs. Hudson will be relieved that there is no longer the threat of an attack on this address once we are gone."

"I should think Mrs. Hudson would have gotten used to that by now," Sarah whispered to Nan. "It's not as if having Sherlock here didn't invite attacks."

Nan for her part went to Watson's writing desk, wrote a note for Neville to carry to Memsa'b, and gave it to him.

"Do you want to wait for us there?" she asked. He nodded, and Nan looked over at Grey. "Do you want to go with him?"

"Yesssss," Grey replied.

Nan took both birds to the window and let them go. "Let's get on our way," she said to Sarah.

It was suppertime when they arrived back at their flat, and rather than allowing Mrs. Horace to take it upstairs, they shared supper with her in her kitchen. They were familiar enough with it after many sessions of candy- and biscuit-making, familiar enough to note with admiration a handsome set of new knives, replacing the ones she'd inherited from her great-grandmother. After listening to some of the neighborhood gossip and enjoying the soup, egg-salad, and fresh bread, Sarah broached the real reason why they wanted to speak with her.

"We miss Suki, and we've decided to spend at least a week at the school," she said. "Perhaps longer, we'll telegraph you if we do decide to extend our visit."

"Well, that's lovely!" Mrs. Horace replied, her eyes lighting up.

"The birds will be going with you, of course?"

"Yes indeed. We expect to be charged the full rent as usual, of course—" Nan began.

"Well, if you're not worried about me touching your things, I've been meaning to ask you if you could go away for a few days so I can give the place a good turn-out," Mrs. Horace put in, her eyes now definitely gleaming. "You just can't do a thorough cleaning when people are *there*."

"By all means, that would be splendid," Sarah said. "Nothing could be better, knowing we'll come back to a shining clean flat."

"I can even have the sweep in, which I wouldn't *dare* with those darling birds there. The soot would probably be terrible for them." It was very clear that Mrs. Horace relished the chance to get in their flat and turn it upside down and inside out, give it a good shake, and put all to rights again.

"Then it's all settled. We'll just pack what we need and catch the last train." Nan finished her tea and stood up. "I'm glad everything is going to work out for all of us."

"Did you see her face?" Sarah whispered to Nan as they climbed the stairs to their flat. "You'd have thought we'd just given her a new fur cloak!"

"Well, you've seen what she does with her own flat for a spring cleaning; there isn't a dust mote left. And ours hasn't been thoroughly 'done' since we moved it. It must have been driving her mad. And it's lovely that she wants to do it. But I will never understand how anyone can enjoy cleaning, of all things."

They parted company at the door and each went to their own room to pack up what they'd need. It wasn't more than a suitcase each and the bird-carriers, since they both kept an extra wardrobe at the school—it saved on packing and unpacking when they came to visit, and neither of them could bear to let go of old, outmoded garments that still had useful life in them. Even if his Lordship did make gentle fun of them by sending them both yet *another* new dress or waist and skirt any time he caught them in their old, comfortable things.

"Now I wish I hadn't told Neville to stay at the school," Nan said ruefully. "We might have been able to borrow Lord Alderscroft's carriage—"

But just as they left the front door and Nan was about to leave the luggage in Sarah's hands to go look for a cab, a growler came around the corner and stopped right in front of them. Inside were an old man and a young man, and it took Nan a moment to recognize the Watsons.

"This yer party, guv'nor?" the cabby called down from his box.

"That's right, that's right," Watson said, in a raspy voice, and coughed. "Help them with their luggage, there's a good lad."

The cabby had already hopped down to do so, and Mary Watson popped out to give the girls a gentlemanly hand up into the cab. "My word, I do like these trousers," Mary said in a low voice, as the cab moved off again. "I may adopt bloomer suits after this!"

Watson sighed.

They reached the station in plenty of time to catch the last train stopping at the station nearest to the Harton School. Watson wouldn't hear of them traveling second class, so they all shared a first-class compartment and traveled in slightly stuffy comfort. Stuffy, because if you opened the windows, you had a better than even chance of getting smuts from the engine all over you, so your choice was to take that risk and have fresh air, or stay clean but sit there fanning yourself for the entire trip.

They chose stuffy; it wasn't too bad, since it was early evening. And when the train stopped at their little country station just outside of the London suburbs, there was a handsome, tall young man dressed in the manner of an Indian Moslem, waiting on the platform.

Nan was first out of the railway carriage, and greeted him with relief. "Dilawar!" she exclaimed. "I didn't know you knew how to drive!" Dilawar was Selim's nephew, and had, along with the nephews of Karamjit and Agansing, arrived last winter to train under the tutelage of their uncles. Not as replacements, at least not yet, but certainly as their adjuncts.

"Mustafa has been training me," Dilawar said proudly; Nan could not help but notice he was the handsomest of the nephews, with his clean-shaven face and expressive eyes. "He says that the others have 'heavy hands.' I do not know what that means, but I enjoy this part of my duties very much."

Watson was just getting down out of the carriage and heard

this. "He means the other lads pull too much on the reins," Watson said, as Dilawar peered at him curiously.

"I beg pardon," Dilawar said in puzzlement, as Mary Watson got out and directed the porter to bring all their bags to where the Harton School carriage was waiting. "I was told I was to be conveying the Misses, and Doctor Watson and his wife—"

"Shhh. That *is* Doctor Watson and his wife," Nan hissed. Dilawar blushed.

"Begging your pardon," he said, still blushing. "Please to be coming this way."

Nan could tell that John was very pleased Dilawar had not been able to recognize him. Actually, so was Nan. It meant the Watsons had probably been able to leave without being followed. And almost certainly no one had recognized the fresh-faced young man as Mary.

The carriage ride to the Harton School, located in Lord Alderscroft's country mansion (Nan refused to call so enormous a structure a mere "house" or "home") wasn't a long one, but Nan was glad to get there, and she suspected everyone else was too. The sheer relief she felt at seeing the place, the burden that lifted from her even though nothing had been resolved, made her feel her exhaustion all the more. And yet there was no sense of elation along with that relief. In fact, if anything, she felt depression. The situation had not been resolved, the danger, whatever it was, had not been averted, and there still didn't seem a way for them to do anything but wait for the blow to fall and hope they could react to it in time.

Memsa'b and the other two nephews, Kadar and Taral, the nephews of Karamjit and Agansing respectively, stood next to her. Memsa'b was not a beautiful, or even a pretty woman, but she was tall and lithe, and even though her hair had started to go gray she was still striking with her strong features. She half ran down the steps to embrace the girls as they alighted from the carriage, then offered her hand to John and Mary in turn. "Excellent disguises, Doctor, Mary," she said. "If I had not known who you must be, I would never have guessed. Now I am sure you are exhausted from the last few weeks, and we are going to say nothing more about why you are here until the morning. The boys will take your things to your rooms," she continued, as the two young men seized all their baggage as if it weighed nothing while Dilawar drove the carriage around to the stables. "I'm sure you'd all like to get into something comfortable. Sahib and I will see you in his study when you feel ready to have a little refreshment. Girls, you already know where to go, I'll show the others to their room."

Nan and Sarah were only too happy to trot after Kadar up to the rooms they always used when they were at the school. Neville was waiting on his stand in Nan's room, up on one leg and looking contented with his world, when she took her case and carrier from Kadar and entered. Once there, she threw off her traveling gown, rid herself of her corset, gave herself a quick wash in the basin, and put on the lightest gown she could find in the wardrobe. It was an old thing, a little shabby, but too comfortable to get rid of.

Unpinning and shaking out her hair, she tied it back with a bit of ribbon, and emerged from her room to see Sarah had done nearly the same thing. The only difference was that Sarah's gown was an old morning gown, which made her chuckle a little.

"What?" Sarah asked.

"Oh, only that somewhere out there, half a hundred great doyennes of Society are feeling a surge of rage over the third course of dinner, and not knowing why."

That made Sarah chuckle too. "A morning gown worn in the evening! *Horrors!*" They headed for Sahib's study, and Nan, at least, was feeling a trifle light-headed at this point, both from being so very tired and from trying to manage her emotions. She hoped the Hartons didn't intend to serve them anything strong.

But first, a quick reunion with Suki was in order. They went straight to her room and spent a half hour hugging and catching up, and explaining to her with as little detail as possible what they had been and probably would be doing. Suki listened gravely, and with a solemn face assured them that they were doing what had to be done, and she would help the Hartons keep the school safe while they did it.

Fortunately, as usual, Memsa'b had anticipated their needs. As soon as they entered, Memsa'b waved them to a tray with four tall glasses of lemonade, which was exactly what Nan would have asked for if she'd thought of it. They each took one and waited for the Watsons. Sahib said nothing, as was generally his way. Nan noticed that the two gray streaks in his hair, one at each temple, had grown thicker, but otherwise he was much the same, his weathered, strong face set in an expression that always reminded her of his wisdom.

The need to be comfortable and casual seemed to have infected all of them. John Watson was, for the first time in Nan's memory, wearing a vest and rolled-up shirtsleeves. Mary was in a linen gown worn so often it was soft and draping rather than crisp and tailored. Both of them acquired their glasses and sank into Sahib's comfortable leather chairs with sighs that betrayed how long they'd been living with tension.

John took a long drink of his lemonade, then opened his mouth.

"No," Sahib said firmly. "It can wait until tomorrow. We want you to relax and rest and get a good solid night of sleep. None of you look as if you'd had one for a while."

"Although Mary looks remarkably lively for a corpse," Memsa'b observed.

"I'm as much of a corpse as Sherlock is," replied Mary.

"We'd suspected as much," Sahib replied. "And since I suspect that Sherlock's non-demise has nothing to do with your current problems, I would very much like to hear how he survived plummeting off a cliff."

John Watson was only too happy to tell the story again. The Hartons nodded now and again, but did not interrupt him.

"I presume he's engaged in hunting down the last of this Professor Moriarty's men, then?" Sahib asked when he was finished.

"Yes, and he warned us that we might well be a target for vengeance. We seem to have attracted other attention instead," John began, and Sahib held up his hand.

"Not until the morning," he said firmly. "Is there anything else that you can talk about?"

They all exchanged glances, a little nonplussed. The necromancer had been occupying so much of their attention and lives that suddenly they were left with very little to say.

Until Sarah suddenly straightened. "Oh! I nearly forgot!" She closed her hand over the locket she was wearing, and her brows furrowed in concentration, and the misty form of Caro—in her young man's garb—formed in the middle of the room, where they could all see her.

"Sahib, Memsa'b, this is Caro. She's attached to this locket, and she's been helping us. Caro, these are the people I've told you about."

"Very pleased to meet you," came Caro's whispery voice. *"And just as pleased to have a change of scenery."*

"Oh, you'll have more than a change of scenery, my dear," Memsa'b replied with a smile. "There's a small army of young hooligans here, some of whom will certainly be able to see or otherwise detect your presence, and none of whom will be frightened by you. In fact, you are more likely to be swarmed if you choose to make yourself visible to all of them."

"That would be a novelty," Caro replied cheerfully. *"It sounds like jolly good fun."*

Nan was very glad that Caro at least was still feeling cheerful. She was having a hard time maintaining "sober" rather than "hideously depressed."

It looked to her as if the others were feeling about the same. And Memsa'b took over the conversation, relating tales of the pupils—which, when one was running a school in which more than half of the children were gifted with psychical powers, could get interesting. Nan noticed that the lemonade had some herbal quality to it, and that the biscuits Memsa'b handed around had also been subtlety "doctored," and from the knowing look Watson had noticed too. Memsa'b didn't have that kind of knowledge of medicinal herbs herself, so it was probably on her orders, but done by one of the ayahs or even someone like Gupta's wife, who was one of the kitchen wizards.

While she nibbled biscuits and drank lemonade, she did notice that although she didn't feel any happier, she did feel sleepier, and it was clear from the stifled yawns the others were feeling the same. "I cannot keep my eyes open," Mary Watson finally confessed. "And I hate to be—"

"Children rise at the break of dawn," Sahib interrupted. "We should go to bed too. Good night, my friends."

Nan trailed Sarah up to their rooms and bid her friend goodnight at her door. She opened the window for some night air (and to allow Neville to fly off in the morning if he chose) and was asleep almost as soon as she pulled the blanket over herself.

But her dreams were dark, and full of troubles.

17

The Harton School wasn't just a school for children with budding psychical talents and a few who were Elemental Magicians whose parents did not have the means to have them tutored at home—it was also a school for the children of parents who were currently living and working overseas. Their parents were usually in India, although now and again a child from Africa, as Sarah had been, turned up as well. Common feeling was that the climates in these hot places were bad for British children, and unless the parents simply could not afford a steamship ticket, the poor things were shipped back "home" to boarding schools as soon as they could be parted from their mamas, sometimes even before they could speak coherently.

Of course, to these children, Britain was not "home." Britain was an alien, too-cold place, where the food was unfamiliar, the clothing they were put into was uncomfortable and unfamiliar, where the way they were expected to act had changed all out of recognition, and nothing was as it should be.

Most schools ignored all this, and the children were utterly traumatized by nearly everything they encountered, from corporal punishment to rooms too cold to sleep in. The Harton School did not. There were Indian ayahs for the littlest children, no one was put into harsh, itchy woolen clothing, the rooms were kept as warm as possible in the winter, and most of all, the food was what these children remembered.

So there was kedgeree for breakfast.

It had taken Nan a while to get used to this particular food, because unlike most of the children, she had been born and raised in the streets of London. But she had also been so poor that every scrap of food she ate came by fighting for it, so she didn't turn her nose up at it, either.

Now the taste of curried rice, smoked kipper and egg brought back memories of the time in her life when her entire existence had turned around for the better, and she had been happier than she'd ever dreamed of being. And although she had awakened with an aching head and the leaden feeling that she had spent all night chasing something that she could never catch, she cheered up a bit over her plate. John Watson had beaten the girls to the table, and was clearly enjoying his breakfast; Mary had looked at it dubiously and opted for oatmeal porridge instead.

Memsa'b appeared in the dining room like magic, just as they were finishing. "Do you prefer to meet in the study again, or would you rather sit on the terrace in some sunshine?" she asked.

"Sunshine," Mary Watson said immediately. "I know it hasn't been that long, but I feel as if I have been hiding in our flat for months."

"Sunshine it is then," Memsa'b replied. "I'll get Sahib. The girls can take you to the terrace."

Nan took the time to get herself another mug of tea—the school used nice, heavy mugs instead of delicate cups that wouldn't last long in the hands of children, and although the children were given milky tea, the adults had proper Gunpowder Black that would make your hair stand on end in the morning. She still felt . . . well, depressed. If nothing else, a mug of tea would give her something to do with her hands.

The furniture on the terrace, rather than being delicate wrought-iron creations, was all in the Indian style and made of—well, Nan wasn't sure what it was made of. Wicker, reeds, some plant material, softened with cotton cushions. It was very comfortable, and she settled into a chair with a back like a spreading peacock's tail with a sigh, and took in the view of the lawns and the children's cricket, croquet, and tennis fields with melancholy pleasure. She sipped her tea, wishing again she was that young again.

Memsa'b and Sahib appeared about five minutes later and

settled themselves into chairs. "All right," Sahib said, "*Now* let us hear the full story of what has been going on."

Nan let John Watson take the lead on this, only adding details that he overlooked. It all took the better part of an hour to relate, and when he was finished, Watson sighed.

"I don't see—*we* don't see anything more that we can do," he said, as gloom settled over everyone but the Hartons. "I don't know what Mary and I are supposed to do when Alderscroft's entire Lodge can't find this cursed murderer. And as Nan's pointed out, her talents and Sarah's seem even less suited to discovering anything than ours are. And this blackguard has to be building up his power and forces to do something *big*. We're like that fellow with the Sword of Damocles suspended by a hair above his head, and there's damn-all we can do about it."

Nan ducked her head and had a big gulp of tea to get herself under control, but hearing it all laid out like that made her want to sob.

And then Sahib spoke.

"I think there are two things you are overlooking," he said, quite calmly. "One of them is Sarah's friend Caro. She's a resource you haven't yet used except as a contact point with other ghosts, and I think we should consult her to see what else she thinks she can do. We are dealing with a necromancer, after all—so a spirit ought by all rights be particularly useful to us. And the other thing you have overlooked—through no fault of your own—is Sarah herself."

Nan's head came up at that. Sarah's expression went from astonished to indignant. "But I've—" she began.

Sahib held up his hand. "I said, through no fault of your own. Memsa'b and I have been consulting with some *other* Elemental Masters that are not in Alderscroft's immediate circle. The Wizard of London is an admirable man but . . ." Sahib smiled wryly ". . . he's rather autocratic. And there are those who just would rather not be ordered about unless there is an actual emergency. They tend their own gardens, so to speak, unless something comes up that the Lodge needs help with."

"But what has that to do with Sarah?" Nan asked. "She's not an Elemental Master."

"So we've all been led to believe," Sahib countered. "That is, until Maestro Sarasate came into our orbit, so to speak."

"The musician?" Watson asked. "I thought he was a Spirit Master—are you saying—"

"That according to the people we've consulted with, so is Sarah." She held up her hand to forestall everyone talking at once. "Let me walk you through our reasoning," she continued, as Neville and Grey flew in over the game-fields and landed on chairs of their respective girls. "First, most mediums can see and communicate with spirits, but spirits actively seek out Sarah. That's not usual. Second, most mediums can convince spirits to move on. Sarah can open a door to the next world and send them through. That's not usual. Third was the ease, according to Beatrice Leek, with which she learned to step into the half-world of earthbound spirits herself. That is definitely not usual. Fourth is the ability to tell when spirits are bound to *objects,* rather than haunting a place, even when the spirit chooses not to show itself. Fifth, there is Caro, who has willingly volunteered to serve Sarah, which is absolutely unheard of for a mere medium. And lastly, there is Grey." Memsa'b transferred her attention to the bird sitting on the back of Sarah's chair. "Grey, were you given to Sarah because she was going to become a Spirit Master?"

"*Well,* yes!" said Grey, and made a rude noise, as if she was amused that the humans had taken so long to figure out something so obvious.

Memsa'b spread her hands, as if to say, *there, you see?*

"Spirit Masters are incredibly rare," John Watson said into the stunned silence.

"They are also not by any means the most conventionally powerful," his wife pointed out dryly. "That would probably be Fire Masters."

John stroked his moustache. "I'd have to say, if you're not a necromancer, Spirit Masters are probably the weakest of the Elemental Masters. . . ."

"But they do have advantages that no other Master has," Mary added. "We're limited to where our Elementals can go, or the nature of our Elementals is such that without close supervision they aren't reliable."

"Well . . . ghosts often aren't reliable," Sarah said reluctantly.

"And they're limited by how far they can go from the point they're bound to."

"But if there's a sane spirit anywhere near something you want watched? Then you have eyes and ears anywhere within that area," said Memsa'b.

"But how does this change anything?" Sarah wanted to know. "We still don't know where the necromancer is!"

"Ah—but you and Nan know the general area to search now, and you know you're not looking for a mere murderer, you're looking for a *necromancer*. That makes all the difference," said Sahib. When Sarah shook her head—and then, suddenly, her expression changed.

"I'm *not* looking for spirits," she said, slowly, "Because he has almost certainly *bound* the spirits of the girls he killed, and more than likely, they can't move at all from the place where he's bound them. In fact, I doubt very much there is a free spirit *anywhere* around his working space, because he'll have bound them all. So what I'm looking for is an *absence* of spirits!"

Sahib and Memsa'b both nodded, but it was Grey who answered.

"*Ex-actly!*" crowed the parrot. "*Ex-actly!*"

There actually was no place other than the cellars where Sarah could have enough darkness to bring Caro out during the daytime. Everyone agreed that there was no point in trying to cram themselves down there amongst the sacks of potatoes and turnips and whatever else the School cooks had down there in order to speak to her a few hours earlier. *Not to mention the mice and rats*, Sarah thought to herself with a shudder. *And black beetles and spiders*. While the School cats probably did a good job with the former, they weren't going to do much about the latter, and while Sarah didn't at all mind these creatures in their proper places— where she could *see* and avoid them—the idea of having something run over her hand or face in the pitch dark gave her the horrors.

But the mere fact that now they actually had something they could work with and the start of a plan had changed everyone's mood. By lunchtime the Watsons had both lost that look of dim despair and Sarah actually caught them smiling. Memsa'b persuaded them to go on a nature walk with some of the children, including Suki, who adored Mary Watson.

As for Sarah . . . she got out her talisman of oak, ash, and thorn twigs bound in red thread, tucked it into her hatband, and persuaded Nan to go on a walk of their own. Of course, Robin Goodfellow probably had too many things on his mind to turn up just to talk to *them*—but maybe he didn't. And maybe he would. And maybe he could give them some good advice.

Nan gave her a sidelong glance when she saw they were headed to the wildest part of the great estate, toward the grassy little bowl that had made a natural amphitheater. That had been the place where they first met Robin, when they had been "playing" *Midsummer Night's Dream* with each of them taking half the parts.

"I don't know," she replied to the unspoken question. "But if he does, we can at least find out if he has any advice for me."

She had just set foot in that little bowl as she said that, so she was not entirely surprised to hear, from behind her "And what advice would that be, Daughter of Eve?"

"Advice on being a Spirit Master. Advice on dealing with a necromancer. Hello Robin!" she said, turning.

They were never quite sure what guise he would be in when he appeared; today he was the youthful Elven Prince, with a lazy smile and nary a hair out of place. Tunic and some sort of trousers of emerald velvet and silk, silver embroidery ornamenting all of it, and a silver circlet around his head, his green eyes glinted with mischief though his sober expression suggested something other than fun.

"I do wish you'd stop calling us that," Nan sighed.

"Calling you what, Wildwood Rose?" he asked, turning the lazy smile on her.

"Daughters of Eve, although I can't say I like 'Wildwood Rose' any better," she replied, with her fists on her hips. "You should know better than to try to cozen me."

"I suppose I should, but then, that would be very out-of-character for me, wouldn't it?" he replied smoothly. "Necromancer, you say?" he continued, and shook his head. "I am afraid I have no advice for you. I don't meddle with human spirits. The best I can assist with is a charm or two, like I gave Sarah, and I doubt that will be of any help."

Well, this was an unpleasant surprise. "You didn't know I was a Spirit Master? At least, Memsa'b thinks I am," Sarah asked.

Again, he shook his head. "That is new to me. I told you, I don't meddle with human spirits. All that I can suggest is that you trust not your emotions but your intellect. In that half-world where the human spirits still tied to earth are, emotions are tricksy things. They're strong there, and they can lead you astray. Don't trust your feelings. Trust your head, not your heart. Listen to your ghostly companion. And take your feathered friends with you; they'll see true."

"Well that's more than I had," Sarah replied. "Any other advice?"

His brows furrowed beneath the thin silver circlet he wore. "Remember that nothing is exactly as it seems there. For instance, walls might wall something *in*, but not wall anything *out*. What seems familiar may act in unexpected ways. Nothing there is permanent; it's always being worn away by the real world. Things that appear strong might be weak. But conversely, things that appear weak may be strong. If you see something, never take what you see at face value." He shrugged. "Your best rule to follow is that if something seems odd, always ask yourself why. All I really know is that the only true things are the spirits, the rest is made of the dreams of spirits and the mortals with power there, and can be true or false. I do not go there, and I am not sure I could."

Sarah's heart fell. She reminded herself that it was always long odds that Puck could help . . . but it was still a bitter disappointment.

"Mary's sylphs can," Nan pointed out.

"Sometimes the lesser can go where the greater cannot. I don't know why." He smiled suddenly. "I did not make the rules, after all."

"No, but you break them often enough," Nan retorted.

"True, true, but I think this might be one I cannot and should not break. It might be very dangerous for me to be there. It might be very dangerous *to* me. I can't say." He shrugged. Sarah had the feeling he knew a lot more than he was going to tell her. But—that too might be one of those rules he was not able to break.

"I'm sorry," Robin said, softly. "I wish I could help more."

"When I think about how much you helped with that—thing—that was trying to come into our world, how can I cast blame on you when you say you cannot help with this?" Sarah said firmly. "This is the doing of mortals. It's up to mortals to deal with it."

Puck sighed with relief. "So, you see it."

"Much as I hate to admit it," Nan replied reluctantly, "Yes, I do. We mortals made this mess. We should properly clean it up."

"Wise beyond your years," Puck agreed. "Well then, I'll give you both a kiss for luck, and Robin's luck is nothing to be scoffed at!"

Sarah might have said something, but Puck darted in, kissed her on her right cheek, kissed Nan on her left, and vanished in a puff of leaves and the scent of green herbs and wildflowers. Sarah picked the leaves up. Oak, ash, and thorn, of course.

Nan looked at her and shrugged. "Well," she said philosophically. "We tried."

But Sarah had the feeling that Puck had bent the rules by telling them more than he properly "should" have.

I just have to figure out what he meant.

Spencer was not the sort of man to feel glee, but he certainly felt a deep satisfaction. There was no sign whatsoever of Sherlock Holmes, and if not even the murder of Mary Watson had brought him out of hiding, there was no doubt that Spencer would have the Professor safely resurrected long before he showed his face in London again. John Watson was also safely eliminated; Kelly reported that he never ventured out of Sherlock's old flat anymore.

He'd replaced two of the fading ghosts with girls supplied by Shen Li, and shockingly, neither of the two new ones were Chinese. They also didn't speak English, but Spencer didn't particularly care *what* they were, as long as they consented to marry him. Whatever they were, Shen Li spoke whatever babble they called their native tongue, and they said "yes" at the right moment. That was all that mattered.

Shen Li had given him more of whatever the drink was that had rendered Xi'er unconscious so quickly; it had cost him extra, but that was negligible given the convenience it afforded.

Now he was a mere two girls away from having enough power to resurrect Moriarty *and* have plenty left over when that task was done.

Moriarty had stabilized, and he had the feeling that Xi'er was the reason for that. Talking to her amused Moriarty no end, and that kept the Professor from getting agitated—or worse, enraged.

Not having to worry about Moriarty's stability had given him the leisure to lay the groundwork for other plans. He had forged several notes in Hughs' hand to his mother, describing his "change of heart" thanks to the change in scenery, and asking her humbly to intercede in a reconciliation with Hughs Senior. He'd arranged for these to be sent from several different villages in the Lake District. The mother couldn't reply, of course, not knowing where her son was, but when "Hughs" reappeared, everything would be in readiness for Moriarty to become the Prodigal Son Returned.

And tonight he was taking an evening to discuss future plans with Shen Li.

The shop was dark when he arrived, but the assistant opened the door to him as soon as he stepped out of the cab. Once again, the assistant led him to the room that served so many functions. Tonight it was set up as a sort of gentleman's lounge. And tonight, for the first time, Shen Li was dressed as an ordinary English gentleman. Or perhaps not so ordinary; on closer inspection, Spencer realized that his exquisitely tailored suit could only have been bespoke from one of the best tailors in London.

"Ah, Master Spencer," Shen Li said, in warm tones. "It is very pleasant to meet with you in normal circumstances." Spencer was astonished. If it had not been for the long braid of white hair he wore, Spencer would have taken him for anyone he might meet in a good club or at the Stock Exchange. "Please, have a seat. Would you care for a cigar? No? A brandy? Certainly. I think you will approve." He gestured to the assistant, who poured two brandies and handed one to Spencer as soon as he was seated in the overstuffed leather armchair he'd chosen. Shen Li took a similar chair at right angles to his.

He sipped cautiously, and then with more enthusiasm. Shen Li was correct. He did approve. This might be the best brandy he'd ever tasted.

"Now, Master Spencer, since you have made it clear that you would like to conduct further and potentially more complicated business with me in the future, allow me to acquaint you with my real name. I am Vladimir Volkov." He smiled. Spencer smiled back. "And as I told you, I am Russian."

"I appreciate that you have trusted me with your real name, Master Volkov," he replied.

Volkov smiled more broadly. "Now, let us sit here in each others' company and enjoy this fine brandy for a moment or two, before we get down to business."

Spencer was not at all averse to doing just that. It had been a very long time since he had been in the company of a man he considered to be his equal—and there was no doubt in his mind that Shen Li—or Volkov—was his equal in every way but as a magician.

So he savored the brandy, and they spoke of politics for a little while. Volkov was quite versed in the topics of the day, particularly international politics. "Your country is making a mistake," he said finally. "They are counting on the fact that your Queen has so many family ties to Germany. But the Germans do not give a farthing for family ties when their own Imperial interests are on the line. If they elect to annex the Lorraine, they will conveniently forget those ties, mark my words."

"But surely the Russians—" he began.

"The Russian Imperial Family will not move to help France," Volkov pronounced. "Now, if the Kaiser were to also move eastward, that would be a different story." Spencer listened with great interest as Volkov expounded on things he himself knew little of, filing it all away to relate to the Professor. Moriarty's projects were many, varied, and international. This would almost certainly be of great interest to him.

Come to think of it . . . it was of great interest to Spencer. When there was war, there was money to be made.

As if he was reading Spencer's mind, Volkov added, "I have investment in munitions manufacturers all over the world. When war comes, and it will, I shall do very well." He finished his brandy and gestured to the servant to pour them each another. "But, my friend, we are not here to discuss that sort of investment, nor the politics of nations. *You* possess something I know very little about. Magic." His eyes gleamed. "I am self-taught. I should like to know more."

"Surely the Chinese—"

"Do not discuss these things outside of select circles, of which I am not a part," Volkov replied, and bent over his knees. "So. Enlighten me, if you will. The more I know, the better I can deliver what you may need."

"Well . . . to begin with, unless you have both a very disciplined will and a powerful imagination, you have to be born with the ability to manipulate magic power," Spencer told him. "And if you aren't gifted at birth with that ability, you'll spend half your life learning how to wield magic, because only those with the gift can *see* it to manipulate it easily. Those who do so by will and imagination alone will always be handicapped in that regard."

Volkov nodded. "Like a blind man learning to navigate by whistling. I knew a man who could do that, once." He waved his hand. "Not worth my time. What *is* worth my time is getting to know a magician able to put a death curse on Mary Watson."

Spencer tried not to start, but Volkov saw it anyway, and chuckled. "I do my research, my friend. I assume that you can make bargains of your own, irrespective of your duties to Professor Moriarty?"

"How did—"

"I buy and sell information, my friend. And I do not believe that the Professor is . . . shall we say, *entirely* gone? His Organization is still functional, albeit diminished. Would I be mistaken in inferring that your current task is to bring him back, so to speak?"

Spencer managed to keep his mouth shut, but Volkov laughed knowingly.

"Very well, then, I assume you can take independent work?"

"I can," Spencer replied.

"Good. Now, we have established that this sort of magic exists. Tell me about what other kinds there are."

Spencer spent a good hour explaining all five types of Elemental Magic, as Volkov listened intently. "The last is the Spirit Master, who can control human spirits. Ones not still in a body, of course," he said. "Now, as I have explained with the others, the Elemental Masters who shortsightedly choose the path of cooperation instead of coercion are weaker than those who don't. But with the Spirit Master, that is even more apparent. Worse than that, most of them spend much of their time sending ghosts on to whatever their ultimate destination might be, rather than actually making use of them." He snorted, and Volkov chuckled. "But the Spirit Master that chooses domination may be one of the most powerful Masters there is. And that is demonstrated by what he's called."

"And what would that be?" asked Volkov.

It was Spencer's turn to grin wolfishly. "The necromancer. The one magician whose name alone strikes terror into the hearts of those who recognize it."

Volkov sat back in his chair, his expression one of very keen interest. "Now this . . . this is the sort of thing I want to hear about. Do tell me more, Master Spencer."

They talked long into the night. Some of that was negotiation—what Spencer might want for various services. By the end of that time . . . Spencer was seriously considering the option of leaving Moriarty's Organization once Moriarty was firmly in charge again.

He wouldn't *tell* Moriarty that of course. That would be suicidal. He'd merely tell the Professor that he needed time for his experiments. And he might even do small tasks for the Professor, now and again, but his main interest would be working with Volkov.

For one thing, Volkov hadn't attracted the attention of Sherlock Holmes, and Moriarty had. Even if Moriarty finally defeated and killed the consulting detective, doing so would take up an inordinate amount of time that could be used more profitably.

For another, he would never be quite sure if Moriarty had come back slightly damaged. That was a risk in these situations. And a damaged Moriarty could make mistakes that would bring everything tumbling down.

Volkov sent him home at around four in the morning in a small, discreet carriage. By the time he arrived, of course, Kelly was well asleep, and he found he was ravenous. He made a quick meal of cold sliced beef, bread, butter and pickles, and went to bed with his head buzzing with plans.

* * *

The girls and the Hartons met once again in Sahib's study, once the sun was down. Sarah wore Caro's locket, which she had never taken off since Watson had given it back to her. This time, though, the study was crowded with Agansing, Selim, and Karamjit there as well. Sarah didn't even have to do more than touch the locket, and Caro shimmered into being in the center of the room. Still in her male clothing, now she had taken on some of the mannerisms of a young man too, pushing her cap back on her head and slouching a little. Her infectious smile made it clear that she was enjoying herself and being in this guise.

"I've been listening in, and I hope you don't mind that," she said immediately. *"I shan't stand on ceremony. You must be the Hartons,"* she continued, nodding at Memsa'b and Sahib. *"But I don't know who these three fine gentlemen are—"*

"These are our colleagues in the occult, Agansing, Selim, and Karamjit," Sahib replied. "They are also quite skilled in their own fields of combat."

Caro bowed to the three with a little flourish. *"Call me Caro,"* she said. *"Now, actually, when I've not been listening, I've been thinking. And if I'm right about what Sarah can do, I think I know how we can find this necromancer. You said she can likely tell where there are no spirits, because he's bound them. That's where I come in. She can find likely areas, but I can investigate those areas. If it's just a matter of happenstance that there are no ghosts there, I can find that out very quickly. And if it's something more than that, I can find that out, too. Then, when we find the place where the necromancer is, all three of us—Nan and Sarah and I and any little Air Elementals Mrs. Watson wants to send—can investigate further. We'll just need a place where Nan and Sarah can safely leave their bodies."*

Memsa'b, Sahib, and their three companions stared at the ghost. Sahib's mouth had actually fallen open a little. If the situation hadn't been so serious, Sarah would have giggled. She'd never actually seen them dumbfounded before.

As for her, for the first time, her heart rose with hope.

Finally it was Agansing who spoke. "That will be very dangerous for you, my friend," he said gravely. "The necromancer might well imprison you. A spirit such as you, intelligent, strong, would be a great prize to him."

"*He'll have to catch me first,*" Caro replied. "*I can retreat to the locket, and if I'm not mistaken, if I do that, he won't be able to detect me anymore. And I am positive that without having the locket in his possession, he won't be able to extract me from it, either.*"

Agansing looked at the others. Karamjit shrugged. Selim made a gesture that Sarah interpreted as "I don't know." Memsa'b and Sahib looked at each other. "We don't know," Sahib admitted. "This is all new ground to us."

"*I'm willing to take my chances,*" Caro replied firmly. "*You risk your lives all the time. I can certainly risk my un-life. This man is a monster, and we need to stop him.*" Then she smiled. "*Besides, this is more excitement than I ever had while I was alive.*"

"But do you truly understand the danger?" Agansing persisted. "Forgive me for continuing to ask this, but there *are* things that can destroy souls."

Caro sobered again. "*I do. Really. I do. And I will be very, very careful, I promise.*"

"You can't very well forbid her, you know," Sarah put in. "How exactly would you stop her? But Caro, words cannot express how grateful I am to you."

"Then I suppose we must surrender gracefully," Sahib admitted. "And I must admit, this is a good plan. The only flaw in it that I can see is that we must find some place for Nan and Sarah to rest securely."

Now Nan spoke up. "That's what the Irregulars would be good for."

Watson blinked. "By Jove—you're right. The young scamps know every inch of the East End. They'll know exactly where not to go, and where we could rent a room safely for the space of a few hours." He actually rubbed his hands together in glee. "I've always wanted to unleash those lads the way Sherlock does."

Caro took a seat in midair, listening carefully and adding her own ideas while they put together a plan. Selim got a map of the East End from one of Sahib's many filing cabinets, and they plotted out the most efficient way to cover all of it that was serviced by the same sewer network. Knowing that this was going to go long into the night, and that the birds needed plenty of sleep, they'd left Neville and Grey upstairs in their rooms—but every now and then, Sarah felt a sleepy nudge in her mind, and she quickly told Grey if there had been anything new in the plan—then Grey would go back to sleep again.

It was nearly three in the morning when they all considered that they had thought of everything they could. Alderscroft would have to be told first, of course, and that meant getting him to come out here. No one wanted to take the chance of communications being intercepted.

"That's the main problem, really," Watson fretted. "We only have rumors of what necromancers can do. We don't actually know the extent of their powers."

"It won't be the first time all of you have faced that problem," Caro reminded them. "Sarah told me about that horrible creature you faced in that other . . . world? Reality? Well, none of you knew anything about that."

"We had a great deal of help," John objected. "Including from Sherlock."

"And Sherlock has faith in you," Caro said. "So have some faith in yourselves."

18

Nan woke to discover Neville sitting on the foot of her bed and staring intently at her, as if he had been trying to wake her by sheer force of will. When he saw she was awake, he *quorked* and projected a very familiar image into her mind—the image of Lord Alderscroft, sitting on the veranda of his country bungalow on this very estate, sipping his morning tea.

"You mean he's *here?*" she blurted. Neville bobbed his head and *quorked* again.

Well, so much for getting any more sleep. She dragged herself out of bed, yawning fit to split her face in half, pulled on whatever clothing came to hand, and stumbled out the door of her bedroom, to find Sarah doing the same thing. "Grey told me," Sarah said, and yawned again. "Should we—"

Nan held up a hand. "Wait, let's see if the others are awake first. I don't want to do anything unless Memsa'b and Sahib give us their blessing first." she consulted her pendant watch, which she had somehow managed to put on. "If they are following their normal schedule despite being up half the night with us, they should be in the dining room, having breakfast."

With the birds clinging to their shoulders, they trotted downstairs to the dining room, once the site of many elegant dinners, now laid out in the manner of a school dining hall, with two rows of tables placed end to end running the length of the room, and the table for the adults bridging the two at one end. Most of the children (including Suki) had already had their breakfast and were at their first lessons, but Memsa'b and Sahib were just finishing theirs—and looking as sleepy as Sarah and Nan felt.

"Neville and Grey flew over to Alderscroft's bungalow this morning, and he's there," Nan said, without preamble.

"Excellent! That saves us a journey. *And* we can use Neville as our messenger and invite him here for tea without any worries." Sahib didn't have to elaborate on "worries"—any time a telegram was sent, there was always the chance someone could intercept it before it got to its intended recipient. Alderscroft might not have watchers on him . . . but chances were, he did. No point in drawing attention to the school at this point in the game.

Sarah ran for pen and ink and paper while the Hartons finished their breakfasts, and Sahib wrote out a note giving a brief explanation and an invitation to turn up at teatime. He folded it and handed it to Neville, who took it with grave dignity, and Nan walked him over to the window and let him go.

"You and Sarah look like a pair of unmade beds," Sahib said kindly, as she turned back to the room. "Why don't you both go back to sleep. I'll wait for Neville to bring back the answer."

Nan had been considering a lot of strong tea, but sleep sounded much better. "We'll see you at luncheon then," she said gratefully, and the two of them went back to their rooms and resumed their interrupted slumbers.

Nan and Sarah had been spending as much time as they could with Suki since they had arrived—it was Summer Term, so academic lessons were minimal, giving the children plenty of time to play outdoors, learning things like riding and archery. But Suki had picked up on their anxiety, which was not exactly surprising, given that she, like Nan, was a reader of minds. Nan was expecting questions from their little ward, so she was not at all surprised when Suki finally asked those questions after luncheon as she was reviewing the map of the East End.

She was also not surprised when Suki chose her to answer them. They were both children of London's darker streets, and no matter how much Sarah loved the little girl, when Suki wanted straight answers, she came first to Nan.

"Somethin' bad is going on," Suki stated.

Nan nodded. "It's a very wicked magician. He's killed a lot of girls, and he nearly killed John and Mary. We have to find him, and we have to stop him."

Suki considered this and sat down next to Nan on the sofa. "Is it as dangerous as the monster was?"

"I have to say that I don't know," Nan admitted. "Robin told us that he can't help us, so we're more or less on our own—but he *is* only a man, and not a monster. And really, before we can do anything about him, we have to find him. That's what we'll be doing tonight, and probably for several more nights."

"And I can't help." Suki sighed. "This is *hard*!" she exclaimed mournfully.

Nan hugged her shoulders. "I know. Having to be the one who sits and waits is the hardest thing there is. And I'm sorry. But I promise you that when you can help, we'll ask you. And soon you'll be old enough to help all the time. Sarah and I weren't much older than you when Memsa'b started asking us to help." She didn't tell Suki some pretty lie about how they needed her here at the school to keep everyone safe. And she didn't make false promises that everything was going to be all right. "The problem is this man already tried to kill Mary and John, and came very close to doing it too. If it hadn't been for Grey and Neville, he might have done it. We don't know everything he can do, and we're not sure that what *we* can do is going to work on him."

Suki gazed earnestly into her face, and finally nodded. "I love you," she said, her big brown eyes growing bright with tears. "Please come back."

Nan gathered the child into her arms. "I love you, too. I will try my best."

Suki sobbed on her shoulder for just about a minute, then got her composure back, and Nan let her go, handing the child her own handkerchief. Suki sniffled into it and dried her eyes. "I'm goin' to go tell Sarah I love her now."

"Go do that," Nan urged, and watched, her heart aching, as the little girl pulled herself up bravely and trotted off to find Sarah and do just that. Like Nan, Suki had seen plenty of death before she found safe harbor with the girls. Like Nan, she understood it at a very young age. So she understood, far better than most people realized, that sometimes people don't come back from danger, no matter how badly they want to.

On the one hand, Nan would have liked very much to be able to take that knowledge from her.

On the other hand. . . .

Nan sighed, and went back to her map.

The meeting lasted from teatime through supper and beyond, but in the end nothing substantial came of it. Other than that now Lord Alderscroft was informed, that is. In the end, even he couldn't think of any way he could help them.

But to say he was gobsmacked by the idea that Sarah was a Spirit Master was an understatement. In fact, he was speechless for many minutes.

When he finally *did* speak it was with a rueful astonishment. "This makes complete sense," he said, shaking his head. "I can't believe I didn't see it before this. And yet—no one ever looks for Spirit Masters. They're ridiculously rare."

"I wish they were correspondingly powerful," Sarah sighed.

"No, you don't!" exclaimed the three other Elemental Masters in the room.

"Think of how much more powerful the necromancer would be if they were," Alderscroft pointed out.

Agansing, Selim, and Karamjit were not present this time; they had been unable to think of anything they could contribute to the discussion, so instead they had tasked themselves, and their nephews, with reinforcing the protections, physical and magical, on the school and its grounds.

"I do have a suggestion," Alderscroft said, after a moment. "There are certain associates of the Hunting Lodge who are . . . ah . . . rough-hewn . . ."

"You mean that since you took over the leadership, you've been seeking out and recruiting outside of the titled and wealthy," Mary put in with amusement. "Although why you can offer associate membership to street thugs and ruffians but not to women does escape me."

Alderscroft turned a bit red, but carried on. "The point is, these young men would be very useful to Nan and Sarah, and they are likely to warn away strictly mundane trouble by their mere presence."

"He's right," Mary admitted. "Especially if you both dress as boys."

"I wouldn't go—" Alderscroft began, but was interrupted by Memsa'b.

"I think that's a capital notion!" she enthused.

"As do I—especially since I understand Holmes himself had been giving you girls lessons in such disguises?" Sahib put in.

"He had," Sarah confirmed. "And I do like that idea. We were going to go as lads anyway, but we'll be a lot less conspicuous in a crowd of other lads, especially if they loiter along and stop to drink or smoke. And if they are magicians as well, that's all the better."

Alderscroft opened his mouth—probably to object—then shut it again, looked thoughtful, and nodded reluctantly. "Dash it all, that is a good idea. I don't like it one bit, because my sense of propriety is utterly revolted by it, but it is a capital idea. My propriety will have to reconcile itself. All right, the sooner we can get this search started, the better. John, Mary, I assume you want to be in London for this?"

They nodded.

"Then you'll stay with me in my townhouse. I'll telegraph the servants that I'm returning with guests. I assume the telegraph in the butler's pantry is still working?"

Memsa'b nodded. And once again Nan was struck by the fact that the very rich were so very different from her. When she needed to send a telegram, she went to the nearest post office to do so. She knew Alderscroft had wires strung to his bungalow, and it appeared he also still had them here.

"Nan and Sarah, would you rather work from your home or mine?" he continued.

"Yours, I think," Nan said, after deliberating for a moment. "I'd like to keep scrutiny as far from Mrs. Horace as possible. I don't *think* the necromancer has deduced we are working with

John and Mary, but it is better that he not associate our address with them if he has."

Alderscroft nodded, and turned to the Hartons. "For now, I cannot think of any role your associates can play except to stay alert and keep the children safe."

"Nor can we," Sahib agreed. "This is magic, and we are of little use to you in this."

"Then shall the five of us return to London tonight?" his Lordship asked. "While your hunt is safest done by daylight—"

"Well we *can* do a great deal by daylight," Nan offered. "We only need Caro's help when we find spots that are free of spirits. Sarah can tell they're there—or not—by day as well as by night."

"Only once we have those areas will we actually have anything to investigate," Sarah agreed.

"Good, that narrows things down a bit. Let's return to London tonight. I'll summon my ruffians in the morning and introduce you tomorrow evening and you can show them your plan. After that meeting, it will all be up to you." Alderscroft looked at the both ruefully. "I don't much care for not being in control of this, but I cannot see any other way. And it isn't as if you four haven't proven yourselves perfectly capable in the past."

Nan looked to Sarah, then they both nodded. "We'll get the birds and our things," said Sarah. "We'll be ready in an hour."

Alderscroft smiled a little. "I may not be psychical, but I had a premonition I would need the big carriage. I brought it from London to the bungalow, and rode in it over here tonight. We can continue this discussion as we drive."

As they went upstairs to their rooms, and Alderscroft went to telegraph his staff—or rather, he went with John Watson who, thanks to his Army experience, knew Morse code—Sarah shook her head at Nan. "You *told* me we'd need to bring our lad's clothing, and I didn't believe you."

"It was a hunch," Nan admitted. "Nothing more. But it's not as if it was going to take up much space in our cases."

They parted at their rooms and packed up everything they had so recently unpacked. Neville didn't even complain that his sleep was being interrupted. He jumped down from his perch as soon as Nan shut the latches on her case, strolled over to the open bird carrier, and settled down inside.

"Did you know this was going to happen?" she asked him before she closed the door.

He just opened one black eye, gave her a long look, and closed it again.

It was a little bit of a squeeze even in Alderscroft's big carriage to get them all inside, but Nan didn't think any of them minded. Thanks to his Lordship's telegraph ahead to his servants, when they arrived just past midnight everything was in readiness. There were even improvised perches in each of the girls' rooms, made of tobacco stands. There was one for each bird, with old newspapers spread beneath, and food and water cups where ashtrays would have been.

Nan had never stayed overnight in Alderscroft's townhouse before—there'd never been a need, since they already had a flat of their own here in London—and she was a little in awe of how luxurious it was. Despite the townhouse having been in his family for several generations, he must have had modern alterations made to it, as it had gaslights as well as the most up-to-date of bathrooms with hot and cold running water laid in. The room had been papered in neutral blue, gray, and white stripes, with soft carpets on the floor. She thought the furnishings were probably mahogany, and seating was upholstered to match the wallpaper. It was all very modern. There was, however, an oil lamp on the bedside table, so she wouldn't have to turn off the gas then stumble to her bed in the dark. She told the maid that she wouldn't need any assistance in getting undressed, did just that, had a brief wash, and slipped into her bed.

Her very luxurious bed. So luxurious, in fact, that she could scarcely believe how soft the bedding was. The sheets felt like cream on her skin. She hadn't thought she would be able to fall asleep in a strange bed, but she did, and slept soundly too.

So soundly that she didn't awaken until a maid tapped on the door and brought in breakfast on a tray. Breakfast! In bed! The only other time she'd had that had been in the winter when she'd gotten up long enough to poke the fires up if it had been her turn, wait for Mrs. Horace to bring up the food, make *herself* up a tray and scuttle back to bed to luxuriate in the warmth. She suspected on those mornings that Sarah did the same, but she was too busy eating toast while swathed to the ears in an eiderdown to check.

Despite having associated with his Lordship for quite a long time, this was the first time she'd gotten a glimpse of what his life might be like.

It was seductive, to tell the truth. And when the maid reappeared to take the tray again, and asked her diffidently if she needed assistance in dressing, and would she like a bath now or before dinner, it became even more seductive.

And for one tiny moment, she felt a torrent of envy wash over her.

But then she remembered the look on Alderscroft's face when she'd casually stated that she and Sarah were going to disguise themselves as young men. And it came over her how much her life would be restricted if she had been born into a family like this. She knew, from books, magazines, and the society articles in the newspapers, just how confined the life of a "mere" female was in these lofty families. A girl was inconsequential when young, valuable only when between the ages of sixteen and twenty-five, and thereafter, if not married, inconsequential again. And while that *might* be different in the families that boasted Elemental Magicians and Masters in their ranks, it wasn't going to be *that* much different.

In fact the reason that she and Sarah were useful to his Lordship was precisely because they hadn't been brought up like that. Alderscroft saw no need to impose the rules of his class on people who were—to be honest—of a much lower class.

I'd rather be me, she thought defiantly, then got dressed to go down and confer, at need, with Alderscroft.

Five young toughs clattered down the steps of the omnibus, laughing and elbowing each other. They were all attired mostly alike, with flat caps, second- or thirdhand and badly creased trousers, coats and vests, yellowed shirts, and scarves around their necks. They also wore thick, lace-up boots, the better to kick someone in the head with. They were also all wearing heavy leather belts with big metal buckles, which for most street gangs doubled as weapons.

Most of the noise was being made by three of the five as they hopped down to the pavement. Two were smaller, slimmer, and quieter than the rest, but the first three were making so much chatter that most probably no one would notice.

Sarah was one of the two quiet ones; Nan was the other. Sarah was quiet out of necessity, since she was concentrating on sensing ghosts. Nan was quiet to keep anyone from noticing she had a higher voice than the other three.

Those three were Eddie, a Fire Magician, Fred, an Air Master, and George, an Air Magician. Sarah liked them immediately on meeting them; despite how they were acting now, they had been cheeky but respectful with Alderscroft, and admiring when she and Nan proved they could defend themselves. George had taken an immediate fancy to Nan, impressed with how she handled her Gurkha knives. All three of them looked pretty much alike—light brown hair, blue eyes, round faces that showed they'd suffered the pinch of hunger now and again, at least in the past. George was a bit more handsome than the other two, but all of them were decent lookers.

"Left at the next corner," Fred said in an undertone, as they slouched their way down the street in a group, hands thrust into pockets, caps pushed back on their heads at a jaunty angle. Fred had the map with the serpentine route they were going to take laid out over the neighborhood served by the sewer system the bodies had washed out of. They planned to weave back and forth, advancing toward the river every time they turned, until they reached the Thames. Sarah didn't think that they'd make it all the way to the river today—but they might.

Neville was following along overhead; Grey had her claws fastened firmly in the cloth of Sarah's jacket shoulder. A parrot on someone's shoulder wasn't exactly a common sight around here, but Grey wasn't colorful, and might be overlooked. Sarah didn't want to take the chance that gulls, crows or jackdaws would attack Grey and hurt her before Neville could come to the rescue.

The group wasn't exactly moving at a brisk pace, but then, people were actually crossing to the other side of the street to avoid them, so it didn't matter. They *might* be in trouble if they met with another gang, but the boys didn't think that likely, not in daylight. And they planned to be off the street by nightfall.

Besides, the boys all knew which gangs held which districts, and if challenged, intended to give the right name.

Sarah didn't have much attention to spare for the "sights." Granted, she didn't have to slip into the spirit world, but she *did* have to devote most of her attention to "looking" for the faint signs of ghosts that were all she could "see" during the daylight hours.

Unsurprisingly, there were a lot of them. Most buildings had at least one. Usually there were several. When she concentrated, she got a sort of overlay of the spirit world onto the material one, and she could count them, since they scarcely moved during the day. It was much easier to do this than it used to be. She wondered whether Puck's "kiss for luck" had anything to do with that.

As far as she could tell, most ghosts were recent, the confused little shades of children that died suddenly and, for whatever reason, whether through fear or bewilderment at suddenly finding that no one could see or hear them, missed passing over to the other side. Or at least, missed passing over initially. Most of them seemed to disappear within a few days to a few months, or at least that was what she had noticed in her neighborhood, so she had the feeling these little ones often got escorted when they couldn't find their way on their own.

But there were plenty of older spirits here too. After all, the East End had been a terrible place to live since the 1700s, and there were plenty of people who *wouldn't* cross over, knowing what their likely "welcome" would be. But of course, as the years went on, these spirits grew tattered and faded, and eventually. . . .

Well, she actually didn't really know what happened to them "eventually," unless what happened was someone like her. She could open doors and trick them across the threshold—according to Alderscroft, she could *force* them over the threshold too, but only if she herself was in the spirit world. But when there wasn't someone like her? She had no idea. Did they just fade and vanish? Did they lose whatever tenacious hold they had on the material plane and get pulled over?

All things to explore another day. Right now, their presence was the marker that what she was looking for wasn't here.

She lost track of time as they all sauntered along, the lads occasionally calling out compliments to women they saw and laughing when the woman either hurried away or made an equally cheeky response. Shopkeepers moved into the entrances of their shops to block the gang from entering as they passed. Finally, Fred said "Left here," and they turned a corner, walked for a while, and then—

There it was, off to the left: an area without a single ghost in it.

"Stop," she whispered.

They didn't actually *stop*. They slowed until they found a good place to loiter, a building with a blank wall to lean against. Sarah and Fred did just that, while the other three stood as a screen between them and the rest of the street, talking and smoking— and drinking a little out of hip flasks. She and Fred sketched out the rough area on the map where there were no ghosts, and when she was satisfied, he gave the signal to move on again.

She was used to doing a lot of walking, but by the time they reached the river, she was footsore, hot, and wanting a bath so badly she could hardly bear it.

But it was about an hour till sunset, and they actually had managed to cover the entire area, finding five spots free of spirits.

Now they walked along the embankment, heading for something else entirely—a Thames waterman with a boat big enough to ferry five, tied up at a particular spot on the bank. The tide was in, which made this possible, since there weren't many watermen willing to risk damaging their craft on the rocky, debris- and garbage-strewn shoreline at low tide. By this time Sarah's feet hurt so much she could hardly bear it, and shoes that had been too large at the beginning of this trek were now tight.

The waterman, a weather-beaten, graying specimen wearing an outfit identical to theirs and a suspicious scowl, was tied up at the bottom of a set of stone stairs nearly identical to the ones they'd used to get to the river when John Watson had called up a Jenny Greenteeth. "Alderscroft sent us," Fred called from the top of the stairs, which turned the scowl into a grudging nod.

"Good. Git in," the waterman replied, and they made their way carefully down the slippery, wet stairs and gingerly clambered into the boat, arranging themselves on the plank seats according to his direction. Sarah was alone in the prow when the waterman untied the boat, tossed her the rope, and skillfully began rowing upriver. Just getting off her feet nearly brought tears of relief to her eyes. Grey, who had been completely silent all this time, bent down and caressed her cheek with her beak. "Home soon," the parrot said soothingly, as Neville flew over a roof and down to Nan's shoulder.

"*Arrr! Pirates!*" Neville said cheerfully, surprising a laugh from the waterman.

"Yer a cheeky bugger, ain't ye?" he called over his shoulder to where Nan was sitting behind him.

"*I'm a right old barstard,*" Neville replied, making the waterman laugh harder. "*Gi' us a kiss, sweetheart!*"

"Blimey," the waterman said, bending his head to wipe the tears of laughter out of his eyes on his shoulder. "If I'd known I was gonna get a music 'all show, I'd'a paid th' Lion, 'steada 'im payin' me."

"Don't encourage him," Nan cautioned, but it was too late. Neville was in rare form, tossing off quips that had the waterman wheezing by the time they pulled up to the dock at the end of their journey. Sarah made the rope fast to a wooden ladder, and one by one, starting with her, they made their way up it to a wooden walkway.

The walkway passed between two buildings and came out on the street, where a carriage was waiting. "This's where we leave ye fer now," Fred said cheerfully. "Might be seein' ye if ye need us fer escort, like."

They all shook hands solemnly, Fred passed the map to Nan, and the three lads went on their way, while Sarah and Nan climbed into the carriage.

"Oh, my feet," Nan groaned.

"I *know*," Sarah echoed. Since the carriage had two seats, they sat across from each other and rested their poor aching feet on the seat opposite. The birds perched on their legs, while they leaned back.

"I want a bath and a foot soak," Sarah added after a moment. "We walked everywhere in Wales—why are our feet so sore now?"

"Paving," Nan told her. "I'm just glad we were wearing these heavy boots. Can you imagine what our feet would have felt like in ladies' boots?"

"Agony. Thank God we won't have to do this again."

The carriage didn't drop them at the front of the townhouse; instead it went around to the carriage house in the back, because obviously a couple of young ruffians would not be allowed inside the front door. They came in through the back entrance, and the servants, who had been told what to expect, hurried them up to their rooms. This time Sarah accepted the help of the maid in getting out of her clothing, especially her shoes. The maid *tsk*ed over the state of her swollen feet, immediately poured the washbasin of fine china full of cool water from the ewer for her to soak her feet in, and hurried off in search of something to add to the water, while Sarah unbound her breasts and pulled a cotton wrapper on over her chemise and knickers.

Then she sat down and gingerly put her feet into the basin.

It felt like heaven.

The maid returned in a few moments with a larger basin and a pail of steaming water. "Miss Nan is having a bath," the girl reported. "So we'll soak your feet until she is finished, and I'll draw you another."

"God bless you, Lily," Sarah sighed as the maid put the tin basin down on the floor with a towel under it next to an easy chair, prepared the basin with the hot water, poured the water out of the china basin into the larger, tin one to temper the heat, and added mineral salts. Sarah walked over to the armchair, put her feet into the hot water, and sat back.

And the next thing she knew, the water was cold and the maid was shaking her, telling her that her bath was ready.

After one of Lord Alderscroft's amazing dinners, the girls, the Watsons, and Lord Alderscroft gathered in his study over the map.

"More than I like, but fewer than I feared," Alderscroft pronounced.

"This certainly has yielded better fruit than anything I could have suggested," Watson agreed. "All right, tomorrow I'll unleash

Irregulars to find places we can safely put Nan and Sarah. Should we do our initial investigations by day?"

Alderscroft looked at Sarah. "Will daylight be all right?" he asked.

"The spirit world doesn't have day or night," she replied. "Daylight should present no problems—except that when we actually *do* determine which of these sites belongs to the necromancer, we will have to be exceedingly careful. He'll be awake, and he might sense us."

"But it will be safer in the material world during the day."

"I can't argue with that," Sarah admitted. "But the real question is, when we find this, and if we escape undetected, what is our plan of attack?"

Alderscroft hesitated for a moment. "I have done a little more research into necromancy," he said, finally. "And although it is perfectly possible for a necromancer to bind and use or use up spirits on a temporary basis, if he wants to continue using them, it appears he needs a part of their former physical body."

Sarah didn't quite understand his hesitation. "Yes? And—"

It was Nan who understood what he was hinting at, and both her hands flew to her mouth in horror. "Oh my God! *The heads!* He's collected the heads!"

Alderscroft nodded. "Exactly. All this time we had been wondering why he beheaded his victims. Now we know. Or at least, I am fairly sure we know."

Sarah suddenly felt sick. "So . . . wherever he is, he is probably keeping the heads, or what's left of them, in his workroom?"

"That's the most likely. And while this is extremely unsettling, this is actually good for us."

"Of course it is!" John Watson exclaimed, pounding the arm of his chair. "We can use Lestrade, the Yard, and the local constables!"

"Exactly my thought," Alderscroft agreed. "The only question is how you give them a reasonable explanation of how we found the bounder."

"It's going to involve a lot of lying," Watson said ruefully.

"Well," said Mary. "Sherlock's explanations usually begin with dirt."

"That's as good a place to start as any. I'll make up some gibberish about the composition of some earth we found—oh bother. Where? It's usually on the bottoms of shoes, but obviously that won't work."

"The shoes were too big on a couple of those girls," Sarah recalled. "In the paper stuffed in the toes?"

John nodded. "All right, earth. Now how do we narrow that down to *that* house? I'm going to assume it's a house. I cannot imagine anyone beheading young girls in a flat and getting away with it for long."

"White threads from their gowns caught on the side of that sewer exit into the Thames?" Mary suggested. "I can't think why anyone in the East End would waste perfectly good fabric by sending it into the sewer, so any thread, we can say, would have to come from their clothing."

"That's a start . . ."

From there, they considered and discarded a number of possible explanations that might have led Sherlock to hit upon a particular dwelling. Finally Nan snapped her fingers.

"We're making this too complicated," she said. "The easiest is that someone complained about Chinese girls going into the house. While an East Ender might be able to afford a servant girl, they're absolutely not going to hire a 'heathen Chinee.' And they'd resent anyone else who did."

"Oh! And that's another point," Mary exclaimed. "John, you said you can't imagine anyone being able to get away with this who has rented a flat, so it must be a house. Well, all we have to do is tell the Irregulars to make sure to look for houses in those five areas. If there aren't any, we can eliminate the areas that don't."

Alderscroft raised his leonine head with a look of triumph. "Excellent," he said. "We have our plan for the next stage, and we have the means to surround the place with Police and the Yard. On that note, I think we have earned our rest.".

19

Nan, at least, woke the next day with aching calves and feet, so gladly took breakfast in bed followed by a soak in a hot bath, followed by going back to bed and begging the pardon of Alderscroft due to indisposition. Neville regarded her with sympathy from his perch, after having his own breakfast of chopped meat. She had just settled in when the housekeeper knocked on the door and came bustling into her room with a basket over her arm.

"Now, miss, I have just the thing for those feet," she said. "That is, if you don't mind servant's remedies—"

"Good gad, no," Nan responded immediately.

"Well, we're on our feet morning till night, and some of us aren't as young or as light as we used to be," she said with a laugh. "So I've brought you some things."

"Some things" proved to be quite a lot. More herbs and salts to put in a foot bath, a salve that smelled of lavender and peppermint to rub all over her feet and ankles, and salicylate powder to take with water. By luncheon the aches had subsided to the point where walking was bearable again, and she went down.

"Ah good, you're feeling better," said John Watson, looking up from his meal. "I've sent the Irregulars out, and we can expect a report by teatime."

"That soon?" she said with surprise, sitting next to Sarah and accepting the offer of something she didn't recognize from the footman. Whatever it was, it was very good.

"They're efficient, those lads," Watson chuckled. "Young Tommy has them all coordinated, splitting up to canvass every inch of the place and report back to him. He'll bring us the précis."

"I think they must be the secret to Sherlock's success," Sarah chuckled.

"He certainly couldn't do without them," John agreed. "They've been mourning him, you know. I thought Tommy would break down in front of me when he said it would 'do them all a bit'a good to be *doin'* agin.' I very nearly told him the truth."

No one needed to caution him not to do that.

Evidently as soon as luncheon was over, everyone had the same idea—go to Alderscroft's magical library, a room separate from the library that any guest might go to and browse through. John and Mary both seemed to know what they wanted and made for two different sections. Sarah consulted the catalogue and made her own selection. That left Nan, indecisive.

Finally she, too, consulted the catalogue, not really certain what she was looking for until she spotted it—and it turned out, when she looked for the book, that John Watson had it already.

Bother.

"Here," said Mary Watson, and handed her a leather-bound book with a few places already marked. "Annals of the London Hunting Lodge. I've marked the places where they encountered necromancers."

"Thank you," Nan said with gratitude, then perused the handwritten volume until teatime.

They were just finishing up when Tommy Wiggins turned up. And although they were all more than eager to hear his results, after seeing his longing gaze at the remains of their tea they sat him down and stuffed him with tea and sandwiches and biscuits until it looked as if he was satisfied.

"All right, Wiggins," said John. "Report."

Tommy pulled a somewhat grimy and much-folded copy of the map out of his pocket and spread it out on the table. "'Ere, 'ere an 'ere, there ain't no 'ouses," he said, pointing to ghostless areas on the map that he had put a large "X" through. "In fact, there ain't no flats, neither. Just rooms."

"That already makes our lives easier," Mary exclaimed. Tommy nodded.

"Now, Oi made a liddle number every place where they wuz a room, cuz they ain't no 'otels near them two good places," he continued, and pulled another piece of folded paper from his other pocket. "'Ere's th' list uv th' landladies. If hits gotta star arter th' name, hit's a good 'un, 'cause the landlady don't care long as she gets 'er money. Arf of 'em are drunks, an' th' rest rents t' hoors." He suddenly realized who he was talking to, because he got very red, and mumbled, "Beggin' yer pardon ma'am, miss."

"'Ere naow, 'oo ye think yer talkin' to, Tommy Wiggins?" asked Nan in her best street accents. "Me mam wuz a hoor, I knows the word!"

Tommy stared at her with a look of shock on his face, while Sarah and Mary giggled, although Mary was every bit as red as Tommy.

He gulped. "Yiss, miss," he said, then gathered his courage in both hands and went on. "T'other ones 'ud do in a pinch, but they're nosy parkers. If'n one feller and three gels goes traipsin' up stairs, they're like to wanta know why."

Watson picked up the list and perused it, then looked at the map. "I think there's enough incurious ones to satisfy our requirements," he said, and handed Tommy a soft leather purse that jingled. "The usual distribution to the lads, and many thanks, my boy." Tommy took it, shoved it in his pocket, slapped his cap back on his head and stood up. "Thenkee guv'nor," he said. "An' thanks from th' lads."

The footman showed Tommy Wiggins the way out and they all crowded around the map. "This one is closer," Sarah pointed out, her finger on the map. "I think there's enough time before sundown to investigate it."

John Watson straightened up and looked at her sternly. "There is, but *only* if you promise that if you find something, you don't linger to take a better look at it."

Sarah held up her hand, as if making a pledge. "I promise. And I'll have Nan and Caro with me to keep me sensible."

"All right then." John perused the map again. "We can take a growler and not be conspicuous to *here,* and walk to the first of the starred lodgings *here.*"

Nan tried not to groan at the word "walk." "I'm ready now," she said, instead.

"As am I," replied Sarah.

John looked all three women over to make sure they would not stand out in that part of the East End. They must have passed muster, because he nodded. "All right then," he said. "Let's go."

Tommy had been right. The landlady looked as if she'd already downed a full bottle of gin by the time they got there and was starting another. She clearly was not in the least interested in why they wanted her room, only that they had the money. Once the fourpence she demanded went down the front of her dress, presumably to rest between two pillow-like breasts, she waved them to the rickety stairs and said "Nummer Tree" and paid no more attention to them.

"Number three" boasted a completely filthy bed and two hard wooden chairs, and nothing more. The window was covered in brown parcel paper, and there was neither candle nor oil lamp. Nan had come prepared however, with a bag that held a number of useful objects. This was not the first time she'd been in such lodgings, although the last time had been much more than a decade ago. She spread a waxed oilcloth over the top of the bed; hopefully any bugs, bedbug or otherwise, would have a hard time getting through that. Then she and Sarah laid down; it was a straw mattress but at least the oilcloth kept the ends from poking them. John wrenched the window open and the birds flew in to perch on the foot of the bed. She shut her eyes—

And didn't even have time to relax before she was *yanked* into the spirit world.

"Oi!" she said indignantly, glaring at Sarah who was still holding her ghostly hand.

They stood in the faded, gray spirit-world version of this room. Caro stood at the foot of the bed, petting Grey's spirit self. Grey seemed to enjoy it.

"I'm sorry," Sarah murmured. "I'm just in a hurry to get on with this."

"So am I," said Caro. *"I believe we want to go that way."* She

pointed, not to the window, but to the wall opposite.

Nan took a moment to get her bearings. "I think you're right," she said. "Lead on."

They were accompanied by a swarm of sylphs as well as Neville and Grey. Once they drifted out of the building, the sylphs flew on ahead of them, playing scout, as they had the last time the girls had made a similar excursion.

Once again, Caro was dressed as a boy, with her bow in her hand and her quiver hanging from her belt. Nan gave her a sideways look. Caro shrugged. *This feels right. I think I was meant to be a boy,*" she said. Nan nodded, and turned her attention to the environment around them.

The gray and misty streets looked pretty much like the last time they'd ventured here into the spirit realm; empty of traffic or any sign of all the people that there were in the material world. There were, however, more ghosts. Many, many more ghosts than there had been in their home neighborhood. Most of them were sad little children wandering aimlessly down the empty streets. The rest were tattered wisps, vaguely shaped like humans. No threat there.

But that didn't mean there might not *be* a threat, as they moved further away from their bodies.

They hurried in the direction of the "ghost-free" zone, trying not to attract any attention. But it appeared that didn't matter. Nothing was giving them any attention anyway. The sad little ghosts met up in the streets sometimes, and seemed to talk for a bit, then began wandering again. Were they looking for home? Parents? Siblings? They began to prey on Nan's mind, and she knew that Sarah wanted to stop and send every single one of them onwards—but they couldn't stop to do that. "Sarah, at least these spirits aren't hungry and cold anymore," she murmured, when Sarah paused once again to look at a pair of little girls holding hands.

Sarah nodded, stiffened her shoulders, and moved on.

It was odd that they hadn't yet encountered anything clearly dangerous, as they had on their first foray. Perhaps that might be because the spirits *were* affected by day and night in the material world, and only the most harmless ones wandered by day, leaving the dangerous ones to appear by night.

Maybe it was because they were just lucky about their route, and it didn't intersect with any of the dangerous spirits. She began to feel fairly confident, however, and pushed the pace a little.

Until suddenly, Caro stopped.

Sarah looked at her askance. "We're not that far from the locket," she objected.

"That's not it. There's something in there—calling me. If I go any closer, I don't think I can resist it—" And in fact, Caro started to back up. *"I've got to go back!"* she said, in something a little like panic. *"If I don't—"* She didn't finish the sentence.

Then she was gone, fleeing back toward the rented lodging.

"Do you feel anything?" Sarah asked Nan. Nan shook her head.

"No," croaked Neville, and Grey shook her head as well.

"So . . . it's not the ghosts." Sarah looked in the direction of the center of the zone. "It could be the necromancer. . . ."

"But we need to be sure," Nan pointed out. "We can't go back now, not when all that we know is that there is something in that direction that called to Caro." Sarah sighed with relief; clearly she felt the same way.

But they proceeded with utmost caution; whatever was there was strong enough to influence Caro at the distance of about half a mile, and all they knew about it was that it "called" to ghosts.

None of the sylphs had returned. Was that because they had nothing to report? Or was it because they'd been trapped by whatever was in there?

Finally they drew near to the center of the roughly circular area on the map. On their map, that center had been occupied by an unprepossessing Methodist chapel; a small, plain building that could barely hold thirty people if they all stood very closely together.

But as soon as they clapped eyes on it, they knew why this was a ghost-free zone.

The front door of the chapel had been replaced with something else. A Door. The kind that Sarah created, but much brighter, and clearly much more powerful, if Caro could feel it at the very edge of the zone.

And, just as clearly, it was imbued with some sort of magic that called ghosts to it.

The Door was beautiful; it poured its brilliant light out onto the street, a light pure, silvery, and welcoming. The sylphs sat or hovered in front of it, as if they were warming themselves by a fire on a cold day. There was no doubt in Nan's mind that whatever had made that door was good. There was also no doubt in her mind that it was not something for her. Not yet, anyway.

"I think—" Sarah said, hesitantly. "I think that there must have been a Methodist minister in the past who was also a Spirit Master, and he put this in place to last past his own death, so he could go on helping lost ghosts." She sighed. "I can hear it singing."

Nan cocked her head to the side, and . . . listened. And even *she* could hear it, faintly, a siren song of peace and promise. Even the sylphs seemed entranced, though when Sarah called them, they came flitting back to her side readily enough.

"Well," Sarah said, a little deflated. "It's not a necromancer."

"But that means we now know where he is," said Nan.

"I have a proposal," said John, when they reached Lord Alderscroft's townhouse and joined him for tea. "Is it logical to assume our necromancer is at the center of the remaining blank area?"

Sarah looked thoughtful. "I suppose it is," she agreed.

"Then I would like to talk to Lestrade and have him send a few men to scout the area—" John began.

"I have a much better idea," Alderscroft interrupted him. "I'll send Fred, George, and Eddie. They won't attract any attention and they won't look like constables. What is it you want to know?"

"What it looks like. Doors, primarily. Windows too, any points of exit. I don't want to come this far and have the blackguard escape us." There was a deep anger under his words, and Nan didn't blame him. "Actually I'd like them to do that for every house on that block. Just in case the one we want isn't in the exact center." Alderscroft nodded.

"You're right. And once the girls do *their* reconnoiter we'll know which house is the correct one. We've come too far. The last thing we want is to slip up by being careless. You go speak to Lestrade and let him know we think we're close to finding the bounder. I'll contact the lads."

John took his hat and left the room, Alderscroft a few paces behind him. Nan, Sarah, and Mary looked at each other and sighed.

"Well, all right then. Is there anything *we* can do?" Mary asked.

"Complain about being made redundant," Nan said sourly. "Men!"

"Well, Lestrade won't listen to us," Mary pointed out. "It was all very well when it was 'please help me solve this,' but once he thinks he has a chance of closing this case, he won't listen to a mere female telling him 'wait, wait'."

Nan snorted, but agreed. "You're right, he won't. And he *will* listen to John, because he knows John is backed by Alderscroft."

"*And* Mycroft Holmes," Sarah added. "Well, is there anything we can do in the meantime?"

"You're in a new area of London," Mary pointed out. "*You* can certainly practice your skills as a Spirit Master by crossing over, building a Door, and either leading or forcing spirits through it."

"Oh . . . that's right. I can." Sarah brightened. "Nan do you—"

"Do you actually need me? If you do, I'll go, but to tell you the truth, I don't like that place and I'd rather stay out of it." The words were out of her mouth before she thought, but as soon as she spoke them, Nan realized they were the truth. She hated the spirit plane. And she'd much rather not go there again until she had to. Besides—

"I do have Caro," Sarah said thoughtfully, as though she had just picked the words out of Nan's head.

"Exactly!" Perhaps Sarah had been afraid that Nan would feel jealousy; all she felt was relief that *she* wouldn't have to go, and that Caro could do just as good a job of protecting Sarah as Nan could. Better, perhaps. "And if anything happens, you can send Grey back to get me."

"In that case, I'll take a book and come sit in your room to keep an eye on things and send my sylphs with you. They can bring me messages as well as Grey can," Mary offered.

"There. Everything is taken care of," Nan told her.

"But what are you going to do?" Sarah asked.

She smiled. "Probably scandalize his Lordship's servants by practicing my knife and stick work."

And that was exactly what she did. There was a bit of walled-in yard at the rear of the townhouse. She changed into her practice clothing and did all the exercises Agansing, Gupta, and Karamjit had taught her. Selim did not have as much to teach her, because he had a knife style of his own and didn't want to interfere with the Gurkha style Agansing was teaching her. Gupta taught her short stick, and Karamjit taught her staff.

She caught sight of some of the servants gawking at her from the windows and kitchen door before the housekeeper or cook shooed them back to their work.

She soon discovered what they thought of her. When she finally finished, dripping with sweat and more than ready for a bath, and walked in through the kitchen door, all the work stopped. The kitchen staff—all female, since unlike many of the rich or noble, Alderscroft employed a cook rather than a chef—stared at her with wide eyes.

She stopped in the middle of the kitchen grounded her staff, and said "Ask me anything."

The staff looked to the cook. The cook tried to look stern, failed, and said, "Fifteen minutes by me timer, *if* ye keep workin'!"

"Miss!" the girl in charge of chopping vegetables raised her hand, then dropped it to go back to chopping. "What was ye doin'?"

She explained the three fighting styles she had been practicing, and after that the questions came thick and fast. Finally, when the fifteen minutes were almost over, the scullery maid, up to the elbow in suds and greasy pots, asked wistfully, "Could *we* learn thet?"

"Not this, no," Nan said, to sighs of disappointment, "But if you want to learn how to protect yourselves, I can teach you some simple things that will make anyone that tries to snatch your purse or interfere with you regret the day he was born."

"Ye'd do that?" the cook said, wonderingly.

"Happily." She held up a hand as the babble started. "I'm doing something for his Lordship right now, but as soon as that is over, we'll arrange an hour a day, or every other day, and I'll come over to teach you."

With that, she left the kitchen buzzing, feeling an odd sense of accomplishment.

* * *

A hot bath and a change of clothing later—Lily carried away the practice clothing with the promise that even though it wasn't laundry day, she would have them clean and dry by tomorrow— Nan checked on Sarah. Grey looked like a stuffed parrot, she sat so still. Mary Watson looked up from her book, smiled and nodded. That left Nan free to call Neville in from where he was hanging about on the rooftops bullying the jackdaws and bring him inside to do more research in Lord Alderscroft's library until dinner. She didn't find a great deal of information she could actually use, unfortunately, and she looked over at Neville, who sat on the back of a chair with a bit of newspaper under him. "I'm beginning to feel rather useless," she confessed to him. "My talents don't seem to have a great deal of application right now."

"Hurr," Neville agreed.

"I think I am a bit jealous that she can do all these new things," Nan continued, then shrugged. "Then again, it means she has to spend time in the spirit plane. Thank you, no."

Neville bobbed his head.

Their conversation was interrupted by a footman, who had come to tell her that "The gentlemen are back, miss, and dinner will be served in fifteen minutes."

A moment later Sarah appeared, looking—contented.

"How many?" Nan asked.

"Lots," Sarah replied. "I lost count. I can't imagine why Lord Alderscroft never noticed this house had six separate ghosts in it!"

"I suspect they stayed out of his way," Nan observed. "Servants?"

"I think so. Most of them were just threads of their former selves." Sarah reached up to her shoulder to give Grey a head scratch. "I could do this a great deal, I think. Or I could find out how that Methodist minister made that permanent Door and start placing them all over London."

"Well, right now you can turn around and come with me to dinner," Nan told her, holding out her arm to Neville, who hopped to it with three flaps of his wings.

They reached the dining room just as the butler was poised to sound the gong. "Everyone's here, Charles, I don't think we need that," Alderscroft said. "We'll just go in now and you can serve."

Alderscroft waited until they had all been served the first course. "The lads will have us exterior plans of the houses by midmorning tomorrow. So that's done. John?"

"I managed to hold Lestrade off, but it was a near thing. There've been more bodies turning up, and he was ready to marshal a small army and search every house in that block—and I have to say I was tempted to let him." John paused while he finished his soup. "We won't be able to hold him off for long."

"Then we should get to that lodging house as early as we can tomorrow morning," said Nan, and Sarah nodded. "The sooner we can confirm the exact location of the necromancer, the sooner we can let Lestrade unleash his hounds."

Nan was amazed at the level of professionalism of Alderscroft's servants. Here they were, discussing Inspector Lestrade of Scotland Yard as casually as Mrs. Horace spoke of her butcher, and talking about necromancers, and they weren't turning a hair. The reactions of the kitchen staff were fairly extraordinary, too. They'd wanted to know how *they* could be trained, and hadn't reacted with horror or affrontery at the sight of a woman doing what she had been doing.

Or maybe it was something else entirely. It would make good sense for a man like Alderscroft to have carefully tutored his staff in the basics of some magic, so they would be prepared for the unusual.

And it wasn't as if they could gossip about this to other servants. Who would believe them?

"We haven't got much of a plan once we *do* discover where he is," John observed. "Just you and some members of the Lodge watching the front door, while Lestrade, the Yard, and the local constables break in the back, and Sarah, Nan, and Caro keep watch to try to prevent him from any dirty work until he's in irons."

Alderscroft made a face, but it was Nan who replied. "We can't do much more of a plan than that, John. Do any of you actually know what a powerful necromancer can do?"

They all shook their heads. "And we also do not know what he has *been* doing, besides murdering girls. The way they are dressed suggests he is performing some sort of ceremony that I am not familiar with," Alderscroft added.

"So we clearly don't know what we need to prepare for," Nan pointed out. "That's the other reason for our foray. To see if we can deduce that."

"I'm ready, and so is Caro," Sarah said confidently.

"Then the best thing we can do is get a good night's sleep and start early in the morning, and see what happens from there," said Alderscroft. "Next course, please, Charles."

"We," of course, did not include Alderscroft, Nan noted wryly as she rose with the sun in the morning. She was dressed long before Lily arrived to see if she needed help, and went quickly downstairs to fortify herself for the expedition to come.

They were, of course, all dressed very shabbily, and got into the carriage in the carriage house to avoid anyone seeing a lot of tramps leaving the house. The driver made sure there were no witnesses when he dropped them off as well, just outside an East End warehouse.

This time the person in charge of the fourpence lodgings was a man instead of a woman, but he was just as incurious as the woman had been once their fourpence was his.

The room showed every sign of having been used last night, and why it was vacant now, Nan had no idea. But at least in this room there was glass in the windows, and the mattress on the bed was cleaner.

This time Nan was ready for Sarah's impatient tug, pulling her into the spirit plane. There were not nearly as many ghosts this time, either, which made Nan wonder what it was about that other neighborhood that had made it so thick with them. Had their been a cholera outbreak? That would certainly account for all the children.

They had chosen a lodging as near to the edge of the ghostless zone as they could, and within a few streets it had gone from the usual East End squalor to a better neighborhood altogether. There were actual *houses* here, just as John had predicted. Proper, detached and semidetached *houses*. To be fair, this was hardly the East End at all, not as Nan would have called it, but it was served by the same sewer system as the real slums were.

"Are you hearing or feeling anything like you did the last time?" Sarah asked Caro.

"No, not at all," the ghost replied, shaking her head. *"If there's a door to the other side around here, it's certainly not calling me."*

Encouraged by this—and by the utter emptiness of the streets—they stopped trying to be stealthy and just moved as swiftly as they physically could. Which still wasn't as fast as they could run, or even walk, in the real world. It was as if there was something here that resisted them moving about. Perhaps it was just the link to their physical bodies holding them back, although the birds seemed to have no trouble flying.

They had both memorized the street map and were on "foot," following it religiously to the center of the zone. And then they turned the last corner, and there was absolutely no doubt that they had found their goal.

The house—the second from the corner—had a sort of "anti-glow" to it. If shadow could radiate, that's what this house did.

"Something tells me we're going to have trouble getting through the walls," Nan murmured. Sarah shrugged.

"I'll see what I can do," she said. "But first, let's try."

They walked up to the side of the house, and it was exactly like walking into the side of a normal house. Caro actually bounced off, landing on her rump. *"Ow!"* she exclaimed, rubbing her head where she had banged it against the wall. *"I—didn't know this was possible!"*

Sarah slid her hands over the wall; Nan had no idea what she was doing, but evidently she had something in mind. "The power and protections aren't evenly distributed," she said. "It's thinning out as I move toward the corner."

"Why?" Nan asked.

"Magic likes circles," Sarah replied absently. "Let's see if we can get through the corner."

The moved along the side of the house to the corner, with Sarah keeping one hand on the wall the entire time. "It's definitely thinner here," she said with satisfaction as they reached the corner. She put her hand against the wall there, and pushed. Slowly her hand, then her lower arm, then her other hand and arm disappeared. Then she pushed her entire self past the wall and disappeared. Grey followed, though she managed to get through faster. Without hesitation, Nan placed both hands on the walls, one on either side of the corner and pushed as hard as she could, Neville on her shoulder.

All of a sudden, whatever she was pushing on "gave," and she tumbled into a sitting room on the other side of the wall. Neville jumped off her shoulder as she fell, and ran out of the way. A moment later Caro stumbled through as well.

"I'm sorry I couldn't tell you—I was working on making a temporary opening," Sarah apologized, as Nan picked herself up off the floor.

"Never mind that—what in the name of God are *those*?" Nan pointed at the farther wall, where a faint suggestion of a glass-fronted cabinet stood. Crowded onto where the shelves would be were . . . things.

Some of them glowed, and not in any way that seemed healthy, or anything but *wrong*. Some of them moved—not a lot, but enough that Nan had the impression the things were alive.

All of them were contained inside tiny bubbles of power. All of them were half-in, half-out of the spirit world and clearly magical in some nature.

"The sign we have the right place, I suspect," said Caro. *"Let's see what else we can find."*

"No, not yet," Sarah overruled. "We need to be physically closer to this place before we take a deeper look. And I think we need Lestrade's men and the Lodge. Let's go."

20

"I still don't know about this rally point business," Lestrade muttered, as one of his men, an expert locksmith, broke into the back door of a vacant house about a block from their target.

"Well, we can coordinate our forces here, where we are close to the target, can make changes in our plans easily, and can slip up on the house in twos and threes, thus giving the quarry no warning, or we can do it in the police station, and draw attention to ourselves when we all roll up in Black Marias, thus giving the quarry a chance to escape," John Watson pointed out.

Lestrade sighed. He still wasn't reconciled to Alderscroft's "Queen's Special Agents," which was what he was claiming the members of his Hunting Lodge were. And he didn't at all like breaking into private property to take it over, even for a day.

He'd have been even more upset if he'd known the three "lads" that were along as "Special Agents" were Mary Watson, Nan and Sarah. But Alderscroft had a paper signed by the Prime Minister (courtesy of Mycroft Holmes) authorizing him to do this, and another from the Chief Inspector tell him to cooperate, so he really didn't have any choice in the matter.

The lock yielded, and both parties traipsed in. Alderscroft immediately set up in the kitchen, since there was still a huge wooden table in the middle of it—it was so big that clearly the reason why it was still there was that it was impossible to fit through the door. One of the Lodge spread out a detailed map of the area. Everyone crowded around, obscuring the fact that Mary, Nan and Sarah slipped away, found the staircase, and went up to find a room on the side nearest the target house.

The house was overly warm due to the closed windows, and smelled a little of mildew and dust. But at least it didn't smell of mice.

Mary spread a comforter on the floor to make it a little less punishing to lie on and dropped two small pillows on it, while Nan opened the window, and the birds flew in, bringing a welcome breeze of fresh air with them. They hadn't had the birds with them, of course. That would have been a complete giveaway to Lestrade that two of the "men" weren't what they seemed. But Nan had been very nervous the entire time the arrangements were being organized; if they couldn't get into place by sunset, they'd have had to smuggle the birds in their jackets and take the risk of being spotted.

Nan was barely lying down when she found herself back in the spirit world with Sarah, Caro, and the birds already there and waiting impatiently. Getting their bearings, they hurried toward the house. Contacting Lestrade and Alderscroft and summoning the Lodge and Lestrade's men had taken a much longer time than any of them had liked. The sun was about to set—and while that would make surrounding the house and setting watch on the front and back doors a great deal easier for the combined forces of Lestrade and Alderscroft, they were now entering the necromancer's favored hours, putting him at a distinct advantage. Even Caro sensed that the situation was a good deal grimmer now; her face was set in an expression of determination, and she had none of her quips ready. She just listened to the plans, nodded, and followed.

They forced their way inside at the corner of the house, and already there was a change. The strange objects in the sitting room moved restlessly inside their confining bubbles; when they saw the girls, some of them even flung themselves against the sides of their prisons, as if trying to attack.

When they came to a stair leading up, and a door that presumably led to the cellar in the wall opposite, Nan looked at Sarah. "Up or down?" she asked quietly.

"The last magician we dealt with had his workroom in the cellar," she pointed out.

"Down it is," Nan said, when Caro held out her hand to stop them.

"Can't you feel it? And hear it?" the ghost asked.

Nan tried, and had to shake her head. "Nothing—"

"No, Caro's right," Sarah said. "It's faint, but it's there. Something . . . nasty. And it's up, not down. The top floor, I think."

Nan shrugged, and turned to lead the way up the stairs.

Only to encounter a door at the top of the stairs leading to the third floor. "Huh . . . I think you must be right," she said, "I can't imagine why there'd be a door here unless there was something to hide." She hesitantly laid her hand on the door, and after a moment of resistance her hand went right through it. "And whatever magic is on the outside of the house isn't on the inside nearly as strongly."

But Caro and Sarah had both gone into a defensive crouch, as if they both sensed the enemy near. *"It's close,"* Caro whispered. *"We need to be really, really careful."*

"Well . . . we can go through walls. Let's go through a wall instead of a door. And let's put our heads through first. . . ." Nan suggested.

"From near the ceiling and hope whatever is in there won't look up." The tension in Sarah's voice put the hair up on the back of Nan's neck. Whatever she could sense was not good. Nan took a tentative sniff of the air to see if she could at least *smell* anything, and at that point realized that the spirit world was devoid of any scent whatsoever. It was just chill, mostly quiet, and very dim, as if the entire world was one vast, clean cave.

Then Nan had a better idea. "We'll go up to the attic," she responded. "And look down through the floor." They drifted upward, following the staircase, as the best way of avoiding being spotted.

The attic, unlike the sitting room, had nothing in it in this spirit-world analog of the real house. It was also one, long, peaked-ceilinged room, with no indication of what or where the rooms beneath it were. The got down on their hands and knees, even Caro, and worked their way along the floor until Sarah whispered "here," and Caro nodded in confirmation.

Then cautiously, they pushed their heads through the floor; there was more resistance, not as if Nan was pushing her head through thick goo, but more as if she was pushing it through an elastic membrane, even though the floor itself didn't stretch or deform in any way.

The first thing that Nan saw when the front of her face got below the level of the ceiling was so fantastic that she frankly did not believe her eyes. It was a Chinese girl, exquisitely beautiful, in the most fantastic robes Nan had ever seen in her life. Her face was as perfect as a porcelain doll's. Her robes had huge, hanging sleeves and enveloped her from throat to foot in layer upon layer of soft pink, lavender, and pale green, held to her waist with a heavily brocaded belt. Nan had never seen a woman with "bound feet" before, but those tiny brocaded shoes, no bigger than you'd put on a toddler, were almost certainly bound. Her hair was held into an impossible coiffure of twists, braids, knots and loops with jade pins. More jade beads hung about her neck. Wide cuff bracelets of gold were connected to golden chains, but Nan's attention was so riveted upon the girl that for a moment she couldn't look away.

She sat in a jeweled throne, and her demeanor was so haughty that in that moment, Nan was convinced they had found their necromancer.

And yet—

And yet there was no sense of power about her.

And she didn't seem to be a mortal crossed to the spirit plane. Something about her, some faint transparency, told Nan that this was, in fact, a ghost.

But what would the ghost of a high-caste Chinese girl be doing here?

Two more Chinese girls knelt at her feet, one holding a jade cup, the other a jade plate full of sweets—at least, Nan assumed they were sweets. The girls were each dressed in much more simplified versions of the first girl's robes; their hair hung loosely down their backs, and they too had cuff bracelets and chains, but not of gold.

Finally Nan tore her attention away from the first girl to follow the chains—to discover they led to yet another group of spirits, all girls, this time mostly very ordinary creatures she wouldn't have been surprised to see walking the streets of the East End. Though there were four Chinese girls among them, huddled away from the rest. None were pretty, though all wore white gowns, or white shirtwaists and skirts. Here, at least, were the missing ghosts of all those victims—and more. Many, many more.

Nan now noticed that there was a sort of bubble, a transparent shell, around the girls and most of the rest of the room. "Is that . . . ?" she breathed to Sarah.

"I think it is," Sarah replied. "Some sort of shield. I think it's backward of what you'd expect. It isn't to wall anything *out,* it's to keep whatever is inside that bubble *in.*"

"*I probably shouldn't cross it then,*" Caro observed.

As they watched and took mental notes, another spirit faded into view in the center of the room; this time a man, with white hair closely cropped to his head, a face that would have been handsome if it had not been so cold, and the aura of great power that was absolutely missing from the Chinese girl on the throne.

As if to prove this, the Chinese girl flung herself down from the throne to the floor at the man's feet. "*Husband!*" she cried. "*I have been chastising your concubines, and we have filled yet more orbs with the blood of heaven!*"

The man smiled faintly, and reached down to caress the side of her face. "Very well done, Xi'er," he said, the lack of a "hollow" tone to his words telling Nan that *this* was their necromancer. "Tonight will be the night. The man is ready, we have sufficient power, and the stars align." He moved across the room, apparently picked up something from a shadowy table, and removed a piece of cloth from it.

And a third spirit appeared; a powerfully built man that Nan recognized with a start from John Watson's memories. *Professor Moriarty!*

Now it all made horrible sense!

"Well, Professor Moriarty, the time has come at last to give you a new mortal shell. The first of many, I do believe," the necromancer said, in a voice as smooth and bland as cream. Beside her, Nan sensed Sarah's sudden shock and dismay. "If you will retire to your talisman, I will begin the ritual."

Squinting, Nan was able to make out the faint form of a young man lying on what looked like an altar between Moriarty and the necromancer. The Professor nodded with what looked like immense satisfaction, then vanished.

They both pulled their heads back up. "Good God!" Sarah exclaimed, her eyes wide. "*That's* what's been going on? Sherlock surely had no idea Moriarty had a necromancer in his employ!"

Caro looked puzzled, but then her expression hardened. "*I don't know who this Professor is, but he's allied himself with someone who has murdered nearly two dozen girls for his benefit, and I am* not *going to let him profit from his evil!*"

"I'll tell Mary," Nan said, and willed herself to wake up.

In the next moment she was sitting bolt upright, with Neville shaking himself awake beside her. "The necromancer is in Moriarty's employ, and he is about to resurrect the Professor somehow—"

"Dear God in Heaven," Mary breathed, shocked. "We can't let that happen!"

"You run and let His Lordship know—" Nan hadn't even gotten the words out before Mary was on her feet and running to inform the men. Or Alderscroft, at least; what Lestrade would make of such words, Nan had no clue.

"You go with her and protect her," she told Neville. He *quork*ed and flew out the window. She laid back down and—

Couldn't get back into the spirit world. With a cry of frustration, she tried to *will* herself there, when suddenly she felt Grey wake up, hop onto her arm, seize her wrist in her beak and—

There she was. Except this time she was lying on the floor, and Grey was still holding Nan's wrist in her beak. Nan shot to her feet as the parrot let go, and both of them raced back toward the necromancer's house across the shadows of this empty part of the spirit plane.

Grey flew through the corner; Nan pushed through in the same place in the parrot's wake, finding it much easier to get in this time. Grey arrowed upward through the ceiling, and Nan followed, ending up at the far end of the attic from where Sarah and Caro knelt.

"Did you—" Sarah whispered.

Nan moved silently toward them as Grey landed next to Sarah. "Mary's telling the men," she whispered back. "What's going on?"

"I think it might be a long ceremony," Sarah breathed. "He is back in the material plane, and he seems to be setting up a great many arcane artifacts."

"I hope it gives the men time to get in place," Nan replied. "Is it safe to look?"

Sarah shrugged, so Nan cautiously stuck her head through the floor again. It appeared that the ceremony was in already progress. Moriarty stood inside a circle of shadow, while the necromancer, a shadow-form himself, half-in, half-out of the spirit plane, gestured and muttered.

And that was when Nan noticed that the bubble keeping everything inside it was gone. But if the necromancer's prisoners noticed, it didn't matter to them. Perhaps the chains kept them prisoner even when the bubble of power did not.

Every ghost in the room stared, mesmerized, at the necromancer. Even Moriarty, who could not seem to take his eyes off the man.

Nan glanced at Sarah—*Sarah* was not staring at the necromancer. Sarah stared fixedly at a point just beyond the huddle of ghosts.

And a tiny point of light formed there. It began to grow, from a point, to a disk, from a disk to a window, from a window to—a Door!

And Sarah darted down into the room, followed by Caro. And luck was with them, for now at least, for Spencer was so wrapped up in his ceremony he did not notice them.

At that moment, Nan felt a shock go through her even as she recognized the source of the alarm. Neville! He was trying to tell her something was happening in the real world!

She pulled her head back in and ran to the window; she narrowed her focus to allow her to stare into the material plane, and to her horror saw that a mixed group of Lestrade's Bobbies and Elemental Magicians were locked in combat with what looked sickeningly like animated corpses. And even as she gasped in a surge of sickening terror, more of the monsters poured out the front door.

"Oh God—" she moaned in indecision. Join the fight, or rejoin Sarah?

No, it really was *no* decision. The fight was a mere diversion—something to hold off the attackers while the ceremony took place. The important thing was the ceremony, because if Moriarty got a new physical body—

She wrenched her attention entirely back to the spirit world, dove through the floor, and joined her friends.

Sarah had gotten hold of one of the girls and was dragging her to the Door. The ghost-girls didn't seem to understand that she was trying to help them; they clawed and scratched at her in a typical fashion for East End street waifs who found themselves weaponless.

Caro held off the necromancer, keeping him from using any of his powers on her, Sarah, or the girls by firing arrow after arrow at him. From the way he yelped as they hit, although they probably weren't doing him any physical harm, they certainly *hurt*, and broke his concentration. That left Moriarty, who clutched the end of the shadowy table the young man lay on, staring fixedly at him with an expression of fierce hunger.

She hadn't even had a chance to make up her mind what to do when Sarah finally managed to shove one of the girl-spirits through the Door. Not only did the girl vanish—but the chain ran rapidly in through the door, as if something was pulling on it. The next girl on the chain found herself jerked away from Sarah, and pulled through the Door. And the next . . . and the next . . . Sarah jumped back out of the way before a loop of the chain tightened around her ankle and watched as the girls were yanked off their feet and on to the other side . . . and whatever awaited them there.

The elaborately gowned girl that the necromancer had called "Xi'er" began screeching, and tried to loop her golden chains around the throne. But the other two Chinese girls threw their burdens aside, each of them taking one of her golden chains, and ran toward the Door. Unable to do anything to stop them, tottering on her tiny, bound feet, Xi'er found herself pulled off balance. She landed on her back, shrieking and cursing in Chinese as she slid on her back in the direction of the Door. The two girls dove through it, hauling Xi'er with them. The last Nan saw of her was the trailing sleeves of her silken robe vanishing into the darkness of the Door, as Spencer tried desperately to get past Caro to stop it all.

Before Nan could act, Moriarty came to life. *"Finish the spell, you damned fool!"* he shouted *"Before your power runs out!"*

The Professor tried to come to the necromancer's aid, but Nan jumped down to intercept him. She *thought* she had the upper hand since she was equipped with a little round shield and her bronze Celtic sword, but the professor shocked her by turning to meet her with a cavalry saber in his hand. With her heart in her mouth and the metallic taste of fear, all she could do was deflect his blows. He was bigger and stronger than she was, despite his age, and his sword had the same properties here as it would have had in the real world. It was steel, and her little wooden shield and short bronze sword were no match for it. Even fighting defensively, her shield soon had deep cuts marring its surface, and bits were missing from the edge of her blade. Moriarty clearly knew how to use what he wielded.

So she stopped fighting defensively—and ran, hoping he would follow.

But he didn't, and at that same moment, as the last of the girls hurtled through the Door, pulled by the chain that had bound them all together, Sarah flung herself at Caro, holding her back with one hand while desperately trying to get the Door shut.

In that moment, the necromancer acted.

He bellowed some words, and to Nan's horror, the transparent image of a young man in his early twenties emerged from the shadowy man-shape on the table, and snapped through the Door as if he'd been shot out of a cannon.

Startled, Sarah let go of Caro, who moved just as quickly.

But not through the Door.

She made a dive for the man-shape . . . and disappeared. Into it?

Moriarty howled with fury, and contorted himself into shapes no human could take, trying to force his way into what had been the young man's body. But Caro was not to be dislodged, no matter what he tried.

"It's too late! Back in the talisman, Professor!" the necromancer cried. "The police are coming up the stairs! We must escape while we can!"

But Sarah was quicker than that. She rushed Moriarty while he was still concentrating on the body that was supposed to have been his. She was half his size, but she caught him off guard, and with a wail of despair, he, too, vanished through the Door.

The necromancer vanished.

"Where?" Sarah cried in anguish, but Nan already knew the answer.

She moved her vision into the real world, just in time to see the necromancer snatching up something from a small altar-like table beside a second table holding a young man's body. He dashed out of the room—but Nan ran after him in spirit form. *I can't do anything to stop him, but at least I can see where he's going!* As quick as thought, Sarah was right behind her.

He pulled down the ladder to the attic, scrambled up the ladder, dashed across the empty attic, opened the window, and pushed a ladder he had waiting right there by the window out across the space between the houses. Like a cat, he got out the window on the ladder and started walking across to the next house.

"He's going to get away!" cried Sarah—and Nan knew with a plummeting heart that she was right. Even though the night was now bright with the lanterns the Scotland Yard constables had brought with them, no one was going to look up—

It was clear he'd had this means of escape there all along, and had planned and practiced this maneuver until he was as good as a circus rope-walker. And there was nothing they could do to stop him. He had the talisman, which probably meant he could bring Moriarty *back* from whatever punishment he'd gone to, and this would only begin all over again.

Except now he'd probably do it somewhere other than England, somewhere remote, Egypt or India or Hong Kong, which meant even if Alderscroft warned every Elemental Master and Hunting Lodge in Europe, by the time anyone found out about this, it would be too late. It wouldn't even be difficult for him to find another young white man whose body he could steal.

With a cry of despair, Nan threw her spectral bronze sword at his back.

It passed right through him, of course.

But the ebony form of an angry raven, flying up into his face from below, did what she could not.

With a screech, he lost his balance and tumbled off the ladder, to land four stories below.

"Back!" cried Sarah, and in the next moment, Nan lurched to her feet, slightly disoriented, but grimly determined. She stumbled out the door and down the stairs, hearing Sarah's equally unsteady footsteps behind her.

They ran as fast as they could to where they had seen the villain fall. But by the time they got there, there was already someone standing over the crumpled body.

Nan braced herself, getting ready for a fight—

But the person was in the uniform of a London constable, holding a lantern. And when he looked up, his face clear in the lantern-light, Nan saw with a shock of recognition it was Sherlock Holmes.

"Inconsiderate bastard broke his own neck," he said crossly, "Now I won't be able to uncover the rest of the Organization without a deuce of a lot of legwork."

Neville dropped down out of the darkness to land at Holmes' feet, as Sarah fell on her knees beside the body and began rummaging frantically through the pockets. "Here!" shouted Grey from the darkness, and flapped to Sarah with what looked like a small glass bottle or vial in her beak.

Sarah took it and dropped it on the ground next to Nan, who understood what she wanted and ground it to powder under her heel. Sarah took Holmes' lantern, opened the side, stuck in a twig to get a light and flung the twig on top of the fragments of the vial and its contents.

They all three jumped back as a tongue of flame as tall as Holmes leapt out of the spot, presumably releasing all that was left of the magic that could call Moriarty back from the dead once more.

"Well," Holmes said, still obviously irritated, looking at the body of the necromancer. "I suppose at least we won't have to worry about *him* anymore."

"No," Sarah replied, looking at the scorched earth with exhausted relief. "No, we won't."

The room next to John Watson's surgery had a bed where he occasionally kept patients he didn't want to send to a hospital, and that bed was occupied by a haggard young man who would probably be quite handsome when he recovered from the terrible experience of going through opium withdrawal. His cheeks and eyes were sunken to the point where his head looked like a skull, his hands trembled, his skin was sallow, and his eyes looked as if someone had rubbed burnt cork under them. But there was a faint smile on his face whenever he looked down at himself that made Nan very certain he was going to come out the other end of his experience just fine.

"How are you feeling, Ca—I mean, Peter?" Sarah asked with concern.

"Like hell, but it's getting better," replied Peter Hughs. Or Caro, in Peter Hughs' body. *I have to get used to calling him Peter. Though he seems to be used to it already.* Grey nudged his hand, and he continued gently scratching her neck. "It helps that I finally feel *right* for the first time in my life. I kept saying I should have been born a boy—not only to you two, but to my own father and brother—and no one took me seriously, but I really *did* feel . . . wrong, inside my own skin. Now I feel right. As for the rest—" he shrugged. "I may be miserable, I may vomit more than I eat, and I may shake as if I had a fever, but it's easier than dying was."

"Well, you can thank Lestrade for finding all those papers who told us who Peter Hughs was, and who his friends and family were," Nan observed. "He might be pedantic, but he's a bulldog when it comes to persistence."

Peter nodded. "Watson made up some faradiddle tale about going on a walking tour to ease his sorrows over his dead wife and finding me half-dead of pneumonia in a shepherd's hut. That covers all my symptoms, at least to the uninitiated. Peter's old friends *might* have had some suspicions, but they've hidden them well, and they certainly aren't going to bleat to Peter's family."

"Are you going to meet with them?" Sarah didn't bother to contain her curiosity.

Peter smiled shakily. "Already have. The father's stiff as two boards, but genuinely broke down when Watson told him I'd been near death. The mother's a smotherer; I'll have to take her in hand a bit. The sister's a sweet little thing. It helps neither parent actually knew a whit about Peter; I was pretty well able to pull the wool over all their eyes, and Watson's told 'em my memories are half gone, and I may never get them back, so that's all right." He brightened. "And when I mumbled something about going back to University to get a law degree once I was well, I thought the old man was going to do a double backflip in joy. I always wanted to go into law, but of course, even if I'd been well, I'd never have been allowed to."

"*Good, good,*" croaked Neville from the foot of his bed. Neville flew to Nan's shoulder, and Grey walked ponderously across the bedclothes to be picked up by Sarah.

"It sounds as if you have everything in hand," Nan said with relief. "But you look ghastly, so we'll come back and visit you again later. Tomorrow, probably."

"I feel ghastly, but I'd love to see you. Peter's friends are a lot of addle-pated poets and artists, and there's only so much empty-headed prattle I can stand before I pretend to go to sleep so they'll go away." Peter smiled again. "I never thought when you found my locket I'd end up with my dearest and most secret dream coming true. I don't know how I can ever thank you enough."

"Don't try, just get well," Nan advised. "You can pay us back with free legal advice when you become a barrister."

"That's a bargain," Peter agreed, and shut his eyes as they left.

They went up the stairs to the Watson's flat-of-record, where Holmes, the Watsons, and his Lordship were having a late tea. It was the first time they had all gathered together since the night of the raid. Nan was looking forward to giving Holmes no mercy about why, if he'd been keeping track of them all along, he hadn't *helped* them.

"Well, here is our Spirit Master at last," said Alderscroft as they opened the door to the flat. "*And* our Spirit Magician!"

"Spirit—what?" Nan was taken completely off guard and stared at him in shock, while Neville laughed wickedly, as if he had known this all along.

"After a great deal of consultation among the Lodges of Paris, Venice, Rome, Marseilles, and Nuremberg, who are the only ones who actually have currently, or have had recently, Spirit Masters, we are all certain that not only is our Sarah a Spirit Master, but you, my dear, are a Spirit Magician as well. It's the only reasonable explanation for why you could have mastered the spirit plane as quickly as you did," Alderscroft explained. "I was just telling John and Mary about our discussions."

"And *now* you have no excuse for excluding females from the

Lodge," Mary said tartly. "Unless you intend to keep the only Spirit Magicians in England out."

Grey made a rude noise.

Alderscroft coughed uncomfortably. Nan took pity on him, and rounded on Holmes. "What I want to know is, if you knew what we were doing and how many dead ends we ran up against, *why didn't you help us?*"

"Elementary, my dear," Holmes replied. "It was obvious to me when I had eliminated every other explanation that these were ritual killings of some—" he coughed "—arcane sort. The usual mentally damaged ritual killer escalates. He no longer receives the thrill he once got from the murder alone. He begins to elaborate into torture before murder, and he takes riskier and riskier chances to obtain victims. And he invariably begins to taunt the police. Our killer did none of these things, so he was killing, not as an end in itself, but as a means to an end, in a way that he did not dare to change. So I stayed out of the picture, and began following the leads you took me to." He actually beamed at Watson. "Good work, old man. Good, solid work."

Watson's expression softened into one of embarrassed pride.

"What *was* that madman trying to do, anyway?" Holmes continued.

Alderscroft immediately jumped in. "Gathering power to use to influence the minds of those of the Organization that were left to allow him to take Moriarty's place," he lied.

"Ah, something like . . . oh . . . psychical manipulation?" Holmes hazarded.

"Something like that, yes," said Alderscroft.

Nan kept her mouth shut. So did everyone else.

"So there is justification to the fairy tales that ritual sacrifice creates power," Holmes said, making it a statement rather than a question. He shook his head. "Is he the only one of Moriarty's Organization who could do this sort of thing?"

"I'm reasonably sure of that," said Watson. "Lestrade is going over every scrap of paper we found in that house, and it appears he was the highest ranking of Moriarty's minions and the only one with any sort of pretense to esoteric abilities."

"That is a great relief." Holmes nodded. "In that case, I can leave the cleanup to Lestrade. He's as dull as a tarnished spoon, but he's doggedly persistent, and this is *exactly* the sort of thing he's good for. I'll be going over to France to deal with whatever viper's den Moriarty left there. From there—I'm not sure. Perhaps as far as Russia. But I will be back, and I will leave you some information on where letters might find me."

"I believe I will remain 'dead' for a while longer," Mary told him. "It gives me a great deal more freedom to operate. Eventually, perhaps after you return, John can 'marry' someone else called Mary—or at least allude to doing so in those tales he writes." She patted his hand fondly.

"Good, and I expect you and Nan and Sarah to continue your lessons in disguises," Holmes told her, with feigned sternness, as Watson looked decidedly uncomfortable. He handed her a card. "I want you to go to this lady. She's truly an expert. She has even gammoned *me* a time or two, in my younger days."

"Only a time or two?" Watson asked archly.

Holmes ignored him.

"We'll certainly do that," Sarah agreed. Nan might have said something, but she was still turning the fact that *Alderscroft* had deemed her an Elemental Magician over in her mind. She decided that she was ridiculously pleased with the fact. After all, this should mean that Alderscroft would be trusting the two of them with even *more* interesting work.

"I will definitely be back," Holmes continued, smiling. "I'm definitely looking forward to our adventures together in the future. This is certainly not goodbye."

"*Au revoir!*" said Grey.

"Precisely," said Holmes.

ABOUT THE AUTHOR

Mercedes Lackey is a full-time writer and has published numerous novels and works of short fiction, including the bestselling *Heralds of Valdemar* series. She is also a professional lyricist and licensed wild bird rehabilitator. She lives in Oklahoma with her husband and collaborator, artist Larry Dixon, and their flock of parrots.

www.mercedeslackey.com

ALSO AVAILABLE FROM TITAN BOOKS

THE ELEMENTAL MASTERS
Mercedes Lackey

Mercedes Lackey's bestselling fantasy series set in an alternative
Edwardian Britain, where magic is real—and the
Elemental Masters are in control.

The Serpent's Shadow
The Gates of Sleep
Phoenix and Ashes
Wizard of London
Reserved for the Cat
Unnatural Issue
Home from the Sea
Steadfast
Blood Red
From a High Tower
A Study in Sable
A Scandal in Battersea
The Bartered Brides

"Fantastic… this is Lackey at her best." *Publishers Weekly*

"Intriguing and compelling." *Library Journal*

"Colourful characters… great fun." *Booklist*

"Innovative historical fantasy." *Romantic Times*

TITANBOOKS.COM

ALSO AVAILABLE FROM TITAN BOOKS

THE COLLEGIUM CHRONICLES
Mercedes Lackey

Follow Magpie, Bear, Lena and friends as they face their demons and find
their true strength on the road to becoming full Heralds,
Bards and Healers of Valdemar.

Book One: *Foundation*
Book Two: *Intrigues*
Book Three: *Changes*
Book Four: *Redoubt*
Book Five: *Bastion*

"Lackey makes a real page-turner out of Mags' and the collegia's
development... this book's outstanding characters, especially Mags, will
greatly please Valdemar fans." *Booklist*

"The tone, characterization, and rampant angst recall Lackey's earliest
Valdemar books... this is a worthy entry in the overall saga."
Publishers Weekly

"Lackey's Valdermar series is already a fantasy classic, and these newest
adventures will generate even more acclaim for this fantasy superstar."
Romantic Times

TITANBOOKS.COM

ALSO AVAILABLE FROM TITAN BOOKS

THE HERALD SPY
Mercedes Lackey

Mags was a Herald of Valdemar. But he had once lived the brutal life of a child slave. When he was Chosen by his Companion Dallen, his young life was saved, and he slowly adjusted to being well fed, educated, and treasured as a trainee in the Herald's Collegium at Haven. Singled out by the King's Own Herald, Mags would thrive in his secret training as a spy. His unusually strong Gift—an ability to Mindspeak and Mindhear anyone, not just others who were Gifted—made him a perfect undercover agent for the king.

Closer to Home
Closer to the Heart
Closer to the Chest

"A welcome addition to the Valdemar canon…a fast, page-turning read."
Shiny Book Review

"You can feel Lackey's passion for her characters…
funny and entertaining." The Qwillery

"Mercedes Lackey is a master storyteller and *Closer to Home*
is a masterful, satisfying visit to Valdemar." Bitten by Books

TITANBOOKS.COM

For more fantastic fiction, author events, exclusive excerpts,
competitions, limited editions and more

VISIT OUR WEBSITE
titanbooks.com

LIKE US ON FACEBOOK
facebook.com/titanbooks

FOLLOW US ON TWITTER
@TitanBooks

EMAIL US
readerfeedback@titanemail.com